WORDS TO DIE BY . . .

Hickey scanned the burning forest with the NVGs. The light reflected from the fires lit the scene brightly in the light-amplifying goggles. There were destroyed vehicles everywhere. Tanks flipped over on their sides, fighting vehicles upside down, burning. Here and there, on the outer edges of the blast area, a few doomed Soviets staggered about. The carnage was complete

"Take a look, Ty."

As King surveyed the destruction, Hickey began to chuckle.

"What you laughin' at?" King asked, not taking his eyes off the terrible scene of devastation before him.

"Just thinkin' of something ol' George Bush said once," Hickey answered. He raised himself up off the ground and shouted, "There's a thousand points of light for you, ya' commies!"

Berkley Books by James B. Adair and Gordon Rottman

The WWIII: Behind the Lines Series

TARGET TEXAS
TARGET NUKE

WWIII: BEHIND THE LINES
TARGET NUKE

James B. Adair and Gordon Rottman

BERKLEY BOOKS, NEW YORK

WWIII: BEHIND THE LINES
TARGET NUKE

A Berkley Book / published by arrangement with
the authors

PRINTING HISTORY
Berkley edition / November 1990

ISBN: 0-425-12346-4

A BERKLEY BOOK® TM 757,375
Berkley Books are published by The Berkley Publishing Group,
200 Madison Avenue, New York, New York 10016.
The name ''Berkley'' and the ''B'' logo
are trademarks belonging to Berkley Publishing Corporation.

PRINTED IN THE UNITED STATES OF AMERICA

10 9 8 7 6 5 4 3 2 1

*We dedicate this book to
the Special Operations troops, who
labor and often die in causes unknown and unsung*

"Twenty miles or so south of Belgrade, we emerged on the main road and joined a continuous stream of Red Army trucks, tanks, and guns flowing northward into battle. One thing in particular struck us now, as it had struck us from the first, namely, that every Soviet truck we saw contained one of two things: petrol or ammunition. Of rations, blankets, spare boots or clothing there was no trace. Almost every man we saw was a fighting soldier. What they carried with them were the materials of war in the narrowest sense. We were witnessing a return to the administrative methods of Attila or Genghis Khan, and the results seemed to deserve careful attention. For there could be no doubt that here lay one reason for the amazing speed of the Red Army's advance across Europe."

—Fitzroy McLean, *Eastern Approaches*

ACKNOWLEDGMENTS

We wish to thank Jim Morris, our editor at Berkley, for his neverending patience and encouragement.

All characters and political organizations in this book are fictitious. The military units are not, nor are their aims and missions.

Kreuzadder, *n.* (lit.) cross adder—crossed snake. A mythical German snake. Said to be highly venomous, it was difficult to detect due to its crossed (X) marking pattern and coloration. It would be found in unlikely places and fatally strike without provocation at the most unexpected times. It would then rapidly disappear, seemingly into thin air.

★ Prologue ★

There was a red dawn on Christmas Day. Wave after wave of Soviet tanks, armored fighting vehicles, and self-propelled guns roared across the East German border, grinding fifty years of peace beneath their treads. Soviet and Warsaw Pact aircraft darkened the sky, seeking targets in Germany and Belgium. Short-range missiles flashed across the sky, too, filled with nerve gas to render airfields and command centers useless by frying the nervous systems of their defenders.

The Soviet 8th Guards Tank Army, supported by the 1st Guards Tank Army and the 34th Artillery Division, hit the U.S. V and VII Corps with nine divisions. The Reds had blown right through the 2d and 11th Armored Cavalry Regiments and would have swept immediately on to Frankfurt but for ceaseless air attacks by the A-10s, F-4s, and A-7Ds of the Air Force Tactical Fighter Wings. The pilots bought with blood the precious hours needed to move NATO's armored forces into position. Even so, NATO units were fighting against Soviet forces two and three times their size.

Lulled by promises of reduced tensions and troop cuts, the NATO nations had happily cut the hearts out of their units facing the Warsaw Pact. Despite seventy years of Soviet deceit, the nations of the West believed that the Russian bear had somehow become a lapdog. Now that lapdog was at their throats, and the tanks, planes, and fighting vehicles needed to save the gullible Europeans were burning in a hundred scrap yards. Political expediency became national suicide.

In America, Soviet Spetsnaz groups had attacked critical transportation and logistics sites, as well as the military units that would be mobilized first to reinforce the units already in Europe. The Air Force's Air Material Center at Tinker Air Force Base in Oklahoma City had been heavily damaged by a fire started when a Spetsnaz team exploded a tank truck full of jet fuel at the base's main refueling facility. In Houston and New Orleans, ships had been sunk in the ship channels and huge container bombs had wrecked the loading docks, virtually closing both ports. The smoke from scores of burned tanks and armored fighting vehicles still drifted over Fort Hood, in central Texas.

At Fort Hood, there had been a warning, if too late. Richard (Jinx) Jenkins, a former CIA contract employee, and BJ Kirkley, an Army National Guardsman, had uncovered the Soviet attack plan. Like Cassandra, their warning went unheeded.

In the attack that followed, Jenkins was vindicated, Kirkley wounded. The surviving Spetsnaz attackers safely escaped into Mexico. Like the two Americans, they were soon on their way to join the fight in Europe.

Once again, America had chosen to ignore history, hoping that hope alone would be enough to turn ruthless men from their plans. Once again, that naiveté would cost thousands of American lives.

★ 1 ★

Senior Lieutenant Fedor Zakharov was bursting with excitement. The An-2's engine throbbed, vibrating through the aircraft's body and into the paratroopers' bodies. Outside the aircraft's skin all was blackness, fog, and cold. Zakharov and his thirteen *raydoviki* were six minutes away from their parachute jump into West Germany. It was Zakharov's first combat mission, and he was eager to get on with it. After he joined the ranks of the combat veterans, perhaps the other more experienced officers would treat him with the respect he deserved.

Standing behind him, Sergeant Blinov was also about to burst, but not from excitement. His bladder was throbbing and only the knowledge that they would jump within six minutes prevented him from running for the tiny funnel at the back of the An-2. Aside from the fact that he would have to unbuckle his parachute harness to get to his aching organ, it would damage his image with the younger paratroopers. He could wait. There would be plenty of time to piss while the group formed up on the ground.

Their mission was to establish an antitank ambush on the E30 Autobahn east of Braunschweig. They were to destroy, or at least delay, any NATO units moving in march formation from their peacetime bases to their mobilization defensive positions just west of the frontier. The big biplane droning over the treetops had darted across the frontier into West Germany at 06.12. The war had begun on the other side of the world, in America, twelve minutes earlier. It had begun here, too, but few actually knew

3

it . . . yet. The first missiles of the main strike force had not yet struck the airfields and prepositioned equipment storage sites in the NATO countries. Tonight, Christmas Eve, the NATO air defense networks were not fully alert. Their short hop across the frontier had gone unchallenged. The ambush, too, should be easy. The days to follow would be harder. After they ambushed the NATO combat unit, Zakharov's raiders would remain in the area, attack targets of opportunity, and report troop movements. It would be more difficult to ambush other units, as they would be prepared for such attacks. Their orders were simple, disrupt enemy forces until relieved by advancing Warsaw Pact forces. Zakharov's group was one of scores crossing the frontier tonight, by light aircraft, helicopter, and foot. No group knew the missions of the others.

The biplane made a hard bank to the left. Sergeant Blinov held the door frame to steady himself as the An-2 made its turn, coming back finally to a course that would take it west over the drop zone. The An-2 was the infiltration aircraft of choice for the Spetsnaz. The aluminum-skinned biplane, adopted in the 1950s, was still a workhorse. It had an operating radius of 450 kilometers, a top speed of over 200 kilometers per hour, and excellent low-level performance—they were even used as crop dusters. The spacious cargo compartment could accommodate up to fourteen jumpers, making it ideal for infiltrating Spetsnaz subunits behind enemy lines. Under each wing was a PDSB-1 equipment container loaded with heavy weapons and ammunition, each with its own parachute.

Two minutes out, the yellow "make ready" lights came on and a horn sounded. The An-2 climbed steeply to 200 meters, its thousand-horsepower radial engine roaring.

Zakharov clung to the edge of the door, faced his men, and shouted, *"Stand up and make ready!"*

The men hooked their white static lines to the anchor cable and quickly checked their equipment's fit.

The loadmaster made his way back to the door on the aircraft's left side, swung it into the plane, and latched it to the inside of the fuselage. The paratroopers moved forward, the first stopping a meter from the open hatch. The aircraft leveled out and throttled back to 160 kilometers per hour.

The lights went green, the horn sounded a continuous blast, and the first *raydoviki* dove headfirst out the door.

* * *

For the tenth time in an hour, Captain Ivan Budnov scanned the maze of huge metal warehouses. Letting the van's side window curtain drop, he set his B-7 binoculars on the floor and eased back in the comfort of the seat. The four other men in the van were either dozing or absorbed in their own thoughts. He glanced at his watch—only 06.14. Again he thought about the vagueness of his detachment's mission. He knew that sometime after 06.00 an attack was going to be launched. When exactly he knew not, nor even the method of attack. It would likely be an air strike or missiles. Nuclear? He certainly hoped not, they were awfully close to the target to survive a nuclear strike. For all he knew, it could even be a ground attack. What he did know was that he and his men must accomplish two main tasks: reconnoiter the target and report by long-range radio the results of the attack. He would then be told whether to await a follow-on strike and report its results, attack the target with his own Spetsnaz detachment, or withdraw and be assigned a new mission. Because of the target's massive size and the small size of his force, he dearly hoped the strikes, regardless of what form they took, were successful.

His thirty-six-man detachment had been brought into the Netherlands by East German Transport International Routier trucks three days before. Hauling commercial goods, the trucks were protected from customs inspection by international agreement. The Warsaw Pact states naturally took advantage of this agreement, using the trucks to collect information on NATO dispositions and to monitor their military exercises. Two frozen agents had supplied them with a safe warehouse in nearby Brunssum, three vans, a small enclosed truck, and information about the target and the local area. Each of the detachment's vehicles were now positioned 1500 to 2000 meters from the facility, in an empty shop parking lot, a roadside rest area, and beside a service station . . . waiting.

Across the mist-hazed fields were over a dozen huge silver warehouses, service buildings, and empty parking areas, all connected by concrete roads. The site's 116-acres were enclosed by a barbed wire-topped chainlink fence. A solitary Dutch civilian security guard drove a small car slowly along one of the roads. None of the 1200 Dutch employees or the one-hundred American soldiers assigned to the site were present early on this Christmas morning.

This site was the 18th Combat Equipment Company's

POMUCUS (prepositioned material configured to unit sets) facility near Brunssum, the Netherlands. Brunssum was one of many such facilities scattered across the Netherlands, West Germany, Belgium, and Luxembourg.

Though Budnov's mission was vague, he had been fully briefed on the significance of the POMCUS sites. The aggressive, but money-pinching, Americans had agreed years before to commit ten combat divisions to NATO. There were, however, only four American divisions in Germany. The political officer had explained that, in order to save money, and to permit the use of the divisions elsewhere in the world to further their imperialistic goals, the Americans had promised their NATO puppets that they could deploy the remaining six divisions to Europe within ten days. Their plan was simple. It was less costly to maintain two complete sets of combat vehicles and major equipment for each division than to actually station the troops in Germany. The sites also served as a threatening reminder to the Warsaw Pact states that the Americans could quickly come in force. American soldiers, with only their personal gear and small items of unit equipment, could be flown to Europe in a massive airlift, man the POMCUS vehicles, and move to the battle zone. They practiced this every year in the form of the Reforger (*return of forces to Germany*) exercises. The vehicles left in America would then be loaded on ships and sent to Europe to replace battle losses. The Americans had even coerced their NATO puppet allies into paying part of the construction costs of the expensive POMCUS sites. Their construction had begun in the late 1970s and continued well into the '80s. They and the Reforger exercises had become a hated symbol of American imperialism and aggression to the peace-loving, fraternal Warsaw Pact states.

Budnov knew now that the long shaky peace was about to end. He did not question who was responsible for ending it; he *knew* without a doubt that the war-mongering American government and capitalist industrialists were solely responsible. He did not question his nation's leaders, his commanders, or his orders. He had trained for this day and was prepared to accomplish his mission regardless of the consequences.

It hardly seemed that he was out of the plane before his D-5 parachute jerked him upright, the static line breaking away, and the small extraction parachute, its job done, falling limp on the main canopy.

Zakharov looked up quickly to check the white canopy, then fumbled for the release that would drop his equipment container, attached behind his hips, to the end of its ten-meter line. It took a moment to find the releases. Zakharov pulled hard and the heavy pack fell away. It hit the ground before it got to the end of the tether. Instantly, Zakharov brought his feet together and braced for the impact. A second later, he was on the ground. A thud nearby caught his attention. Zakharov heard the man get to his feet, then heard a moan and a deep sigh.

"Ochen horosho!" the figure sighed.

"Comrade Sergeant Blinov?" Zakharov asked quietly.

"Just so, Comrade Lieutenant," the sergeant responded. "have you seen the others?"

By way of answer, two figures laden with equipment loomed up out of the darkness. One of the heavy equipment containers bumped to the ground behind them.

"Welcome to the Federal Republic of Germany, comrades," muttered Sergeant Blinov.

Senior Sergeant Sergei Zhivkov, sitting in the front passenger seat, suddenly straightened, looking quickly to his right, toward the POMCUS site. Budnov grabbed the side-door window's curtain and looked at the site himself. A series of mist-enshrouded flashes were bursting over the warehouses.

"Down!" screamed Zhivkov.

Mesmerized, Budnov watched the clouds of fine, expanding mist ripple into a blinding white nebula. Someone grabbed him around the waist and pulled him to the mud-encrusted floor.

KA-KABOOM-BOOM-BOOOOM!

The little van rocked like a toy as the safety glass windows exploded into a million particles, peppering the inside of the vehicle. A second later, the vacuum caused by the instantaneous burning of the very air under the massive explosions caused gale-like winds as air gushed into the void.

A quiet *"Ochen horosho"* was muttered by someone beside Budnov.

All that could be heard was a high-pitched whine from the POMCUS site, probably a ruptured natural-gas line. There was a faint ringing in Budnov's ears. His head throbbed and his throat hurt. There was a salty taste in his mouth. His fingers traced the taste to his bleeding nose. The others were sitting up, shaking their heads and working concussion-jarred jaws. Strelbitski, the driver, was slumped over the steering wheel, his head and shoulders ripped by glass fragments. Blood was running from his ears.

"Mother of Christ," breathed Zhivkov.

Budnov struggled to his knees and pulled the shredded curtain open.

What he saw before him was a devastated tangle of collapsed smoking structures. Everything was blackened, twisted, and distorted into unidentifiable forms. Even lengthy sections of the perimeter fence were down. There were only a scattering of small, flickering fires.

"What in God's name was that?" mumbled Zhivkov. His mouth had been open as he had shouted the warning, saving him from ruptured eardrums.

"I believe it was fuel-air warheads on missiles, probably several in each missile," Budnov answered. "We have been developing them for years. They were classed as weapons of mass destruction along with atomics and chemicals sometime ago."

Everyone was peering at the total destruction, oblivious to poor Strelbitski.

Zhivkov was the first to regain his faculties. "An excellent lecture on the superiority of Soviet weaponry, Comrade Captain, but it would perhaps be wise if we were to depart this area. This no doubt will attract some local attention!"

"Yes, of course!" Budnov laughed as he lightly slapped his radio operator on the arm. "Call the other groups. Have them withdraw to the warehouse! We will make our damage report from there. I think there will be no need for further action here!"

Zhivkov pulled the moaning Strelbitski from the driver's seat and slid behind the wheel. The other men dragged the wounded driver into the van's rear as the radio operator called the other groups on a civilian hand-held CB radio.

As they drove slowly through the back streets of Brunssum, Budnov could not help but wonder what that old Dutch security guard thought in his last moment of life.

Late morning found Senior Lieutenant Zakharov's small group of raiders dug-in in shallow slit trenches on the south side of the E30 Autobahn. In a clump of bushes about fifty meters from the autobahn's shoulder were three men with an AGS-17 automatic grenade launcher, called "Flame" by the troops, and several RPG-22 disposable antitank rocket launchers. They were also well supplied with hand grenades for close-in protection, including RKG-3M antitank grenades. About 200 meters to the right of the Flame's position and a 150 meters from the paving were two men with an RPG-16D antitank rocket launcher. Another pair of similarly armed men were positioned 150 meters to the Flame's left. Three hundred meters from the autobahn, Sergeant Blinov and a machine gunner with an RPKS-74 watched over these three weapons crews. Several hundred meters to the west were two men in a security outpost. Connected with Zakharov by radio, they served to alert the force when an enemy column approached. Zakharov was positioned with a two-man AT-7 missile launcher crew on a small knoll 600 meters from the autobahn. They were aligned with a long straight stretch of highway where it curved in front of the group's emplacements. This positioned them to launch the wire-guided missiles down the length of the autobahn, enabling them to attack the vehicles' rears. With a range of 1000 meters, Zakharov hoped his launch team could fire all three of its high-explosive antitank (HEAT) missiles and destroy tanks on the straight stretch.

The AGS-17 grenade launcher was not primarily an antitank weapon, but Zakharov had insisted on including it over Sergeant Blinov's opposition. Zakharov was counting on it to destroy a large number of armored personnel carriers with its belted HEAT rounds as they deployed off the road. It was well sited in a well-protected position. The Flame crew had even brought along twenty empty sandbags to further protect their little fortress.

Traffic on the autobahn had been surprisingly light until 08.00. The raiders knew that the war had already begun, but the only indications were occasional low-flying fighters, both Soviet and NATO. After 08.00, German refugee traffic had then begun to pick up rapidly, all heading west. Military traffic was almost nonexistent. Small groups of cargo trucks, mostly German Territorial Army, did rush by heading east.

The R-126 radio's headset crackled in his left ear. Junior Sergeant Abramov, in the security post, spoke in German. The little radio had no secure voice capability. Speaking in German would hopefully delude any NATO intercept operators.

"Robar, Robar, come in, this is Gerhart," the earphone said.

"Gerhart, this is Robar," Zakharov spoke into the cheek microphone.

"Anna-one-zero, Gregori-four, Gregori-five, Elena-three,"

responded Abramov giving the Soviet phonetic word for each letter.

After writing the characters down, Zakharov quickly opened his notebook to a tabbed page. Across the top margin was a row of Cyrillic letters. A column of numbers edged the left margin. In a grid of hand-drawn boxes were abbreviated words and standard map symbols. By connecting the appropriate letter column and number line, Zakharov was able to translate the simple message. It was impossible to break such a code as the code sheet was prepared by the end user.

"Battalion, tanks, APCs, British," translated Zakharov to the missile launch crew. "Prepare to fire on my command, comrades!"

The gunner was already checking the optical tracking sight and his assistant readied the launch tube containing the next missile. The AT-7 missile's launch would signal the other ambushers to open fire.

If only everyone holds their fire, thought Zakharov.

Peering through the bushes to his left, Zakharov could see two little Ferret reconnaissance cars darting down the highway—the lead reconnaissance patrol. Minutes later three FV432 armored personnel carriers of the advanced guard rumbled down the paving. British soldiers stood in the open-back hatches with rifles and machine guns pointing to the roadsides. A troop of three massive Challenger tanks clanked past next, their 120mm guns angled to the right and left.

A continuous and seemingly endless column of assorted APCs of a tank-reinforced infantry battle group rattled by. Zakharov sensed the gunners becoming nervous at this display of armored might.

"Steady, comrades," muttered Zakharov. "Stand by."

Another troop of green-and-gray Challengers clambered pass.

"Track the last of the three tanks, comrades. Attack it first, then work forward."

The gunner strained to concentrate on the tracking sight. More APCs rumbled to their left.

"Stand by."

Zakharov wanted to allow as many of the following APCs as possible to come into the sectors of fire of the AGS-17 and two RPG-16s. He could take advantage of the missile's longer range and allow the tanks to get farther away.

"Stand by . . . stand by," Zakharov muttered. The assistant

gunner patted the next missile, ready to eject the spent launch tube and replace it immediately.

"Fire!"

There was no hesitation, the launch motor whooshed instantly. The missile screamed toward the tank leaving a white trail of smoke. The gunner continued to track his victim by keeping the sight's crosshairs trained on the vulnerable rear of the turret. Two loud double bangs signaled the firing of the RPG-16s as their launch charges expelled the rockets, followed instantly by their booster charges igniting. The Flame immediately began to rattle 30mm rounds into the flanks of several APCs, the flashes crackling on their sides. One lurched to a stop with smoke pouring from the open troop compartment hatches.

The missile struck the rear Challenger with a flash and a boom. The entire turret erupted into an orange fireball, burning main gun rounds arched through the air. The assistant gunner slammed the next missile into the launcher assembly. The gunner was already laying the tracker's crosshairs on his next target.

"Ready!"

"Fire!" screamed Zakharov.

The second missile screamed on its way. Zakharov saw that the lead tank had turned off the road presenting a flank shot.

Why had not the gunner fired at it? Because he had been told to work forward, thought Zakharov in frustration.

The column of vehicles was in pandemonium. Most were turning off the autobahn in their direction. Red machine-gun tracers laced across the fields. The RPGs, almost in unison, fired again. Several APCs were burning or smoking, victims of the RPGs and the Flame. The black oily smoke, propelled by the brisk northerly wind, wafted across the rolling fields and over the ambushers' positions. British infantrymen, in camouflaged winter uniforms, were stumbling out the back of some APCs. A six-man section rushed into the snow-patched field spreading out on line. The RPKS-74 machine gun spoke for the first time and hosed a steady stream of tracers into the advancing men, felling two.

He must have emptied the entire forty-round magazine, Zakharov thought.

Caught up in the excitement of the slaughter, the young officer shouldered the assistant gunner's AKS-74 assault rifle. He began firing short full-automatic bursts into the still-advancing British. More Englishmen tumbled to the frozen ground.

"Comrade Lieutenant!" screamed the gunner. "May we fire?"

He had allowed himself to become too absorbed in the killing. *"Fire! Fire!"*

The missile roared, the backblast overpressure again popping his eardrums. He saw the second tank blazing fiercely, burning fuel flowing down its flanks.

To his horror he realized that the lead tank was rumbling down the autobahn shoulder toward them, its massive gun aimed straight at them! Machine-gun bullets cracked through the tops of their bushes. The missile struck the turret's front slope to the right of the gun mantle with a flash. But still the main gun fired.

An armor-piercing penetrator slammed into the ground just meters from their clump of brushes, sending a shower of dirt clods on top of them. The British had been expecting to meet Soviet tanks in their first engagement. The tank discharged its smoke grenades to conceal it from further fire. The grenades burst across its front in sprays of red phosphorous.

Looking in the direction of the grenade launcher's position, he was shocked to see it erupt into orange flashes as hand grenades descended on it. Simultaneously, something, a rocket launcher or recoilless rifle, had ranged on the RPG position on the far right. The bushes concealing it were shredded by blast and fragmentation. More infantrymen were rushing across the fields. Some of the APCs had turned into the fields as well, their machine guns sending streams of tracers into anything that might conceal the enemy.

Several detonations rippled across the fields spraying dirt clods and chunks of turf toward the advancing British infantrymen. Sergeant Blinov had fired the four MON-50 mines hidden in the bushes. Copied from the U.S. claymore mine, the mine fragments ripped into the thin green line of soldiers sending many tumbling backward onto the snow-patched ground.

Zakharov grasped the PG-431 illuminating rocket and fired its three red flares toward the enemy so that his men would be able to see it, their attention being focused on their targets. The surviving positions began hurtling RDG-1 smoke grenades to conceal their withdrawal.

"GO, GO!" he screamed at the missile launch crew. The gunner, clutching the AT-7 tracker and launcher assembly, lunged out of the bushes followed by his assistant, who carried the tripod. Zakharov stumbled out after the pair. He was barely

on his feet when he felt a sharp stab in his right thigh. In front of him, the gunner's chest erupted as two bullets passed through his torso. The gunner dropped his weapon and tripped over it. Ignoring the dead gunner, Zakharov and the assistant gunner ran into the woods that sloped to the south. He could only hope that most of his small band would make it to the assembly point beside the pond. Behind him, the sound of heavy machine-gun fire grew louder.

★2★

As he pulled around the corner onto Caroline Street, near downtown Houston, Platoon Sergeant Bobby Daniels thought the scene looked like any other weekend drill at Company G (Long-Range Surveillance), 143d Infantry Regiment, Texas Army National Guard.

One group of men in BDUs and maroon berets were piling equipment into a company two-and-a-half ton truck parked on the grass strip, running back and forth from the large double doors on the ground floor. Another group stowed rucksacks and duffel bags in a Greyhound bus parked in front of the tall front steps that led up to the front door of the stately old armory.

Built in 1924, the building was a tiny Gothic fortress. The oldest armory still in use in the state, it had been built with the Houston Light Guard's own funds. The Light Guard was the oldest National Guard unit in the state, dating from 1873. Turreted and crenellated, the armory stood like an outpost in the dingy neighborhood that had grown up around it, a ghetto Fort Zindaneuf.

Daniels had seen the place look just like this a hundred times. The first difference he noticed was the sandbagged M60 machine guns on both front corners of the roof. He could see the gleam of the bright cartridges in the ammunition belts. This was no drill; this was the war they had trained for, worried about, but never really expected. Daniels fought back the thought that many of these men, these friends, had only a few more days to live.

14

Long-range reconnaissance was a risky business in peacetime. In war, it was almost suicide.

Well, hell, he thought, it's not the first time a National Guard LRRP company has gone to war. An Indiana company had spent a year in Vietnam, did a good job, too.

He parked in the lot next to the armory and walked around to the front. Staff Sergeant Stanley Bicknell and his little brood from the Selection and Training Section were on the steps. They had their M16s at port arms, guarding the front door. S&T, as they were called, trained the newly assigned men in LRRP skills and culled out the quitters before they were assigned to a recon team. This morning, since they were not part of a team, they were guarding the door.

"Mornin', Stan," Bobby said as he mounted the steps, "CO around?"

"Upstairs in operations, Bobby. Where you been, man? Lieutenant Tightlips is jumpin' through his ass!"

"I'm a shift supervisor. Couldn't just walk out of the chemical plant. They had to roust out another supervisor to relieve me."

The group parted to let Bobby pass. He walked through the metal front doors into a babel of noise in the armory. Men in uniform ran up and down stairs, carrying papers, equipment, weapons, the tools of war. On his left the door to the unit museum was closed and locked.

I guess it's gonna have a whole new set of displays soon, Bobby thought as he crossed the foyer to the stairs and went up to the operations center.

Captain Wally Schultz, commanding officer of Company G, was on the phone in his adjoining office. Every line on the phone was blinking. Normally a quiet, taciturn fellow, Wally was clearly stressed.

"That's right, 152 men and their equipment, tonight. Yeah, I'll hold." He motioned to Daniels to sit down. "Okay, I'll see you tonight."

Schultz hung up the phone and rubbed his face.

"I can't fuckin' believe this, Bobby," Schultz said. "A fuckin' Soviet attack on Fort Hood!" On the desk was a morning copy of *The Houston Post*. Its headline screamed FORT HOOD AT-TACKED!

Daniels said nothing, just looked at the CO.

"We need to be at Hood tonight, and on the way to Germany day after tomorrow. I still can't believe it!" Schultz leaned back in the old wooden desk chair and lit up a Marlboro, his tenth of the morning. "Did you hear about Kirkley? He and some CIA spook got on to the Russians and fought them at Hood, got wounded. First Purple Heart of the war." Schultz was wired. Daniels had never seen the CO so wound up.

"You really do need to quit smoking, sir. Where do you want me?" Daniels asked quietly.

"I want you to take your platoon right on up to Hood with the bus as advance detachment. Get things sorted out and lined up for the rest of the company. The first sergeant will go with the trucks. Third Platoon should already be there when you get there. We'll assemble in the 163d MI's area. They're supposed to have some quarters laid on. I'll be there later tonight when I get this madhouse shut down. Do your people have all their stuff?"

"Yes, sir. We're ready to go," Daniels said, standing. "As ready as we'll ever be."

"I hear that," Schultz replied. As Daniels walked away, he picked up the phone and pressed one of the blinking lights.

"Captain Schultz," he said for the umpteenth time.

The unit had conducted real world missions before, which included clandestine antidrug surveillance missions with the Border Patrol in the Big Bend area since 1988, but this was a different matter altogether.

Daniels threaded his way downstairs through the stream of men coming up from the supply room.

"Hey, Bobby," Tom Slater, the supply sergeant, called, "I thought you'd gone to Canada, man!"

"Not a bad idea, Tom," Daniels answered as he shouldered his way into the rapidly emptying supply room. "Got any masks?"

"Just yours, Bud," Tom answered, tossing Daniels an M17A2 protective mask. "Want a gun?"

"Sure, why not?" Daniels surrendered his weapons card as they walked across the weapons cleaning area to the arms vault. He had carried the card in his wallet for years. Now he wondered fleetingly if he would ever get to trade the weapon back in for that card.

The bus was nearly full when he got back outside. Daniels walked back to his car. He unlocked the trunk of the Oldsmobile and took out the big gray-and-green Alpinist II rucksack and nylon load-bearing equipment. He lugged the gear over to the bus, then made a second trip back for his duffel bag. Dropping the nylon olive drab bag to the ground, he grasped the trunk lid to shut it and found that he could not let go. His hands were quivering, clutching the lid. Forcing his grip to relax, he took a deep breath, slammed the trunk shut, and slowly walked to the bus. Daniels stashed his gear in the bus's baggage compartment and went back into the armory to round up his platoon and find the operations sergeant, Kurt Hagger. There were about fifty things they had to do before departing. He had better check everyone's state of mind while he was at it.

When the news of the Soviet attack finally set in, many people panicked. Afraid the hydrogen bombs would be falling on them, thousands of Houstonians hit the road. It was the same all over the country. The police, sheriff's department, and National Guard were trying to keep the roads open, but about the best they could do was to keep the protected bus transit lanes clear for official traffic. Bobby's little convoy would use the bus lane as far as it went, then hope for the best. Outside the city, the Highway Patrol would run interference for them.

BJ Kirkley hung up the phone and sighed. He gently ran his fingers over the thick cushion of bandage that covered the right side of his head. Underneath, the skin was sore. He still got dizzy when he stood up, but the doctor said that would pass in a few days if he took it easy. What a joke, take it easy! All of Company G would be at Fort Hood tonight. In two or three days, they would be in Germany, deep in the enemy's rear areas. This was the easy part.

"So, BJ, what's the word?" Captain Pat Peterson's voice rang from the other room.

"Main body'll be here at 2030 tonight," BJ called back, "if the roads stay clear."

Pat's dark face appeared around the corner.

"How you doin', baby?" she asked. "How's your head?"

"It's okay, Pat. Really."

"Listen, why don't you get some Zs until your people show up? Nothin' to do till then anyway."

That was a lie, of course. There were a thousand things to do to get a combat unit ready to deploy. When the rest of Company G arrived, they would have to be processed into the Active Army, get new ID cards, get their shot records updated (a process that scared some of them more than the prospect of combat), fill out dozens of forms, and get their equipment ready to load on C-130s and C-141s. Pat was cutting BJ some slack, and he decided to let her.

"Okay, I think I will, Pat. Thanks."

"Here, take my car and rack out in my room"—she rummaged in her bag for a second, then tossed BJ a key ring—"I'll call you when your guys show up."

West Fort Hood was a hive of activity with troops of the 504th Military Intelligence Brigade loading vehicles with all sorts of strange equipment. Gray Army Airfield was a parade of air transports. C-130s, C-141s, C-5Bs, even civilian 747s, L-1011s, and DC-10s landed and took off in a continuous stream. The air bridge to Europe had begun, and not too far behind schedule.

Passing the shattered control tower and burned Mohawks, he drove down Base Road from West Fort Hood and turned onto Highway 190 to take him to main post. Shattered civilian vehicles had been cleared to the side of the highway overpass at the intersection. Firemen still hosed water on the ruptured fuel storage tanks on the other side of the highway and railroad tracks. Entering the sprawling post on Clear Creek Road, he had to wait as IDs were checked. Fort Hood was still smoking. All the fires were out, but there was still smoke drifting off the burned-out hulks that had been the tanks, infantry fighting vehicles, self-propelled artillery, and other combat vehicles of the 1st Cavalry and 2d Armored Divisions. Fort Hood Army Airfield was littered with the wreckage of dozens of helicopters. Not as bad as that freak thunderstorm in '89, BJ thought. It had wrecked 200 helicopters, half of them Apaches.

Salvage crews were tearing the damaged vehicles apart, harvesting what parts they could to send to Europe. Without the tanks and IFVs to send as reinforcements, the spare parts would be critical to fix what was already there.

The railhead was just as busy as the airfield. M1 tanks and Bradley IFVs were lined up, waiting their turn to drive onto a railroad flatcar for the trip to Houston and then on to the ports of Beaumont, Orange, and Galveston. All other rail traffic between Killeen and Houston was shunted onto spurs. The tanks had first priority. It would take them at least a week to get from Texas to the Netherlands and Belgium by ship. This war could be lost in a week. He had wanted to drive down North Avenue to view the devastated motor pools, once lined with hundreds of combat vehicles, but the road was blocked off. Pulling into a parking space at the BOQ, he was surprised to see medics carrying bodies out of the Officers' Club across from the BOQ. Helluva strategic objective, he thought.

Armed guards were everywhere now. The MPs were all nervous and trigger happy, still scared spitless after their firefights with the Spetsnaz.

Pointless, now, BJ thought. If these guards had been in place and trigger happy on Christmas Eve, they could have prevented a lot of damage. But, instead of defending the base, all the MPs did was law enforcement and traffic control. Their security training had been almost nonexistent. He wondered if the MPs in Germany were any better prepared? Oh, well . . .

In Pat's BOQ room, BJ flopped down on the bed. A thousand thoughts raced through his mind, but his body overrode them and in less than a minute, he was asleep. His system seemed to know that soon sleep would be a luxury, and it was trying to stock up.

Sleep, he told himself, sleep now while you have the chance. The flight from Grenada to Angola would take at least eight hours. Now was the time to sleep, later there would be little chance.

Major Aleksei Bodnya took a deep breath and leaned his head back against the canvas seat, pulling his blue beret over his eyes. The flight from Nicaragua to Grenada had been tense. The Americans had aircraft that could have reached the Aeroflot Il-76's flight path, but none had been spotted. Cubans flown in from Angola had taken the airfield at Point Salinas, Grenada, on Christmas Eve at the same time Bodnya's Summer Harvest force had attacked Fort Hood. The Cubans had landed a civilian airliner on the runway and simply taken the terminal and tower by storm, much as the Israelis had taken Entebbe.

After invading Grenada in 1983, the Americans had completed the 10,000-foot runway the Cuban military engineers had begun. Now the island was again in Cuban hands. The Americans would be too preoccupied in Europe to worry about it. From Grenada, Bodnya's men would fly to Luanda, Angola. From there the Il-76 would take them due north across Africa to Libya. They would refuel again in Libya and make a dash across the Mediterranean. They would fly over Greece. A member of NATO, the Greek government had for years parroted the party line from Moscow. A joke in the Soviet Army was that

Greece was the only Warsaw Pact country that was part of NATO. The Greek fighters would not challenge them. The only real danger might be from the U.S. Navy, and possibly the Turks. Israel was certain to side with NATO, but would probably stay out of a direct confrontation with the Soviet Union. Bodnya assumed that the Soviets would encourage Syria and Iraq to attack Israel.

Unfortunately, the Syrians had not performed well against the Israelis in the past, and the Iraqis were bled white by the long war with Iran. In any case, the crossing over Greece would be short. Once north of Greece, they would cross over Bulgaria and land at Odessa. From there, on to Germany.

To do what, he wondered. Bodnya hoped that he would command a strike force operating in the NATO rear areas. He had studied the accounts of the predecessors to the Spetsnaz—the partisans and special detachments in the Great Patriotic War. In one operation in 1943, "Operation Concert," the partisans had wrecked hundreds of trains, blown hundreds of bridges, and killed thousands of German troops. It was Bodnya's dream to wreak such destruction. For now, he had two days to dream, to sleep and to dream.

Finally, he thought as the little C-12 turboprop lifted gently off the ground and climbed into the thin clouds over central Texas, finally I can get some sleep.

Since daybreak, Richard (Jinx) Jenkins had been grilled and regrilled about the Soviet attack on Fort Hood. He had talked to the Army's Intelligence and Security Command people; the Defense Intelligence Agency people; the National Security Agency people; the FBI, whose two dead agents in Austin had finally been recovered; the Immigration and Naturalization people who wanted to know how the Russians had gotten into Texas; and outfits he had never heard of like the Department of the Army's Assistant Chief of Staff for Intelligence's Foreign Intelligence Directorate's Soviet Division . . . whew!

The Spetsnaz attack was now the hottest show in town. Before he could not even give away the idea of a Soviet attack, now everybody wanted to hear about it! There was even a captain for the 902d MI Group's Resident Office, responsible for counterintelligence functions on Army posts, wanting to know why Jinx had not come to him. No doubt the man was trying to insure that his own ass was covered.

But, last of all, his employer, the CIA, wanted to talk to him. The pair from the Agency were tight-lipped and taciturn. Jinx detailed his mission in Nicaragua and specifically named Russell as the man who was more interested in getting rid of Jinx than in gathering information. At the end of the interview, Conklin, the agent from Austin, gave Jinx a copy of his walking papers from the CIA. In typical Agency fashion, they were going to keep Russell and fire Jinx. When they left, Pat Peterson had come in with orders for Jinx returning him to active duty and assigning him to Military Intelligence. He was ordered to report to Intelligence and Security Command— INSCOM—headquartered at Arlington Hall Station, Virginia, by the first available transportation.

Now, at dusk, he was on his way. Jinx was sure that Arlington Hall would be a repeat of the debriefings at Fort Hood. He unbuckled his seat belt and stretched out on the floor, using his bag as a pillow. The droning and vibration of the plane was already draining his tension. The flight was only four hours, but four hours' sleep was better than nothing. It might be a while before he got another chance.

Time was out of whack. Everything seemed to be moving in slow motion. He could see the muzzle of the pistol swinging toward him, lining up with his head. He fought to bring up his own weapon, but it seemed to be made of lead. The little man with the gun was smiling, but the smile was a rictus smile, a smile of death. BJ saw the finger tighten on the trigger. Fire blossomed from the muzzle and BJ's head began to ring. He screamed as the dream vanished and he sat up straight in . . . Pat Peterson's bed.

The ringing phone sounded miles away. It took a second for the nightmare to fade enough for BJ to function. He reached over for the receiver.

"Kirkley."

"BJ, are you okay?" Pat asked, her voice filled with concern. "The phone rang about ten times!"

"Yeah, Pat, I'm fine, just dead to the world."

"Well, you better wake up, baby, your people are here. We're moving them into some quarters now."

"I'll be right there, Pat."

"Okay, bye."

BJ swung his legs over the side of the bed, then stood slowly and walked into the latrine to splash cold water on his face.

How many nights am I going to see that gun in my face, he asked himself, forever?

At the barracks, 2d Platoon's six recon teams were milling around, waiting for someone to come in and start making work assignments. BJ didn't expect the reception he got from the members of his own platoon. They looked at him like he was a stranger, like they had never seen him before.

He was still BJ Kirkley, recon team leader and noted eccentric, but now he was something different. He had fought the Russians and won. The bandage on the side of his head spoke proudly of that fight. He was different from them, and they knew it. The distinction wouldn't last long. In a week, everyone in 2d Platoon would be different. Everyone who was still alive.

Bobby Daniels broke the ice.

"Good thing you got hit in the head, Beej," Daniels said, peering around at the bandage that covered one side of BJ's face, "no vital organs there."

"Nice to see you, too, asshole," BJ answered with a grin. Then everyone was crowding around, slapping BJ's back and carrying on.

"Okay, okay, let's get on with it here," BJ finally said. "Where's the CO?"

"He'll be here later with 1st and Commo Platoons," Daniels answered. "Third Platoon's been here awhile. It's a shorter trip from Austin."

"Okay, we'll give him some time to get here before the routine starts. The processing people want the whole outfit to run through at once. They'll convert us to regular Army, we turn in our pink ID cards, get issued new green cards, get everyone's pay records straight, and turn us over to the medics," BJ went on, ticking the steps off on his fingers. "The medics will make sure you're breathing, then bring your shots up-to-date."

The mention of shot records drew a moan from the crowd. No one liked the prospect of mass inoculation. Daniels especially dreaded it. It had long been a Company G tradition that the platoon leaders and platoon sergeants gave each other shots. The medics had always gone along with it, but maybe they'll be too rushed, he thought.

"After that, we just wait for the next available transportation.'' BJ concluded his checklist. "We're priority, folks, so we won't have to wait long.''

The kidding and bs stopped right then. For years, they had trained for this day, but that training had been fun and exciting. Hard work, too, but exciting nonetheless. What would come now was exciting, but real, deadly real.

"We do have one interesting development," said Daniels. "There're four guys that want out of the company. They say it's their right since it's a volunteer unit.''

"Ya? What's the Ol' Man and Top say about that?'' asked BJ.

"Top passed the word that they're right, anyone can request a transfer out . . . once we get to Germany. Then they'll be shipped to the 22nd Replacement Battalion for reassignment to a mechanized infantry battalion. The Ol' Man says they can think about their judgment call while they fry in an armored personnel carrier that sucked up an RPG.''

"Sounds good to me," said BJ. "I don't want someone like that on my team.''

The CO and the rest of the company showed up around midnight. By noon the next day, Company G, 143d Infantry, had been processed into the Army and was ready for shipment to Europe. At 1520, the four C-130s brought down from the Air Guard unit at Dallas lifted off for the first leg of the long transatlantic flight. Their vehicles would follow on C-141s. Men crowded around the tiny round windows, trying to get a last look in the fading light. The burned tank parks were still smoking, a grim reminder of what awaited them in Germany. Each man wondered if the ruined post would be the last look at Texas he would get.

★3★

Finally, Bodnya thought as the dark blue of the Mediterranean flashed beneath, finally we are out of Africa. It wasn't a moment too soon for him. If all our allies are that stupid, that lazy, and that cowardly, he decided, we will have to win this war alone.

The Il-76 was hugging the ocean to avoid radar detection by the U.S. Navy. It was risky to fly so low in a plane this size, but not as risky as detection by a pair of F-14 Tomcats. They would be out of the American area in an hour and safely inside Greek airspace. After that, it would be routine to Odessa.

The Libyans had been so repulsive. All their warlike bluster had disappeared when the Soviets had attacked NATO. Supplied by the Soviet Union with the latest export weapons, Libya had twisted the tail of the NATO countries and terrorized the countries around it in North Africa for years. Now the normal rules were out and the Western democracies were committed to war. If they repelled the Soviet thrust in Europe, they would doubtless come around to square old debts with Libya. The Libyan Air Force commander in Benghazi had flatly rejected the notion of sending fighter escorts with the Il-76. He wanted the Russian plane refueled and on its way. Kovpak had been disgusted with the man, calling him a coward to his face. The Libyan had been furious.

"Well, Comrade Ensign, you made a new friend today."

"Comrade Major, the man is a coward, like most of those African monkeys," Kovpak answered. "A month ago, they were training terrorists and bragging about striking fear into the very

24

heart of America. Now, all they want to do is to jump on a camel and ride into the desert. None of those people has the stomach for a fight. I would trade the lot of them for a company of *Basmachi*.''

''I cannot argue with you there,'' Bodnya answered, laughing. His experiences with Arab troops had not impressed him. None of the Arabs were a match for the Afghans, but then, who was, really?

''If we had an army of *Basmachi* fighting for us, we would be dining in London in a week, Comrade Major,'' Kovpak added.

''Perhaps an army of Cossacks will suffice.''

Bodnya decided to stretch and walked up the steps to the flight deck of the transport. There an argument was in progress. The flight engineer, Senior Lieutenant Pyotr Gontar, was clearly upset about the low-altitude flight across the Mediterranean and was lecturing the pilot, Major Lovchikov. The engineer's voice was cracking with fear.

''Comrade Major, I must point out that this aircraft is not designed to operate at such a low altitude, especially over the ocean.''

''What difference does the ocean make?'' Captain Shatlov, the copilot, asked.

''The salt vapor in the air seriously reduces the life expectancy of the aircraft systems, especially the engines and electrical components,'' the engineer flatly stated. ''I must insist that . . .''

''I must insist that you shut up, Comrade Lieutenant!'' shouted the pilot. ''This is not a training flight! We are easily within range of American carrier aircraft. If we are detected by these aircraft, the salt vapor will not be a problem. One of their air-to-air missiles will reduce the life expectancy of this aircraft and its occupants to zero! Now be quiet and return to your station! *Do you understand me?*''

All eyes in the cockpit were on the young engineer. He seemed to deflate, to get smaller.

''Yes, Comrade Major, I understand.''

He turned back to his console.

''Pyotr,'' Lovchikov said quietly, ''this is war, now. None of the rules are the same. The only rule is do your job and stay alive.''

The engineer was silent.

* * *

It's a cold, hard world, Jack thought as he slowly scanned the snowy hillside, not to mention hostile and deadly.

Captain Jack Connauer and the five other members of Operational Detachment A-12, 1st Battalion, 10th Special Forces Group (Airborne), had been inserted by one of the 160th Aviation Regiment's HH-60D Nighthawk helicopters less than four hours ago, after a harrowing flight through the massed Soviet air defenses. The Nighthawk's AN/APR-39 radar-warning alarms had buzzed and beeped constantly as the dark green special operations chopper had threaded its way at treetop and below treetop level to their landing zone seventy kilometers behind the Warsaw Pact juggernaut advancing across the IGB—Inner German Border. Since their insertion, the team had occupied its observation post and begun setting up shop. The night had been filled with the sounds of distant jets and helicopters, but their hillside had been quiet.

Already the cold was taking its toll. Jack's knees were almost numb from kneeling in the snow. Behind him, he could hear the other five team members quietly cursing to themselves as they tried to dig into the frozen ground. It would be light soon, already the eastern horizon was a pale gray line. They would have to be dug in and camouflaged before it got light.

"Cap'n, we can't get through this frost layer," SFC Dan Dionopolus whispered from behind, "it's like asphalt."

"Do the best you can, Dan." Connauer answered. "Use the pine needles and snow to hide the gear in that little draw, we need to be operational by daylight."

The operations sergeant returned to his task and Connauer again used his binoculars to search the gloom. The highway, E8 Autobahn, was now visible in the weak gray light, a four-lane line of concrete, dark against the snow-covered fields. E8 ran west-southwest from the southern outskirts of Berlin, its path coming to within 500 meters of the low hill on which the split A-team now waited. E8 was the major route west across the North German plains into West Germany and to Hannover.

Connauer's Green Berets were there to monitor traffic on the highway and laser-designate selected targets for air attack by the 2d Allied Tactical Air Force. The other half of A-12 was on an identical mission farther south on the E6 Autobahn. In the four days since the balloon had gone up, the 1st Battalion, 10th SF Group, had deployed nearly all its A-teams. The 10th had been lucky, in a way. Nearly all of the troops were still in Germany on Christmas Eve. Many combat units had as much as one third of their personnel scattered all over Europe and America. The 1st of the 10th had been ready to go on Christmas Day. By December 27th, they had almost all their thirty-six A-teams deep in enemy territory, all along the NATO Central Front, most of them across the IGB from the V and VII U.S. Corps. Others, like A-12, were deployed farther north to support NATO's Northern Army Group (NORTHAG) pending the arrival of the U.S. III Corps. Unhappily, some of those teams had not been heard from since.

Movement in the distance caught his attention. He studied the highway through binoculars, trying to identify the line of vehicles moving down the road. They were wheeled vehicles, not tracked. He counted fifteen of them before the first one got close enough to identify. They were BTR-60s, eight-wheeled armored personnel carriers. Not exactly the latest Warsaw Pact equipment, enough vehicles for half a motorized rifle battalion, probably East German.

"Sparks!" Connauer called softly to the radio operator, "get your radio up, we have a target."

Raymond "Sparks" Posey, the commo man, dropped his entrenching tool and rapidly set up the AN/PSC-3 satellite communications radio, adjusting its tiny dish antenna to point at the geocentric satellite high above. This would enable the team to transmit a message on a very narrow beam, at a high angle, making it almost impossible to detect it. Posey encrypted the message into the required format. He then pulled the Digital Message Device Group (DMDG) from his pack and began to input Connauer's message.

"Read back the message."

"Fifteen BTR-60PBs moving west on E8, followed by a six-digit grid coordinate and the time. No ADA."

"Go with it."

As Sparks attached the DMDG that would transmit the entire message in one second-long high-speed burst to the radio, and set the frequency, Connauer watched the BTR-60s pass.

"Ready to transmit, sir."

"Send it."

Sparks pressed the X-mit button on the DMDG, sending the short message. He waited a few seconds, then sent it again, waiting for a confirmation signal from their communications base south of Hannover. As Sparks sent the message the second time, Connauer watched the line of BTRs suddenly turn off the road, their tires churning the light snow. All fifteen of the personnel carriers were off the road in a wide line making their way across the frozen fields at the foot of the hill.

"Jesus Christ! They're heading this way!" Connauer shouted to the team. "Get your shit and move out!"

The team wasted no time in pulling out. Each man had his gear collected and rucksack on in under a minute. Only Sparks was slower, packing up the radio gear. As he pulled on the sixty-pound pack, Connauer watched down the hill as the BTRs pulled on line, disgorging dozens of AKM assault rifle armed troops. Connauer knelt down beside a pine tree and focused his binoculars on the long, ragged line of men advancing up the slope. Their uniforms were steel-gray with a round white patch on the left shoulder.

"East German Workers Militia, for Christ's sake!" Connauer said over his shoulder.

"Come on, sir," Posey replied. "Move it!"

Connauer took the sergeant's advice and followed the team, which was now loping toward the crest of the hill. Burdened with their heavy rucksacks, they looked like a hunchback track team.

How the hell did they find us so fast, Connauer wondered as he forced his pack-laden body up the hill. This was not a good sign. They were in East Germany to kill tanks, not run track and field. Aside from the danger, they would not be effective on the run. They would move over to the next hill, half a kilometer away, and see if the Germans pursued them farther. At least he hadn't seen any dogs.

The hill was growing light as A-12 slipped over the crest and made its way west along a saddle between the two low, rolling hills. The road was no longer visible behind them. The neat German forest had no underbrush beneath its tall evergreens. It made movement easy, but stealth difficult. At least the snow was patchy here. It would not lead the militia right to them. Another 200 meters and they would stop for a moment to watch for pursuers. Connauer's heart was pounding. The rucksack felt like an anvil, its straps biting into his shoulders. The cold air burned his lungs. No amount of training could prepare you for running with a loaded ruck, but fear was a powerful motivator.

They started up the saddle when Connauer felt, rather than

heard, movement behind him. Looking over his shoulder, he caught a glimpse of a rifle butt just as it hit his left temple. Reeling back, he could vaguely hear shots and muffled shouts, but they seemed to come from far away. The world rapidly narrowed to a long, dark tunnel with a Russian at the end of it. He fumbled for his M16, but his hands had grown boxing gloves. The rifle butt appeared again, and Connauer's brain erupted in a flash of dark red pain.

We're fucked, he thought. Then the ground came up and the tunnel went black.

★4★

"I wondered if we would ever see the Rodina again, Comrade Major," Kovpak said as the Aeroflot transport made its final approach to the military airfield outside of Odessa. Their last leg—from Libya, across the Mediterranean, and across Greece, over the Black Sea, and into Mother Russia—had been particularly unnerving for the Spetsnaz raiders.

"We will not see it for long, my friend," Bodnya replied. "We will very soon be on our way to join the fight in Germany."

Kovpak had been nervous during the flight over the Mediterranean. Now he was all smiles. He was back in Mother Russia. Many Soviet soldiers reacted this way when returning from overseas assignments. They were unhappy and uncomfortable outside the Soviet Union, too many decisions, too many people watching them, and it was always so "foreign." It was as if they drew strength and comfort from the Russian soil itself. Bodnya thought it was because, when overseas, the Soviet system was not there to make every decision for them. Without the constant regulation, they felt lost. Even Ensign Kovpak, with all his experience in foreign countries, was sometimes inflicted with this discomfort.

Kovpak did not answer. In truth, he was not looking forward to joining the fight in Germany. The attack on Fort Hood had been easy. The Americans had not been expecting them, and they had fought only ill-prepared military police. Now they would be up against an enemy who was expecting them, on guard for them; for certainly many enemy units had already felt the bite of Spetsnaz wolves. It would be easier to survive this war behind Warsaw Pact lines, but it was clear that the major was looking forward to fighting behind NATO lines. Perhaps he would be lucky and the war would be won before they were committed. The role of occupier was more appealing to him than that of martyr to the struggle to defeat the forces of darkness. He would relish an opportunity to enjoy West German abundance, not to mention the fräuleins.

Landing at Odessa was a dreary homecoming for the Operation Summer Harvest survivors. Totally blacked out, there were few aircraft at the usually busy base. The fighters, bombers, and transports had deployed either to bases in the western USSR or had dispersed to satellite bases. Sentries from the base guard company were everywhere, standing in the shadows of hangars, marching pairs alongside the taxiways. Sixty-two of the original ninety Spetsnaz paratroopers were still with the group, along with the eight members of their An-12 transport's crew. One of their wounded had died while refueling at the clandestine airstrip in Mexico. Eight wounded had been left in Cuba before the group boarded an Il-76 transport bound for Libya.

Several of the remaining men bore minor wounds, but had remained with the group. The others had perished at Fort Hood, Texas, on the eve of the Warsaw Pact offensive into West Germany. They could only hope that their sacrifice had not been in vain, that they had in fact delayed the departure of III Corps' reinforcements to Europe.

The weary paratroopers, chilled by the cold air and still wearing American battle dress uniforms, were hastily off-loaded from the transport as its engines powered down. To a man, they had donned their blue berets. Most had slipped on their traditional *Telnaishka*, the paratrooper's blue-and-white striped undershirt, a bizarre combination with the American camouflage uniform. Instructed to leave their weapons and equipment aboard, they were hastened to a large dark hangar not far from the airliner's parking area. Leading the men through the small personnel door set in the hangar's main door, Bodnya could make out a large group of men in the darkened hangar's center. A cold feeling began to creep into his stomach.

"Aleksei . . ." muttered Kovpak at his side, "I have an uncomfortable feeling . . .'' The door slammed shut with a tinny bang.

Blinding lights suddenly flashed on from the hangar's ceiling. Arrayed before them was a full Air Force band decked out in their sky-blue parade uniforms. The bandmaster, an ensign, lifted his baton high and the band burst forth with the stirring strains of the ''Soviet Army Song.'' Written on the twenty-fifth anniversary of the Soviet Army and first sung after the 1943 victory at Volgograd (Stalingrad), it was dedicated to the soldiers defending the Motherland. From the side an Air Force chorus bellowed the rousing lyrics . . .

> *"Valiant and legendary,*
> *In battle having tasted the joy of victory,*
> *To you, admired Army,*
> *Our Motherland sends its greetings in song!"*

Bodnya was almost overwhelmed by pounding waves of emotion. Tough little Kovpak's hands were shaking. His paratroopers were stone still, most with tears in their eyes.

Scores of draped flags of the Soviet Ground and Air Forces provided a colorful backdrop. A huge, quickly painted banner hung above the flags. It portrayed a pack of gray wolves pulling an armored, battle ax-armed warrior from his black steed. The mounted warrior, ''The Destroyer—the Phantom Warrior,'' was the symbol of the American III Corps. The symbolism was not lost on the paratroopers; the Spetsnaz wolves, their traditional symbol, unhorsing the armored warrior. A group of generals and colonels in Ground Forces sea-green and Air Forces sky-blue uniforms marched forward. The ragged group of paratroopers began to stumble into some semblance of a formation. A signal troops lieutenant general, almost certainly GRU, stepped before Bodnya, firmly clasped his shoulders, and peered into his eyes.

''Lieutenant Colonel Aleksei Bodnya,'' he bellowed over the martial music, ''the President, the Congress of Peoples' Deputies, and the Soldiers and Workers of the Union of Soviet Socialist Republics send their greetings and appreciation to you and your brave soldiers!'' He embraced him in a bearlike hug kissing both cheeks. The general stepped back, a major carrying a red satin-covered board appearing at his side. The general pinned the modestly small and simple red ribbon and plain Gold Star of a Hero of the Soviet Union over Bodnya's heart. This was followed by the more elaborate, but lesser, Order of Lenin. Handing him a deep red leather-bound citation from the Presidium of the Supreme Soviet, the general again stepped back.

Bodnya could barely manage the obligatory, "I serve the Soviet Union!"

"Comrade Guards Lieutenant Colonel Bodnya"—the general smiled at him—"your unit has struck the first blow against the enemies of the Motherland. Striking into the very heart of the enemy's machine of aggression, under the most demanding and arduous of conditions, the 800th Construction Training Company has provided an example to be emulated by all special source units and subunits!"

Bodnya was shocked. No one had previously used his unit's deception designation openly.

The other generals were pinning the Order of Lenin on his officers and the Order of the Red Star on his paratroopers. The band had changed to the quite lilting tune of "The Guardsmen in Berlin." The chorus quietly sang the opening verses, pausing after each as the tune slowly built in tempo and volume . . .

> *"The Guards greeted the spring in Berlin,*
> *In the year 1945 . . ."*

The general spoke again. "To merely award soldiers with the honors they so richly deserve, having risked and sacrificed so much for the Motherland, is not enough to honor such a unit!" The music swelled in intensity, the chorus' deep voices boomed . . .

> *"We had seen so many orphans and dead,*
> *We were as wrathful as devils . . . "*

"The 800th Construction Training Company is redesignated the 800th Guards Independent Special Purpose Battalion, the first unit to be so honored since the Great Patriotic War in 1945!" The ballad reached its resounding final verse . . .

> *"Peace is not signed on a piece of paper*
> *But with a Guardsman's Bayonet!"*

The generals began pinning Guards Badges on the paratroop-ers' right chests. Bodnya was stunned by the presentation of such an honor.

The band switched to the solemn "Meeting March" as a Guards paratrooper colonel came forward bearing a red Ground Forces unit colors streamer emblazoned with a gold hammer and sickle. Beneath the hammer and sickle was embroidered their new cover designation, 800—й Гвардийя Отдельнайа Воздусэно-Десант Батальон —Guards Independent Airborne Battalion. From the staff dangled a red-and-gold Гвардийя — "Guards" ribbon. Another ribbon was inscribed Техас —Texas. So, their new unit would also bear that honor title in its desig-nation, just as earlier units bore "Berlin" and other liberated cities.

"Ensign Kovpak!" The little Ukrainian rushed to his side. The colonel gave the colors to the general, who, representing the Minister of Defense, presented it to Bodnya on behalf of the President of the Supreme Soviet. Bodnya in turn pivoted and passed it to Kovpak. Kovpak dipped the bloodred colors once and shouldered the short, thick oak staff on his left shoulder. He recalled seeing that done in his old tank unit. The troops, too, were stunned by the wealth of honors.

Bodnya turned and motioned Senior Lieutenant Sukharev and Master Sergeant Ratnikkov to flank Kovpak as an ad hoc color guard. They slowly marched the short length of the formation from its left to right flank.

Bodnya thought to himself, It is the commander's duty to self-lessly defend the colors to prevent their capture by the enemy. If the colors are lost, the commander and the responsible serv-icemen are brought to trial by a military tribunal, and the unit is disbanded. He would see to it that such a thing never took place.

Speeches were given and presentations of flower bouquets were made by female Air Force lieutenants and sergeants to all ranks. The band played light music accompanied by the chorus' quiet mournful singing of the Soviet Army's legendary deeds in the Great Patriotic War. During the remaining speeches, the troops eyed a long, food-laden table bedecked with flowers.

The taste of victory is indeed sweet, thought Bodnya. Glanc-ing down at Kovpak, the little Ukrainian returned a big smile over his equally large mustache and winked. Bodnya suddenly realized the smile and wink were aimed at a comely young Air Force junior sergeant across the hangar. Some things never change, thought Bodnya.

The taste of victory *will* indeed be sweet, thought Kovpak.

★ 5 ★

Arlington Hall had been a whirlwind. He had been interviewed, questioned, processed, the whole works. What was that line like from "Alice's Restaurant," he'd been inspected, infected, rejected, and neglected. No, not neglected. Everything but that. Jinx had been the center of attention at the Intelligence and Security Command. They were very interested in Jinx's report. As far as INSCOM was concerned, the Agency had blown the chance to head off another Pearl Harbor, and INSCOM, along with DIA as part of the military side of intelligence, was all set to jam it down the CIA's throat.

None of that mattered to Jinx. He was back in the Army, and on his way to Germany. Jinx doubted that anyone had been processed into the Active Army so fast. He got an instant Form 20 and updated 201 file, promotion orders to major, green ID card, dog tags, one set of BDUs, a field jacket, a set of mustard-brown major's oak leaves, and a pair of rose (for knowledge) and sword (for strength) MI branch collar insignia. The rose and sword were known as the "pierced pansy" to insiders. He also got orders assigning him to the 588th MI Detachment, somewhere in Germany.

Now, sitting on the landing gear of a Blackhawk helicopter packed inside a C-141 flying over the Atlantic, Jinx wrote his name on the BDUs with a magic marker borrowed from the loadmaster. He wouldn't have time to get name tapes sewn on.

How many of these things do they have, Caporal-Chef Henri Bouchet wondered as he watched the huge silver plane touch down. The C-141s were landing in a continuous stream now, once every minute. The routine was always the same, ground crews would unload the palletized load as fast as possible while the plane was refueling. As soon as the plane was fueled, it took off for the U.S. via Canada, again to bring another load of weapons, supplies, ammunition, or troops.

Once unloaded, the cargoes and soldiers were whisked off the base. There were no buildings left on base for processing and the risk of chemical contamination was still there. Henri was not worried about chemicals. His decontamination team had scrubbed the concrete areas of the base first, and was working around the clock to clear the grassy areas. If they stayed on the concrete, they would be all right. He tried not to look too much at the ruins of the base.

Liege-Bierset had been the home of the Belgian 1st and 8th Squadrons dedicated to the 2d Allied Tactical Air Force. At 1900 hours on Christmas Eve, the base commander, Colonel Jean-Luc DuBarrai, had been assassinated in his home, along with his wife and two of their three children. At 0400 hours Christmas morning, the power lines to the base had been cut, and at 0628 hours, Liege-Bierset had virtually been destroyed, from what he could gather, by two Soviet missiles carrying multiple fuel-air warheads that had exploded over the base. The blast from the fuel-air warheads was nearly atomic in force. The horrendous overpressures caused by the detonation of the volatile aerosol clouds dispersed by the warheads had collapsed most of the buildings and damaged the hardened structures where two squadrons' Mirage 5BAs were hangared. Reflected blast, dynamic pressure, and mechanical impulse had combined to cause further damage. The second series of blasts, five minutes later, set fire to the collapsed buildings and shattered some of the hardened structures. The two squadrons of ground attack fighters were crushed inside their own hangars. Twenty minutes after the second blast, as rescuers were searching for survivors and fighting the dozens of fires, another missile with a chemical warhead went off. A thick mist of Sarin, a persistent nerve agent, quickly covered the base in a huge elliptical pattern. Anyone caught without a protective mask and suit died in minutes. The mist coated the ground, the buildings, and the people, making them all lethal carriers of the nerve agent. At the hospital in town, two nurses and an orderly had died when they got the chemical on their skin, trying to treat other victims of the attack.

The base had been closed until Henri's decontamination unit had arrived. Their high-pressure hoses had cleaned the runway and hard stands so the base could be reopened, but it took hours. Henri tried not to think about where the contaminated water went as it ran into ditches and drains. The first C-141 had landed an hour after the runway had been cleared of ice left from the decontamination foam. The fires on the base had burned themselves out. No attempt was being made to search the rubble. Anyone in there was dead now, either from the poison gas, blood loss, or shock aggravated by the cold. All new arrivals were rushed off the base to a processing center in town. The townspeople were all terrified, fearing another chemical attack on the processing center, and were fleeing the small town, choking the roads to the west. If the purpose of the Soviet attack had been to destroy the base at Liege-Bierset and to create chaos in the NATO rear area, it was working perfectly.

The bell scared Jinx awake.

"Indian territory," the loadmaster said as he made his way toward the rear of the aircraft.

Jinx stood up and stretched. They were entering the European Theater, off the coast of England. For all intents, the Theater began at the outer limit of Soviet fighters. Su-24 Fencer fighters based at Templin could strike west of the Irish coast.

A pair of Royal Air Force Phantoms had picked them up and would escort them to Liege-Bierset airbase in Belgium. From there, Jinx would have to hop a transport headed for Bonn. That would not be any problem, everything moving was headed east.

As the C-141 made its approach to Liege-Bierset, Jinx saw the effects of the Soviet attack. Bulldozers had cleared most of the wreckage and chemical decontamination teams were at work on the base. Yellow plastic tape and yellow triangular signs marked the many still contaminated areas. Jinx knew it would be months before all the contaminated soil was scraped off and carted away. Until then, only the concrete areas were safe.

A Belgian *premier sergent* met them on the ramp.

"Keep inside the taped areas," he said through a bullhorn, his voice muffled by the protective mask. "Keep your masks on until you are clear of the base."

Jinx suddenly felt naked without a mask.

"Major Jenkins?"

Jinx turned to find a tall, thin, very female, but masked Spec. 4 standing next to a jeep, holding a German protective mask.

"I'm Jenkins."

"Jenna Collingsworth, sir. I'm here to pick you up. I thought you might need this," she said, handing him the gas mask. "They never think to issue them in the States. We have a few extra since the balloon went up. You have any baggage?"

"Just this," Jinx answered, tossing his AWOL bag into the back of the jeep.

"Great, let's go," she said over her shoulder as she climbed into the jeep and kicked the engine back to life. "We're goin' to have to get you a pot and chem suit, sir." Jinx was barely in the seat when the jeep lurched off and slid deftly between two five-ton cargo trucks headed for the airbase gate. Once out of the gate, she gunned the open jeep around the lumbering trucks and made for the open road as fast as the jeep would go. She drove fast, but skillfully. The cold wind forced Jinx to pull his gloves on and put his earflaps down.

"Sorry about this old quarter-ton," she apologized, raising her voice to be heard over the engine and wind noise. "All the Hamm-Vs were sent to units at the front. They pulled them all out to replace battle losses. We've lost a bunch of them, a bunch of everything. We're clear now."

She pulled the hooded mask off and carefully laid it between the seats. Jinx removed his own and replaced it in its gray bag.

Jinx hadn't expected anyone to meet him, much less a nice-looking, blond cheerleader type like Spec. 4 Collingsworth. Her casual style intrigued him. Here they were driving toward the war zone, and she acted like it was a joyride in the country. Besides, when he had been on active duty there had not been that many women in the Army, especially in troop units. Her blond hair streamed out behind her helmet, against regulations, and even the baggy camouflage-patterned chemical protective suit couldn't conceal a pair of very long legs. She was close to six feet tall, Jinx guessed.

Handing Jinx a small olive drab plastic box, Collingsworth shouted over the wind, "Decon your boots and drop the wipes in the trash bag in back. Just a precaution since we weren't even required to be MOPP'ed up."

Popping the top off the box, marked "M258A1 skin decon-taminating kit," he discovered six OD mylar packets. Half were marked "1" and the others "2." Hesitating a moment, he shyly asked, "How do you use this?"

"Where have you been, sir? Haven't you ever taken an NBC proficiency test?" Collingsworth was eyeing him with mild disbelief.

"I've been out of the loop for a while."

That was an understatement if there ever was one, he thought. It's been years since I've had to do real Army stuff.

"Eh, just read the instructions on the box, sir." Being in an MI unit she was fast to catch on and asked no more questions. Reading the instructions, he tore open a "1" packet and began wiping his boots down.

"We pulled back to Koblenz yesterday," she went on. "We should be able to stay there for a while if the center doesn't collapse. I don't think it will. I don't think they'll be able to get through Darmstadt."

Jinx gingerly dropped the wipes into the trash bag and wondered if he had gotten anything nasty on his leather gloves.

Ahead, a group of civilian cars and commercial vans were stalled in the road. Jenna steered around them, driving off onto the frozen field. The knot seemed to be a collision between an Audi and Mercedes sedan. Behind the wreck, the road was solid cars as far as Jinx could see.

"Civilians. Gas killed a bunch of 'em Christmas Day. The rest hit the road. They don't know where they're goin', just know they don't want to be where the Russians are. The roads are all fucked. Even the armor units can barely get through. The autobahn looked like a parking lot the first two days. It cleared right up, though, after the Feldjägers hung a couple of motorists from the overpasses with signs around their necks that said, 'I Blocked the Road.'"

"The what?"

"The Feldjägers—Field Police, German Military Police—strung up a couple of Kraut civilians who blocked the road and wouldn't get their cars off to let military traffic through. Left 'em hanging, too." She hooked her finger back over her shoulder. "Those folks back there had better straighten out that mess pretty quick, or they may get the same treatment. The Belgian Gendarmes are beginning to get just as serious about clearing the roads."

Jenna deftly steered back onto the shoulder and gunned the

jeep past the stalled column of cars. It took four hours to get to Koblenz, where the 588th MI Detachment had set up its base.

The headquarters was in a small *gasthaus*. The only real indication that it was a military facility was the communications van and dish antenna parked next it. Jenna pulled around back, parking the jeep in the long covered parking garage.

"It's not much, but we call it home."

Inside the place, it was warm and busy. Every room downstairs was crammed with whatever furniture the small unit could scrounge. There were a couple of desks and all the tables from the dining room had been shanghaied for the communications gear and computers. As Jinx rubbed his face to get some feeling back, he heard a voice behind him.

"Major, I'm Thomas Tucker, this is my facility," a short, studious lieutenant colonel said from behind him. Jinx turned to meet the commander of the 588th.

An English teacher, Jinx thought as he stuck out his hand, the man looks like a college English professor. He even has a New England accent. The rock-hard handshake the man offered didn't feel academic, though.

"Richard Jenkins, Colonel." He handed him the brown envelope containing his orders and 201 File.

"Your timing is excellent. I want you to meet the gentlemen you'll be interacting with. Come this way, please."

Tucker led the way up the stairs to a room on the second floor, as he flipped through the 201 looking first to see if his Top Secret clearance also cleared him for Special Compartmented Information and included the requisite Special Background Investigation. In a former guest room were two officers, one a recruiting poster model and the other a tame bear in a uniform.

"Major Jenkins, since you're former Special Forces yourself, you'll be working with these two on one of our projects, Operation Kreuzadder. That means 'crossed snake' in German, a mystical creature." The two officers nodded.

"You'll be employed for liaison with III Corps' 504th MI Brigade, 10th SF Group's elements up here, the German ANB—Federal Defense Forces Intelligence Office—and any other organizations and agencies involved with cross-FLOT (forward line of troops) operations. The operation's goal is to place specially trained SF teams in Soviet uniforms deep behind their lines to harass and pillage . . . general brigandage. The teams will spread the belief that they're deserters from Soviet Central Asian republics who refuse to fight for the Soviets. We hope to divert many of their rear-area security units to search for the Kreuzadders rather than our own special operations elements, as well as accomplish intelligence collection, disrupt their lines of communications. We feel that the Soviets will overreact and go to excessive ends to eliminate this 'counterrevolutionary' threat within their ranks, simply because they cannot afford to permit it to spread. The team members were individually selected for their experience and physical similarity to Central Asians . . . not Oriental, more Turkish or Arabic in appearance,'' Tucker remarked seeing Jinx's questioning look. ''They're versed in Russian, the appropriate dialects, customs, and mannerisms. Your duties will also involve coordinating the intelligence they collect and relaying it to the appropriate NATO command. The more we can hit them behind the FLOT, the easier it will be to stop them. I'll have to excuse myself and leave you with these two. They'll take you in hand and fill you in on the details.''

With that, he dashed off down the stairs.

''A man of many words.''

''Yeah, but when he speaks, folks listen.''

The uniformed bear stepped forward. ''I'm Lou Bennett,'' the major said, ''this is Fred Haskell,'' nodding to the crew-cut captain.

''Richard Jenkins,'' Jinx said, shaking the two offered hands. ''This is quite a plan. Obviously, you guys didn't just think this up.''

''Not hardly''—Bennett laughed—''we came up with the idea a couple of years ago during an exercise. When we ran it through ASOCOM, Army Special Operations Command, they loved it, but the Pentagon people—Office of the Deputy Chief of Staff for Intelligence—went nuts. Said that the U.S. Army does not practice 'black' operations, could not engage in piracy and atrocities as a matter of practice, and told us to forget the idea and destroy all documentation about it.

''Naturally, we figured that was a good indicator that it was an excellent plan, so we went back and refined the concept. We put together four A-teams dedicated to Kreuzadder. They look and act the part. The Anglos on the teams are Russian speakers, and act the part of Russian deserters. All of 'em have been trained on the Soviet armored vehicles and equipment at Combat Maneuver Training Center at Hohenfels, so they can use any they find. We even sent them through our own 'School of the Young

Soldier,' Soviet basic training, so that they know how to act like Soviet soldiers. Their orders are to harass Soviet units, recruit real Soviet deserters, and establish a fifth column in Ivan's rear. They have carte blanche on how they go about it. The only standing order they have is to attack any Soviet nuclear assets they encounter."

"These teams are already in place?"

"They went in last night by chopper during an EW jamming storm. Lost a returning special ops Chinook to friendly fire, but all the teams got in. They should be in business today."

"Changing the subject a bit, just what kind of MI unit is this?"

"Odd," said Haskell.

"Unusual," said Bennett, "but interesting. It's a TDA (table of distribution and allowances) unit. It doesn't have a table of organization and equipment, like real units, so we can be structured as the mission requires. We're under SOCEUR (Special Operations Command Europe) down in Heidelberg, for now anyway. Our job is to represent SOCEUR up here in the north, coordinate special ops activities with NATO's NORTHAG (Northern Army Group) and U.S. forces; that means III Corps. We rely on the 504th MI Brigade for some of our support such as integration into the MSE (Mobile Subscriber Equipment) communications system, ASAS (All-Source Analysis System), and general service support like mess, vehicle maintenance, and admin."

Jinx was totally lost on the systems they spoke of.

It is a new Army, he thought. "What's the rest of the detachment do?" he asked.

"Good question," responded Bennett. "We're divided into cells . . . compartmentalized. Unless you have a need to know, don't ask. Shop talk over dinner is not a good practice around here."

"I can understand that. Besides you two, am I working with anybody else?"

"Me," Jenna's voice twanged from the door, "I've been assigned to do the ASAS computer work and fill you in on our allies, Major."

The two Green Beret officers exchanged glances.

"And Staff Sergeant Lomas, the intel analyst," Jenna went on, "he's over at the 504th now."

"And who does what to whom between you two?" Jinx asked the two officers.

"I'll be the operations officer and handle current ops," said Bennett. "Haskell is the plans officer, and worries about what happens next and how to do it."

"Okay, so where do we stand now?"

"We wait. There is no set reporting schedule. These guys are supposed to be Soviets, so they will act the part. If they need help, if they find some really terrific target, or hot intel poop, we'll hear from them; otherwise, they won't make contact with us at all. They have all sent their initial entry reports and are in good shape."

"So what are we here for?"

"To wait and listen."

"Don't you mean to hurry up and wait?"

"That, too"—Bennett laughed—"that, too. But, I can imagine that once things start popping, it'll become more interesting."

"Sir," murmured Collingsworth from the door, "I can brief you now on allied special ops. I'm sure that things'll get more interesting, too."

★6★

Lying on a muddy camouflage shelter cape was a pathetic excuse for a soldier. His camouflage cold weather suit was mud-splattered, the knees torn from being dragged. Blood was caked on his face, having seeped from beneath the thin, blood-soaked Soviet field dressing binding his head. His face was grimy, appearing even more filthy from the dark green camouflage paint smeared on it. Though wounded and unconscious, his wrists and ankles were bound with insulated wire.

Captain K. V. Yakushev regarded the ragged figure before him not as a wounded enemy soldier, but as an asset . . . an intelligence asset. Granted he was a soldier, of sorts, a reconnaissance-diversionary soldier, little better than a terrorist. An enemy agent provocateur, sent into a brother Warsaw Pact state to spread terror and bring death and destruction to the combined armies of the Warsaw Pact as they executed their sacred Internationalist duties.

"Drag it over to that tree," Yakushev commanded the two Border Troops privates, indicating a thick pine tree. He went back into the headquarters building, a schoolhouse on the edge of Wollin, southeast of Potsdam. The German militia troops had done well in this operation, he thought. Their first real success to date, and a combined operation at that! The one-hundred-man company, or century as they called it, from the "Hans Beimler Kampfgruppen (Combat Group)" Battalion had performed well for part-time soldiers past their prime. Maybe there was something to the much-vaunted traditional German efficiency. A German civilian had spotted the American terrorists as they crossed a dirt forest road. He had been out for a late night stroll, walking his dog of all things. Here massive armies clashed, waves of combat aircraft passed overhead, thousands were dying, and this old German shit was out walking his dog through the forest on a freezing winter night! When Yakushev had been told this he had questioned the German People's policeman who had received the telephoned report, as to what this man was doing walking about the forest at night. The German assured him that it was a common practice. These Germans!

Regardless, this was a piece of luck. Just the sort of cooperation expected in a People's war, civilians aiding the protecting soldiers. The KGs had dispatched an alert squad, traveling to the area in two privately owned cars, dismounted on a forest road, and began searching the forest in pairs. The men knew the area, had hunted small game and hiked there. One pair spotted the Americans as they moved into position on a hillside overlooking the autobahn, another piece of luck. The pair returned to the cars, and, not waiting for their comrades' return, drove back to police headquarters to sound the alert. The police had already called the 2nd Battalion of the Soviet's 92nd Border Troops Regiment headquartered in Wollin, just south of the autobahn. The battalion's first officer had alerted the 5th Company at Ziesar, farther to the west. The first officer then got in touch with the KG battalion and coordinated the operation over a civilian telephone line. The 5th Company mounted its trucks and traveled the back roads south of the autobahn, linking up with the KG alert squad at an agreed-on crossroads. With the two KG soldiers leading the way, and the 5th Company in radio contact with the BTR-60 mounted KG-reinforced company-sized "century" on the autobahn; the Border Troops dismounted, formed a line, and moved quietly north through the forest toward the Americans' hill. The KG "century" announced they had turned off the autobahn, dismounted themselves, and were sweeping up the hillside in a broad crescent formation. The next report announced they had seen a man running south through the forest.

It had been over within seconds, almost as much of a surprise for the Border Troops as for the Americans. The small band of terrorists were suddenly among them and the dark pine trees. The number of shots fired had been surprisingly few. The end result was one dead and two wounded Border Troops; four dead Americans, a fifth that died in convulsions on the muddy cargo bed of a truck on its way to Wollin, and this sorry soul propped up against a tree.

The 92nd, Captain Yakushev's regiment, had been flown into Berlin two days before the war began. Captain Yakushev headed the 2nd Battalion's Special Section—Osobye Otdely—00, the small KGB Third Directorate element attached to all unit levels of the armed forces to insure their loyalty to the State. The 00 were responsible for counterintelligence, surveillance of officers and soldiers to detect potentially anti-Soviet tendencies, observing political attitudes, and interrogation of prisoners of war. In the regular armed forces of the Ministry of Defense, the Ground and Air Forces and Navy, the 00 were only attached to regimental or equivalent level. Due to the sensitive duties of the Border Troops, however, there they were attached to battalions. Staffed by KGB officers and sergeants, they did not wear the KGB's royal blue collar tabs and shoulder straps, but rather those of the unit to which they were attached; in the case of the Border Troops, green. The Border Troops themselves were under the control of the KGB, but as any 00 officer was quick to point out, they were not *real* KGB.

Yakushev was painfully aware that officers assigned to the KGB's other directorates and chief directorates did not consider the 00 officers to be *real* KGB either, but merely the watchdogs of the armed forces. He had long aspired for a transfer to an operational directorate—had studied English in school, done well in his other studies, advanced beyond most of his fellow students during his four years at the Higher Border Troops Military-Political Red Banner School in Moscow, excelled in his Komsomol work—and while accepted into the KGB, had only drawn an assignment in the Third Directorate—armed forces. The reason was simple, he lacked the family political connections. He had not let this dilute his determination; in fact, he redoubled his efforts to attain his goal. He had volunteered for Afghanistan service, for which he was held in some awe by the regiment's officers, as few had served there. It was in a Border Troops mobile group operating in northern Afghanistan that he had discovered an initially disturbing personality flaw. After two years in Afghanistan, he now looked at it only as a mildly disquieting character trait.

"Comrade Captain," said Junior Sergeant Nedozorov, his section's only sergeant. Nedozorov was a youngster perpetually excited by this great adventure. "The prisoner has come to and I have given him hot tea as you ordered."

Blowing lightly on his perfectly inked notes, Yakushev closed his report book, snapped the cap on his French fountain pen, then slipped a triangular file and side-cutting pliers into his trousers pocket.

Back to work, he thought.

The prisoner stared stupidly up at him, no doubt dazed, probably with a concussion. What the prisoner saw was an six-foot, thin, wiry Russian officer. A dark green, red-piped, billed service cap crowned a close-cropped blond head. His perfectly fitted camouflage Border Troops uniform displayed green collar tabs and green piped shoulder boards with four small stars. Dark brown eyes glared down at him from hollow cheeks. His hands were thin and long-fingered, feminine.

"We have much to talk about Captain"—Yakushev glanced at the green military ID card—"Jack Connauer."

"I'm not telling you a damn thing, Bud!"

"They always say that, *Bud*, but they *always* do." Not wishing to waste time with verbal fencing, he ended the conversation, for now, with a kick to the solar plexus.

"Nedozorov, a hand here!"

Yakushev shoved the gasping American over on his side and turned him around. Cutting the wires securing his ankles, he told Nedozorov to grab his right ankle. He took the left. The two pulled the man's crotch into the tree truck, his legs straddling it. Nedozorov rewired the legs together while Yakushev, after pulling the man's arms over his head, tied the wrists to a nearby sapling.

Stretched out and immobile, the terrorist considered his plight. He had regained his breath, but was now . . . dismayed. Yakushev began to feel the familiar warmth creep through him, reaching into the depths of his Russian soul—his *dusha*. He welcomed it from its long absence. Not since Afghanistan, eighteen long months, had this feeling coursed through his veins, the feeling of total domination, complete control. But it was more than those simple base feelings that excited him. Hidden in this man's mind was information . . . secrets he desired, held within a labyrinth of gray matter, only millimeters from his grasp. He had but to find the right passage into the maze of secrets. He *always* found that invisible passage to receive his personal and the State's reward. The ability to find that passage, and extract the secrets from within the labyrinth, were the true gratification he sought.

He had been instructed to find only two items of information. What was this terrorist's subunit's mission and how to use the Communications-Electronics Operating Instructions found on the radio operator's body. The first item would allow countermeasures to be taken in the event that another subunit was sent. The second item was needed by the *front* radiotechnical reconnaissance regiment to aid it in countering special operations radio transmissions from behind Warsaw Pact lines.

Tugging on his leather gauntlets to tighten them, he stepped over to the American and withdrew the file from his pocket. The American's eyes went wide and his lips tightened into a thin line. Ramming a knee into the American's solar plexus, Yakushev squatted on the man's chest, locking the head between his knees. He punched the American in the mouth, then deftly pried it open with the file. Yakushev then jammed a half-inch-diameter, ten-inch-long stick into the man's mouth, levering it open. The file fell in the mud and snow. He recovered the now muddy file.

A few fast, hard rasps with the file cut the teeth, lips, tongue, and gums and exposed the nerves deep inside the American's jawbone. Yakushev withdrew the file and stick, watching the American closely. His eyes were shut as tight as his mouth, and his chest heaved as he breathed rapidly through flaring nostrils. His body twitched against the wire bonds that held him.

"What excellent dental work," Yakushev said sweetly, "I have never seen its like." The American did not reply, but only clamped his bleeding lips together again.

After a moment, Yakushev repeated the process, inflicting more damage, then again withdrew his instruments.

Straightening up, he whispered, "I have questions."

Spitting blood and tooth fragments, the American managed to mumble, "I'm naw 'elling you a 'amn 'hing, 'mudder fucker!"

Yakushev repeated the process again.

"Jesus Chriss! Stick th' file up your ass, commie bas'ard!" Tears flowed down his cheeks mingling with the blood and spittle around his mouth.

Yakushev sat bolt upright. Commie? He meant it as an insult, calling him a "commie." The thought had never occurred to him. But why not? We call them capitalists and imperialists. A most interesting concept.

"There are only two ways to end this. You tell me what I must know or you die."

"*Sosi khui*—fuck you!" hissed Connauer, almost exhausting his Russian vocabulary.

Yakushev jumped on the American and worked the file with a vengeance for almost half a minute. He stopped and again peered into the American's eyes. The tear-filled eyes flickered open. A deep rattling moan erupted. No more words of defiance. He was following the usual pattern right on schedule. Let us see how hard this man is. He lightly tapped a serrated tooth with the file. Another prolonged moan, followed by some gagging coughs.

"Wha'? Wha' you wan'?"

He looked down at the prisoner, his back arched off the muddy ground in agony.

"*Zhit' budesh, no est ne zakhachesh!*—You will live, but you will not feel like fucking," Yakushev said, parroting the traditional welcoming to new gulag prisoners. He had found the right passage into the labyrinth. He always did.

Yakushev turned the detailed report containing the requested information over to the regimental 00 chief in person.

"You have performed well, Comrade Captain. This information will greatly aid our efforts in combating enemy reconnaissance-diversionary troops," rumbled the major. "It is most sad that I must lose your services. We have just received orders to dissolve the battalion special sections in order to conserve manpower. You are being reassigned to the KGB Directorate in Potsdam. I am confident that your performance there will be as exacting and professional as it was here."

Snapping to attention, Yakushev responded, "I serve the Soviet Union!" He had opened the way to yet another passage.

★ 7 ★

I'm gonna be sick, Ben McCullough thought as his stomach slammed up into his throat again, this time for sure.

The flight was the roughest he had ever flown. The MC-130H Combat Talon jumped and twisted like a lizard on a griddle. Contour flying they called it. The special operations transport followed the roll of the terrain, making it harder for radar to detect it. Only their seat belts kept McCullough and the other eleven Green Berets in their seats.

The seat belts held them onto the red nylon benches that ran the length of the cargo bay of the huge transport. The cold draft that came through the vents was not cold enough to dry the sweat on the faces of the men of the two split A-teams strapped into their parachute harnesses, their huge camouflaged FPLIF ruck-sacks hanging between their legs like grotesque swollen scro-tums.

Take it easy, breathe through your mouth slowly and deeply, McCullough told himself. It's not like this is serious, you're just parachuting into East Germany with an A-bomb between your legs.

Even over the roar of the engines, McCullough could hear the loud squawking sound of the radar-warning receivers. So far, the squawks were short, the enemy radars "flashlighting," searching for targets. If a radar picked up their plane, the squawks would get longer as the radar "painted" them. A long, continuous tone meant that the radar had them "locked" and that missiles or high-explosive incendiary rounds were on the

51

way. The MC-130H Combat Talon was equipped with the latest in radar-jamming devices, the ITT AN/ALQ-172 Pave Mint, but the flight crew would use it only if they were ''painted.'' The jamming would draw attention to itself if used indiscriminately. The crew would rely on speed, maneuvering, and terrain-following to get past the first echelon of the rapidly advancing Soviet forces. Visibility was zip. They were flying to the drop zone strictly by the transport's Adverse Weather Aerial Delivery System—AWADS, an advanced navigation system.

Once in the rear, they would continue to hug the ground, skimming the trees until it was just short of one of the two team release points. Then the big transport would pop up to 400 feet, drop one of the teams, and go back down on the deck. When both teams were inserted, the Combat Talon would head back west, popping up several more times. By morning, Mc-Cullough's Atomic Demolition Munition team would be on the ground and operating in East Germany.

The other team, ADM-032B, seated forward, was on an identical mission. Although ADM-032B was the other half of his own A-team, McCullough knew nothing about their target. If captured, what he did not know, he could not be forced to tell.

Before the war, three days ago, McCullough's team had practiced this operation many times. They had joked about being a nuclear hand grenade team. Now the joke was hardly funny. In one of their rucksacks was the ''device,'' the 0.10-kiloton atomic bomb that they would place under the railroad bridge. If detonated, the bomb would collapse the bridge and seal off both the rail line and the highway that ran under it from any traffic from the east. It would take weeks to clear the rubble and reopen the highway, if it could be reopened at all. But first, they had to get there.

McCullough looked down the row at the rest of his team. Bob Thompson, the engineer, was next to him on the seat. Thompson looked bad. He had his hands up in the red seat webbing behind his head and was breathing slow and deep, fighting the nausea. On the other side of McCullough was Gunter Malle, the weapons man. As usual, Gunter was a rock. Nothing seemed to faze the big German, least of all a rough flight. The others, Taggart, Cohen, and Mitchell, were lost in the darkness. A loud groan announced someone's impending airsickness.

Think about something else, McCullough told himself, focus

on the mission plan, it'll give you something to think about other than your stomach.

The plan had been worked out a year ago. Back in the early 1980s there had been an outcry from the Germans because of the ADMs that Special Forces kept in Germany, a fact pointed out by the Soviets. They had, in the spirit of goodwill, been removed, for a while anyway. When A-032 had been tasked with the Atomic Demolition Munitions, SOCEUR had run dozens of map exercises and FTXs to train the chosen A-teams. McCullough's six-man team had been assigned two targets, Bergfreide and Swiecko. Using computer simulation, the team had planned and executed five different attack scenarios for each target. Of the ten, this scenario had scored the best.

The railroad bridge, located between Bergfreide and Taterberg, was on the direct rail line to Wolfsburg on the border between East and West Germany. The track crossed into West Germany and went west to Hannover. The bridge crossed over Highway 188, a major east-west avenue. Cutting the track, and keeping it cut for more than a few days, would halt the flow of supplies and reinforcements to the Red forces advancing on Hannover and slow the Soviet push into northern Germany.

The plan was to emplace their atomic demolition device under the railroad bridge. The device was equal in power to 200,000 pounds of TNT. Its detonation would obliterate the bridge and blow a hole forty feet deep in the highway underneath, fracturing the roadbed for another one-hundred feet of its length in either direction. Repair time for the bridge and the highway underneath, including radiation decontamination, was estimated, under optimum conditions, at six days. A war fought during a North German winter was hardly optimum conditions. The railway and main road to Wolfsburg would hopefully be out of business for weeks. All traffic would have to be diverted to other routes, choking them and making the supply convoys more vulnerable to allied air attack.

All the attack plans had been in a target folder when the balloon had gone up. McCullough's team had spent only four hours in isolation preparing for their missions, an hour of that waiting for the MC-130 that would insert the team. The other three hours were spent in communications briefings, determining the various frequencies to be used on the mission, and going over the nuclear device release procedures. They ran a team movement formation and some quick immediate action drill rehearsals.

McCullough's bomb would be used only on the order of the president, releasing theater tactical nuclear weapons. That release would only come if the Soviets used nuclear weapons first or if the Soviets managed to break through the NATO defenses before reinforcements arrived from America. Until the order came, his half of A-032, now designated ADM-032A, would cache their ADM, monitor and report Soviet activity in their area of operations, and maintain contact with the Special Forces Operations Base (SFOB).

All that seemed so simple when they planned it in Flint Kaserne. It seemed much less so now hurtling through the cold night in the heaving belly of the Combat Talon.

Down the row, another belly heaved and McCullough heard Mitchell, the commo man, gag and yell, "Fuck me!" into the darkness. To his left, McCullough heard the Air Force loadmaster muttering, "Oh, wonderful." McCullough clutched his own little white "burp" bag even harder.

The loadmaster would be happy to get the puking "snake eaters" out of his plane. They would be happy, too, to be out of the plane and on the ground. McCullough felt that if the jumpmaster told him to stand up, remove his chute, and exit the aircraft, he would gladly do so. The mission would be a gold-plated bitch, but at least this gut-wrenching flight would be over.

The loadmaster spoke briefly into his helmet microphone, then leaned down to Master Sergeant Larry Taggart, the operations sergeant, seated across from McCullough. Taggart nodded and got to his feet, taking the offered intercom headset, and stepped over to the back to the portside door with the loadmaster.

Taggart was the team's "dad." As operations sergeant, he ran the team day to day. Although McCullough was the team commander, he was an officer and knew well that the men on the team, all NCOs, looked to Taggart for direction. Lean and wiry, Taggart was a savvy NCO, as skilled in the politics of the peacetime army as he was in combat.

At the door, the loadmaster turned the handle, popped the door in, and pulled it up. A maelstrom of wind and noise battered the Air Force sergeant as he locked the door up and stepped back into the hollow tail of the aircraft. From where they sat, the jumpers could see only vague shapes and patches of fog whipping by in the darkness outside. The nausea of the plane ride was quickly replaced by a rush of adrenaline that put all other sensations on hold. The red lights on the leading and trailing edges of the jump door and on the aft anchor line cable supports came on, surprisingly bright in the darkened plane. When the red lights went out and the green lights next to them flashed on, ADM-032A would be out the door.

"Six minutes," Taggart shouted at the seated jumpers.

Taggart turned toward the troops and got his balance next to the large roll-up door. He snapped his own static line onto the overhead cable and passed the excess yellow static line to the loadmaster to control. Spreading his legs for more balance, he thrust his hands out in front of him, and screamed, *"Thirty-two-Alfa, get ready!"*

The five other men of 032-A unbuckled their seat belts and shifted forward in their seats.

"Stand up!" He brought both hands upward.

The five struggled to their feet, holding the nylon seat webbing and anchor line cable for support.

"Hook up!" pumping his arms up and down, fingers forming hooks.

Each man reached up over his head and grasped the taut steel cable that ran the length of the plane. Steadied by the cable, he used his free hand to unfasten the oval metal static line hook from his reserve's carrying handle and snap the hook onto the cable. They fumbled with their safety pins, finally managing to insert them in the too-small hole and bend them.

Secured to the cable, the men gripped the yellow nylon static lines for support, looking like large mutant fetuses at the end of thin yellow umbilical cords.

"Check static line!" His fingers formed the "OK" sign as he worked his hands back and forth.

The command was redundant. Each man was testing his static line with each lurch of the plane. But each made certain that the man's line to his front was not misrouted around a piece of equipment or, worse, himself.

"Check equipment," crossing his forearms and slapping his hands on opposite shoulders.

With their free hands, each man quickly checked his own gear; making certain the rucksack's H-harness was snapped to the parachute harness D-rings, weapon container properly secured on his left side, helmet chin strap fastened, no balls under the leg straps.

"Sound off for equipment check!" He cupped his hands behind his ears.

Each man in turn, from the front of the aircraft toward the door, shouted his stick number and "okay!" as he slapped the man in front on his rear. The man nearest the door pointed at Taggart and shouted, *"All okay!"*

With that, Taggart shouted, *"One minute!"* He pivoted into the open door and stuck his head out, the wind pulling his face into a skull mask. Jumpmasters no longer hung out the door thrusting their bodies into the hundred-mile-per-hour prop blast as they had in the old days. Now they just looked out enough to check for any problems and clearance. There was no way to see the drop zone anyway, as low as they were and with the dense fog. He pulled back in and spoke quickly into the intercom mike, then pulled off the headset, faced the jumpers, and pointed to the door.

"Stand in the door!"

Staff Sergeant Paul Cohen was first in the door, gripping its edges and staring straight out, oblivious to everything before him. The team medic, he was, at five feet seven, the shortest man on the team, but considered himself the intellectual giant.

Behind him was Sergeant First Class Sylvan "Mitch" Mitchell, the communications specialist. Mitchell was the product of an Ivy League prep school; he and Cohen endlessly debated the ways of the world.

Behind Mitchell was Staff Sergeant Bob Thompson, the engineer, a marathoner, intense, and gung-ho.

McCullough was next in line, and bringing up the rear was Sergeant First Class Gunter Malle, the weapons man. Gunter was the giant of the team, a six-foot-four Aryan warrior.

The tension and anticipation in the plane was so great now that the air seemed to crackle with electricity. There was a smell to it, a pheromone that transmitted excitement to anyone else who smelled it. Cohen said it was the smell of testosterone. Whatever it was, McCullough had never felt it stronger. This was the Big One, the one they had planned for but never really expected. A scene from the movie *Dr. Strangelove* flashed through McCullough's mind; Slim Pickens in a B-52 telling his crew, "This is it, boys, nucle'r combat, toe to toe with the Rooskies!"

The plane suddenly lurched upward. McCullough held tight to his static line for balance. Taggart clutched Cohen's left arm, keeping him in the door. This was the 400-foot pop-up for the jump. As suddenly as it had pitched up, the plane flattened into level flight.

"Ten seconds!" the loadmaster shouted the final warning required for an AWADS jump. The seconds crawled by.

"GO! GO! GO!" Taggart screamed as he slapped Cohen on the rear. Next to him, the green light beckoned.

The five men plunged out the door into the darkness in less than five seconds, Taggart immediately following his brood into the howling darkness.

The six taut static lines streamed out the door. The loadmaster checked to the rear for a towed jumper as the aircraft dove for the treetops. He and A-032B's jumpmaster hauled in the lines and their flapping deployment bags.

To the others left in the plane, it seemed that the six had just vanished into thin air over East Germany, which, of course, they had.

The honors and glories of Odessa were far off in distance and memory, if not in time, for the cadre of the 800th Guards Independent Special Purpose Battalion. The more pressing realities of the cold and mud and filthy snow at the Edgar-Andrae Training Center were now of more real concern. The battalion's cadre, the Summer Harvest survivors, now numbered fifty-six. Six of their lightly wounded were not permitted to accompany their comrades to the combat zone. Arriving at the battered, formerly American, Templehof Airfield in recently liberated West Berlin, they were quickly loaded on captured West German Mercedes buses and taken to the training area near the town of Lehnin, southwest of Berlin. The troops were starved for news of the war they had helped start, but all they heard were rumors. A Commandant's Service traffic control officer confided in Bodnya that there were still small groups of American and British soldiers holding out in the suburbs. He also reported that the East German Frontier Troops and 1st Motorized Rifle Division had had a very difficult time routing the understrength American, British, and French brigades from their West Berlin sectors. Soviet and East German reinforcements had been called to their aid.

The Edgar-Andrae Training Center was an East German-controlled facility. Scattered among the dark pine forests were firing ranges, demolition training sites, areas containing mockups of West German combat vehicles, obstacle and physical training courses, and a collection of ramshackle unheated wooden barracks and support buildings.

Bodnya had not really known what to expect on arrival at the base. Years of peacetime soldiering and a structured career had not prepared him for the confusion of an all-out war and its effect on a burdensome military bureaucracy. Much to his surprise, twenty-four GAZ-66 2000-kilogram cargo trucks and eight UAZ-469 command cars awaited them.

"What are we going to do with these trucks, Comrade Major"—Senior Ensign Kovpak still occasionally called him by his old rank out of habit—"haul war booty?" he asked hopefully.

There was no other equipment, no weapons, no radios, nothing, not even rations. The following day a GRU liaison officer arrived with a small entourage of rear service, transport, and billeting service officers. They brought a truck load of "dry rations." The GRU major seemed to be ill at ease, for he knew who Bodnya was.

"Comrade Battalion Commander"—once the two of them were in Bodnya's barren office—"I have your unit's orders and the authority to coordinate the necessary support to fully form your battalion. You must please remember that the war has stretched our material support resources to the limit and that we are hard-pressed to even maintain committed combat units."

"Yes, Comrade Major, I fully understand. My men have already tasted combat and wish again to fight in defense of the Motherland," Bodnya replied. "Any assistance in accomplishing that task will be appreciated."

"Then I am certain we can work together to accomplish that task," babbled the major. "Tomorrow your full complement of weapons and combat equipment will arrive at the Lehnin rail yard. The material support unit there is short of soldiers and will require the assistance of your men to drive the trucks and load the materials. Your trucks are required there at 09.00. The officers, sergeants, and soldiers needed to bring your battalion to strength will also arrive tomorrow. They are now at Spandau in Berlin and will arrive by train in Lehnin at 04.30. They will be brought here by bus."

Bodnya was quickly making notes. "Comrade Battalion Commander, the troops will be a draft from two sources." The major seemed uncomfortable. "The first unit is the 358th Independent Special Purpose Battalion. It was flown in from the Byelorussian Military District and committed to attack combat units of the

British and Netherlands Corps as they moved from their peacetime stations to the front. It will provide 248 troops.''

Spetsnaz battalions averaged 400 to 500 men, depending on its specific mission. The 358th must have had a very rough time indeed, thought Bodnya.

''The other troops, 128, will come from''—the major hesitated a moment—''the 192nd Independent Flamethrower Battalion.''

Bodnya quickly looked up from his notes. ''Those are not Spets, they are not even paratroopers! What am I supposed to do with a batch of chemical warfare troops!''

''I am sorry, Comrade Battalion Commander, but they are all that is available at the moment and should be compatible to your unit's mission,'' apologized the major.

''And what might that be?'' demanded Bodnya.

''You will find your mission in your sealed orders, comrade. I do not know the details, of course. I must return to Lehnin Government Center. You can reach me at this number.'' He handed Bodnya a sheet torn from his notebook. ''I am assigned as your unit's liaison with 1st Western Front GRU 3rd Department and the KGB Directorate in Potsdam.''

''KGB?'' hissed Bodnya. ''This is a KGB operation, Comrade Major?''

''It is, comrade. But some things are best left unspoken for the time being. I will be in touch with you tomorrow, comrade.''

''KGB . . . indeed,'' muttered Bodnya as the major retreated out the door. The major is right of course, some things are best left unspoken . . . for the time being. He quickly added up his troop totals, 432. ''KGB . . . chemical troops, indeed!'' he again muttered. ''Kovpak!''

''BJ, you've been here before, where the hell are we?'' Hickey asked.

''We're in Germany.''

''Oh, thanks, that's a big help.''

''It's the best I can do, Shannon, okay?'' BJ shot back. ''I didn't get a chance to memorize every foot of West Germany when I was here on exercises. I think we're near Essen, since that's where we set up last year.''

''It would have been nice if we all could have gone on the last Reforger, not just the headquarters bunch,'' Wally Kosinski chimed in. ''The brass got to come over and ski, and the rest of us got to run around in the Sam Houston National Forest and pretend it was East Germany.''

The truck suddenly lurched to a stop in front of a brick building.

''Okay, everybody out!'' a voice called from the tailgate. The troops spilled out and formed into five platoons, with the little S&T Section down on the end, on the snow-covered grass strip in front of the low modern building.

First Sergeant Cordes put the company at ease and made the equipment off-loading assignments.

''This school's been appropriated for the signal company of the 303d MI Battalion and Company G. Each team will be assigned a classroom both to live in and use for isolation. Your platoon sergeants have the assignments.'' He pointed back past the school. ''Across the playground there, on the other side of the road, is a small field that will serve as a helipad for team launching. Let's get everything unloaded and into the rooms. Headquarters and Commo Platoons, you know what to do. The vehicles will arrive later tonight. After you're unloaded, the patrol platoons will assemble in the gymnasium. Some are going to work tonight. Welcome to the war. Let's do it!''

Company G's 196 troops fell out and scattered to their assignments.

''Damn!'' Murphy remarked. ''I'm glad Top reminded us it was a war. It felt like just another exercise for a minute there!''

''That'll change soon enough,'' BJ muttered under his breath, touching the bandage on his head.

Bodnya's two remaining captains and Kovpak sat before him with their mouths literally hanging open.

"KGB?" groaned Noskov.

"Chemical troops?" gasped Yurasov.

"Rear-area protection?!" exclaimed Kovpak.

"Yes, comrades," said Bodnya, "after proving ourselves with the most difficult of tasks, we are now to be little more than militiamen—policemen, with firebugs, and under the command of the KGB!"

He relied heavily on these two officers. Noskov had a special knack for planning. He felt cheated of having experienced real combat because his group had destroyed the vehicle storage facilities of the Texas National Guard's 49th Armored Division and met no resistance whatsoever. Yurasov was a real fighter. His group had disabled almost every combat vehicle of the 2d Armored Division while encountering heavy resistance. The group tasked to attack the 1st Cavalry Division's motor pool had not been so fortunate. Though partly successful, many of the group's subunits were lost along with their commander.

Bodnya continued, "The situation is simple, the 1st Western Front's chief of the rear cannot neutralize the enemy diversionary-reconnaissance troops operating in his rear areas. He has under his control two KGB Border Troops regiments recently brought in from the Motherland, twelve German Combat Groups of the Working Class battalions, and units of the Volkspolize—People's Police—VOPOs, all coordinated by the

KGB and German VOPOs. They have accomplished little to prevent NATO reconnaissance patrols and raiders from collecting information on our units' activities and movements, directing air strikes, and executing raids on our rear services.''

"What are these 'Combat Groups of the Working Class'?" inquired Yurasov.

"That is almost twenty battalions of rear-protection troops, Comrade Lieutenant Colonel," asked Noskov, "what do they expect one more battalion to accomplish?"

"Then the trucks really are for booty!" quipped Kovpak.

"One at a time, comrades!" Bodnya bawled. He quoted from the information sheet that accompanied his unit's orders.

"The Combat Groups or KGs, what the West calls Workers' Militia, are German volunteer workers who train one weekend a month and attend one or two week-long exercises a year. They are formed into motorized battalions centered around their place of employment, such as factories or collectives. They are well armed and are motorized with trucks belonging to their work establishment, though some have old-model armored personnel carriers. Many have completed their military service in the German National People's Army and they do know the area in which they operate. Their training is limited though and most of what they do is guard airfields, bridges, factories, government buildings, utilities, and so on. They are under the command of the County Offices of the VOPO KG Section."

Bodnya looked up at his staff, then went on.

"As far as what we have to do with ridding this threat from our rear areas is also simple, comrades. The Combat Groups simply guard rear-area objectives. They have very little inclination or skill to chase after NATO commandos. The Soviet Border Troops are better trained and equipped, but their past experience has been guarding borders with brother Warsaw Pact states. They have no combat experience, not even Afghanistan, though some Border Troops units were deployed there. They, too, have shown little desire or ability to dismount their vehicles and hunt down enemy diversionary-reconnaissance troops. These enemy troops, little better than terrorists, have proven to be adapt at evading searches for them. Indeed, some have been discovered and neutralized. But the only successful methods used to date are those employed in the 1950s when our internal security organs destroyed the Ukrainian National Army bandits.''

Bodnya glanced at Kovpak, but he showed no sign of concern,

the UNA had been *Western* Ukrainians for the most part, not trusted *Eastern* Ukrainians like himself. Bodnya continued, "These methods have been the encirclement and sweep. They take a great deal of coordination, manpower, and time, and still the enemy commandos sometimes slip through the net. What we are expected to offer, comrades, is a combat-experienced unit that does have the skills, the physical conditioning, and the initiative to dismount from our trucks, put on rucksacks, and hunt the terrorists down. We will be employed as a pursuit battalion and will use the same field skills the enemy uses to evade our forces to find and destroy them!"

The two captains were obviously already considering ways to adapt their special skills to deal with this new threat. Kovpak, too, seemed to be calculating, but of what, Bodnya did not wish to even hazard a guess. Whatever it was, it would certainly work, but it would, somehow, even if indirectly, benefit the trusted *Eastern* Ukrainian.

"And the KGB, Comrade Lieutenant Colonel?" asked Noskov.

"They will not be a direct threat to us, comrades." The officers laughed and Bodnya hoped that statement was true. "They merely coordinate the activities of the different rear-area protection organs and conduct various counterintelligence functions. Actually, we will be working more closely with the German District VOPO Security Command."

"But what about the flamethrower troops?" asked Yurasov.

"I unfortunately do not have a nomogram," Bodnya answered, referring to a complex series of standard formulas used by the Soviet armed forces to calculate variables pertaining to combat actions, "to determine how they will preform!"

The officers laughed again. "I do know that this flamethrower battalion was all but destroyed valiantly liberating West Berlin. They are reported to be tough troops who have gained a great deal of combat experience in just a few days. If they can run through city alleys with twenty-four-kilogram LPO-50 flame throwers, they can certainly carry a rucksack and assault rifle!"

It was a long night for the four officers. On paper they integrated the draft troops into the battalion's organization, discussed and diagrammed methods of employment and tactics, made officer duty assignments, prepared a short training schedule to maximize the far too brief time allotted them, and made a lengthy list of tasks to be accomplished before their deployment.

"Comrade Captain, what would you have us do with the bodies?"

"Do not disturb me with these petty questions, Sergeant," the captain answered, brushing a few snowflakes from his brown field uniform. "Do with them as you like."

"Just so, Comrade Captain!"

The stocky senior sergeant returned to the knot of enlisted men waiting near the pile of corpses. At his direction, the men dragged the dead men off into the trees that lined the road.

The captain walked slowly around the BTR, searching for battle damage. There was none. He strolled over to the second machine and gave it the same thorough scrutiny. The machines were undamaged. They would be perfect for his needs.

"Comrade Captain," the sergeant was calling him again, his Russian atrociously accented, like that of so many Asians.

"Yes, Sergeant?"

"We are ready to go, Comrade Captain."

"Excellent! Load the men into the personnel carriers. This one will be my command vehicle."

"Just so, Comrade Captain!" the sergeant replied briskly. The sergeant turned and ordered the rest of the men into the BTRs. This done, he turned back to the captain and said quietly in English, "Sir, do we have to talk this way even when there are no Russians around? It's kind of a pain."

"Damn it, Ike!" Captain Conrad (Connie) Harlan, 10th U.S. Special Forces Group hissed in Russian. "Play the role. We are supposed to be Soviet deserters. Let's try to act the part, especially here at the beginning. Can't have any Russians from Malibu."

"Like, fer sure, Comrade Captain," the Oriental sergeant crooned, then snapped to attention and said in his accented Russian, "I serve the Soviet Union!"

"That is much better, Comrade Senior Sergeant."

With that, Master Sergeant Tommy Ikehara, turned and walked away, climbing into the next BTR.

Under overcast skies, Bodnya and his staff stood before the 800th Guards Independent Special Purpose Battalion, paraded in three dissimilar groups of soldiers. The small group of proud

Summer Harvest veterans in their new camouflage uniforms and blue berets was formed to his left, the position of honor in the formation. To his front were the demoralized remnants of the 358th Spetsnaz Battalion in grimy camouflage suits and a mixed assortment of dirty blue berets, field caps, and fur winter caps. Though somewhat sullen, they were obviously fit Russians and other Slavics. To his right were the dispirited survivors of the 192nd Flamethrower Battalion. A few Slavic officers were evident, but the bulk of the soldiers were angry Georgians, bitter Armenians, confused little Kazakhs, and other Soviet Central Asians. They were clothed in filthy and torn brown field uniforms and gray overcoats with soot-smudged steel helmets and mud-matted fur caps. Their arrival that afternoon forced Kovpak to ask, "Is this exercise really necessary, comrades?"

Bodnya had pondered that question himself. If there ever was a unit with a potential for discipline and morale problems, it certainly stood before him now.

Bodnya made the welcoming speech, keeping it short. Captain Noskov, now the first officer, or operations officer, read the citation of the unit's exploits and briefly told the story of Summer Harvest. Even the most slow-witted of the bedraggled soldiers realized that they were now part of an exalted unit. Summer Harvest officers and sergeants moved through the formation pinning Guards badges on the chests of their new comrades. Already the troops' attitude began to change with the presentation of this honor by the very men who had made the legend.

"All officers and ensigns to me!" commanded Bodnya. Master Sergeant Ratnikkov took charge of the formation, split them into two groups, sent one to be fed, and the other to be issued new winter uniforms. The chemical troops happily donned their new dark green, tan, and brown camouflage uniforms and the blue-and-white striped Telnaishka that Kovpak had somehow acquired during a foray into Potsdam. "Dry ration" cans of meat and *kasha*—a fat-laden porridge of buckwheat, onions, and carrots, boiled in 200-liter steel drums. The boiling served to both heat the rations and to remove the protective coating of grease from the unpainted, nongalvanized cans. Cooks from the material support battalion skimmed off the grease, passed out the hot cans, filled mess kit soup cans with hot sugared tea, and handed out packages of dried rye bread. Most of the troops crumbled the otherwise inedible bread into their tea and spooned it down like soup.

Bodnya briefly talked to the officers and Noskov briefed them on their mission, announced the officer assignments, and described how the assets of the draft units would be integrated into the 800th Battalion.

"Now, comrades," announced Bodnya, "the officers' mess is open. We will detail each of you tasks for tomorrow over dinner, be that as it is. After dinner we will begin issuing weapons and reassign the troops to their companies, it will be another long night."

Dawn found the bleary-eyed battalion, after only four hours' sleep, again assembled on the muddy field, but now wearing new fur-collared camouflage uniforms and fur caps, armed with AKS-74 assault rifles, fed, and formed into their new companies. Most of the Summer Harvest veterans and the best of the 358th Spetsnaz had been formed into the 1st Company under the command of Captain Yurasov, following the usual Soviet practice of placing the best troops and commanders in the first subunit. The bulk of the 358th formed the 2nd Company under its only surviving company commander, Captain Shepelev. The 3rd Company was comprised of most of the flamethrower troops under Senior Lieutenant Kashevarov. Many of their surviving officers had previously been reassigned to other chemical units. Some of the sergeants and soldiers of the 358th were assigned to 3rd Company to instill their special skills. Bodnya had considered integrating the flamethrower troops into all three companies, but since many had only limited ability with Russian, he thought it best to keep them together. Service troops from both battalions formed the 800th Battalion's small Headquarters Company under the command of Senior Lieutenant Sukharev, a Spetsnaz rear services officer. A separate entity, an oddity in the 358th, was its Scout-Diversionary Platoon. This subunit had been independent from any of the battalion's companies and intended for some specific mission, apparently one it had never performed as it was still intact.

Bodnya had decided to retain its hand-picked paratroopers as a separate reaction force. Its commander, Senior Lieutenant Dubovik, appeared to be an extremely capable and aggressive young officer.

The battalion was to be entirely truck-mounted with each nine-man squad having its own. There were not yet sufficient trucks to motorize the 3rd and Headquarters Companies, but these were expected to arrive the next day. The companies had three platoons of three squads, though the Scout-Diversionary Platoon had four squads. Bodnya's staff was comprised of Major Serafim Goncharov as his chief of staff. Goncharov, the former CoS of the 358th, was a tough, broad-shouldered three-tour Afghanistan veteran. Tall, with short-chopped black hair and brown eyes almost as dark as his hair, he appeared to Bodnya as the epitome of a Spetsnaz officer, both a fighter and a planner. Major Butakov was the Deputy Commander for Political Affairs—the *zampolit*. Another 358th officer, Goncharov assured Bodnya he was a capable and trustworthy political officer. Besides Captain Noskov as the first officer, his staff also included Captain Milstein as the second officer, or intelligence officer, also formerly of the 358th.

Lieutenant Zimin was the communications officer and also commanded the small communications platoon. Lieutenant Evdokimov was the secret section officer, responsible for maintaining and issuing maps and classified documents. Senior Lieutenant Ivashutin was the deputy commander for technical affairs, responsible for vehicle and equipment maintenance. Since the battalion was short of junior officers, Senior Ensign Kovpak had volunteered to command 1st Company's 1st Platoon. Bodnya knew full well that he did not want to have his movements restricted by being tied to the staff, on which Bodnya had offered him a position.

Training began in earnest with the platoons rotating through driver and vehicle maintenance training, small-arms firing, radio operation, map and compass work, and handling of prisoners, which Bodnya emphasized the most important of all, due to their intelligence value. The German camp commandant had pointed out an elaborate compass course and told them how to conduct it. It was more demanding and complex than most of the soldiers had experienced, especially the flamethrower troops who had never had such training. Bodnya sent his second officer, secret section officer, and *zampolit* to Potsdam in a command car to receive maps and research information on NATO special operations units. He had decided to send the *zampolit* after he had announced the troops needed further political indoctrination, ''to prepare them for their Internationalist duties and the forthcoming struggle.'' Major Goncharov only shrugged his shoulders when Bodnya glared at him.

★ 9 ★

"Two-One," spit Sergeant First Class Hagger.

"Ready!" responded Team 21's leader.

"Two-Two, Two-Three," the operations sergeant shot off rapidly.

Each of the four 2d Platoon recon team leaders responded with the traditional "Ready," stood, and reached for the large black imitation leather pouch handed out by Platoon Sergeant Daniels.

"Two-Four."

"Ready!" BJ accepted his isolation packet. They had trained for years for this, following the demanding procedures for even the simplest weekend missions, the strict premission planning procedures, the isolation requirements, the field training, all the components of Long-Range Reconnaissance.

Now that war had finally come, the same procedures would be followed.

How many times had he taken the same familiar black packet to plan his team's training missions? Dozens, he guessed. He saw now why the Operations and Intelligence Section (O&I) had always demanded Standard Operating Procedures be followed to the letter. No shortcuts, no half-assed exercises like some National Guard units ran, just going through the motions. All that effort had been to prepare them for this day.

It was Hagger who constantly reminded them, "Any bunch of weekend warriors can put on their cammies, load up with all kinds of neat guns and knives, and go out in the woods and play

68

army. But real LRRPs plan their missions, that's the most important half of the game.''

''Let's crack 'em, guys,'' said Hagger.

BJ peeled the Velcro flap open and pulled out the thick sheaf of papers and maps. Hagger ran rapidly through the contents check: company operations order, intelligence summary, analysis of area of operations; team roster; security briefing and statement; several different request forms; recon zone maps; overlay, sketch, and ruled paper.

Hagger talked the team leaders through an initial mission briefing as informally as he had in countless exercise briefings in the armory or in some obscure training area. Their last training mission had only been a month ago. That seemed like a year now.

''The Dutch corps is cracking up fast, guys,'' said Hagger. ''The 2d Guards Tank Army have been piling on the pressure. The Dutch tanks are holding their own against the Soviet T-64s and T-80s, but there's not enough of them. Their APCs are very much outclassed by the BMP-2s. Dutch antiarmor and air defense weapons were also outdated and in limited supply. Their worst problem, though, has not been the equipment, but their soldiers.''

BJ had read an article about the Dutch conscript soldier, who had one of the briefest active duty periods among the NATO armies. They had long enjoyed easy training constraints, imposed by a servicemen's union. They had proved to be no match for the Soviet soldier. The Red Army was not a union shop.

''Third Corps is going to counterattack right through what's left of the Dutch corps, once they all get here,'' continued Hagger. ''We're going to start putting teams in ASAP. You guys are going in tonight.''

''What time?'' asked Ben Stockton, 21's team leader.

''0200,'' said Hagger.

''Shit, Kurt!'' moaned BJ. ''That's not enough damn time for premission! This ain't no exercise!''

''That's right, Beej!'' shot back Hagger. ''This ain't no exercise! Look, guys, things are going to hell in a handbag . . . fast. Things are not going to be like on exercises. And you might recall that the exercises weren't exactly well scripted either. We had to do some real off-the-wall shit during some. But what did we always do?''

''Accomplish the mission,'' mumbled the team leaders in unison.

"Just remember our old maxim," piped in Daniels. "If you think training's screwed up, wait until you see combat!"

"Okay, let's cut the crap and do it," said Hagger. "A few Dutch LRRPs are still out there. Some of their teams from the 109th Recon and Surveillance Company have not even been inserted. We've got to get some teams in to start building a better picture of what the Sovs are lining up back there to throw at III Corps. The 2d Guards Tank Army has not yet committed their second echelon divisions and the 28th Combined Arms Army is following them. You guys are going to set up OPs and keep some autobahns under surveillance. That's all you need to know about one another's missions. Daniels and I'll cover specific missions with you in your team rooms. Let's go down the time lines."

Hagger listed the times for the radio operators' commo briefing, when supplies and equipment would be issued, when the teams would present their briefbacks to the Operations and Intelligence reps, and station time for their choppers. "You've got to get your supply/equipment, commo, and ammo requests in fast. No air item requests, you're going in by chopper."

"Are the commo jerks going to be set up by the time we insert?" asked Will Colly, 22's leader. "Their base station vehicles aren't even here yet! How're they supposed to get up and humming by 0200 much less out to their commo sites?"

"Who appointed you commo officer?" responded Hagger coolly. "They'll be up soon enough, maybe not at zero two, but as quick as they can. That's the best we can do!"

"Aw shit, Kurt! You mean we're going in without commo?" declared BJ. "This is exactly like that exercise at Fort Chaffee when we jumped in without rations and each team had to make it to another DZ by dawn to get rations dropped in so we could eat for the next three days!"

"No, it's not! And one more 'Aw shit' and you're not going on the mission!"

"Aw shit!" chorused the four team leaders.

The open jeep pulled up in front of the school and two captains clambered out. Bounding up the steps, they shook the melting snow from their Gortex cold-weather suits before entering.

Captain Schultz slapped his pile cap on his thigh before shoving it in a cargo pocket. Company G never wore their maroon berets when deployed. Anything that might indicate that they were a long-range surveillance company was banned. Third

Corps patches replaced their traditional "T-Patch" and airborne tab. Gone, too, were jumpwings—foreign and U.S., Ranger and Special Forces tabs, expert infantryman badges, and any other "scare" badges that were the signature of a special unit.

Airborne tunes were not sung. Jumpwings, airborne tab decals, and unit designations were not permitted on notebooks or briefcases. New members were told not to adorn themselves with airborne tattoos.

Neither were Ranger-style white sidewall haircuts permitted. Schultz said, "You might as well drop down, start knocking out push-ups, and screaming 'Ranger' with a haircut like that." There was no place for skinheads in a unit that operated in the enemy's rear.

"I'm glad you pushed the G3 Air rep, Chuck!" Schultz said, turning to Captain Chuck Ranwanz, his operations officer. "He had me believing we'd get a whole Blackhawk platoon, but we're only getting two birds!"

"Apply enough pressure on a staff officer and he'll blurt out the truth!" said Ranwanz.

"Well, right now we've got more pressing problems," said Schultz. "The Sovs are going through the Dutch like a dose of salts through a widow woman, haven't even bothered committing their second echelon, and III Corps's not building up as fast as we hoped. There's no telling when Corps will be able to launch its counterattack."

"Maybe it'll all work out," replied Ranwanz. "You know what happened to the Egyptians in 1973."

"Yes?" Schultz said slowly, sensing another of his ops officer's lectures.

"The Egyptian forces first successfully crossed the Suez Canal at the beginning of the Yom Kippur War. They dutifully followed to the letter the highly detailed operations order prepared for them by their Soviet advisers, who had returned to the USSR prior to the offensive. It was not long before the Israelis executed a counterattack and forced a crossing of the Suez splitting the Egyptian 2nd and 3rd Armies, and getting into their rear. Cut off and with their rear support in turmoil, the Egyptian General Staff quickly turned to the next page of the operations order only to find it blank!"

"Go on," said Schultz, resigned to hearing the captain out.

"Well, in panic the chief of staff telephoned Moscow and asked what the missing page had written on it. 'Oh, that's simple,' replied the staff assistant who took the call. 'It says, retreat to the capital and wait for the winter snows.' "

Laughing, Schultz said, "The only problem is that the winter snows are already here. Maybe they think they won't have to rely on that strategy this time!"

The two officers stopped at a cross hallway as an S&T NCO, pointedly ignoring them, turned into the corridor clutching a large rucksack to his chest. Several softly clucking hen heads protruded from under its flap.

Looking at Ranwanz, Schultz said, "I didn't see that. Did you?"

"Huh uh, man, no way!"

The two stepped into what had been the school's administrative offices, now housing the company's Tactical Operations Center—TOC. The entire O&I Section was busy at work.

Two NCOs bent over a large map board working a coordinate scale and magnifying glass, probably selecting insertion landing zones for the teams. Two sergeants and two corporals operated a small assembly line, compiling isolation packets from two long tables placed end to end and piled with orderly stacks of forms, documents, and maps.

An intelligence analyst, stooping over a copy machine, ran off portions of a map on legal-size paper. Every man on a recon team would enter their recon zone with a map, no matter how simple. If they became separated they could at least find their way to the team rally point. In the corner, a Commo Platoon NCO discussed the commo plan with an assistant operations sergeant.

Surveying all this activity, Schultz said, "Busy as little bees, your boys are."

"Keeps them out of trouble," replied Ranwanz. "You know what happens when their minds become idle."

"Hey, sir," Staff Sergeant Janecky, the intel NCO, called out, "you've got a call from the Brigade S3 Air."

"Shit," moaned Ranwanz, "he probably wants to know if we'll accept a hot-air balloon insertion!"

Out in the hall the S&T Section trainees, wearing black running shorts and sweatshirts, thundered past and out the front doors into the swirling snow. Each clutched a flapping chicken in his left hand and a single-edged razor blade in his right.

"Well," commented Schultz, "now we know what we're havin' for dinner tonight!"

★ 10 ★

Senior Ensign Kovpak slammed open the barn's side door allowing a blast of frigid air to rush into the cavernous room. Banging the sides of his paratrooper boots on the door frame to knock off the mud, he surveyed the pitiful 800th Spetsnaz Battalion's ''temporary'' headquarters. After permitting maps, papers, straw, and manure dust to be blown about, and ignoring angry shouts from the staff, he finally banged the door shut. The barn's interior temperature was only a few degrees warmer than the freezing wind outside. A small commandeered gas stove sat in a corner hissing as it struggled to perform its impossible duty.

Bodnya, seated in a metal folding chair, his hips on the edge, shoulders resting on the back's top edge, and his legs stretched out before him, paid no attention to the intrusion. His thoughts raced back and forth between his battalion's pursuit mission and the misfortune of having received that mission. He should, at this moment, be far behind enemy lines preparing to attack a key NATO headquarters or major communications facility. His staff fumbled with developing a plan of action. Spetsnaz officers were not used to this sort of operation. There was no clearly defined objective to study, no infiltration factors to calculate, no means by which to make an analytical estimation of how the enemy would respond to specific courses of action. There was not enough information to impact on the dialectic. Besides, this filthy barn was no better than a shithouse!

The battalion had been moved from its training area to this farm complex near the East German town of Irxleben, about ten kilometers west of Magdeburg. The E8 Autobahn, a main supply route for the 3rd Shock Army, was just to the north of the town. Because of this, the British Special Air Service had been extremely active in the area. The farm complex and some resident rear service units had suffered an attack by British Tornados the previous night, no doubt targeted by the SAS terrorists. Wrecked Soviet vehicles were still strewn about the area.

Kovpak stomped over to the little stove and made a show of removing his gloves and warming his hands, the combat soldier posturing before the staff, safe in its protective shelter.

Norms and nomograms were of no value when their mission was simply to wait for the enemy to reveal himself. They had analyzed the rear-area objectives that might be of interest to an enemy reconnaissance-diversionary force and the vulnerabilities of those objectives. They had identified which main routes the enemy might wish to place under surveillance, and developed response plans with the local VOPO, Combat Groups, and Commandant's Service traffic control points. Bodnya and his staff had been briefed on the local rear-area protection measures that had been taken. Small units and headquarters in the area had been sited together to make them less vulnerable to attack. Checkpoints had been established on roads, small convoys were marshaled into large ones. Strict camouflage measures were enforced. A dusk-to-dawn curfew for civilians had been ordered. Observation points were established overlooking large areas in an attempt to detect infiltrating terrorists moving cross-country and on the lookout for enemy helicopters and parachutists. His companies were conducting mounted and dismounted patrols on the area's secondary and back roads as they continued their training.

Bodnya fully realized the importance of maintaining a stabilized rear. The never-ending flow of supplies and materials could not be disrupted. The attacking forces could not be permitted to grind to a halt for lack of the ammunition, fuel, spare parts, and rations needed to fuel their insatiable appetite.

Stalin had said, "No army in the world can be victorious without a stable rear. An unstable, and yet more, a hostile rear will without fail transform even the best, most compact army into a crumbled mass." It was as true today as it had been in 1918.

"But, why me?" he stormed. "Why me?"

He had never given much attention to NATO's special operations forces. Why should he? They were of no interest to him. His mission was the same as theirs, destroy rear-area objectives or collect intelligence information. Until now he had not considered that they may one day meet on the battlefield. It was no more than a policeman's task to chase after the West's many "Rambo" units.

Kovpak pulled out a combat knife and began scraping mud from the sides of his boots, scanning the room for something to eat.

Bodnya recalled, during his days at the Ryazan Higher Airborne Command School, once being given a lecture on NATO parachute formations. They were shown a newspaper from the American 82d Airborne Division by a GRU analyst-instructor.

Apparently published by a servicemen's collective, the issue compared the lone American parachute division to the Soviet's, pointing out that it took two Soviet divisions to equal the American.

What good was one large division, difficult to airlift, to resupply, and far too large to manage on the ground in the confusion of an airdrop and the modern high-intensity battlefield? That was why the Soviets possessed six smaller, but far more deployable divisions, the GRU officer had reasoned. He had gone on to describe the comparisons the Americans made between their division and the Soviet's, between weapons, manpower, and tactics.

Bodnya saw the point, they were acting like they may one day face the Soviet paratroopers. It was a waste of time. If dropped into the rear of Soviet forces, the division, or its units, would face massed combined arms units, not Soviet paratroopers. That is why the Soviet airborne assault divisions were equipped with air-droppable armored infantry combat vehicles armed with tank-killing weapons, providing the secondary mobility needed to maneuver on the ground, as well as self-propelled artillery. They *knew* they would face enemy armor. The American paratroopers were foot-mobile, relied on light towed artillery, and had only limited antitank weapons. They would be slaughtered if committed into the Soviet rear.

Bodnya savored that thought for a moment. He had begun to realize that almost overnight he had come to hate the NATO special operations units. He had been diverted from a higher calling to challenge the threat they posed. The vulnerability of his own detachments in Afghanistan and during exercises in the

Motherland and East Germany nagged at him. Skill and sheer determination had insured the accomplishment of their missions and survival.

He truly looked forward to crushing the floundering little bands of terrorists sucking around in his sector of responsibility.

He slowly became aware of Kovpak clomping across the straw- and manure-covered floor.

Why now? Bodnya thought. He only wished to wallow in the comfort of his misery.

"I have a question, Comrade Battalion Commander. What does the commander wish for most at this moment?" Kovpak asked reviving their old game.

"A parachute, a rucksack full of SZ-2 concentrated charges, and a NATO division headquarters," Bodnya growled.

The ever-present smile disappeared from Kovpak's face. He pulled a packing crate over and sat down before his commander and friend. This was not good!

Looking around at the barn's squalor, he brightly offered, "I can send some of my boys down to the town, commandeer some paint, put plastic sheeting and blackout curtains over these broken windows, sweep the cow shit out, and replace the door hinges. Then your headquarters will be raised to the standards of a shithouse!"

Bodnya contemplated his only true friend from under half-closed eyelids. "You are right, my friend. I was just thinking myself that this place is a shithouse. It is time we make it look like the headquarters of a Guards unit!"

Rising to his feet, Bodnya shouted, "Major Goncharov! I am stepping out to discuss Ensign Kovpak's progress. Have this shit-house cleaned up and looking like a headquarters by the time I return!"

He filled a cup of hot tea from a battered samovar and handed it to Kovpak. Officers and sergeants were already scurrying about as the two paratroopers stepped out the door.

"What are your feelings about the battalion, Pavel Pavlovitch? It is a mixed bath of soldiers thrown together under unusual circumstances. I am especially concerned about the 3rd Company's flamethrower troops."

Kovpak wrapped his hands around the hot cup and looked up at his commander. "The firebugs are the least of our concerns. They appear grateful that they have been accepted into a unit such as this. The simple act of giving them the paratrooper's

Telnaishka and Guards badges has raised their morale to new heights. They are working hard to achieve the training norms you have placed on them. Now that they have been issued their trucks, even if they are those old GAZ-63A 'Molotovkas,' they are even happier.

"The problem lies with the 2nd Company. They are behaving well, but I sense a note of discord. I cannot place my finger on it, but there is something they resent. Perhaps it is the fact that their battalion was dissolved and absorbed into this one."

Bodnya thought for a moment, placing one boot on a riddled and twisted truck fender lying in the mud. "I think I understand the resentment. I feel it myself. They, like our unit, performed a heroic mission for the Motherland, and now we are tasked with chasing ghosts. It is a disappointment for such men."

"Perhaps, my friend, but there is something else. I do not know what. The 358th Battalion soldiers in the 1st Company appear to have no complaint. They are working well with our boys."

"What about the Scout-Diversionary Platoon?" asked Bodnya. "They were part of the 358th Battalion. I am relying on them as our main reaction force, should I still? You do seem to be on good terms with Senior Lieutenant Dubovik."

"The Scout-Diversionists are a good group. They seem to hold themselves apart from the other 358th troops. I hope to work closely with Lieutenant Dubovik. He is aggressive, wants to do well, and is, after all, a brother Ukrainian!"

"I was afraid of that. I take it you have contacts in all the companies by now," said Bodnya. "Perhaps I should reassign you as our special section officer. You seem to have a flare for monitoring the troops' attitudes."

Indignant, Kovpak raised to his full height. "Comrade Battalion Commander, I am no Chekist! I am a special source paratrooper performing my sacred duties for the Motherland!"

"And, for yourself, I think," Bodnya replied, smiling. "Just an observation, my friend! You need not be concerned, I can better use your skills as a hunting dog than a watchdog!"

Both men turned as four GAZ-66 trucks snorted up the muddy farm track past the burned-out house and toward the barn. The lead square-nosed truck mounted a twin-barreled ZU-23 antiaircraft gun. The tail-end truck mounted a ZPU-1 "Vladimirov" 14.5mm, very heavy machine gun. The paratroopers of the

Scout-Diversionary Platoon huddled in the back of the trucks, assault rifles projecting over the sideboards.

"Do you think those will shoot holes through some ghosts, Comrade Battalion Commander?"

"Where did they get those?" puzzled Bodnya.

"We found them in a convoy on the shoulder of the autobahn," replied Kovpak. "The convoy had been hit by air attack. Lieutenant Dubovik and I evenly distributed the abandoned weapons."

"So your platoon is similarly equipped?"

"Of course, Comrade Battalion Commander! Our platoons were rehearsing sweep-and-block techniques when we happened on the convoy."

"Indeed! Are you certain the convoy was actually destroyed, Ensign?"

"Within reasonable doubt, Comrade Battalion Commander!" The Ukrainian put on his look of total innocence. "I must return to my platoon to continue the training."

Bodnya watched the little ensign scamper down the road, waving at the approaching trucks. He could just see Kovpak's own trucks parked in a clump of trees.

"Within reasonable doubt?" Bodnya muttered to himself. "Just exactly what did that phrase mean?"

He started back to the barn, but turned when a command car honked its way past the mud-covered trucks. Struggling up the road, the little vehicle fishtailed its way slowly up the road leaving a rooster tail of flying mud. Bodnya stood with his hands in his pockets watching its creeping approach past a burned-out communications repair truck. As it slid to a stop beside him, he saw it contained three men topped with green Border Troops caps and wearing immaculate green-on-green camouflage uniforms. A tall, thin captain sat in the front passenger seat, a junior sergeant was behind the wheel, and a lieutenant nestled in the back between canvas clothing bags.

The captain looked distastefully at Bodnya, who wore only mud-splattered olive drab mountain trousers and a camouflage jacket devoid of insignia, a habit from Afghanistan.

"Soldier," the captain snapped, "do you stand with your hands in your pockets when approached by an officer?"

A KGB Border Troops shithead, thought Bodnya, certainly not a *real* KGB officer! He withdrew his hands and snapped to attention, saluting.

"Do not salute me in a combat zone, you fool!" The captain admonished him as though he were a raw recruit, "Is this Unit 8217?" rattling off the battalion's field post number.

"Exactly so, Comrade Captain!"

"Where is the headquarters, soldier?"

"In the barn, Comrade Captain, you may park on the far side!"

"Very well, I will tell your commander that you were of aid to me," as he eyed Bodnya's muddy trousers. "Continue on!" he snapped at his driver.

"Just so . . . Comrade Captain," Bodnya responded with a faint hint of dryness.

The command car slithered up the track and around the barn.

"KGB dog turds!" Bodnya snorted under his breath. Shoving his hands back in his pockets, he stomped down to the destroyed farmhouse and its outdoor latrine.

★11★

"You guys good to go?" BJ asked, looking at each of the four LRRPs lined up for inspection.

"Fuckin' A!" shouted Tyrone King. "Let's do it!"

BJ attributed King's outburst to boyish enthusiasm or possibly the accidental ingestion of lead-based paint as a child. The other team members merely nodded their heads or gave a thumbs-up sign.

Team 24 formed up in its team room, their weapons slung and their big gray-and-green rucksacks on the floor in front of them. BJ ran his eyes over each of his four men's faces. All, except PFC King, were in their early or mid-20s and had completed a number of years on active duty. Some had taken a rank bust to get into Company G. His enlisted men had regularly outshone the other students at the Guard's Leadership Development Course at Camp Mabry in Austin. Company G expected motivation and initiative from its enlisted men. When offered a chance to go to Officer Candidate School, Company G EMs declined, saying they would rather be a corporal in Company G than a lieutenant in the 49th Armored Division. It was that kind of spirit and dedication that made the company good.

The TOE called for six-man recon teams, but most fielded only five, the preferred size in Company G. Most NATO LRRP units used four- or five-man teams. The U.S. Army had adopted a six-man team for one reason only. A captain at the Fort Leavenworth Combat Arms Development Center had been tasked with writing the doctrinal concept proposal for the new long-range surveillance units. His only qualification to do so was that he was Ranger qualified. He had never served in a LRRP unit.

The captain had recommended a six-man team so they could be paired off as "Ranger buddies." Although the Ranger Course used combat and reconnaissance patrols as a vehicle to teach leadership skills, it did not even pretend to teach deep penetration LRRP skills—that was not its goal.

While a worthwhile concept, each man watching out for his buddy, it did not justify adding an additional man. The West German LRRPs had long since found that for each man added over four, the team's chance of detection was increased by twenty percent. The larger team also required the construction of a larger observation post and more helicopter space. Company G had worked effectively for years with two-man and three-man elements in each team.

"Maps," said BJ, breaking out of his reverie. Each man withdrew his waterproofed recon zone map from his left trousers leg cargo pocket.

"No marks on the map?" The team members were constantly reminded that nothing was to be marked on a map—ever!

"Check your notepads. No unit ID, no intel info." The men removed the small dark green notepads from the map cases and flipped through them.

BJ quickly gave each man a once over, looking for missing equipment items. Each LRRP wore protective clothing in layers: thermal underwear, Army-issue sweater or British "wooly pully," BDUs devoid of any insignia, and four-color woodlands-pattern camouflage Gortex cold-weather suit. This two-piece suit was a lifesaver and so popular that they sometimes jokingly called themselves the "Gortex Rangers."

The Gortex fabric "breathed," permitting moisture vapor to pass through its water and wind repellent layers to prevent excessive sweating during movement, one of the principal causes of hypothermia, the loss of core body temperature. Hypothermia, or exposure, was the greatest fear the teams had when operating in extreme cold for prolonged periods with little chance of drying out or warming up. While well-suited for movement, the lightweight clothing offered only limited protection when they remained static in a team site, such as an observation post, objective rally point, or laager, for any length of time.

When stationary the men crawled into their sleeping bags, keeping them unzipped. If additional cold protection was needed, they could always don the chemical protective suits carried in their rucksacks. This way the teams could travel "light," retaining freedom of movement.

Their ensembles were completed by Gortex insulated gloves, wool scarf, various models of insulated boots running the range from German paratrooper boots to commercial Gortex-lined models. BJ's team's winter headwear were forest-green, wool-knit skull caps. They also carried issue pile caps for use when stationary. The teams were given some leeway in the selection of their headgear, just so long as everyone in the team wore the same. This was a key recognition feature at night when, often, only a man's silhouette could be seen.

Each LRRP carried on his person specific mandatory items. His compass, Army-issue lensatic or Silva orienteering model, was in his left chest pocket secured by a string of "dummy cord." In other pockets were a pocket knife, some form of fire-starting device, water purification tablets, and a mylar thermal survival blanket. In the right trousers cargo pocket was an emergency ration made up of the main components of three MREs and LRP rations, sealed in a bag. These simple items provided a LRRP with minimal essentials if his web gear and rucksack were lost. He could still navigate, retain body heat, and eat.

On the web gear were two pouches each containing three thirty-round magazines for their M16A1 rifles, first-aid pouch with two field dressings—for entry and exit wounds—and one or two canteens. If only one was carried, it was on the hip opposite from the man's shooting arm. This way he could reach for his canteen with his opposite hand and keep his weapon ready with the other. Additional canteens were carried on the rucksack. Some carried a sheath knife on the belt. The company had always discouraged expensive fighting and survival knives. The knife was regarded as a tool rather than a weapon. The loss of an eighteen-dollar Air Force survival knife was easier to tolerate than a 150-dollar "Rambo" special. The eighteen-dollar knife could kill someone just as well and skin a rabbit far better than a stiletto fighting blade. Nothing was permitted to be carried on the web gear's suspenders. It would tangle with rucksack straps and catch on vines.

Each man also had a SERE (survival, evasion, resistance, and escape) kit attached to his belt. This was a nonstandard item, assembled by each man following minimal guidelines. First-aid items, survival materials, and navigation aids were configured and supplemented as the individual desired. It was a custom-made survival kit assembled at his own expense, insurance that he would care for it. Besides his rifle, various fragmentation, white phosphorus, and CS (tear gas) grenades were carried to assist in breaking contact. Last, but not least, was the M17A2 protective mask with all of its associated decontamination and protective items carried in a canvas case on the left thigh.

BJ stepped up to his assistant team leader, Sergeant Shannon Hickey, a twenty-seven-year-old machinist in civilian life. He had been in an 82d Airborne Division battalion scout platoon, but had not joined the National Guard for a couple of years after getting off of active duty. He had missed the bush and the jumping. Hickey could have had his own team long ago, but liked the lesser responsibility of an ATL. He had even run Team 24 for almost a year when BJ had done his turn as an S&T NCO, but was happy where he was. Married, he had three small kids with a fourth "standing in the door," probably another motivation to get out of the house once in a while. He spoke only when absolutely necessary, and when he did have something to say it was brief and to the point.

"Show me our surveillance sector, Shan." Hickey, using the tip of a retracted ballpoint pen, traced a three-kilometer sector along Highway 75 heading southeast out of Hamburg and just east of the intersection of the north-south Highway 3.

"I don't like operating so close to an intersection, Beej. Too many baddies," grumbled Hickey.

"Me neither, Shan, but Highway 3 is only secondary to us, we won't really be able to see it if we've got 75 under surveillance."

That had been a continuing problem with the MI folks. They expected a team to be able to observe every highway, railroad, and foot trail in the area from their OP just because it appeared so close on the map. In reality, because of terrain, vegetation, weather conditions, and distance, this was usually impossible.

Another continuing problem was that higher headquarters always wanted to pinpoint the exact location of the OP when assigning missions. A site might look great on a map, but once the team was on the ground, they usually had to select their own. O&I assigned a team a surveillance sector on the targeted highway and the TL selected his own OP site after a ground recon, then reported its location.

"We're going to be way ahead of the game if I can locate the

OP we used last year,'' said BJ. During a NATO LRRP exercise he had been attached to a Danish Jaeger Corps team, who had proved to be some of the most effective LRRPs in NATO. They had constructed an elaborate OP in the area assigned him now, which was why he had been so fortunate to draw this mission.

BJ moved over to his senior radio operator, Corporal Troy Murphy. The twenty-six-year-old electrician had served six years in the Marine Corps as a radio teletype operator. He had come out of the Corps and directly into the unit when he found he could go to jump school. He had been taking business courses at a community college so he could go into business for himself. The team's joker, he was single and a ladies' man. He could make the radio hum and burn through to a base radio station when many teams had called it quits.

''First day's freq, Troy,'' BJ asked his SRO.

Murphy rattled off the first three days frequencies.

''I know you have the emergency crypto system down pat,'' said BJ. ''Where's your crypto bag?''

''Left cargo pocket where it always is,'' said Murphy as he pulled out the sage-green bag secured with dummy cord. It held the communications-electronic operating instructions and one-time pads, each in its own Ziplock bag. The other team members craned their necks to see for themselves where it was, to reinforce their memories. That little bag was the team's salvation, as were so many small items of their equipment.

BJ moved next to Corporal Walter Kosinski, the scout.

''The NVG check out okay, Wally?''

''She's workin' fine, boss,'' said the scout as he leaned over his rucksack and removed the night-vision goggles from the top compartment. ''It's even got all four lens caps!''

Kosinski would have the NVGs on when they off-loaded the chopper. He was the team's pointman, a job he rotated with the radio operator. The twenty-four-year-old Kosinski was loud and obnoxious in the armory, but in the field he moved with a silent grace, a skill he had picked up deer hunting in East Texas pine forests. BJ was never certain what form of employment Kosinski would announce he currently held at each drill, but it was always outdoors work: land surveyor, roofer, barge crewman. Though uncharacteristically quiet about it, BJ knew that he was concerned about his live-in girlfriend. She almost fainted when Kosinski had boarded the bus for Fort Hood.

He had been a combat engineer for three years on active duty, most of it spent in the 3d Infantry Division in Germany, a valuable background. He had joined a National Guard engineer battalion to be eligible for the Texas Veteran's Land Grant Act. After making his first few drills he had watched a helicopter return a Company G recon team from an exercise. The chopper had landed at his unit since Company G's armory had no helipad and a truck had been sent over to pick them up. The team had been sloppy in their on-loading procedures. The platoon sergeant, who had been aboard the extraction chopper, had dropped the team for push-ups while they still wore their rucksacks.

Kosinski showed up at Company G's armory on Monday morning wanting to know if he could transfer. BJ valued his engineer route reconnaissance skills and his ability to rate bridge load capacities.

"What's our route to the ORP (objective rally point), Wally?"

"First to the stream on 345 degrees for 350 meters, then 800 meters to the forest road on 20 degrees where we confirm our location in reference to the crossroads just to the east. Then it's 1800 meters on 350 degrees. We'll cross three forest roads on that leg. After the third one we move about 300 meters, establish the ORP, and you and I locate your old OP several hundred meters to the north."

"Good going, Wally."

"You hanging tight, King?" BJ asked, looking up at PFC Tyrone King, the team's radio operator. The new TOE called for only one school-trained radio operator, but Company G trained one of the team's scouts as a backup RO.

"They're hanging, but it's my asshole that's tight, Beej," responded the six-foot-four, 208-pound "King Kong."

King was the team's quiet brute strength. Whenever there was extra equipment to carry, he always quietly accepted it, never complaining. BJ sometimes thought he would carry every man's rucksack if asked, not told, to. At twenty years, he was also the team's youngest. Born and raised in Louisiana, he had come to Texas to live with an uncle while he attended the University of Houston, where he majored in engineering. He had joined the Guard to make himself eligible for resident tuition and help pay for school. He had never been on active duty. The only time BJ had ever heard him complain was the day they arrived in Germany, "I hope this doesn't mess up my schooling."

"How about the beacon, King?" asked BJ.

"It's packed, padded, and waterproofed. I've checked the bat's and the spares. I double-checked to make sure the freq is not set on the actual.''

"Good work. Your load okay?" asked BJ. "That's a lot of extra weight."

"I can handle it, man."

"When do we make our initial entry report?" asked BJ.

"When we get to the ORP."

"Okay," said BJ, "I want each of you to show me the exact location of our insertion rally point and the primary RP on your maps."

Platoon Sergeant Daniels led the four teams across the playground, a bordering street, and into the field that served as the unit's helipad. "Guys, dump your rucks here on the sidewalk and keep them separated by team so you don't mix them up when the choppers show. Move everyone into the shelter when that's done."

Some of the Headquarters Platoon had rigged a large canvas trap as a windbreak and partial overhead cover. Some park benches had been moved into it.

"Make sure your weapons are clear, but that the magazines are handy," said Daniels. "Once you're situated I want to see the TLs out here. Don't let anyone drop off to sleep. You guys need to be alert when the choppers arrive."

BJ knew that was bullshit. No one would be able to sleep now. Maybe if they lived a few days or weeks, they might develop the combat soldier's ability to sleep anywhere, anytime. Tonight, the pucker factor would prevent any rest.

"And don't talk to the other teams," BJ added quickly. "What they're doin' is none of your business and vice versa."

The four team leaders clustered around their platoon sergeant, hands in their pockets.

"All your guys okay?" asked Daniels.

A muttered "Ready" came from each man.

"There's not anything I can say to make this any easier except to repeat Hagger's advice," said Daniels in a low voice. "Do it just like you did in training. You developed good habits, so don't try something new. Take it easy and stay flexible."

"Just don't forget to pick us up this time, asshole!" Colly said in his best imitation whine. The other TLs chuckled, all recalling the time Colly's team had been left in Sam Houston National Forest. Three choppers had been extracting teams and there was a mix-up on which teams each would pick up. The missing team had not been discovered until the choppers returned to the Air Guard's Ellington Field. The birds were out of blade time and Daniels had immediately jumped in a van and drove ninety miles to the training area. He had found the pissed-off team trooping down the shoulder of a farm-to-market road on their way to the interstate highway. He had bought them lunch to atone.

"We aren't going to forget you this time, but if we do, I'm not driving out there to pick your asses up!"

Two similar-sized figures walked up to the group.

"Everything all set, Daniels?" asked Captain Schultz.

"Yes, sir. As ready as it can be."

The CO turned to the teams huddled under the shelter. "Everyone wide awake and set to go?"

"Ready!" came the response in unison.

"Well, I guess you are awake. It's almost 8:00 P.M. in Texas. You'll be alert during the most critical stage of the mission, the insertion, but come dawn your eyes are going to start telling you it's bedtime. Stay on your toes and make sure the whole team doesn't crash in your OP at the same time."

"I do have some good news," he went on. "The 6th Cav Brigade is unable to support us right now, too many missions and not enough assets. Instead we're getting two HH-60 Nighthawks from the 160th Aviation Regiment, special ops types. They have a detachment up here supporting Special Forces, but they've been released to us for the night. That means much better navigation capabilities and survivability."

The team members all stared at their CO.

What the hell do I say to these guys? How do I get them to focus their minds on the mission so they stop worrying about the infiltration, the acknowledged most dangerous phase?

Captain Ranwanz came to his aid, "I want you guys to do one thing for me. Picture in your mind your team's recon zone map. Think about where your rally point is. Telescope in on that point on the map and burn your RP's location into your brain. Just picture it on the map so you can look at it and find it instantly!"

The dull pop of rotors arrived on the wind.

"Luck, guys!" shouted Schultz as the two Nighthawks settled on to the field, guiding on the strobe light held by an O&I NCO.

* * *

Donna Vasquez, the shortest Chief Warrant Officer Two in the Army, and the only female HH-60 Nighthawk pilot, set the big chopper gently down on the field, guiding on the chemical light sticks and flashing strobe. The second bird came down behind her. The four teams crouched on the grass beside their rucks, their backs turned to the whirling storm.

"There're our passengers, Tommy," she said as the ship settled.

"Meat on the table," Tommy Cox, Donna's copilot, replied. The two pilots were the original odd couple of the sky. Donna was short, bright, eager, and relentlessly perky. Cox was tall, taciturn, cynical, and misanthropic. Donna had once asked Cox if he had been assigned to her as a test. He replied that he thought so, but couldn't decide which of them was being tested.

As the chopper settled, BJ's and Colly's teams quickly walked to the lead chopper's doors, the teams boarding from opposite sides. As BJ helped his men into the chopper, a decidedly feminine voice called out, "Beej! Is that you?"

BJ peered through the pilot's side window. Inside, Donna leaned close to the partly open window and shouted, "It's me, Donna Vasquez!"

Through the Plexiglas window, BJ could just make out the tiny smiling face framed by the huge green flight helmet.

"Donna, what the hell are you doin' here?" BJ shouted through the window's opening.

"I work here, Bud," she called back. "Jump in, we're goin' for a ride!"

The two team leaders handed Tommy Cox their insertion instruction forms, listing the primary and alternate landing zones, team call sign, air-to-ground frequency, and desired landing heading. The infiltration route had been preplanned and coordinated with the aviation unit by the O&I Section, the corps' engineer terrain detachment, and the corps' Combined Air Space Management Element. The route had been selected to avoid known enemy units—especially air defense, and power lines, maximizing the use of hills, ridges, valleys, and tree lines as a nap-of-the-earth flight route. Each course change of the preprogrammed route had been punched into the Nighthawk's on-board inertial navigation computer. The big chopper would almost fly itself to the landing zone with the pilot controlling the altitude and watching for obstacles and radar contacts.

The teams placed their rucks on the floor between their legs and held their weapons muzzle down.

BJ reached up and pulled down the intercom handset from its ceiling recess.

"Long time no see, Donna!" shouted BJ over the rotors. "How the hell did you get here?"

"It's a small Army!" replied Donna. "I wanted some excitement, so I called back some favors! Which team's goin' in first?"

"I am. Two-Four on the sheet. Wish we could visit!"

"Me, too, but it's showtime!" shouted Donna.

With that, she snapped her night-vision goggles down, and as BJ locked his seat harness on, she pulled power and the dark special operations helicopter lifted into the very hostile eastern sky.

★ 12 ★

The sound of the column reached Harlan first. The grinding of gears and the dull throb of diesel engines carried clearly through the wet fog that clung to the ground, turning the pass into a gray blue of shadows and half-seen shapes.

"Here they come!" Harlan hissed. "Wake em up, Ike!"

"On the way," the blocky little Hawaiian answered as he slithered over the rim of their fighting position and made his way quickly down the length of the ambush.

During the night, Harlan's Kreuzadders had parked their captured BTR-80s in a draw two kilometers away. After a hurried march to the ambush site and two furious hours digging in along the narrow ridge, the fire teams had settled in, waiting for a column. Harlan suspected that most of the teams were now sound asleep. He wanted them to be at least awake enough to remember where they were when the shooting started. Harlan hoped this first ambush would go as easily as had the capture of the BTRs.

They had caught the three vehicles at a road crossing. The crews were a motorized rifle platoon who stood arguing over a map, pointing in different directions. Absorbed in their argument, they had not heard Harlan's men slipping up to the vehicles. A few short bursts had killed the entire Soviet party. The three BTRs were captured intact. In one of the vehicles was an extra treat, two AT-7 "Saxhorn" missile launchers and eight extra missiles. The AT-7 was a Soviet wire-guided tank killer.

Harlan knew this ambush would not be that simple, but if the column was not heavily defended, it should be easy enough.

Ikehara moved quickly from one position to the next, making sure that each man was awake and alert. The sound of the trucks was much louder now, although the thick mist still hid the vehicles. Some of the Kreuzadders were dozing, but most were awake, stretching and working the kinks out of their muscles before the fun started. When he was convinced that everyone was ready, he scurried back to his hole at the far end of the ridge.

I wish these Soviet launchers had thermal imagers, Harlan thought, they would make it a lot easier to see through this soup. What the hell, the fog hides us as well as it hides them.

"Ready, Comrade Captain," Ikehara whispered as he slid back into the shallow hole.

"Ike, why are we whispering?" Harlan asked, straining to see a moving shape in the thick whiteness. "Those trucks are loud enough to wake the dead."

"Because it's a secret, Comrade Captain." Ike smile slyly.

"Oh, right."

The first movement was the boatlike front of a BTR personnel carrier. It slid through the fog like a dark finger pointing the way for the others to follow. At the sight of it, Harlan and Ikehara slid back down into the hole. Through gaps in the rim of the hole, they watched the entire column enter the pass. The BTR-80 armored personnel carrier led the way, followed by two fuel tankers and another pair of BTR-80s. The BTRs were painted with white bands that ran the length of the vehicle. Behind the BTRs, another fuel truck and half a dozen Ural 375 trucks with trailers lumbered along. At the rear of the column, one of the Urals had a ZU-23 twin 23mm antiaircraft gun mounted on the back of the truck.

Fuel and ammo, Harlan thought, the standard load, escorted by some traffic control BTRs and an antiaircraft gun.

The BTRs' commanders were standing up in their hatches, straining to see through the fog. As the lead BTR-80 began to disappear into the mist at the far end of the kill zone, Harlan tapped the gunner next to him.

"Now!"

Senior Private Walter Nolan had been tracking the BTR with his gunsight since it had come into view. He pulled the firing trigger and waited for the backblast, trying not to flinch as the missile suddenly exploded from the tube. The Saxhorn missile took only three seconds to cover the 500 meters to the BTR. It followed the personnel carrier into the mist and a second later a roar and a huge red fireball announced its arrival.

The ridge line was silent for a second after the Saxhorn fired, then it came alive. Every weapon fired at once, the noise drowning out the rumble of the trucks now swerving wildly to escape the storm of metal ripping into them. An RPG-7 rocket turned the antiaircraft gun at the rear of the column into a brightly burning hulk, trapping the convoy. The two remaining BTRs spun their turrets, searching the murky walls of the pass for targets. Half a dozen RPG-7 and RPG-22 rounds fell on the pair. The second BTR-80 immediately disappeared in the smoke of four exploding rockets. A single dazed and bleeding crewman stumbled from the stricken vehicle. As he stumbled away from the smoking machine, a stream of 5.45mm rounds from the ridge slammed him into the slick surface of the road.

The remaining BTR-80, somehow unscathed, turned and started up the steep slope. The BTR commander dropped into his hatch and began raking the top of the ridge with his 14.5mm and 7.62mm machine guns, searching the mist for the phantoms who were killing his convoy. His shots went high over the ridge. An RPG round took off the left front tire, slewing the boatlike personnel carrier to the left. Smoke canisters flew from the rear of the BTR's small turret, too late to hide it from the gunners on the ridge. Two more RPG rockets hit the crippled BTR, one above the driver and one directly atop the turret. The BTR shook, then just sat there. Black smoke curled up from the blown open hatches.

With the BTRs out of action, the trucks were sitting ducks. Several of the drivers abandoned them at the first shots, running for the safety of the mist. Only a few of them escaped. The Kreuzadder's RPKs and PK machine guns raked the far slope. As much as possible, the fuel and ammo trucks were to be spared. The Kreuzadders wanted them intact.

The first fueler swerved around the burning wreckage of the lead BTR and tried to escape. A single RPG-22 flashed down from the ridge and hit the fueler near the rear of its tank. The whole truck seemed to leap off the road, bending in the middle as it jumped up in the air and exploded. A huge, fiery black mushroom cloud disappeared up into the mist as the twisted wreckage came back down in a heap. The burning fuel fell on the remains of the already burning BTR.

"Holy shit!" Ikehara said as the tanker went off. "Look at that!"

"Damn this fog!" Senior Lieutenant Arkady Yemenev said for the hundredth time that morning. "Will it never lift?"

If the fog could have hidden Yemenev's column from the enemy's bombers, it would have been a godsend. Since the bombers could see right through it with their devices, all it did was to hide the slick road and slow his column even more. As it was, the column was poking along at thirty kilometers an hour.

They were well into the pass before Yemenev even realized it. The steep slopes rose up into the thick mist on both sides.

Yemenev clearly heard the missile launch above him. He swiveled his head up, looking for the source of the sound. He just caught a glimpse of the missile before it hit the lead tanker.

"Ambush left!" Yemenev screamed down to the driver. He dropped down into the small turret and jerked the turret control handle to the left to bring the gun around to bear on the ridge. He pulled the firing levers of both the 14.5mm and the smaller 7.62mm, spraying a long burst from both toward the ridge above him. He knew that he was firing wild, but hoped the return fire would put their heads down for a moment. Yemenev could hear the pinging of bullets on the skin of the BTR and thanked the nonexistent God for the thin layer of steel around him. The driver was gunning the engine, trying to climb the slope. Yemenev peered through the view block, looking for flashes that would give him a target.

A loud bang signaled the first RPG hit and the BTR suddenly pitched to the left. Yemenev's head slammed against the receiver of the 14.5mm. He shook off the impact and went back to the gunsight.

Smoke, he thought, fire the smoke grenades, quickly.

Yemenev was so busy with the smoke launchers, he didn't notice that the BTR had stopped moving. He pressed the firing switch, launching all six smoke canisters toward the ridge.

The sudden blast inside the BTR deafened him, blocking out the driver's screams. He didn't hear the RPG round that hit the turret next to his head. The jet of fire from the shaped charge burned through the thin armor and right through Yemenev's helmet. He fell headless into the scorched interior of the burning BTR.

When no more movement was visible on the road, Harlan passed the word to cease fire. He waited a moment for the firing to stop, then ordered his search teams into the pass. As they made their way carefully down the slope, the missile teams at each end of the ambush moved to their blocking positions to watch for any more traffic. In the kill zone, the search team began its work.

The searchers were swift and methodical. They first swept through the vehicles and set out security teams beyond the kill zone to thwart any counterattack. This done, they searched the dead truckers for any intelligence information. One "dead" trucker proved to be quite lively, but when he came up with an AK-47, he instantly rejoined the dead.

Two of the fueler trucks and three of the Urals were still intact. As it turned out, only two of the Urals were full of weapons and ammunition. The other had rations and even a case of vodka! All in all, it had been an excellent morning.

★13★

Once the hole cover was in place, BJ turned on his flashlight and with the blue-green light scanned the interior of the hide-hole and its small side sleeping bays. It was still in good shape. The walls were sound and only a small puddle of water had collected in the center of the damp floor. The ceiling sagged only slightly, but they could prop that up with a few stout limbs.

It had taken BJ and Wally the better part of an hour to find the old OP, searching about in the darkness for the landmarks that had changed with the season. They had listened for traffic sounds from the highway, but only heard light truck traffic. When he scanned it with the NVG, Wally saw only widely spaced pale green blobs drifting west on the highway, a supply convoy.

The two returned to the ORP, where they had left their ruck-sacks, and led the team back. Shedding their rucks, they wiggled into the hole and quickly picked their own spots. Hickey snapped a pale green chemical light stick and hung it from a ceiling beam. BJ and Wally rigged a poncho blackout curtain to block off the entrance from the rest of the compartment.

"King," BJ said softly, "take your E-tool and dig a sump over there against that wall, that'll drain off that water."

"Roger, Beej," the huge black PFC said, turning his ruck over to get at the folded shovel stored on one of the equipment loops. In minutes, King had dug a hole against the wall, scraped a small trench to drain the water into it, and filled the center of the hide-hole with the loose dirt from the sump. The others situated their rucks and checked weapons. Hickey placed several grenades in a niche by the entrance as he kept watch over their immediate vicinity. From one of the narrow sleeping bays, BJ pulled a folded bundle of dirty plastic sheeting and, with the help of the others, spread it on the floor.

"Four walls and a roof, what more can you ask for?" whispered Troy Murphy.

"King, take the first surface watch," directed BJ. "Wally, take your Kukri knife, slip out of here, and cut three limbs to prop up our roof. Cut some one-inch sticks so we can weave a grating for the sump. Remember to smear dirt over the tree's cut ends. Do a 360 security check while you're out and don't forget the password. King, try not to shoot him when he comes back."

"Wally, why don't you leave your Rolex here . . . just in case?" suggested King.

Wally slipped off the watch without a word and handed it to King, who, smiling, shoved it into a pocket.

King took out the DMDG (digital message device group) and took up his watch position. Murphy was already setting up the AN/PRC-70 radio without removing it from his ruck.

"We'll run the antenna wire out when Wally gets back. It'll take both me and King to camouflage it."

"Tell me again how you know about this place, Beej," Hickey asked as the team busied themselves, the tension and fear of the insertion and cross-country move seeping slowly out of them.

"We dug it over a year ago during a NATO LRRP exercise," BJ answered as he dug deep inside his rucksack and produced what looked like a black metal dildo, three inches wide and about eighteen-inches long. "Some Danish Jaegers and me. We watched the highway for almost a week. The OPFOR had trackers out looking for us, but they never found us."

"I hope it works that well again," Hickey said, backing into a corner. "I'm afraid to ask, but what's that thing for?"

"Periscope. We built it just for this kind of hide-hole."

BJ extended the telescoping black tube and twisted it, locking it into place.

"We just push it up through the little hole in the roof and check out the neighbors without having to poke our heads out or make a vision slit. The night-vision gear fits on with this adapter."

Murphy had the radio and DMDG set up by the time Wally came back from his woodcutting chore. Those inside the hide had not even heard King challenge his return.

"Real quiet on the highway," he said. He and Hickey began shoving the support limbs into place, first ripping a slit in the floor plastic and placing flat rocks to support the posts.

"You guys ready to put up the antenna?" asked BJ.

"King, bring the white tape, I've got the antenna reel," said Murphy.

"I need my watch back"—Wally smiled at King—"and you might as well leave me yours . . . just in case."

King handed over the two watches and Wally slipped them both on his left wrist.

BJ quietly went about extending the homemade periscope to its full length and working it up through the roof lattice. It emerged in the shell of a hollow rotted log that had been placed over the opening, making it almost invisible. Through it, BJ could see the highway to the north. With the adapter for the NVG, it was almost as useful at night as during the day. It would permit the team to stay in the hide-hole as long as they needed to.

When the periscope was in place and secured to the ceiling with a bungee cord, BJ made a slow scan of the sector. He stuck small strips of fluorescent tape to the ceiling, each a reference point for a specific landmark and the limits of the periscope's scanning sector. He made a sector sketch on a notepad page identifying each point and taped it over the periscope's eyepiece. In this way, he could quickly turn the periscope to a specific point, much the same way a mortar crew uses aiming stakes to lay in their mortar on specific targets.

In the next few hours, Highway 75 carried a steady stream of vehicles. Small convoys, with vehicles spaced at one-hundred-meter intervals, paralleled each other on the westward lanes, moving through the night guided by tiny lights on the vehicle ahead. He saw a truck break down. It was quickly pushed off the road to be repaired or towed off. Nothing was permitted to stop the flow of traffic. BJ figured that by now the big combat units moving to the front had gathered in assembly areas to hide out during daylight. At one point on the highway, a commandant's Service traffic control point routed vehicles around road repairs left unfinished, weaving one convoy through another.

Hickey worked up a situation report that would give the team's OP location and current status. Added to this would be a spot report detailing activity on the highway. He read off the report to BJ line by line. When Murphy returned, he began encoding it by substituting the words with three-digit groups of numbers taken from the brevity code section of the CEOI— communications-electronic operating instructions. He then opened the transmit booklet of the two one-time pads and substituted each three-digit number for single letters arranged in groups of five. When he was through, he had King double-check the results of his encoding and encryption.

Murphy watched King type the message into the DMDG, a cigar box-sized microcomputer with a typewriter-style keyboard and a thirty-four-character plasma display. Once the message was in the machine, Murphy scrolled the string of letters across the display checking them against the one-time pad's pages.

Thus encrypted, the message was impossible to break. The only existing key to his particular pair of one-time pads was in the Communications Platoon Headquarters where the messages were decoded and decrypted. Each team had its own unique set. The next message he sent would be encrypted using new one-time pad pages with an entirely different random mix of letters. In effect, each message a given team transmitted, and received, used a different encryption system. No one message was long enough to establish a pattern.

Coupling the DMDG's cable to the AN/PRC-70 radio, he turned on the power, set the frequency, tuned it, and pushed the DMDG's X-mit button. A minute later he repeated the process. King turned the frequency knobs to hide the frequency while Murphy tore out and burned the one-time pad pages he had used.

BJ and Hickey took first surveillance watch, alternating as observer and recorder. The recorder maintained a tally sheet marking stick numbers of vehicle types in convoy groups along with their pass times. Only one event of real note happened during the first watch. The sky was just getting light as BJ watched a column of widely spaced trucks begin snaking past the repairs, the trucks began bunching up behind each other on the outer lane.

Poor driver training and convoy control, thought BJ. He would include that in the next report.

Most of the trucks had gone through when a battalion of T-80 tanks rolled up to the repair detour in the westward inside lane. The traffic control officer halted the steel monsters and continued to wave the trucks through. The officer in the lead tank of the halted column jumped down and began to berate the traffic control officer, apparently demanding that his tanks should go through, and failing to consider that it would completely disorganize the truck convoy. On the tail of the convoy a second tank battalion rumbled up as the first battalion's officer ran back to his tank. He hastened back to the traffic control officer when he realized the other unit was attempting to pass his battalion. The traffic officer flagged this unit to a stop and he found himself in a three-way shouting match. Finally, the two tankers fell to blows in the center of the highway, while their troops climbed up on their tanks to get a better seat for the fight, each unit cheering on their champion.

"Hey, check this out," BJ said.

"What is it?" Hickey inquired from his seat on the dirt pile.

"Two Red tankers are dukin' it out in the road."

"Say what?" Hickey asked, moving up behind BJ.

"Check it out."

Hickey slid up to the eyepiece and focused.

"Jesus Christ, they're beating the shit out of each other."

"Idiots," Lieutenant Vladilen Osipov muttered, *"dristui."*

The two diminutive tankers, both platoon commanders, were thrashing around on the ground, pounding the stuffing out of each other. Their tanker helmets' earflaps and intercom cables flailed as wildly as their fists.

"Get back to your tanks!" Osipov shouted at the pair. "You will both get your chance to fight!"

The two black-clad tankers either did not hear or, more likely, did not care. They continued to punch and gouge with gusto, cheered on by their troops in the half light of near sunrise.

This is out of control, Osipov thought, watching the fight. He wished that a senior Commandant's Service officer was present, but they had all been placed to control traffic at the more critical highway intersections.

If the major comes along, Osipov worried, it will be my fault, not these two fools'. He turned to his three-man patrol standing by a BTR-70 painted with the distinctive red-and-white Commandant's Service band.

"I have had enough of this. Shoot them!"

The patrol did not react at first. "Did you hear me?" Osipov yelled over the roar of the fight crowd.

"Just so, Comrade Lieutenant!" Junior Sergeant Lubkos answered quickly.

The sergeant barked at the patrol and immediately three AK-

74 muzzles came up. Three rapid bursts caught the two pugilists and sent them rolling across the pavement leaving a splattered trail of blood. The staccato barking of the rifles stopped the crowd noise like a switch. Empty cartridge cases rolled across the concrete toward the still bodies.

"Now," Osipov screamed at the two columns, "get these tanks moving. Do you hear me?"

The crews of the two nearest tanks dropped into their T-80s, and for a second Osipov wondered if they would fire at him. They did not. Russian discipline had them by the throat, as usual.

The commander of the first battalion came running up with one of his company commanders, the pair closely followed by the chief of staff of the other battalion. On seeing the two blood-ied black bundles locked in each other's arms, the officers stopped in stunned amazement. One began drawing his pistol, but still eyed the torn bodies. Tatters of crimson-stained white fleece clung to the wet pavement.

The rifles of Osipov's patrol were pointed at the officers.

"Comrades," Osipov shouted in his most authoritative voice and placing his hands on the hips of his black leather uniform, "these servicemen were fighting on the highway, obstructing the movement of military units in a combat zone. You may recover the bodies, but these units must move immediately, they are blocking other units."

The officers of each unit had one of their tankers remove the identity books from their dead platoon commanders and roll the bodies into the ditch. There was no place to carry corpses when going into combat.

The tanks roared to life and, at Osipov's direction, threaded their way around the repairs, one battalion at a time, their crews peering at the bodies in the ditch.

Osipov turned the direction over to his admiring sergeant, walked around behind the BTR-70, and found it almost impossible to light a cigarette.

"Holy shit, Beej," Hickey exclaimed, "the traffic cop shot 'em both. Look."

BJ moved back to the eyepiece. The matter had been finally settled by the traffic control officer, whose troops shot both men as they rolled around on the concrete. Traffic resumed a minute later, presumably after a quick set of battlefield promotions.

BJ recorded that they had observed a possible discipline breakdown.

An hour later, after dawn broke, BJ figured he had observed two tank regiments and assorted support units making their way west. They were not hiding out during daylight, but kept moving. It was obvious that some big push was on. The flyboys would love targets like these.

He woke Wally and gave him the text of the second radio message from the hide-hole. Detection by Soviet radio direction finders was the least of his worries. The antenna was highly directional and the single sideband radio used a skip-wave transmission, bouncing its transmissions off the ionosphere. Their three base radio stations, deep behind friendly lines, were spaced many miles apart in positions dictated by the radio wave propagation tables. These took into account the terrain, atmospherics, weather, and other aspects of the region's ether. The digital data burst capability of the DMDG burst transmitted the message in mere seconds, barely enough to tickle an intercept radio's detection dials.

The day saw an endless progression of Soviet vehicles down the highway. The entire inventory of Soviet might was rumbling and clanking westward, an endless stream of tanks—T-80s and T-89s; BMP-2 infantry-fighting vehicles; their antitank counterparts—PPVs; BTR-70 and -80 wheeled armored personnel carriers; self-propelled cannon; towed cannon; rocket launchers; air defense missiles; trucks; fuel tankers; engineer and bridging equipment; everything a modern army needs to fight. A road repair crew arrived in midmorning and by noon the repairs were crudely completed. The traffic control troops departed with them.

The highway had been cleared of dozens of wrecked civilian vehicles, whose burned and twisted hulks littered the roadside. BJ did not see any bodies around the wreckage, but the angle kept him from seeing into the ditches. That was fine by BJ. There was nothing he could do about those people. The best he could do for the thousands of German civilians desperately fleeing the Soviet advance was to help keep some of the bastards from getting that far. Besides, he had seen plenty of dead bodies already, and expected to see more.

The targets continued to rumble by with the team transmitting spot reports almost hourly. By 1630 hours, when the sun began to set, BJ's team had watched two complete tank divisions and dozens of combat support units roll by. No strike aircraft had appeared. The frustrated team kept a watch to the southwest, hoping to see A/F-16s making repeated runs through columns of black smoke. They never did.

"What kind of crap is this, Beej?" groused a disgruntled Murphy. The whole team's mood had turned foul.

"Ya, why the fuck are we out here puttin' our butts on the line and the 'remfs' (rear echelon motherfuckers) can't get their act together to flatten these assholes on the road!" grumbled Wally Kosinski.

"Look, guys," pleaded BJ, "we don't know what the score is. Maybe they're hitting them farther to the west, or they're suckering them into a trap. Maybe they don't have anything left to hit them with!"

"Oh, great!" growled Hickey. "Here we are, Lord only knows how far behind their lines, and they've got nothing left to hit them!"

"I *meant*, that they could spare to hit this deep! Maybe they're going to hit them tonight. We're not the only ones out here watching them, and as they move closer to the front, they've got other means to monitor their movement."

These guys are getting an early case of cabin fever, BJ thought.

When the sky was finally dark, BJ allowed each man out of the hide for a brief time to relieve himself, bury their plastic piss bags, and get some much needed fresh air. Most of the men had been eating their MRE (meal, ready-to-eat) barbecue bean packets, enabling them to purposely fart. It was an effective method of covering the sour odor of urine. After eating a hot meal, they mellowed out a bit.

"Predict! *Predict*, Major Goncharov?" Bodnya's voice was as cold as the wind outside the barn. "What is this *predict*? Fortune tellers predict! Staff officers *forecast*!"

Major Serafim Goncharov, chief of staff of the 800th Spetsnaz Battalion, stood beside the working map, his arms hanging to his sides.

"Comrade Commander, I apologize for my choice of words. I was attempting to convey that this mission is *Ne Po Shablonu*—not by pattern. The nonstereotyped behavior of NATO reconnaissance-diversionary forces do not permit us to employ the standard tactical norms, nor does it offer the requisite quantitative data for calculations. Our troop control under present-day conditions constitutes an objective necessity for which we must obtain the requisite quantitative data for correct situational estimates and for reaching well-substantiated decisions.''

Goncharov looked at Bodnya, stretched out on his folding chair, his hands behind his head for support, and realized that he had again made an incorrect statement. What now?

Bodnya slowly eased himself to an upright position and stared at the freshly swept floor for a moment, before looking at his chief of staff.

What was the word that one of the agents in Texas had used to describe a troubled situation blighted by nonsense? *Bullshit!* That was it. No word in the Russian language seemed to describe the situation as well. It had that certain American sound, as did so many of their swear words, blunt and disgusting.

To the side sat Captains Noskov and Milstein, the first and second staff officers, the newly arrived and still highly embarrassed KGB Captain Yakushev, and Major Butakov, the *zampolit*. Butakov could see that both officers differed in their view of the present conditions, the required troop control measures, and the correct situational decisions. As the deputy commander for political affairs, his duties included the unit's ideological-political training and reliability, military education, recreational activities, leadership of the Komsomol organization, prevention and correction of morale, discipline, and personal problems, and the harmonizing of political programs and combat readiness.

It was obvious that the two senior officers of this unit were in direct conflict with each other and Butakov was in a position to understand both viewpoints. His duties required him to support the commander. However, he owed certain loyalties to Major Goncharov.

They had done much together to prepare the 358th Battalion for their first mission; a mission that had proved fatal for many of that once-effective unit. Goncharov had supported him in all his recommendations to the former commander. Ideologically and doctrinally, Goncharov was correct in his estimate of the dynamics of the present conditions and the manner in which he had arrived at the normatives he recommended.

On the other hand, due to the nonstereotyped nature of the enemy, he could understand the different form of initiative that Bodnya desired to counter their actions, or as the colonel aptly put it, ''Grind them into the mud!''

Bodnya looked like a hungry wolf . . . perpetually on the

prowl. Now would not be a good time to make a vocal stand in support of Goncharov. His political didactic skills would be better directed in support of the battalion commander. But his timing must be precise.

"What I want," began Bodnya in a low rumble, "is a simple plan of action to enable this battalion's subunits to be deployed in the most effective manner to counter the *possible* actions of enemy reconnaissance-diversionary subunits. Not absolute forecasts or *predictions* as to where and when they will strike. Because of their patternless manner of operations it is quite impossible to forecast such events!"

"Comrade Battalion Commander," began Butakov, "if I may interject a thought." Bodnya turned slowly to face him, his eyebrows knitted, giving his eyes a distinctly hooded appearance.

"Yes, Comrade Butakov," sighed Bodnya, "by all means do make any observations that pertain *directly* to this discussion."

Butakov began hesitantly, "It appears that this discussion of the unit's manner of deployment is confused by a misunderstanding in terminology . . ."

"Thank you, Comrade Butakov," cut in Bodnya. "In order to conduct an intellectual conversation, or combat operation, the participants must have a common vocabulary. I hope that all officers now present were able to absorb the requisite knowledge during the three or four years they spent at their service academies!"

Goncharov noticeably winced.

"What I was going to say, Comrade Commander," Butakov said as he stood, almost in disrespect to the still-seated commander, "is that the enemy reconnaissance-diversionary subunits rely solely on only one of the seven principals of war . . . *zapnost*—surprise. We do not know where or when they will strike. They dictate both the spatial and temporal aspects of the battle . . ." He paused a moment.

"Go on," said Bodnya, leaning forward in his chair, apparently unfazed by Butakov's show of disrespect.

"I am having trouble finding the correct terminology, maybe there is none," continued Butakov. "But, it would seem to me, by deploying our subunit in a manner totally unexpected by the enemy, we could, to some degree, control certain spatial and temporal aspects of this form of warfare.''

''Yes,'' said Bodnya thoughtfully. ''Step up to the working map, Comrade Butakov, we have some work to do!''

★14★

"Glad to meet you, sir," said Captain Schultz, offering his hand. "What can we do for you?"

"My detachment represents SOCEUR in NORTHAG's sector and we're coordinating cross-FLOT special ops," Jinx answered.

"Well, let's step into my office." Schultz turned to Sergeant Tarpley, the intel NCO. "Fetch Captain Ranwanz and have him come to my office."

Jinx looked back over his shoulder. Jenna Collingsworth was already cornered in the hall outside by three O&I members and two LRRPs from uncommitted teams.

She can probably take care of herself, Jinx thought.

"Do you have a Sergeant Kirkley around?" asked Jinx.

"BJ? Most certainly," said Schultz. "He's on a mission, though."

"He's a friend of mine. How's he doing?"

"He's okay and his team's sending in a lot of good solid reports," said Schultz. "You know he was involved with screwing up the Spetsnaz attack on Fort Hood?"

"Ya, I heard about it."

"I'm surprised that SOCEUR has taken an interest in us. Long-range surveillance units aren't considered special ops as far as 1st SOCOM is concerned. What's up?"

"We have a monster on our hands. It appears that no one ever fully considered the control and coordination problems that

106

would develop with so many elements operating across the FLOT. Frankly, it's a total cluster fuck.''

The two took seats in the office marked VORESTEHER, the former principal's office.

''You don't sound like the typical 'echelons above God' staff type,'' said Schultz with a smile.

''This isn't what I usually do,'' replied Jinx. ''But there are a lot of things falling through the cracks. From what I've seen, the various units are reasonably effective, but meshing it altogether, and acting on the intelligence information they've collected, has left a lot to be desired. I've also seen some very unrealistic ideas suggested, based on some real stupid preconceived notions.''

''We can identify with that!'' exclaimed Schultz. ''During most of the command post exercises we've been involved in, when we mentioned infiltrating LRRP teams into East Germany, some corps' staff rat would freak out and say we couldn't cross the Inner German Border! Christ! Why not? They only just fucking invaded us!''

''Believe it or not, there are still some staff rats saying that.''

''Bizarre!'' said Schultz. ''We've been barraged with some pretty farfetched ideas as far as our deployment, too, ever since the unit was formed, and usually from folks that had no idea of what LRRPs actually do, how we do it, and what our limitations are.''

The operations officer came through the door.

''Major Jenkins, Captain Ranwanz,'' introduced Schultz.

''Chuck Ranwanz,'' the ops office said, extending his hand.

''The major's from SOCEUR and wants to discuss some cross-FLOT special ops problems with us,'' said Schultz.

Eyeing Jinx's MI collar insignia, Ranwanz said, ''And, I hope, intel processing problems as well!''

''That, too,'' said Jinx.

''That's been our biggest problem so far,'' said Schultz. ''What did you find out at corps, Chuck?''

''Well, they got a rump corps TOC up and running. But they're still lacking many of their commo support elements. The 504th MI Brigade is going full tilt collecting info. That was one of the best moves they've made, bring the collection assets over on the first lifts so they could begin building a data base. Right now the problem is that they have more intelligence info than they can process, analyze, and disseminate.''

"We've seen that all over," said Jinz. "The analysts have been forced to adopt a form of triage, a priority in selecting what info to process. They're going crazy."

"I can vouch for that from just what I've seen up at corps," responded Ranwanz.

"I think I now understand what our CO meant," Jinx said slowly, struggling to remember the exact words, "when he said, 'The Soviets will strive to overload the enemy's collection system with information, regardless if it's real or deceptive, so as to turn his collectors against him and create doubt in the value of the information.' "

"And I've seen that happening up at corps," said Ranwanz. "Most of our deployed teams have been sending in a lot of information. Some excellent targeting information has come in and we've sent it to corps ASAP. But this afternoon we've had three teams, keeping highways under surveillance south and southeast of Hamburg, ask why there's been no air strikes. They've turned in some incredible targets."

"For example?" asked Jinx.

"Entire tank and motorized rifle regiments in march formation in broad daylight! One artillery and engineer battalion after the other, every kind of support unit you can think of," said Ranwanz in exasperation.

"Did you find out what they're doing with the reports at Corps?" asked Schultz.

"Same ol' crap! It's received, logged in, sent to a couple of different cells, and *filed*! Nothing's been sent to the Air Force. They're running around in circles worrying only about the close-in battle. All this talk about the AirLand Battle, deep attack of the follow-on forces, is just that . . . talk!" Ranwanz looked like he was about to burst a vein in his forehead.

"What's the progress of getting the reports from the LRRP teams to corps?" asked Jinx. "I'm familiar with Special Forces' system, but not with LRS's."

"It's basically similar to SF's, but on a different scale and aimed at a different end user . . . the corps," said Schultz as he began jotting a diagram on a notepad. "The teams transmit whenever they have useful info, there's no scheduled transmission windows like SF usually uses."

"What kind of commo gear do they use?"

"Prick-70s and the DMDG, same as some SF," said Ranwanz.

"The teams transmit using skip wave and our base radio stations have to be at least one hundred miles away for best results," went on Schultz. "The three base radio stations are deployed in depth, maybe ten to twenty miles apart. It all depends on the propagation tables. A given transmission may be received by any one of the BRSs, or all three."

"Or, sometimes none," chimed in Ranwanz, "but that doesn't happen too often."

"Doesn't that leave the teams kind of wondering if they're received?" asked Jinx.

"No. Any BRS that receives a message transmits a confirmation, a code word," answered Schultz. "They use a Prick-109 coupled to a DMDG with a printing attachment so they can get a hard copy. They give it to the radio teletype operator who transmits it to our Communications Center here at the company."

"Does the BRS decrypt it?"

"No, sir," said Ranwanz. "That's done by the Comm Center. They give it to the Ops and Intel Section in the TOC where they extract the in-house info—team's condition, current location, and so forth . . . the stuff nobody outside the company needs to know—reformat it, and give it back to the Comm Center. They use a secure facsimile to fax it to the Corps intel cell."

"How long does all this take?"

"Under an hour, most of the time," said Schultz. "Sometimes we get a backlog, but they clear out fast. It's near real-time intel."

"Then?" asked Jinx.

"What Chuck said earlier, sir. More often than not it's filed and forgotten."

"That's probably some of the best deep targeting info they'll get," stated Jinx. "I visited I German Corps this morning, up north. Their intel officer told me they count on their Fernspah, what is it . . . ?"

"Fernspah-Kompanie—long-range scout company," Schultz helped. "We've worked with them, very good."

"Ya. He said they expect better than sixty percent of their hard deep intel to be from their LRRPs. And they use the info too, targeting Luftwaffe Tornados on the really hot targets."

"These guys don't want to talk to the Air Force," said Schultz bitterly. "They've got almost nothing that can reach back to the

Soviet operational second echelon, except Lances . . . maybe, sometimes, but no way they'll get the flyboys in on it!''

"Inter-service rivalry?" asked Jinx.

"I wish it were that simple," said Ranwanz. "They just don't want to fuck with it! They're only concerned with what's right in front of them now."

"I assume that you have copies of today's messages on file," said Jinx.

"Yes, sir, every one of them," said Schultz.

Jinx pulled out his security clearance papers and a letter of authority from Commander, USAREUR—U.S. Army Europe, and handed them to Schultz.

"If you let me into your TOC, I think we might be able to get things moving a little faster."

"You bet!" exclaimed Schultz.

"What the hell is this?" bellowed Master Sergeant Ratnikkov. His six-foot, lean, hard-muscled frame stood beside the GAZ-63's tailgate with his hands on his hips, surveying the scene before him.

Soldiers stumbled into a staggered line at attention. All except one who remained facedown on the ground, his camouflage trousers pulled down to his knees revealing battered and bloody buttocks. His field jacket and torn paratrooper's undershirt lay trampled in the snow and mud. Brown leather belts with bloody brass buckles also lay on the ground, where the man's assailants had dropped them. The victim struggled to his hands and knees, his head hanging in shame.

"Stay put, soldier!" shouted Ratnikkov. The man immediately flopped back into the mud.

Ratnikkov was the 800th Battalion's master sergeant, the unit's senior sergeant. In the West he might be considered equivalent to a sergeant major, but in actuality he was more akin to a senior foreman. His principal duty was to relay orders from the staff to the unit's other sergeants. He did not have the supervisory responsibilities of NCO training and management, nor was he an adviser to the commander on enlisted men's affairs as his Western counterpart. But there was one thing he did have in common with his Western counterpart, he was the unit disciplinarian. He had more power, though, and he wielded it in a far different manner.

"Who is senior here?" he demanded, looking at the six soldiers. All were Russians or other Slavics, staring straight to their front. He recognized most of them as being former 358th Battalion paratroopers now assigned to the 3rd Company.

Senior Sergeant Druzhinin of the 3rd Company had reported to him that he was having problems controlling his troops. A faction of 358th Battalion soldiers were harassing some of the ethnic soldiers of the former 192nd Flamethrower Battalion. It was unusual for a company senior sergeant to report such difficulties to the battalion master sergeant. They normally took care of the situation themselves, using other sergeants and selected senior privates to handle, one way or the other, any problems involving troop control and morale. Reporting such problems was normally considered a sign of weakness. It had apparently gotten out of hand in the 3rd Company.

Ratnikkov had decided to pay the 3rd Company area an evening visit to see for himself. The company's trucks were scattered about in a small copse of trees. Because of a lack of tents, the soldiers slept in their trucks. He visited each platoon's area while they ate their evening meal. He used that as an excuse for the visit. The battalion commander expected him to see to it that the troops were well fed.

"Again! Who is senior here?" he all but screamed.

A tough-looking twenty-year-old took one step forward.

"What is your name, soldier?"

"Senior Private Lyubimov, Comrade Master Sergeant!" he responded in a clear voice.

"Are all of these soldiers from the 3rd Company, Comrade Lyubimov?" Ratnikkov asked quietly.

"In no way, Comrade Master Sergeant." He suddenly sounded less confident.

"I thought so . . . *Well!*" Ratnikkov shouted.

Two more soldiers stepped forward, their eyes fixed on some invisible distant object.

"What company?"

"Second company, Comrade Master Sergeant!" said the taller of the two.

"What is this shit? Why are you two here? Why are you out of your company area?" Ratnikkov fired at them.

The senior man, apparently feeling he had found a justifiable defense, immediately answered.

"Comrade, this *zheltoe gavno* (yellow shit) has repeatedly said that the paratroopers are hollow heroes, that anyone can wear the striped paratrooper's shirt. He has dishonored the unit and the real soldiers, paratroopers, who have won these honors!''

Ratnikkov punched the man in the throat, sending him reeling into the truck's side. He fell to his knees, gagging and clutching his throat. None of the others dared move.

"This nonsense has taken place only because this soldier is a Nerusskie, a non-Russian!'' Ratnikkov shouted. "I am Ukrainian, do you call me a *khokhol*!'' He referred to the Russian slang term for a top-knot of hair that described the stupidity and stubbornness of Ukrainians. "Do you call me a *makaronik* (a macaroni-man)?'' This was a common name for Ukrainian career sergeants, the macaroni referring to sergeant stripes. Eastern Ukrainians made up the largest percentage of Soviet sergeants.

"In no way, Comrade Master Sergeant!'' coughed out the senior man, who had shakily risen to his feet.

"Are you this mob's grandad?'' asked Ratnikkov, forcing himself to take a calmer course.

"Exactly so, Comrade Master Sergeant.''

He was referring to the conscript soldier's unofficial system of hierarchy. A "grandad" was a senior conscripted soldier who was about to be demobilized and released into the reserves upon completion of his two-year service to the Motherland. A new untrained conscript was called a "raw soldier.'' After six months he became a "bootlace,'' having just learned the basics of soldiering. When he had completed one year he was called a "lemon''—sour because he still had as much time to serve as he had already endured. At eighteen months he became a "senior'' and later a "grandad.'' The higher in the hierarchy a soldier rose, the easier his life, for the junior soldiers did minor chores and errands for the seniors, such as make their bunks, wash uniforms, and clean weapons and equipment. They also drew most of the subunit work details. While unauthorized, the system was condoned and encouraged by the officers and sergeants since it made their job easier, and because it was also a means of maintaining discipline. There were cases of abuse, with "seniors'' forcing "raw soldiers'' to exchange their newly issued uniforms for their worn ones, extort them for their pitifully small pay and food parcels sent from home. It was also a means of harassing ethnic minorities like the little Uzbek lying in the mud. The nearest Western equivalent to the system was in prisons where convicts were permitted to control internal affairs.

"Each of you give me your names, numbers, and subunits!" Ratnikkov yelled as he pulled out his notebook. When he had taken the information he ordered them each to report to their company senior sergeant and confess their offenses, which he enumerated for them in detail and at some length.

"If we were not in a combat zone, you all would be in the guardhouse awaiting transport to a penal battalion!" he shouted. "Now get out of my sight and return to your subunits!"

The paratroopers scurried about retrieving their belts.

Ratnikkov looked down at the Uzbek still lying in the mud.

"On your feet, *churka* (worthless wood-chip)!" The man snapped to attention, his trousers still around his ankles. "Make yourself look like a soldier!"

He hastily pulled his trousers up over his scrawny, muddy legs and struggled into the jacket and torn undershirt. Ratnikkov walked around him as he dressed; blood was soaking through the trousers' seat.

"Comrade, did you say that paratroopers were hollow heroes?" he asked from behind the Uzbek.

"*Nyet Russkie, Tovarich Starshina*—No Russian, Comrade Master Sergeant."

The little slant eye cannot understand Russian, but he has followed all the instructions I have given him, Ratnikkov thought. He probably did call us hollow heroes.

"Hooligan!" snarled Ratnikkov, kicking the soldier as hard as he could in the ass, sending him crashing into the truck's wheels. He walked back to the battalion headquarters debating whether to report the incident to the chief of staff.

" 'Hamburg has many faces,' " Murphy read from the guidebook. " 'A trip through the canals makes you realize why it is called the Venice of the north.' "

The entire team was awake, and Murphy was reading to them from a tourist book about Germany. " 'A walk down the neon-lit Reeperbahn at night assures you that it is the wickedest city in Europe.' "

"A walk down the Reeperbahn tonight would assure you of a chestful of full metal jackets," Kosinski snorted.

"That's what we love about you, Wally, you're such an incurable romantic," Murphy shot back.

"I'll buy the incurable part," Hickey chuckled.

"What a bummer," Murphy went on, reading from the dog-eared guidebook, "listen to this. 'The Colibri is not for prudes. Its shows, depicting the most lurid forms of sexual intercourse between man, woman, beast, or whatever, are among the most erotic you'll see in Germany.' Think of that, guys, a mere fifteen klicks from our snug little home here."

Murphy's smile was appropriately lurid as he read the list of live sex show bars from the book. The review, punctuated by Murphy's editorial comments, soon had everyone in the hole giggling.

"Murph, will you knock that off?" BJ said, suddenly irritated by the conversation. "I seriously doubt that any of those bars are still open, and if they are, the shows are long gone."

"Well, excuuuusseee me!" Murphy said in his best Steve Martin impression. "I forgot that for a minute. Jeez!"

The others were quiet. Murphy's guidebook had provided the first real tension relief of the mission. BJ was still uptight, running on nervous energy. Everyone else slumped back against the walls of the hide and turned his thoughts elsewhere. They had been on the ground only twenty-four hours, but time became relative in the dark, confining hole. It was 0300 hours and everyone was wide awake, still affected by jet lag.

"I'd like to see one of those beast and whatever shows, I think," King said quietly.

"You could *be* the whatever, Ty," Murphy piped up.

"No, man, the whatever is yo' mama!"

It was too much, everyone broke out in giggles. This time even BJ smiled.

"I'd like to check out that street with all the hookers," Kosinski said. "What's it called, Murph?"

"Herbertstrasse."

"Yeah, Herbertstrasse. It sounds like a fucking supermarket."

"You mean a *fucking* supermarket."

"That's what I said."

BJ turned back from the periscope. "You guys better remember that Hamburg has the largest gay community in Europe. The Reeperbahn is probably crawling with AIDS."

"You know, BJ, I wish you could guarantee me that I'd die of AIDS," Murphy said, leaning against his pack. "Then I'd know that I had a few more years to live. That highway out there is the Grim Reeperbahn. What it's crawling with makes AIDS look appealing.''

Everyone nodded at that, even BJ.

''Murph, you and King take over, I'm getting some Zs.''

BJ crawled back to his rucksack and stretched out against it. The others could do without him for a while. He gingerly fingered the side of his head. The wound was healing, but it was still tender. The watch cap covered most of it, so BJ had stopped wearing the bandage.

He thought about Donna Vasquez. She and BJ had met two years earlier on a training exercise and hit it off immediately. She was a bundle of energy, built like a short centerfold, and always cheerful. The two of them had planned to spend a weekend together, but she had gotten a posting to Germany before they could get back together. Since then, they had been in touch off and on, but BJ had not seen her since that exercise. It seemed odd to run into her here, but logical, given their jobs. He fell asleep thinking about her.

★15★

As the first thin line of color appeared on the horizon, Murphy slipped out of the hole and checked the antenna's camouflage and fastenings. The last message was more of the same, a catalog of Soviet hardware, all headed west. It looked like they were receiving additional supplies flown into the Soviet airhead at Hamburg.

Back in the hole he and King went through the routine of transmitting the message. A few minutes later the confirmation arrived with a lengthy message included. Recorded on the DMDG, he ran it back across the visual display, writing down the strings of letters. Using the receipt one-time pad and the brevity code, he went through the lengthy task of manually decrypting the message and turning the digital data burst into a detailed change-of-mission order.

"What is it, Troy?"

"We're instructed to activate the radar bombing beacon on our location and set it to broadcast no later than 0450," Hickey read from the notepad. "After we have the beacon in place, we're to depart the area for pickup at CCP (communications checkpoint) Blue, five kilometers south of here, at 0530. All the beacon data is included."

"Shit! That's only an hour from now! That's it, guys, saddle up," BJ snapped. "King, you got the beacon?"

"Right here, BJ," Tyrone answered, plumbing the depths of his rucksack. He brought out the radar beacon, a rectangular black metal box the size of two cigarette boxes with a fruit juice can-sized projection on top.

BJ and Murphy opened the CEOI to the beacon bombing report format. They quickly prepared the message with the necessary data and encoded and encrypted it. King checked it and the message was transmitted.

'How do they know where a target is?'' asked Wally. "All they know is that we're reporting columns of vehicles going by.''

"They've got something," said BJ. "Probably based on our info and supplemented by air recon, radio intercept, shit . . . national assets for all I know!''

"What's national assets?'' asked King as he helped Murphy pack the radio.

"Recon satellites and real high-level commo intercept, stuff like that,'' said Hickey.

BJ took the beacon and ran though the operational test and set the preselected frequency. He glanced at his Seiko and set the delay on the timer and the transmission time interval. When the timer went off, the beacon would be prepared to accept an interrogational signal and broadcast a powerful directional, line-of-sight radar signal for the set time interval. The signal would be picked up by the inbound bombers and contain coded ground location information. Even in the worst weather and in total darkness, the beacon would signal its location to the bombers. Using the offset bombing mode of the aircraft's on-board computer, the radar's crosshairs are placed on the beacon while the bomber attacks the target that is offset at the prescribed range and bearing from the beacon allowing it to hit with pinpoint accuracy. The bombers would come in at treetop level to avoid detection and be gone before their bombs detonated. They might even attack the target with the new stand-off weapons, launching them miles from the target.

By the time BJ had the timer set, the rest of the team had their gear stowed and was ready to go. Hickey was doing a final check in the corners and sleeping bays making certain nothing was left behind.

BJ and Kosinski bent over a map and hurriedly plotted a route to a possible pickup zone near the CCP.

"Wally, you take the point," BJ said as he stuffed his gear into the huge rucksack. "Make sure your compass is okay.''

"Roger," Kosinski answered. He pulled the compass out of

his chest pocket and flipped it open. The dial glowed softly in the dark. King took out his and they compared the north arrows.

"Good to go," said Wally.

BJ shouldered his rucksack and switched off the blue-green flashlight.

"Let's go."

As silently as they had arrived, the five men slipped out of the hole and moved into the sparse brush nearby. BJ lashed the radar beacon into a Y shaped fork in a bush, then joined the team. Without a sound, the team made its way off into the darkness with the sound of the Soviet juggernaut loud in their ears.

At 0500, a flight of F-111F fighter-bombers from the 48th Tactical Fighter Wing at Lakenheath, England, would pick up the radar signal and lock their on-board computers onto it. Once locked, the computers would guide the bombers to their targets. The Soviets would get the same warning that the 48th had given the Libyans in 1987—none. Cluster bombs would decimate the vehicles caught on the road before the heavy GBU-10 Paveway bombs cratered the highway. The damage would stop traffic on the highway for only a short time, but during that time, the Soviet advance would stall at that spot while road repair crews went to work on the shattered pavement and roadbed. Masses of armored vehicles and trucks would collect there, another tempting target for later the same day.

By the time the F-111s arrived, BJ's team would be safely away.

"Talk to me, Tommy," Donna's voice came over the intercom, "how we doin'?"

"We're dead on, about three klicks out," came the reply. "We should be able to see the antenna tower in thirty seconds."

"Easy does it, I don't want to overshoot and that transmission tower may be blown down."

Sure enough, lying across the ground was the broken latticework of a downed 200-foot radio transmission tower right where it should be. It glowed almost white against the dark ground in the night-vision goggles.

"Way to go, Tommy," Donna trilled. "Right on the money."

The Nighthawk banked into a low turn around the collapsed structure as Donna transmitted their call sign.

"Echo Five Delta, this is Papa Seven Tango, over."

Three tries were all they were allowed. If they received no response, they headed for home.

Her headset immediately crackled.

"Papa Seven Tango, Echo Five Delta, one-six-eight degrees. I say again, one-six-eight degrees, over."

"Roger, one-six-eight degrees, over," Donna said with ill-concealed relief.

Cox brought the bird around to the heading on 168 degrees and flew it slowly at treetop level. Both of the aviators searched through the light fog for the flash of an infrared strobe light.

"We hear you," came a brief transmission.

Donna could begin to make out the lighter shade of darkness indicating a clearing. The infrared strobe flashed green in her NVGs.

"I've got it," she said, taking control of the chopper. Cox lightened his grip on the stick, but kept his hand on it and the collective in case his pilot was hit by ground fire.

A group of running figures broke from the tree line in a ragged V formation as the helicopter flared over the clearing's edge. Donna eased the chopper onto the ground.

"Clear to the rear," said the crew chief.

Cox turned around and pointed to the figures approaching.

"There they are!"

Bobby Daniels, acting as air guide in the troop compartment, nodded, then grabbed the headset and slipped it off over his field cap. As the running figures neared the chopper, Daniels and the gunner jerked open the sliding door and helped pull each heavily laden team member into the HH-60. As the last man clambered in the gunner reported that all were aboard. Daniels retrieved the headset.

"Everybody okay?" Cox asked over the intercom.

"Roger that," Daniels replied, "no casualties."

"Great, now sit tight and buckle in," Cox said, "this'll be a wild ride home."

Donna turned the stick over to Cox after they lifted off. The taciturn Cox proved to be a master of understatement.

Ilya Cervik was positive he would freeze to death. The temperature was above freezing, but his uniform was soaked inside from sweat and now it seemed to suck the warmth right out of him. His little apartment in Lvov seemed like a dream to him. The place was tiny, a single room with a stove and a toilet at the end of the hall, but now it seemed like a palace compared to the inside of the 2S6 antiaircraft gun's turret. The only way to escape the cramped turret was to stand up in the hatch and freeze in the open air.

I should be through with all this, he thought dejectedly, I did my two years. Now, just as he was finishing his studies to be a teacher, here he was, yanked back from the reserves to active duty in a war with the West.

The radio crackled to life.

"Air defense section! Targets!" cried some unseen fire control officer. "Ninety-five degrees relative, very low altitude, helicopter!"

"Wake up, Dimitri!" Cervik yelled as he dropped into the turret and flipped the switches on the radar set. He jerked the turret around to the east, searching for the approaching helicopter.

"It is behind us?" Dimitri screamed. "Where, where?"

"Shut up, Dimitri!" Cervik yelled. The driver was always terrified of any enemy behind them. He knew just enough military theory to know that penetration into the rear was a prelude to disaster. It seemed to escape him that aircraft could attack from any direction.

Cervik scanned the area to the east with the radar, trying to separate the intruder from ground clutter.

"Where is it?" Dimitri yelled again, the fear rising in his voice.

"I do not know, Dimitri, now . . ."

The screen suddenly glowed large near the center.

"*Vot kok!*" Dimitri screamed, pressing the trigger. "It is right on us!"

The hammering of the four 30mm guns drowned out the sound of the rotors as the helicopter flashed by overhead. Cervik cringed as it passed over, waiting for the explosion that was sure to follow. It did not come. Surprised, Cervik swung the turret around to track the fleeing intruder. There was nothing on his scope but ground clutter. For a second, Cervik wondered if he had even seen the helicopter at all.

How did they get so close? he wondered. Did they travel underground? His heart was pounding, his breathing fast and ragged. Damn it! Once again, the inside of his tunic was soaked in sweat.

* * *

"We're hit, Donna!" Cox shouted into the intercom. "Starboard side!"

Donna felt a shell slam into the Nighthawk. Now she could hear screaming in the cabin. Both pilots craned their necks to see where the 30mm shell had ripped into the ship. At the base of the right door, there were two jagged holes nearly a foot long. Inside the cabin there were torn spots in the liner where fragments had ripped into the chopper's interior. Donna searched her instrument panel looking for warning lights or dropping pressure gauges. Nothing—so far.

In the back, soldiers were scrambling around, making the ship rock.

"Tommy, what the fuck's going on back there?"

A deep voice came over the intercom.

"We got a man hit back here!"

"Roger that, take care of him, we're doin' the best we can," Donna shot back, trying to keep her voice from shaking. "Hang on for another ten minutes."

Flying right above, and sometimes just below the trees, Donna raced for the specific point where they would reenter their own lines. Cox's eyes were glued to the instruments, looking for signs of damage.

"How we doin', Tommy?"

"So far so good," the copilot replied casually, his usual calm returning. "Our Lady of Perpetual Airworthiness is watching over us, I guess."

As they flashed over the river that marked the edge of the battle area, Donna keyed the radio.

"Sierra Four Bravo, this is Papa Seven Tango One Four."

"Papa Seven Tango One Four, this is Sierra Four Bravo."

"Inbound with casualties, request ambulance."

"Roger, Papa Seven Tango One Four, you're cleared for approach."

"Roger, Papa Seven Tango One Four out."

Donna switched from the radio to the intercom.

"Hang in back there, we're almost home!"

"I don't think we're in any hurry, now, ma'am," the deep voice answered, "he's dead."

★16★

The medics were waiting on the emergency pad when BJ's team landed. They were already moving up to the door as the chopper settled down. The first face he recognized was Captain Schultz, who hauled back the door.

"BJ, you okay?" Schultz asked over the whine of the engine.

"Yeah, I'm okay," BJ answered, looking back over his shoulder into the dark interior of the chopper. "Bobby Daniels got hit on the way out—shrapnel. He's dead."

The words seemed to hit Schultz like a hammer. He had seen dead men before, but this was one of his men, a friend.

The other team members helped the medics, lowering Daniels' body into a black plastic body bag. BJ could see the dark stain that covered the right half of Daniels' BDUs. Daniels' head lolled back, Shannon Hickey moved to support it. It seemed obscene to put a man they all knew and liked into that . . . trash bag. BJ just stood there, watching helplessly as the medics hoisted the bag onto the stretcher and carried it to the waiting ambulance.

Donna was out of the chopper and walking slowly around it running her gloved hands over the skin in the darkness, looking for more holes in the stricken bird. She saw BJ standing, watching the medics and the team walk off.

"Sorry about your guy, BJ," she said, touching him on the sleeve.

Her voice seemed to startle him. He looked around and put

his hand over hers. The faint glow of predawn could be seen on the eastern horizon.

"Thanks, Donna," BJ said softly. "He was an old friend."

"This is a bad time to be old friends, I guess."

"Yeah."

"Say, BJ," Donna said brightly, trying to break the sadness of the moment, "you ought to see the swell place they've hooched us up. It's about a klick up the road." She switched on a Mae West voice, "Come up and see me sometime. Come tonight, it's amateur night."

The pointer jabbed at the working map, specifically at a small blue X marked with a date and time, 30.12 0140, this morning. The blue X and manner in which the date and time were written identified it as an enemy action. If it had been in red and the date and time reversed, it would have identified a Soviet action.

"The SAS gangsters attacked a damaged vehicle collection point on the E8 Autobahn this morning . . . only six kilometers from where we now stand," whispered Bodnya. "Nine combat vehicles and four trucks were destroyed, eight Soviet soldiers died."

The assembled company commanders and main staff officers stood in a loose semicircle around the map, With them, unusually, was a German VOPO major from the VOPO's County Security Section. All were steeling themselves for the ravages of the impending storm they knew would break shortly.

"Our subunits have been deployed to provide rear-area protection to the most vulnerable facilities in this unit's sector," Bodnya went on. "Additionally they have conducted both mounted and dismounted patrols on the roads and in the forests. They have seen nothing. They have accomplished nothing . . . except for smashing one of our trucks into a self-propelled howitzer, damaging farm gates and fences, running over two cows, the theft of countless pigs and chickens, and the rape of a German girl!"

Fixing Senior Lieutenant Kashevarov, the 3rd Company's commander, with his gaze, Bodnya asked, "And what has been done about that last matter, Comrade Kashevarov?"

"Comrade Battalion Commander, the culprits have been found and turned over to the Commandant's Service at the Magdeburg Government Center."

"That is not the kind of rear-area protection I expect this unit to provide, comrades,'' said Bodnya softly. ''What I want to see are the bodies of British terrorists, wrapped in shelter capes, dumped in front of this headquarters! The concept of deployment for this unit was to exploit our special skills to hunt down enemy diversionary-reconnaissance groups using the same methods of operation . . . 'To catch a thief, set a thief,' '' he quoted.

The group of officers chuckled. The fear of a storm had subsided. The commander appeared to be caught up in his enthusiasm for a more meaningful operation.

''I thought that to be a fitting comparison myself,'' remarked Bodnya. ''During these first two days of deployment we have made the mistake of attempting to protect what we had analyzed to be the most likely targets for attack. We have also attempted to determine when and where the enemy would attack. Our efforts have achieved nothing. Our protection methods are no different from what other security organs have been doing with equally little success. We are merely reacting to the initiatives of the enemy.'' He paused a moment to let his officers mull over the problem.

''Obviously a different method of operation is required by the current conditions,'' Bodnya continued. ''Comrade Guards Major Butakov will outline our new deployment plan.'' He handed the pointer to the *zampolit* as an operations clerk replaced the working map with another.

Butakov was mildly surprised. He had not expected to brief the commanders on the new plan himself. It was a rare sign of confidence from the battalion commander. Even the insertion of ''Guards'' in his rank was unusual and unexpected. Bodnya had previously neglected to include it when addressing the political officer.

Accepting the pointer, he stepped up to the new working map. Bodnya, Butakov, and the rest of the staff had worked on the tactical plan until the early morning hours. Their tactical sector of responsibility stretched thirty-five kilometers along the E8 Autobahn and its paralleling Highway 1, from just west of Magdeburg, the district capital, westward to within five kilometers from the border. Here East German Frontier Troops maintained security. Though the offensive had moved well into West Germany, the East German frontier barrier was maintained. It effectively served as a movement control line for Warsaw Pact convoys and troop units, aided straggler control measures, limited the infiltration and exfiltration of enemy special operations forces, and had proved to be an extremely effective catch line for rounding up enemy air crewmen downed in East Germany. The flyers' ground tactical skills were no match for the Frontier Troops and their sophisticated modern barrier system as they attempted to evade back to friendly lines.

The map sector was divided into three color-shaded subsectors, each ten or so kilometers across and roughly twice that wide, centered on the autobahn. The westernmost subsector was red—1st Company's, 2nd Company's was in the center—green, and 3rd Company's, the easternmost, was yellow. The battalion headquarters was still located outside Irxleben on the western boundary of 3rd Company's subsector.

"Comrades," began Butakov, "we have divided the battalion's sector into three company subsectors for which each company will be solely responsible." He pointed to the color-coded subsectors. "We are attempting to receive approval to relocate the battalion headquarters to Uhrsleben so that it will be in a central location for more effective troop control," pointing to the small town on the north side of E8 in 2nd Company's subsector. "Regardless, the Scout-Diversionary Platoon will be relocated there to serve as a response force for all three companies. Coordination is being conducted with the German Frontier Troops to have two Mi-8 helicopters on standby for rapid deployment of the platoon to your subsectors. Keep in mind that if committed in this manner they will be without secondary ground transport. Each company is to field all of its platoons, but one of your most effective squads will be retained at your company headquarters as a local response subunit. The battalion commander recommends that you reinforce this squad with two or three more soldiers and additional machine guns."

"I expect the company commanders to personally lead their response squad when it is committed," injected Bodnya. That should prevent an overresponse to every suspected report of enemy activity, he thought, looking from one company commander's face to the next.

"The key to this tactical plan is not to attempt to second-guess the enemy diversionary-reconnaissance groups as to when and where they will attack," went on Butakov. "That is the responsibility of the unit and facilities that may suffer such attacks. We have, with the aid of the VOPO"—Butakov nodded at the thick-necked VOPO major in his gray-green service uniform not unlike his Second World War forefathers'—"identified the areas that the enemy groups are most likely to hide in during the day. The VOPOs and Battle Groups will patrol and search these areas during the day, aided by dogs. At night they will secure the most critical of the rear-area objectives.

"Our platoons will sleep, eat, and conduct maintenance during the day. They will be deployed into these suspected hide areas before nightfall," he went on, looking at his notes, "at approximately 16.30. You will be given overlays with these hide areas marked. When placed on your copy of the working map, which also identifies rear-area objectives of interest to the enemy, you will be able to select flow lines—natural lines of drift across the terrain—that the enemy groups may follow from the hide areas to possible targets." Captain Milstein was passing out the overlays.

"I must caution you," said Bodnya, "that these overlays and working maps must not be taken into the field. Follow normal practice and distribute only sketch maps marked with the necessary tactical data to your subunits. Use only nonstandard map symbols on the sketch maps. Lieutenant Evdokimov, the secret section officer, will visit each company headquarters daily to inspect your maps and documents, insure that the previous night's sketch maps are destroyed, and to deliver any new orders and planning documents."

"You will deploy your platoons in a manner that will allow them to ambush enemy groups as they move to attack rear-area objectives," said Butakov. This was out of his depth and he looked over at Major Goncharov. The chief of staff wore a slightly pained expression as the *zampolit* presented the briefing he should by rights be giving. He had done his utmost to participate in the planning after his falling out with the commander, but it was apparent to all that his credibility with Bodnya was in doubt. Butakov still felt an obligation to the officer however.

"Comrade Guards Major Goncharov can better describe this aspect of the operation," he said, glancing in Bodnya's direction. The commander's expression remained deadpan.

Goncharov immediately launched into the briefing, attempting to redeem himself. "Your platoons will establish ambush sites on these possible movement routes. You may use platoons, squads, or combinations of platoon- and squad-sized ambushes. Use caution when employing independent squads. Select only those with commanders you can completely rely on." He looked pointedly at Senior Lieutenant Kashevarov. It was common knowledge within the battalion that Goncharov had little use for the *chuzhoi*—distrusted strangers—of the 3rd Company and that he resented having some of the 358th Battalion's paratroopers assigned to them. "Insure that the actions of the ambush drills are rehearsed, that the sites are carefully chosen and well concealed. The initiation of the ambush must be a complete surprise to the enemy and executed with decisiveness! Your companies will be issued MON-50 directional antipersonnel mines to make them more effective. Make certain that the squad commanders are trained in their use."

"Comrade Chief of Staff," said 2nd Company's Captain Shepelev, "what is the status and disposition of prisoners?" Shepelev, another former 358th Battalion officer was obviously trying to help out the chief of staff.

"Perhaps Comrade Captain Yakushev can better answer that question," said Bodnya.

All eyes turned to the tall, thin KGB officer as he confidently stepped into the semicircle.

"The battalion commander and myself have discussed prisoners in some length," he began, as if to establish his own authority. "Prisoners, especially those belonging to diversionary-reconnaissance groupings, are valuable sources of intelligence regarding their subunits, methods of operations, movement techniques, and future intentions. You must constantly remind your soldiers that it is their duty to take such prisoners. To kill a potential prisoner, when he could have been captured, is considered neglecting one's sworn military duty and punishable under Soviet military law." The other officers uncomfortably shifted their weight and looked around at one another.

That should increase these Spetsnaz bastards' discomfort, thought Yakushev. They were more comfortable going in and killing everything that moved. How often in Afghanistan had their kind deprived him of his needs?

"Is it not difficult to extract useful information from them? They are highly trained and politically indoctrinated," said Captain Yurasov, 1st Company's commander.

"Captain Yakushev has assured me that he will be able to obtain any information we desire . . . quickly," interrupted Bodnya with a tight smile on his normally solemn face. "We all know what has to be done." The smile turned suddenly to a frown. "Comrade Senior Lieutenant Ivashutin will brief you on technical support."

"The Headquarters Company will form a technical support grouping that will visit each company every morning, before 12.00. If you have special needs in ammunition or vehicle spare parts, contact us when your subunits return to your headquarters. The grouping will depart the battalion headquarters area at 07.00. It will be comprised of a fueler, maintenance technicians with a vehicular repair complex, general replenishment supplies, radio batteries, and the day's rations. The *feldsher* will also accompany the grouping to treat any sick and injured, and evaluate them for medical evacuation."

"Comrades, you have your orders," announced Bodnya. "Captain Noskov will distribute copies of the orders. You will return to your companies and relocate them to your assigned subsector immediately. Operations will commence tonight. If you have any questions or special requirements of the staff, take care of that now. If you have any specific questions of myself, I will be in my work area. Good hunting, comrades!"

★17★

"What do you have for me, Major Jenkins?" asked Colonel Tucker, motioning him to one of the overstuffed chairs in his office.

"Can I speak frankly, sir?" Jinx asked, easing himself into the chair's softness. It had been a long, grueling, and sometimes scary jeep trip.

"Of course, Jinx. This isn't the Agency," his CO said with a smile. Jinx noticed the first-time use of his nickname by the normally formal officer.

"To put it simply, sir, I don't think I could have intentionally designed a more ineffective control and coordination system for NATO special ops if I had tried!" Jinx nodded for emphasis.

"It's sad to say, Major, but there is no system," said Tucker. "Oh, there's some agreements between NATO forces and the usual lip service about sharing information, but no real system was ever developed, much less practiced, in the past. Were you able to visit all of the organizations on your list?" The colonel cocked his head.

"It was like we expected, the roads are a mess. Between the refugees and military traffic, it's worse than the Houston freeways at rush hour," replied Jinx. "But I was able to find most of the units."

"Well, let's go down the list," said Tucker. "Give me a snapshot of each organization's situation." He peeled the wrapper off a cigar.

Jinx pulled his notes from his breast pocket. "I'll start in the north and work south, though that's not necessarily the order I visited them," Jinx began. "I never found the Danish Jaeger Corps. Nobody at any headquarters knew exactly where they were. The intel section at HQLANDJUT was receiving reports from them, through the Danish General Staff, but they said that the General Staff was keeping the Jaegers under their control."

"HQ-LAND-JUT?" queried Tucker. "Refresh me, they have more NATO acronyms up there than I can even start to remember." He fired the tip of the cigar with a Zippo that bore the pierced pansy logo.

"Headquarters, Land Forces, Jutland," Jinx replied. "That's the only multinational corps in NATO. Principally Danish and German units responsible for the defense of Schleswig-Holstein. The Jaeger Corps is only a small LRRP unit. A few of their teams are supporting HQLANDJUT, but they think that most of them have been deployed to Zeeland. You know that a combination Soviet, East German, and Polish parachute and amphibious landing took place there and that Copenhagen has fallen?"

"Damn, no!" exclaimed a stunned Tucker. "The first NATO capital to fall."

Jinx nodded. "They say it's real bad up there, sir. They're talking about diverting the U.S. 1st Marine Division up there rather than sending it to Norway. The British 1st Infantry Brigade has already been committed there, straight out of the UK."

Tucker shook his head. "Well, we can't worry about that now. Go on, Jinx."

"First Dutch Corps is next and you know what the situation is in this sector, sir. Maybe you can bring me up-to-date."

Jinx two-fingered a cigarette from his breast pocket. "The Dutch still have some teams from their 104th Observation and Reconnaissance Company operational and reporting," said Tucker, "but the teams that were not committed have apparently been withdrawn to the Weser River. It looks like the Dutch are preparing for a worst-case scenario."

"Third U.S. Corps is building up and appears to have an extremely aggressive intelligence collection plan to assemble a good picture of what their counterattack will run into," Jinx went on. He lit his cigarette and inhaled deeply. "I talked to the CO and ops officer of Company G, 143d Infantry, the corps' long-range surveillance unit. They're doing okay, but they had a legitimate complaint that III Corps was doing little to respond to the deep targeting info they were giving them. They showed me the reports and I went up to III Corps and talked to the intel and deep attack cells. The Air Force liaison officer got involved and they began allocating some deep air strikes.''

''Excellent, Jinx, excellent!'' Tucker smiled. ''That's exactly the kind of initiative I want to see demonstrated in this unit.''

''Thank you, sir. I think that was about the only worthwhile thing I managed to accomplish. The I German Corps is holding its own. They rely very heavily on their Long-Range Scout Company 100, which is fully committed. They have a very good system for passing intelligence information, for internal use. Their teams transmit to base radio stations the same way our own long-range surveillance units do, and the info is sent to corps. But, that's where the similarity ends. Each of the three German corps LRRP companies, even though they're in different parts of Germany, also transmit the info to a centrally located signal evolution company, which sends it directly to the German Army Staff in Bonn.''

''That sounds like a good concept. We'll have to look into it further, if we're able,'' said Tucker, frowning.

''The Germans also have, I think, some line-crossers, under the Federal Defense Forces Intelligence Office. They're real closemouthed about them, sir. They won't really admit they have agents slipping behind Soviet lines.''

''They're probably stay-behind agents, posing as refugees,'' said Tucker. ''Someone said the other day that if they don't have them, they should!''

''The I British Corps has more special ops types then everyone else put together, I think,'' said Jinx. ''They're almost as closemouthed as the Germans, sir. They've got two Special Air Service Regiments deployed as corps patrol units in the LRRP role.'' He grinned.

''Two SAS regiments? That's a lot!'' said Tucker.

Jinx nodded. ''You have to remember, sir, that British regiments are actually battalion-sized. The 21 and 23 SAS Regiments are Territorial Army, similar to our own National Guard. They have dozens of four-man patrols, that's what they call their teams, on the ground in their corps sector. Some are in hides keeping main Soviet lines of communication and supply routes under surveillance and others are operating in troops of three or four patrols executing harassing raids. There are also some Regular 22 SAS Regiment elements deployed here, but the Brits won't say what they're up to.''

"Let's hope it's something as nasty as the Spetsnaz have been doing to us," Tucker mused. "You know, Jinx, in all the exercises I've ever participated in, both field and command post, there was always some form of opposing force special operations play integrated. It was always random small-scale raids, snipings, terrorist attacks, convoy harassment all spread out over the exercise's duration. But never anything like we've seen here."

He shook his head. "I've heard stories and seen some of the spot reports, sir, but what's the big difference?" Jinx arched an eyebrow.

"The attacks occur simultaneously with major Soviet actions. For example, when the Soviets executed an attack along the seam between the Dutch and German corps' sectors, dozens of Spetsnaz attacks hit headquarters, communications facilities, artillery units, and reinforcements moving to the front. Their actions are orchestrated by the Soviets almost like a form of fire support."

Jinx nodded. "Maybe that's how the Soviets look at them, sir," he replied, "as a form of fire support, a combat multiplier. Your mention of fire support reminds me of another Brit outfit, the Infantry Battalion of The Honorable Artillery Company."

"Don't you have that backward, Jinx?"

Jinx smiled. "No, sir, you heard me right. The Honorable Artillery Company is the traditional title of the oldest unit in the British Army. It's Territorial Army and consists of two units, an infantry battalion and an artillery regiment. The infantry battalion is organized similar to an SAS regiment and operates as four-man patrols. Basically they're LRRPs, nonairborne, but their principal role is to act as forward artillery observers for I British Corps Artillery. They often infiltrate behind the Soviet lines to spot deep targets. They've had some conflicts, too. They and the SAS have occasionally run into each other as there's been little coordination between them."

"We've been fortunate in that respect," said Tucker. "The Special Forces teams we have back there have not run into any other NATO special ops elements . . . yet. But I'm concerned with the lack of coordination between our own long-range surveillance, Ranger, and SF elements." He shook his head.

"Have we had many problems, sir?" asked Jinx.

"To an extent"—Tucker nodded—"I've had liaison officers out, but they've gotten very little cooperation. The Rangers in particular have been a problem. The 3d Ranger Battalion seems to think they're a law unto themselves and they don't feel obliged to conduct any more coordination with other organizations than they absolutely have to. Every time we talk to them they tell my people to go through the 75th Ranger Regiment, but that's down south with V and VII Corps.''

"Great. Has SOCEUR been advised of the problem, sir?"

Tucker nodded again and relit his cigar. "Yes, but, like everyone else, they're overloaded with more pressing matters," said Tucker. "What about the Belgians on NORTHAG's southern flank?"

"The Belgian 1st Special Reconnaissance Teams Company, like the Dutch, deployed its teams late since they had to come out of Belgium. The delay proved to be fortunate, because when the Soviet 20th Guards Army attempted to split the boundary seam between I Belgian Corps and III German Corps to their south, they were able to deploy their remaining teams to screen the main routes into their southern flank. They're sharing the information they collect with the Germans and vice versa.''

Tucker nodded. "That's good news for once," he said, "at least some of the Allies are working together."

"What about III Corps' divisional long-range surveillance detachments, sir? Have any of them been deployed yet?''

"There's been some discussion of that with the Corps G2," said Tucker. "Now everyone's seen the coordination problems, they're looking at control measures closely. But, no, none have yet been committed.''

Jinx nodded. "I understand what you're saying, sir. Having our long-range surveillance assets so decentralized makes no sense to me. All the other NATO LRRP organizations are under centralized control for better training management, better coordinated deployment, and smoother flow of intelligence information.''

"You're absolutely correct, Jinx. But that's our job, to try and pull this mess together. Do you have all this ready to go into a report for NORTHAG C2?''

"Yes, sir, Jenna . . . Specialist Collingsworth's entered it into a portable computer during the trip. I'll have it ready this afternoon.''

"Excellent.''

It wasn't a chateau, more a fancy country home for some executive from Essen. It was done up in country French decor, tasteful, if a bit floral. Its main advantage, aside from the space, was the forest that surrounded the estate. The tall pines all but hid the house from view, especially from the east.

Combat engineers had cut some of the trees flush to the ground and used the huge trunks to form hasty revetments inside the tree line. The helicopters could be hidden in the woods for maintenance, refueling, and rearming. All the aviation unit's vehicles were hidden in the trees. Only a single set of tire marks from the driveway to the tree line marked their passing. It was as good a hasty airfield as could be found.

Donna's room was on the second floor at one end. BJ found her sprawled on a large bed, her tight-fitting flight suit a sharp contrast to the white lace canopy that covered the four-poster.

The rest of the room was done in the style of Louis the someteenth, all brocade and frou-frou. An elaborate wood mantel covered the stone fireplace on the outside wall. A divan and wing chair faced the fireplace.

"Nice hooch." BJ dropped his web gear, mask, the bag holding his chemical protective suit, and helmet on the divan. He leaned his rifle against the wall. They had to carry the survival gear wherever they went.

Donna leaned up on her elbows.

"Only the best for our gallant warriors of the sky," she replied brightly.

"You sound like some Air Force puke," BJ said wearily as he plopped down on the large divan.

"You don't have to be nasty."

"Sorry, Donna, I'm just tired. Took two hours to get debriefed. Then we had to clean all the gear. I only got a few hours' rack time."

The understatement of the year, she thought as she looked at the exhausted warrior on the divan.

"We both are." She rolled off the bed and walked over to the huge mirror that hung above the dressing table.

"If it hadn't been for you," BJ said quietly, "I'd be dead meat now."

"That's my job, sugar."

"Great jobs, huh?" BJ said. His eyes took on the thousand-yard stare so common to combat soldiers. "You think we'll survive this war, Donna?"

Donna didn't want this conversation to go the way it was heading, so she turned it around.

"Oh, I don't know," she replied, watching BJ in the mirror, "I survived AIDS, I think I can survive this, too."

She stifled a laugh at the look of blind panic that appeared on BJ's face.

"Uhh, how, I mean, I didn't think you could have AIDS and still fly."

Donna watched BJ's pained expression in the mirror. He was trying to act nonchalant, but failing. She'd let the cocky little sucker sweat for a beat.

"Um, I said, I didn't think you could . . ."

"Relax, sugar," she said, turning to lean back on the dresser, "the AIDS I had was *Aviation-Induced Divorce Syndrome.*"

BJ's face flickered with mixed relief, irritation, and amusement.

"Had you goin' for a second?" she asked, a Cheshire cat smile on her face.

"Thanks a lot."

Donna laughed out loud. She walked back to the divan and dropped BJ's gear on the floor so she could sit down.

"What's this?" she asked, pulling a thin paperback from the pocket of BJ's Gortex jacket. *"Death Commandos #19: The Return of the Impaler."* She shot BJ a sidelong glance and thumbed open the book.

" ' "No, no, no more," he screamed, his agonized cries echoing down the stone corridor long into the night.' BJ, do you really read this shit?" she asked, tossing the book back onto the jacket.

"It passes the vast amount of free time I have."

Donna looked at him for a moment, then slowly walked over to the door.

"I think we can find some better way to pass the time." She closed the door and locked it.

"Why don't you grab a quick shower?" she asked. "That might perk you up."

"This place has running water?" BJ asked.

"Sure, it has its own cistern or something. Hot water, too."

"Oh, baby," BJ said as he walked quickly to the tile bathroom. He began shucking his BDUs as he entered the elaborate bathroom. In a minute, clouds of steam and moans of ecstasy floated out of the bathroom.

BJ was in no hurry to get out of the shower. This was his first hot bath in Europe, and he wasn't about to waste it by rushing.

If he used all the hot water, tough shit. Donna's voice in the steam-filled room surprised him.

"Got room for one more?"

She was standing in the doorway, the zipper of her flight suit pulled all the way down.

"Absolutely!"

She pulled the flight suit off her shoulders and stepped out of it. Under the insulated flight suit she had on a brown GI undershirt and a pair of white cotton panties.

"I hate to let all that hot water go to waste," she said as she slid the panties down her thighs. Her eyes never left BJ's although his eyes were scanning her dark legs and crotch. She straightened up, stepped out of the panties, and pulled the undershirt up over her head. The undershirt caught on her breasts and pulled them up with it. They finally fell free as the shirt went up over her head. As her face emerged from the shirt, Donna was greeted by that expression she knew so well. BJ's mouth was hanging open, his eyes riveted to her breasts.

They're all the same, God bless 'em, she thought as she stepped into the hot spray.

I have died and gone to heaven, BJ thought as she slipped out of her shirt. What a set of knockers!

"BJ, sugar, close your mouth before you drown."

Donna reached past him and took the slim bar of soap out of its niche in the tile wall.

"Turn around," she said to the still-stunned BJ, turning him toward the spray.

"Do I have to?" he asked over his shoulder.

"Yes, I outrank you," she replied, laughing. She soaped his back, feeling the muscles tense, then relax under her fingers.

"God, that feels good," he moaned.

"God's not here, sugar, lucky for us."

BJ leaned forward, putting his hands on the tile wall as Donna ran the soap up over his shoulders and arms, then down under his armpits and around to his chest. She used both hands to lather his chest and stomach, then slowly worked her way down to his crotch.

Things were already happening there. She used the soap to work up a thick lather in BJ's dense pubic hair, then slowly began to stroke his scrotum and his rigid digit with the sweet-smelling foam.

"Oh, Jesus," BJ moaned again. His whole body tensed as

Donna massaged him. She pulled herself against him, rubbing her breasts on his soapy back. A series of animal noises came from his throat as he rocked back and forth.

As BJ's breath began to get ragged, Donna turned loose of his straining organ and ran her hands up his belly.

"My turn," she said, twisting her body around away from BJ, who immediately turned to face the tiny aviatrix. She was so much shorter than BJ that he dropped down on one knee to begin soaping her up. The water spray hit him on the back of the head, but BJ hardly noticed it.

He took the soap from her and ran it rapidly back and forth across her shoulders and back, switching the soap from hand to hand to cover Donna's tiny back. He was surprised at how muscular she was. She was little, but solid. He soaped her back, letting his hands move down to her round rear. BJ kneaded her tight buns, causing a low moan. From her rear, BJ slid his hands around to her front and up over her abundant breasts.

"Uuumm!" they both murmured as BJ's fingers slid up and around Donna's *balcón manifíque.*

He squeezed her breasts, then rubbed her dark nipples and tugged at them as they stiffened. He leaned closer, kissing her soapy back. She began to writhe in his arms. BJ ran his soapy hands down over her flat belly to the dark patch between her legs. She opened her stance to admit his hand and reached back behind her, holding BJ to steady herself.

Now it was Donna's breath that was ragged. She moaned and gasped as BJ soaped the wet slit between her legs.

Abruptly, she pulled away and faced him, putting him at arm's length.

"Sugar, let's finish this shower before we both fall down and hurt ourselves."

They scrubbed the soap off them as fast as they could and dried each other with the thick towels hanging next to the shower.

When they were dry, she reached down and grasped BJ's swollen organ.

"Come on, lover boy," she said as she led him from the bathroom by his throbbing leash. "I have to warn you, though, helicopter pilots don't really fly, we just beat the air into submission!"

"Ooh, be strict with me!" he groaned, following her to the canopy bed.

Donna climbed up on the bed, never losing her grip on BJ.

She flipped him onto his back and quickly sat down on his cock, burying it inside her. She leaned forward and put her hands on his chest, then began rocking her hips back and forth, slowly at first, but then faster and faster until BJ thought his cock would be pulled out by the roots. She began to moan, then to cry out with each thrust of her hips.

This was not the woman of his recurrent fantasy. This woman was as aggressive in bed as she was in the sky. She took control and kept it. BJ hadn't realized just how strong Donna was. Her compact little body was mostly muscle and she obviously viewed sex as a contact sport.

The Donna in his dreams was all sighs and soft caresses. The Donna in this bed was a tiger who lunged, scratched, bit, and turned him every way but loose.

So, what the hell, he thought as she pounded him into the four-poster, he liked this Donna better than the dream Donna anyway. This was turning into the best sex of his life, if he could just survive it.

"Jeez, Donna, if the Reds don't kill me, you will!"

"Don't worry, sugar," she gasped, "you'll make it. I haven't lost one yet."

Her ecstatic cries echoed down the stone corridors long into the night as she welcomed the return of the Impaler.

★18★

In the NORTHAG area, Soviet pressure was steadily increasing. Dutch, Belgian, German, and British units were giving ground, buying each kilometer with hundreds of lives. The plains and tree lines of northern Germany were littered with burned-out tanks and fighting vehicles. In places, ruined vehicles from both sides were mingled in destruction, evidence of failed counterattacks. The doctrine of "Competitive Strategies" had served the Allies well. Soviet losses were appalling, unbelievable. The NATO battle was swift, violent, and frightening in its use of stand-off weapons that destroyed entire Soviet battle formations without warning and without any target for retaliatory fire. The newest generation of antitank weapons gave the NATO infantryman the ability to engage and defeat all armored vehicles. NATO aircraft were more than a match for their opponents in the sky.

Unfortunately, none of these things could counter the Soviets' main advantage—numbers. Each time a battalion was destroyed by an air strike, another battalion moved up to replace it. Division followed division. The Allies were hoist on the petard of their own governments' wishful thinking.

In the late 1980s, the free world media applauded the reduction in Soviet troop strength both in Europe and along the Chinese border. Great pressure was brought on the NATO partners to reciprocate with troop reductions to reduce tensions between East and West. Bowing to the popular will, the NATO governments made sizable reductions in their conventional and nuclear forces.

The fallacy, of course, was that the Soviets pulled the units out of Eastern Europe and off the border with China, but did not disband or significantly reduce their fighting strength. The *perestroika*-induced reorganization of Soviet divisions—the removal of the motorized rifle division's lone tank regiment and a similar regiment from the tank division—was an illusion. The "disbanded" regiments were retained and restructured as independent combined arms tank regiments and brigades. When the war started, the Soviet Union swiftly moved these new units and the previously withdrawn divisions forward by rail, heavy equipment transporters, and air transport. Entire units were moved the 1000 kilometers from the western USSR to Germany in thirty-six to seventy-two hours.

Even the most vigorous NATO defense could not hold against the number of divisions thrown against them.

The Soviet 2nd Guards Tank Army, reinforced by additional Soviet divisions relocated from the Transbaikal Military District, and backed by the East German 5th Army, was hammering its way through the West German I Corps and the Dutch I Corps. The Soviet 3rd Shock Army battered itself against the British, and the 20th Guards Army ripped through the Belgian I Corps. The Soviet units would accept losses that no NATO commander would tolerate, fighting in many cases to the last tank, the last man. If the Allies could buy enough time, the U.S. III Corps would arrive to bolster the defense, and to organize its counterattack. If not . . .

Lieutenant Colonel Tucker looked at the officers assembled in his office. His face bore a pasty appearance that most of the officers took to be fatigue-induced, not an uncommon malady among their numbers. Picking a thin sheet of paper up off his desk, he looked down at the joint message form as if to reconfirm its contents.

"Gentleman," he began, attempting to keep his voice steady, "we have had a major change in the general situation. On the recommendation of the commander, Northern Army Group, due to the rapidly deteriorating situation in the I Dutch Corps' sector and potential for similar emergency developments in other NORTHAG corps' sectors, the Supreme Allied Commander Europe has requested the President of the United States to authorize nuclear release."

Not a word was spoken, each man momentarily lost in his own personal thoughts.

"Well, hell!" said Major Lou Bennett, looking around at the solemn faces. "Does this mean there won't be a movie tonight?"

Some of the others chuckled and one remarked that he thought *Fail Safe* was scheduled. Tucker silently thanked Bennett for the much-needed pressure release.

"Gentlemen," announced Tucker, "I wish the ADM cell to remain here while the others go about their business. I must caution you all not to discuss this turn of events. Release may not be granted, or their use not required."

Slim chance of that, Jinx thought. He had seen firsthand the chaotic state of NORTHAG's corps' headquarters.

"I do want," continued Tucker, "to quietly have each cell conduct refresher training on the use of radiac meters and review the procedures for preparation for a nuclear attack."

Major Francis Ladd, the detachment's Soviet specialist, raised her hand. "Sir, I recall reading a Soviet magazine that described their recommended procedure if they receive a warning that a nuclear attack is imminent."

"Yes, Major," said Tucker, "please share that with us."

"They were having a town civil defense meeting, and the senior civil defense director began asking selected individuals what they would do in such a case. He chose the town drunk, who promptly replied, 'Comrade Director, I would place a sheet over my head and *slowly* walk to the cemetery.'

" 'Why walk slowly, comrade?' asked the director.

" 'So as not to create a panic, Comrade Director!' "

The officers filed from the room still laughing and returned to their work areas. Two officers, the ADM control cell, remained and took seats as Tucker softly shut the door.

"What's your problem," asked First Sergeant Cordes as BJ flopped into the folding metal chair, "you still got jet lag?"

"More like dick lag!" smirked Sergeant Hagger.

"Give me a break, man," moaned BJ as his head lolled back.

"No breaks, lover boy!" said Hagger. "Unless you want a broken leg."

"Fuck off, Kurt, I think I earned a Purple Heart," whimpered BJ.

"But no Good Conduct Medal. This ought to perk your ass

up,'' said Cordes. "You're the new 2d Platoon Sergeant, hard dick.''

"Oh, no, you don't! I don't want it! Give it to Will Colly, he's been here longer than me.''

"Relax, Beej,'' soothed Codes, "it's in name only, for now anyway. We can't afford to lose a team leader right now. Lieutenant Trapley's taking care of it himself. Okay?''

"And the good news,'' chimed in Hagger, "is that your young ass is goin' out again, tonight. I thought I'd give you a break from your chopper jockey.''

"I don't know how to thank you, Kurt,'' BJ said in mock seriousness. "You may have just saved my life by sending me deep behind Soviet lines!''

"Well, you know our motto, LRRPs do it deep in the enemy's rear,'' said Hagger. "Let's go to the TOC. Your isolation packet is ready. I need to give you enough poop so you can give a warning order to your team.''

The two NCOs walked into the Tactical Operations Center. Unlike a conventional unit, most of the activity in a LRRP unit was during the premission and infiltration phases. Now that most of the teams had been deployed, it was relatively quiet. Planning a cross-FLOT LRRP mission for a five-man team was extremely complex and detailed. Outsiders often failed to understand this, for some reason thinking that since it was only a small team, it was as simple as a rifle company sending a squad out to recon a road junction a few klicks away. With eighteen such teams to plan for and coordinate with dozens of outside organizations, it was a monumental and on-going task as teams were continuously inserted, extracted, and recommitted on new missions.

BJ moved two chairs to a planning map and pulled out his notepad while Hagger picked up Team 22's isolation packet. Staff Sergeant Janecky, the intel NCO, came over to the map with Hagger.

"We've got a hot one for you, Beej,'' said Hagger. "Janecky'll cover the general situation, then we'll go into the details.''

"What we've got here is an apparent assembly area on the north side of Autobahn 195,'' said Janecky, pointing to a large wooded area southeast of Neuhaus. "The Sovs are running troop units and supply convoys up 195 from Autobahn 5 out of the Berlin area. Autobahn 195 parallels the Elbe River and the East German border until it runs back into Autobahn 5 and crosses the border at Lauenberg. From there they can take any one of several routes south of Hamburg into West Germany. Autobahn 195 is only a two-lane interregional road and our collection folks didn't pay much attention to it. Traffic on E15 had begun to slack off 'cause our air interdiction strikes were hitting E15 hard. Somebody noticed the lighter traffic and began to look at other routes. It appears they had begun using 195 rather heavily and had quite a deception effort going. Somewhere in this area"— Janecky tapped the wooden area again—"are one or more major assembly areas. It looks like each day different units move into the area for rest, refit, and refueling before barging into West Germany. Follow-on second echelon forces may be building up in there. The problem is that we need to narrow the area down for better targeting."

"We want you to go in, conduct an area recon, and nail it down to the exact areas they're using in those words," said Hagger. "We've got some stuff to hit them with, but we need a smaller CEP (circular error probability) before the flyboys knock the shit out of 'em. Plan for a three-night mission. Go tell your guys to saddle up and you get back here quick so we can hammer out the details."

"We going in by chopper?" asked BJ.

"You bet, but I'll ask them to send someone other than your little friend!"

Captain Yakushev walked into Bodyna's work area yanking off his blood-covered gloves.

"And were we successful, Comrade Captain?" Bodnya queried.

"Exactly so, Comrade Commander!" responded Yakushev. "I will admit that this SAS gangster was one of the more difficult subjects I have had to contend with, but, like all the others, he saw the wisdom of sharing his knowledge." Yakushev set a bloodstained handkerchief containing his side-cutting pliers and three large, partly broken teeth on Bodnya's desk. "Perhaps that is why they call these wisdom teeth in the West."

Bodnya sensed a certain pride in the KGB captain's tone and he fully realized that his special section officer may derive a little too much self-gratification from his intelligence-gathering efforts, but it was the end results that mattered. As far as Bodnya was concerned, the end results were all that mattered, as long as it did not drastically change the dialectic.

"This gangster will most certainly require the care of the *feldsher*. He is rather in a bad way," Yakushev remarked offhandedly.

"But is the information obtained of value?" asked Bodnya.

"Most certainly, Comrade Commander." Yakushev was somewhat perplexed by his new commander. Comrade Bodnya did not appear to be discomfitted in the least by his methods. In fact, he seemed to encourage them. "The gangster reports that he was a demolition specialist belonging to a terrorist gang called a 'troop.' It is composed of four 'patrols' of four men each. His parent unit is the 2nd Squadron of the 23rd SAS Regiment headquartered in Birmingham. They were brought over from England two days after our operations began and infiltrated by helicopter four nights ago. Their mission was to attack convoys on our supply routes. They were instructed to take no prisoners, Comrade Commander."

Bodnya thought fast. This may be an excellent propaganda opportunity. "Do you feel the prisoner might be persuaded to sign a statement admitting to that?"

"Most certainly, Comrade Commander!" Yakushev responded without a moment's hesitation.

"Excellent!" said Bodnya. "As soon as you have accomplished that task, have Major Goncharov contact the Front Intelligence Directorate's 4th Department and pass the signed statement to them along with your finalized interrogation report. He does not need to be attended by the *feldsher* until he signs his name." He knew full well that, besides providing the information to the GRU information department at front, the captain would also pass the information to his own masters. The KGB Directorate in Potsdam would probably receive it before the GRU. The KGB would use it to further its own propaganda efforts.

That was fine, thought Bodnya, as the Chekists could probably make better use of the information than their military intelligence "smaller brother."

"Is there any information regarding his gang's daytime hiding locations, methods, anything?"

"Very little, Comrade Commander. They apparently hide in a different place each day. He said that they will most certainly move to a far different area because of his capture and probably would not strike tonight."

"Too bad," Bodnya mulled. "One less opportunity to catch the bastards at work."

Yakushev collected the grisly objects from Bodnya's desk and withdrew from the room promising to have the final interrogation report and a signed statement by early afternoon.

Bodnya reflected on the past night's events. The 3rd Company had done well, and raised their esteem within the battalion. The Company's 2nd Platoon had established an area ambush on a low-wooded ridge line, covering a junction of three trails. Just after midnight a group of enemy terrorists walked into the ambush site. The trail junction was swept with automatic weapons fire and the bodies of seven British SAS soldiers were left, along with one unfortunate individual shot through both legs.

The British had fought well, they had even attempted to counterattack, apparently in an attempt to recover their dead and wounded, but that, too, had failed with the loss of one more terrorist. Bodnya was greeted at dawn by the sight of eight bodies wrapped in shelter capes laid out on the parking area in front of the small warehouse now serving as his headquarters. Captain Yakushev, unconcerned by the night's little victory, had greeted the wounded prisoner like a long-lost comrade . . . they had much to talk about.

The battalion headquarters had been granted permission to relocate to Uhrsleben on the north side of the E8 Autobahn the day before. This allowed the headquarters to be in a central location for more effective troop control. Another bit of good news had reached them as they moved into their new headquarters. An East German Battle Groups platoon had conducted a linear search along E8 that afternoon, investigating likely sites for enemy observation posts with the aid of a Frontier Troops tracker dog team, when they discovered an OP. The SAS gangsters had attempted to break out of their dug-in OP. Two of the British had died in the attempt, but the other two had run for it. The KGs had hunted them down and killed both in a field. The KGs had lost three men, however. The tide was slowly turning in their favor in this little rear-area war. He and his pursuit troops were anxious to get on with it. They were now looking forward to the sunset. As with all Spetsnaz, the night was their favorite time of day.

"Come on, sir, move it or lose it!" Jenna shouted as she bounded down the stairs with a field file cabinet. Outside, the sound of bombing was coming closer from the east.

Jinx was packing the remaining maps into a waterproof case. The overlays were stuffed inside his BDU jacket. As he rolled the maps and jammed them into the case, the room was suddenly filled with sound. A roar shook the entire house, rising to a scream that felt like two ice picks jammed into his ears. The roar suddenly disappeared like a burst bubble, leaving only a shriek that Jinx recognized as the chemical alarm. Ripping open his mask case, he pulled the black rubber mask up to his face, slipped the straps over his head, and pulled the hood over his shoulders. Through the mask lenses, he watched Jenna drop her file box and grab for her mask. She jerked on the mask, took two steps, then faltered, took another unsteady step, and fell down on her hands and knees. Around her, no one stopped to stare. The clamor of the chemical alarm brought them up short. Everyone caught outside frantically clawed at their mask cases. Many of them got their mask on, only to fall twitching to the ground.

Jinx exhaled to clear the mask, slapping his hands over the inlet valves, then cinched the straps tight in back of his head. He pulled on his black rubber gloves. Outside, Jenna was now spasming, her body wracked with muscle contractions. She was not alone, others nearby on the ground and in the jeeps and trucks were jerking around like puppets. The chemical bombs had apparently exploded in the air, the sound covered by the aircraft noise. The elliptical pattern of the chemical dispersal, its "footprint," completely covered the surrounding area. Caught in the act of moving, the MI detachment was an easy victim.

Jinx vaulted down the stairs, rummaging in the mask case for the antidote injectors stored there.

Someone had turned off the gas detector's alarm, and now the sound of screaming and panic came up from below.

Jinx passed Lieutenant Colonel Tucker on the stairs, staring through the mask.

"Everyone up there masked?" he asked, his voice muffled by his own protective gear.

"Yes, sir," Jinx yelled back. "Only me up here."

"Good, good," the CO yelled. He turned and followed Jinx downstairs, where pandemonium reigned.

"They caught us flat-footed," Tucker yelled at Jinx. "A pair of Su-24s, I think. You stay in here until you get your complete MOPP suit on!"

The colonel then darted out the door, rushing first to Jenna, who lay closest to the door. The colonel, no scholarly academic now, quickly pulled the injectors out of Jenna's mask bag. Tucker removed the smaller of the two antidote injectors from its clip and rolled Jenna over, grasping the long muscle of her left thigh. He pushed the green tip of the injector against Jenna's leg until he felt the needle stab into the muscle, injecting the first part of the antidote. He left the injector in place as he pulled the second, larger injector from the clip. Tucker repeated the procedure, shooting the 2 PAM C1 into the same thigh. While the second injector was in place, Tucker removed the first injector and bent the needle against the ground. This done, he did the same with the second injector.

As Jinx watched from the window, the scene took on a surreal quality. Figures bundled in camouflaged MOPP suits, looking like aliens from a cheap sci-fi film, attempted to treat those unlucky enough to be caught without their masks. Injections of nerve agent antidote from automatic injectors would save those only slightly exposed, like Jenna. Those caught outside unmasked were either dead or soon would be. The nerve agents did not need to be inhaled. Droplets on the skin would kill as easily. Jenny was lucky. The drivers, their masks on the seats of their vehicles, had taken the brunt of the poison.

★19★

BJ's eyes seemed to lose their ability to focus as the Nighthawk plunged toward the clearing. The pair of digital torque readouts between the pilots were a green blur, the numbers changed so fast.

"Stand by," the command came clearly over the troop handset he held to his ear with one hand, his other hand gripping his rifle. The crew chief slid the port door open as his team unsnapped their seat harnesses. The landing gear thumped onto the frozen ground of East Germany.

"Go!" barked the handset.

"Everybody inside, outside!" yelled BJ.

He snapped the handset into its recessed ceiling bracket. Pushing himself out of the nylon seat and falling to his knees, BJ slipped his arms through the big rucksack's shoulder straps. The team, burdened by their rucks, stumbled out the wide side door as a body, and into a wedge formation with BJ at its point. As the chopper lifted off, they moved at a trot into the nearby wood line.

BJ was always amazed at how suddenly it became quiet after an insertion chopper departed. Deadly quiet. He looked around making certain his band was staying together. The first moments after insertion were some of the most critical, and the time when a man could easily become separated. As the team ran, bent under their rucks, they chambered a round, pulled their earplugs out and shoved them into their pockets. Dropping them on the ground would have been like leaving a calling card. The earplugs

148

were essential to insure their full range of hearing after the loud chopper ride. They slowed as they approached the tree line. More than one team had run into a fence at full speed.

As they entered the evergreens, the five men fell into a column formation with the scout, Wally Kosinski, now at the point. BJ was a few meters behind him, followed by Troy Murphy, the senior radio operator, scanning to the right. Tyrone King followed him, responsible for security to the left. The assistant team leader, Shannon Hickey, brought up the rear.

They quietly moved about fifty meters before BJ signaled a security halt. Each man went to a kneeling position and faced in his direction of responsibility. They remained absolutely silent, perfectly still . . . listening. They listened for sounds of pursuit, for other sounds of activity in the area, and to accustom themselves to the forest's night sounds. After several minutes, BJ gave a quiet all-clear and each man checked his gear to make certain it was secure, that nothing had been dropped. They checked their compasses, orienting themselves to the terrain as BJ and Kosinski confirmed the initial movement direction.

The team came to their feet when BJ did and began to slowly feel their way through the pitch-black forest relying on Wally Kosinski to guide them with his night-vision goggles. Their initial direction of movement was different from the one they would actually take to their recon area, an effort to confuse anyone attempting to follow them. After 350 meters, when they reached a small forest road, they switched to their actual movement direction. The road's distance and direction from the landing zone also served to confirm their actual location. It was not unheard of for a team to be accidentally inserted on the wrong LZ. Team leaders wanted to confirm that they actually were where they were supposed to be as soon after insertion as possible.

BJ was concerned about their recon area and its proximity to the East German frontier zone. The zone was a five-kilometer belt paralleling the border and under the control of the Frontier Troops.

Checkpoints were established on all roads entering the zone and the Grenztruppen patrolled all roads and trails. Civilians living within the zone carried special identity cards and entry permits. Some were members of the Frontier Troops auxiliary. All civilians were directed to report the presence of any strangers or signs of unusual activity. Even children were included in this program, as they played in areas that adults seldom frequented and were quick to spot strangers. He was also concerned with local military security since it was an established assembly area. It could get hairy.

The five shadows drifted slowly through the mist-shrouded evergreens. The pine needles that covered the forest floor muffled their footfalls. They avoided the occasional thin patches of snow so as to leave no footprints. Like most German forests, this one was nearly devoid of underbrush. It was very different from Sam Houston National Forest and the many military posts they had trained in. The choking underbrush and "wait-a-minute" vines of the southern U.S. pine forests slowed night movement to a crawl. Here they could move relatively quickly, but it was a trade-off. The bare forest floors offered little concealment. They felt almost naked as they padded through the pines, their breath making little puffing clouds before their faces.

After an hour of slow but steady movement, Wally quickly raised his right hand. Every man froze. BJ signaled a security halt and, again, each LRRP kneeled facing his direction of responsibility. And again they listened. A faint whine came from the far distance. A low rumble disrupted the thin whine, momentarily drowning it out. The rumble throbbed down to a lower pitch and the whine could again be heard.

BJ leaned back to Murphy and whispered, "Power generators. Someone fired up a tank engine. Pass it back."

The team moved forward again, even more cautiously. BJ directed Kosinski to be on the lookout with his NVGs for a laager, a concealed spot the team could lay up in.

Kosinski pointed out a spot to the right to BJ. Passing the spot, the team continued on for another fifty meters and then began to loop around to the right, doubling back to the spot and entering it from the opposite direction. Each man took up his rehearsed prone position in a "wagon wheel" formation. Their feet almost touched in the center of the little circle, enabling them to silently alert the others with a tap of the boot. They removed their rucks and placed them to the front. It was a good laager, under the dense low-hung limbs of an evergreen. Several rocks and small clusters of brush around the tree's drip line offered further concealment. Kosinski covered their back trail.

If anyone was following their trail, the team would see them as they passed and they could either evacuate the site or ambush their pursuers. The latter option was the least desirable. A five-man team deep behind enemy lines had little chance if detected.

Larger forces would be called in and the area cordoned off and swept. East Germany was not Vietnam, where a LRRP team could call for an extraction chopper while on the run. The long-range radios now used could not be operated while moving. There was no voice capability available at the distances they operated, and the messages had to be encrypted and input into the DMDG for transmission. Besides, it took turns to coordinate and plan a helicopter infiltration mission in such a high-threat environment. Their training constantly emphasized that detection or contact in any form was to be avoided at all costs. Their mission was solely to collect and report information, and not let anyone know that they had even been there.

BJ and Murphy, after insuring they were not followed, encoded and encrypted their combined initial entry and spot reports under the concealment of a poncho, while King rigged the antenna. Murphy then transmitted the message.

After the half-hour process was completed, BJ called a conference with the team's heads clustered together.

"We're goin' in slow and easy. We're at least a klick and a half away, maybe more. They generally have security patrols about a klick out. I only want to get in a little closer and find a real good ORP—objective rally point. We'll hole up and go out in two pairs to see what we can. We ready?"

"Ready," came the four whispers.

★20★

The burst transmission took only seconds. Even that time seemed like forever in their exposed position. Murphy, lying flat next to his radio, waited for confirmation that their report had been received. Although the burst had been short, the message was fairly long. It detailed the assembly area hidden in the forest northeast of the highway.

BJ estimated that at least a regiment of tanks was packed into the woods, waiting to be sent forward to punch through the NATO lines. This was a regiment of some second echelon division. If it could be destroyed here, it would take a lot of pressure off the beleaguered defenders along NATO's NORTHAG front. The trick, of course, was that the regiment was too far from the front for artillery fire and there were several air defense units deployed with the tanks, making an air strike extremely risky.

The how was not his problem, though, only the what and where. From their transmission site, BJ could easily hear the clanking rumble of more tanks and combat vehicles joining the other massed units.

Finally, Murphy took down his antenna and slithered back with BJ to the relative safety of the ravine. In the ravine, the other members of Team 24 were busily enlarging the cave. Using their folding entrenching tools, they had enlarged the hole enough to accommodate the entire team. The massive rock slab overhead afforded both cover and concealment. They banked the dug-out earth in front of the entrance. The cave lacked the crude comforts of their previous hide-hole, but it was better than lying out in the open watching the assembly area.

As soon as they were back in the cave, Murphy set about decrypting the message received on the digital message device group. Using the one-time pad and communications-electronics operating instructions, he went through the meticulous task of translating it into English.

"What now, BJ?" Tyrone King asked. "We gonna stay here?"

"We'll know in a minute, Ty," BJ replied, tucking his hands into his armpits to get some circulation back.

"I hope so," King went on, "I'm freezing my ass off here!"

The temperature had dropped steadily since they had been inserted, and a bitter north wind howled and whipped around them. The ravine was some shelter, but the cave was better.

"Murphy, what have you got?" BJ asked the commo man as he finished decoding the message and set fire to the page from the one-time pad.

"STRIKEWARN," Hickey answered, reading from the notepad, "Haymaker. Assess post-strike damage."

"What the hell is a Haymaker strike?" asked Murphy.

"I don't know," the senior radio operator replied as he flipped through his CEOI, "I'm looking."

"I just want them to do it, so we can get out of here before our nuts freeze and fall off," Kosinski grumbled.

"It's going to warm up, Wally," Murphy said as he finally found Haymaker in his code book, "Haymaker—tactical nuclear strike/missile. Kiloton range."

"Holy shit, Jesus," Kosinski whistled. Suddenly no one was concerned about the cold anymore.

"When, Troy?" BJ asked quickly.

"Sometime after 1730 today."

"Well, guys, I suggest we take the time we have left before this event to make this hole a better shelter. We're gonna need all the cover we can get."

"BJ, you don't really mean to stay here while they nuke the place, do you?" Kosinski asked, his eyes wide and darting toward the entrance to the hole as if he were about to bolt out of the cave.

"Wally, I would rather be in here than out there somewhere when that thing goes off." The other team members were silent, watching Kosinski. "We've got to stay here and report the strike results. I don't think we'll find a better place with the time we have left, and I don't want to move around out here any more than we have to. Too much of a chance of running into a security patrol.''

''Shit, man, this rock'll fall down on us and smash us like bugs!''

''I think I'd rather be squashed like a bug than fried like a burger,'' Tyrone King said softly. Hickey and Murphy looked over at the hulking black man and smiled. King had summed up their feelings as well. The three of them went back to digging their cave deeper under the overhanging rock. BJ joined them.

Kosinski still sat nervously watching the others, twisting his pile cap in his hands.

''Jesus, man, I don't want to even think about nukes,'' Kosinski whined. ''Nukes, oh, God.''

''Well, Scarlet, if you think about it today, you'll go crazy,'' Murphy said. ''So think about it tomorrow.''

''If you're still alive,'' Hickey added flatly.

''Right on, Bro,'' King said. He laid on the entrenching tool with even more vigor, showering Kosinski with flying dirt.

There it was again, the metallic sound. Junior Sergeant Gleb Budenny raised his arm and then pointed in the approaching darkness to the rock outcrop that seemed to be the origin of the sound. He then spread his arms out on both sides, the signal for his squad to go on line and prepare for an assault. The rest of the squad nodded and moved quietly from their column file to an assault line. Budenny motioned one of the RPKS-74 machine gunners and the RPG-7 rocket gunner to set up their weapons and provide covering fire for the squad from the flank. The other machine gunner joined the assault line.

When the supporting weapons were in place, Budenny motioned the squad forward. He wished to surprise the intruders and capture them alive, but if they resisted, they would perish. As his squad drew near the dimly seen rock, the sound of digging became louder. A deep voice swore in a foreign tongue.

''*God almighty damn!*'' King shouted, spinning away from the back of the cave and shoving his right hand into his mouth.

''Watch the damned noise! What'd you do, Ty?'' BJ asked as he continued to scoop up dirt and pile it against the wall of the ravine to build up the entrance to the cave.

"Hit my knuckle on a fuckin' rock!" King mumbled, his hand still pressed to his mouth. "Hurts."

"Take a break, everybody," BJ said, slumping back against the wall of the cave. He looked at his watch, "Everyone needs to get into their chemical protective suits. It's gettin' close to showtime."

"Think we ought to have a quick look-see out there?" Murphy asked, motioning toward the cave's dark opening.

"Yeah, Murph, we need to," BJ answered. "We don't want to get too excited about the nuke and forget everything we know. Take Hickey and have a quick peek, then get your ass back in here. It's almost 1730 now."

Murphy and Hickey picked up their M16s and moved out of the cave, one on each side of the rock. The excitement of the strike warning had almost caused them all to forget even basic SOPs, like site security. A couple hours of digging had dulled the edge of that excitement. When Murph and Hickey got back he'd . . .

The two M16s fired as one, jolting the others in the cave into action. They reached for their weapons and jumped toward the mouth of the cave.

Budenny was only twenty meters from the cave when the two Americans appeared. He knew they were Americans by their M16 rifles. The pair had seen him at the same time, dropped to the ground, and fired their weapons. The squad had paused for a split second, surprised by the firing, but were now running forward, firing short bursts from the hip. In the light of muzzle flashes to his left, Budenny saw Private Selunski twist and fall, his rifle falling on its bayonet, sticking up out of the ground. The Americans were suddenly joined by others firing from both sides of the rocks. Private Volnov had dropped to the ground and was firing his RPKS-74 at the right side of the rock, pinning down the Americans. Budenny motioned the squad to assault that side. Grenades began to explode on the squad's left side. Private Shepelev stumbled, but dropped to one knee and continued firing. They had the Americans now. They would close and overwhelm them.

The Russians were right on top of them. If Murphy had waited a minute longer, BJ thought as he scrambled out of the cave, they would have been trapped like rats. At least it was just a small group. If they could take them, they could pack up and split from the area . . . if they had time.

The steady rattle of a machine gun on the left side of the rock was accompanied by whining ricochets and flying rock chips. BJ moved in that direction, keeping his head down. Tyrone King came out of the cave with a grenade in each hand and flung them over the rock, reaching back for his rifle as the grenades exploded in bright flashes. BJ saw the curve of a Soviet helmet appear over the rim of the rock and jerked the rifle to his shoulder. He squeezed the trigger. The figure disappeared in a flash of light that just got brighter and brighter.

"Now," Budenny screamed. "Assault!"

He slapped a fresh magazine into place. Now he would drive his bayonet into the intruders! Budenny ran up onto the rock amid muzzle flashes and streaking tracers. In the ravine, movement caught his eye. He swung his rifle toward the movement, firing as he turned.

The dark interior of the ravine suddenly became light. The American, his rifle firing, was plainly visible. In an instant the American and the ravine disappeared in a blinding flash that seared his eyes like hot daggers. Budenny felt the heat at his back, then a huge hand—the hand of God?—slapped him like a fly. The image of the American was the last thing Budenny saw.

"INNNCOMINGGG!" BJ screamed. "GET IN HERE! QUICK, QUICK."

The warning was unnecessary. The others had been facing toward the assembly area, trading fire with the Soviet squad when the nuclear weapon went off. The flash caught them all by surprise and Murphy had his hand over his right eye as he stumbled and rolled into the cave. King grabbed Hickey's web gear and dragged him in. The Soviets were forgotten as the five Americans sought the salvation of their cave.

"*Mask, Mask!*" BJ screamed as he and the others rolled over the pile of big rucksacks.

The five men ripped their protective masks from the bag strapped to their legs and pulled them up over their faces, tugging the straps tight against the back of their heads and rolling the rubberized hood down over their shoulders. The masks would keep them from inhaling any radioactive particles. The big packs would cover them from flying debris, if nothing else. Huddled together in a welter of bodies behind the tiny protective wall of the packs and earth, each man's eyes were shut tight against the glare that quickly began to fade.

"Open your mouths!" Hickey screamed as the thunderclap struck.

Each man clapped his hands over his ears and opened his mouth to equalize the pressure, an old artilleryman's trick to deal with intense blasts that could puncture eardrums.

Outside the cave, hell was in session. The force of the blast blew the trees away like splinters and hammered the tanks and fighting vehicles into junk. The heat of the explosion set fire to nearly all the fighting vehicles, many of the tanks, and all of the trucks, fuelers, and support vehicles. Men caught out in the open simply vanished. Others inside vehicles died screaming as the overpressure burst their organs and the blast heat turned their vehicles into pressure cookers. The fire blew across the heaving, buckling forest like a hurricane from hell, smashing everything.

In three seconds, an entire reinforced tank regiment of the 90th Guards Tank Division simply ceased to exist. What was left was a forest full of burning metal hulks filled with dead and dying men.

The first blast was followed by a roaring sound that reminded BJ of the hurricane that had slammed into Houston in 1984. The noise rose to a wailing sound as the blast wave screamed past outside. The pressure sucked at the air in the cave, trying to pull the very breath from their lungs. Above them, the huge rock shook. Another wail joined the outside noise. Kosinski was screaming. The others tucked up into tight fetal positions behind the packs and rolled tight against the killing noise and their own fear.

The roaring sound stopped for a moment and Kosinski jumped to his feet.

"Come on! We gotta get out of here!" he screamed, his voice muffled by the mask. He pulled his heavy pack up onto his shoulder, "Come on! We . . ."

Tyrone King jerked Kosinski off his feet just as the maelstrom swirled into the ravine. The blast had sent out a pressure wave that had left a vacuum in its wake. Now that vacuum pulled in another torrent of debris-laden air. Kosinski's muffled howl rose above the sound of the wind. In a minute, the wind and the dust abated. The huddled men cautiously looked up over their packs. The sky outside was dark, but an odd glow lit the night, the light of a thousand fires reflecting off the tons of dust thrown into the air by the blast.

"Hooooeeee, baby!" Murphy yelled. "That was some *shit*!"

No one else spoke, except Kosinski, who wept, the tears leaving streaks inside the eyepieces of his mask.

BJ sat up, leaning back against the wall of packs.

"We should have covered ourselves with ponchos," he said to the others. "We probably got covered with fallout."

"A poncho can melt on you," said King.

"Hang on, I'll check," Hickey said. He brushed the dust from his pack and dug down inside it, coming up with the IM-174A/PD radiac meter. He held up the radiation monitor and slowly scanned the cave, watching the needle in the meter.

"We picked up some hot dust, but not too much," Hickey said as he stuffed the radiac meter back into his ruck. "We need to get out of here, though. Radiation builds up over time in an inclosed area. Once out of the area we can decontaminate some of our gear."

"Right," BJ answered, "Hickey, you and Ty go up and have a look with the NVGs." As the two men made their way out of the cave, BJ turned to the radio operator.

"Murphy, you get a message started. We need to do a strike report on the target and an extraction request. We'll use CCP Bravo. When Hickey and Ty get back, you can get the details." He turned back to go packing up their gear.

Outside, the forested hollow that they had watched all day was gone. In its place was a blackened hellhole that stretched nearly to their own position. There was no trace of the Soviet patrol that had come so close to wiping them out. Nothing. No bodies, no gear, *nada*.

"Where'd them Russian boys end up?" King asked as Hickey turned on the night-vision goggles.

"Who cares?" asked Hickey. "You can bet they aren't coming back for more."

"Huh-uh."

Hickey scanned the burning forest with the NVGs. The light reflected from the fires lit the scene brightly in the light-amplifying goggles. There were destroyed vehicles everywhere. Tanks flipped over on their sides, fighting vehicles upside down, burning. The carnage was complete. Here and there, on the outer

edges of the blast area, a few doomed soldiers staggered about.
A vast central area was denuded of trees and vehicles. It gradually became a zone of stumps, and then changed into a ragged
ring of blown-down, limbless black tree trunks.

"Take a look, Ty."

As King surveyed the destruction, Hickey began to chuckle.

"What you laughin' at?" King asked, not taking his eyes off
the terrible scene of devastation before him.

"Just thinkin' of something ol' George Bush said once,"
Hickey answered. He raised himself up off the ground and
shouted, "There's a thousand points of light for you, ya' commie cocksuckers!"

He laughed out loud. "Come on, Ty, we've seen enough."

The two men slid back down into the cave.

"BJ, those fuckers are gone!" Hickey exclaimed.

"Can you be more specific, Shan?" Murphy asked.

"I'd put the damage at seventy percent vehicles destroyed,
twenty percent vehicles damaged. Casualties maybe eighty to
ninety percent. They got their butts waxed! You ought to see it!
The whole place is on fire! It looks like . . ."

"Murphy, get that into the message and get it off," BJ broke
in, "then send our extraction request. We need to get the fuck
out of here before this place is crawling with Russians. They
might send in some rescue and recovery parties." He looked at
Kosinski, who sat huddled against his rucksack, his knees pulled
up under his chin.

"You okay, Wally?"

Kosinski just looked at him. BJ could not read much through
the protective mask, but it didn't take much to see that Kosinski
was out of it. The nuclear blast had scared him half to death.
They would have to lead him by the hand out of here. If they
got hit again, Kosinski was dead meat.

"Shan, you and Ty get all of the essential stuff out of Kosinski's ruck and stash it in someone else's."

The two men stripped the unresisting Kosinski's pack of the
binoculars and extra radio batteries. They also took the ration
packets. There was nothing else vital in the pack. If they got
stranded, Kosinski could share a sleeping bag.

What a lousy thought, mulled BJ. If they didn't get extracted,
they would have to evade back to friendly lines on foot and the
first thing they would have to do was penetrate the border bar-
riers on the Elbe River.

As they repacked the equipment into their own rucks, Murphy got up and went outside to rig up the antenna. This done, he came back in and took out the radio and DMDG to send the strike report message and the extraction request.

"It's on the way, BJ," Murphy reported when the transmission was completed.

"Okay, we'll move out as soon as the commo gear's stowed," BJ answered, "Get into your protective suits." He slid over next to Kosinski and sat down.

"Wally, we're moving out," BJ said quietly, "are you ready?"

Kosinski looked back and nodded. BJ patted Kosinski's shoulder and stood, helping the frightened soldier into the clumsy protective suit.

"Ready, BJ," Hickey said, closing his pack and shouldering the heavy load.

"Let's go and let's take it easy," BJ cautioned. King led the way with Murphy second. BJ and Kosinski followed with Hickey bringing up the rear.

Outside, a breeze was picking up. The fires ignited by the blast were burning fiercely, fed by the tons of shattered trees. The heat from these fires rose over the detonation site, sucking air in behind it. The resulting breeze, in turn, further fed the flames. A firestorm was starting in the splintered forest. Soon the whole area would be ablaze, the fire spreading out as far as there was fuel to feed it. With luck, they would be extracted before the fire came their way and overtook them. But they had to get there first. The pickup zone was four kilometers away and there was no telling how long before the chopper would arrive. It would be an interesting wait.

★ 21 ★

The horn honked three times. The lieutenant motioned for them to return to the vehicle.

"Damn it! Can we never get a hot cup of tea?" Senior Sergeant Nowak grumbled. "Ignore him."

The lieutenant honked again, more insistently this time.

One by one, the four men returned to the missile transporter, Nowak coming up last, sipping the tepid tea from his tin cup.

"Hurry, you *churkas*," Lieutenant Lavrov shouted through the window of the launcher, "we have a fire mission!"

The crew stopped in their tracks. They had expected to hear that they were moving again. They had moved twice a day since the war had broken out, staying just behind the advancing echelons, hiding from the enemy's aircraft and setting up their launcher in the locations surveyed before the war. The SS-21's range of one hundred kilometers required it to be close to the action. Its atomic warhead was designed to break up enemy counterattacks or to counter enemy atomic strikes.

The order to fire could mean only one thing. The Americans had used weapons of mass destruction!

"Are you deaf?" the lieutenant screamed. "We have a *fire mission*!"

Nowak was the first to respond. He dropped his cup and ran to his station on the launcher.

"On your command, Comrade Lieutenant!" Nowak shouted as the other crewmen ran to their respective launch stations.

"Prepare for launching!" the lieutenant barked.

161

The crew went into action just as they had a hundred times in training. They had never fired a live SS-21 before, but the drill was the same.

After the camouflage nets were pulled off, the sliding doors atop the six-wheeled transporter/erector/launcher slid back, exposing the stubby missile. As Nowak and the others worked the hydraulics that brought the missile up from its horizontal traveling position to its vertical launch position, Lieutenant Lavrov fed the targeting information into the guidance package. It took only fifteen minutes to prepare the missile for firing, as the launcher was already positioned and stabilized.

"Ready for firing, Comrade Lieutenant!" Nowak shouted when the final item on the prelaunch checklist was completed.

"Firing positions!" the lieutenant snapped.

The crew climbed into the troop compartment of the BTR-70 support vehicle tucked into the edge of the forest. There they would await the command to launch the missile and then move to the next firing position. The lieutenant was the only one authorized, and able, to actually fire the missile. He sat with the remote firing control station cradled in his lap, speaking to no one. Nowak and the others sat in the cold belly of the personnel carrier and waited. Each man was lost in his own thoughts.

Half an hour later, the launch command came. The missile roared out in a cloud of smoke, streaked up from the launcher, and slowly angled over to the northwest. The crew did not know its target. That information was classified too far above their level.

As the smoke cleared from around the launcher, Nowak led the crew back. They immediately ran through the post-launch procedures and closed the missile hatch cover. They climbed into the launcher's crew cab. Inside, Lieutenant Lavrov was sitting with the firing console beside him, staring out the front windshield. He seemed startled when Nowak spoke.

"Are you all right, Comrade Lieutenant?" the sergeant asked.

"What? Oh, yes, Comrade Senior Sergeant, I am fine," the lieutenant replied absently. "Are we ready to move to our next position?"

"Just so, Comrade Lieutenant!"

"Excellent. Proceed."

Nowak started the engine and steered the empty launcher onto the narrow road. The next launch position was four kilometers to the south. They would reload the launcher with the missile that would be delivered by the KGB special transport and security section, and await another firing command. The missile just fired would land before they reached the new position. Nowak wondered if they would be able to see the flash from the road. One hundred kilometers was a long way, but an atomic explosion made a big light.

The crew was silent. Each man knew that the war had become an atomic war. Weapons of mass destruction would fall from the heavens like rain now. No one wanted to think of the destruction the American gangsters had unleashed. Surely they were no more than animals to resort to such weapons.

It chilled Lavrov to think of it. Now he was part of the madness, too. This could only end horribly. Lavrov remembered an old saying: When a man rides the tiger, he cannot get off.

It was no trick to find the area, even without the satellite navigation system and the preprogrammed computer with the route memorized. The light from the burning forest lit the sky like a hellish beacon. BJ and his LRRPs would be well away from the flames, of course. At least she hoped they would be. Donna had a knot in the pit of her stomach that got a little worse each day. It was fear. She knew that. What surprised her was that she was more afraid for BJ than for herself. She was always too busy doing her job to worry about herself, but that jerk BJ kept popping up in her mind.

Cox was on the intercom. Donna forced BJ out of her thoughts and tried to hear what Tommy was saying.

"So what do you think?"

"About what?" she replied.

"God damn it, Donna!" the copilot snapped into the intercom, his head swiveling to look at her. "Pay attention! The communication checkpoint is coming up." Cox printed to the lake now visible, its surface reflecting the distant fires. "Do you want to start transmitting now or wait until we orbit the CCP?"

"Start now," she replied calmly, "we don't want to hang around here at all."

"Roger," Cox replied. Tommy was never happy, but he was getting bitchier every day. He had not been amused when she told him this morning that if he was going to be premenstrual, they should synchronize their periods.

As they approached the lake, Donna put the chopper into a lazy bank, circling the lake low and slow. Tommy was broadcasting their call sign, Zulu Niner Tango, and BJ's, Alpha Eight Charlie. It was up to the team to respond with an azimuth for the chopper to fly to the pickup zone. If they did not respond after three tries, the chopper would head for home.

As they made the first lap around the lake, Cox transmitted the call sign for the second time. The knot in Donna's stomach got tighter. She willed herself to think only about her flying.

Cox's voice came up on the intercom. "One more time, Donna, then we're out of here," he said, the pitch of his voice rising with the tension. "If your boyfriend isn't here, we're not . . ."

The voice on the radio broke into Cox's speech.

"Zulu Niner Tango, Zulu Niner Tango, this is Alpha Eight Charlie, over," the voice said, "seven-eight degrees, I say again, seven-eight degrees."

"Roger, Alpha Eight Charlie," Cox responded. "Any hostile, over?"

"Negative hostile. We are contaminated, I say again, we are contaminated, over."

"Roger, Zulu Niner Tango, over."

"Those pricks!" shouted Cox, switching to the intercom. "Everybody mask up and put your gloves on. The team's hot!"

The Nighthawk's crew was already wearing their protective suits. They struggled into their M24 aircraft masks, Donna and Cox switching piloting duties as the other donned the mask and special rubber gloves.

Donna kicked the chopper around to the azimuth and pulled all the power she safely could. The Nighthawk shot across the surface of the lake and climbed over the trees, the compass needle coming around to seventy-eight degrees. All they had to do now was fly until they saw the infrared strobe signal that marked the pickup zone.

Donna almost overflew the signal, it came so soon. The team was only about 300 meters from the lake. She flared out and settled into the small clearing. The team was already running from its cover in the trees.

"Chief, get that door open!" Cox yelled into the intercom. "Get 'em in here, quick!"

The order was unnecessary, the crew chief already had the door open. A moment later, dark figures lunged through the open door and slithered across the metal floor. There was no style in their entry, speed was what mattered. In less than half a minute, the crew chief gave the pilots a thumbs-up and Donna pulled power, whisking the chopper out of the small clearing.

Once above the trees, she flew to the preplanned exfiltration route and let the computer take it from there. The computer would fly a route that would, hopefully, take them back through both enemy and friendly air defense belts.

In the troop compartment, the LRRPs struggled out of their equipment and onto the nylon bench seats, buckling themselves in for the flight.

The voice she had been waiting to hear came over the troop intercom.

"Hi, babe," BJ said breathlessly, "glad to see you!"

Donna turned and smiled at the warrior whose grotesque masked head appeared between the pilots' seats. She realized that he couldn't see her smile and gave a thumbs-up instead.

"Listen, Donna," BJ went on. "you need to get a radiation check on this chopper when you get back. That nuke dusted us pretty good. We decontaminated, but you still need to wash this thing out!"

"Oh, thanks, BJ," she answered, "track hot mud into my ship, thanks a lot!"

"Damn you, Dimitri!" Ilya Cervik shouted. "Calm down! We are still alive, and we are still soldiers!"

The terrified driver was outside the vehicle now and looked as if he were about to run away. Not that there was any place to run to, but panic and terror knew no reason.

"Get back in here!" Cervik shouted from his perch in the turret of the 2S6. "You are safer in here than out there, the vehicle has nuclear protection!"

"The gun will be our coffin!" Dimitri shouted back, his eyes darting around, searching the horizon for more atomic flashes. Cervik had about pissed himself when the flash had lit the sky to the east. Another flash minutes later, much farther to the north, had been terrifying as well, but now the fear had loosened its grip on Cervik.

In desperation, Cervik pulled the Makarov PM pistol from his holster and pointed it at his driver.

"Comrade Private Ulisov, if you do not return to your duty station, I will shoot you where you stand."

"Fine," screamed Ulisov, "you will be doing me a service!"

"Damn it, Dimitri . . ."

The screech of the radar-warning horn broke in on Cervik's exhortations.

"Target!" he yelled. "Dimitri . . ."

Cervik looked up to see his driver running for the woods, screaming as he ran. The man had lost his reason completely. Cervik dropped into the turret and switched the radar from sweep to search mode. In a second, the acquisition radar had a trace, two kilometers out and to the right. Cervik switched to the fire control radar to lock the guns on the target and the turret automatically rotated in the target's direction. He switched off the acquisition radar; it emitted too much of a signal to let it run. The target faded, evading at a very low altitude. The fire control radar lost its lock, but the guns were still following the intruder's predicted course, calculated by the system's computer. Cervik set his gun's fire control switch to engage automatically when the target reappeared, if it did. He kept his finger on the manual override in case it proved to be friendly.

His mind barely registered the blip on the screen before the four 30mm guns opened up, shaking the entire vehicle. The radar screen flared into a green-white haze. Helmetless, and with the hatches open, Cervik screamed as the noise from the rapid-firing guns stabbed into his ears like hot nails. He slammed his left hand up over his ear as he grabbed frantically for the helmet with its protective earphones. He was struggling into it when the firing ceased. The guns had fired a 100-round burst, then lost their target lock. The target was off the screen now, either destroyed or evading again.

Cervik snapped the acquisition radar back on, scanned his sector, and waited, watching his screen. As usual, the engagement had been too short to register much on him. Targets came and went in an instant. It was rare to even see them, even during the day.

Earlier in the day, before the atomic strikes, half a dozen tanks and fighting vehicles had disappeared in smoke and flames without warning, during their movement to this location. The attack was over before the noise of the attacking jets roared over them.

The aircraft, American A-10s someone had said, had dropped a shower of small bombs down the length of the road. Many vehicles were damaged and others destroyed. The hapless motorized riflemen riding on the outside of the vehicles had been riddled. The other 2S6 in his section had been destroyed in the lightning attack and his own gunner, his head protruding from the hatch, had been killed by a small fragment. The SA-19 missile launchers were useless, their missiles used up long ago. No reload missiles had been delivered. His vehicle was now the only 2S6 left out of the original six in the regiment's special air defense battalion. The speed of the enemy aircraft, and their skill at hiding in the trees and behind hills, made Cervik's job that much harder.

At least this engagement is over, he thought, now to find that worthless coward of a driver.

"Radar!" Cox screamed. "Painting, ten o'clock!"

A glance on the radar scope showed the rim that housed the radar-detection display glowing on the left front of the ring. A warbling tone sounded in their headsets.

Cox was frantically arming the chaff-and-flare dispensers. The flares would decoy any infrared missiles, but they would point like a bright finger back to the chopper. The chaff cloud would shroud them from radar.

The warbling tone changed to a continuous tone. "Locked!" Cox shouted. He fired the chaff and began firing the flares in pairs off the back of the chopper.

Donna pushed the stick forward, skimming along the treetops, praying there were no power lines or a lone tall tree ahead in the darkness.

A solid stream of red fireballs streaked in front of the chopper—tracers!

Donna pulled up hard. The Nighthawk jumped into the climb. In the rear, the LRRPs hung on to their nylon seats, their gear sliding around on the floor. Donna heard the pops of the flare dispenser, then the ship was suddenly filled with fire and wind, cold wind blowing through a hole the size of a basketball that had opened at the top of the cockpit between the windscreen and the side windows. The top third of the door frame there was missing, blasted away by the explosion.

Donna's scream could be heard over the sound of the roaring wind. Cox immediately took control of the chopper, which was vibrating badly. He scanned the red lights coming on all over his instrument panel. The left engine was faltering and fire lights were coming on. Automatic Halon systems fired in the engine compartment, trying to smother the flames. Cox shut down the damaged engine and increased power on the good one. The vibration abated, but two of the fire lights remained on.

In the troop compartment, BJ had unbuckled when he heard Donna scream. Her head was back, rolling from side to side with the pitching of the chopper. He moved up behind her seat and peered around her. Donna's protective and flight suits were ripped open across the left breast, a dark stain soaking through the nomex fabric. The peppering fragments had ripped small holes in the face piece and hood of the protective mask. There was also a large gouge on the front of her flight helmet that had bent the night-vision goggles' mounting bracket. The goggles and mask's eyepieces had probably saved her eyes.

Cox was yelling over the intercom to the crew chief and gunner to see if anyone else was hit. None were.

BJ reached for the handles on either side of the wounded pilot's seat and pulled them. The seat back dropped rearward into his arms. BJ pulled the first-aid kit off the top of Donna's seat and held it in his teeth. He pulled the release on her harness buckles and, grabbing her under the arms, pulled her into the troop compartment.

The wound in her chest was bleeding, but no bubbles were visible through the fabric. BJ spat the first-aid kit into his hand and tore open the flap. Inside the kit were field dressings and gauze bandages. BJ ripped open one of the field dressings and slipped off the plastic wrapper. He ripped apart one side and the bottom to make the wrapper into a large flat square of plastic. This done, he pulled the front zipper down and tugged the layers of tight fabric to one side. Donna's large left breast was ripped by a jagged gash about six inches long. BJ's heart sank at the sight. They were still a long way from help. She could bleed to death easily, even drown from blood in her lungs. BJ pressed the plastic square over the wound and pressed hard on Donna's chest to expel any air trapped in the wound. He pressed the plastic down with one hand and retrieved the field dressing with the other. Behind him, Murphy had unbuckled and knelt down to help.

"What can I do, BJ?" Murphy yelled over the wind and engine noise.

"Press hard on this dressing, Murph," BJ shouted back over his shoulder, "so I can tie this thing around her."

Murphy stepped over Donna and put both hands down on the large bandage, covering BJ's hands.

"Okay, now," Murphy yelled, trying to steady himself against the rolling of the chopper.

BJ slipped his hands off the dressing, letting Murphy hold the pressure on the wound. BJ ran his arm around Donna's back inside the flight suit, grasping the long gauge tail on one side of the field dressing. He pulled the tail out around her tiny body and tied it to the one on the other side of the dressing, pulling them tight to keep air from entering the wound, in case her lung had been penetrated, creating a sucking chest wound. The thick bandage was already starting to fill with blood. Donna was so tiny, she couldn't have that much blood to spare.

As he tied the dressing tails together, his hands were shaking so hard he thought he wouldn't be able to tie the ends. She would die because he couldn't get a grip on himself! No, one of the others would do it for him. He paused for a second, then tied the tails in a square knot that held fast. He grabbed another dressing and tore it open, placing it over the first.

Up front, Cox was flying for their lives. He had the ship red-lined, ignoring all sane operating standards. If they crashed, it wouldn't matter if the engine was stressed. His only thought now was to get the crippled ship over friendly forces. After a few minutes, he backed the throttle off a bit and resumed level flight again. A more detailed scan of the instruments showed that the Nighthawk was chewed up, but not falling apart.

"How is she?" Cox screamed over his shoulder.

Murphy pulled down the intercom handset and pressed the talk button.

"She's hit bad. In the chest. We got her bandaged, but she needs help quick!"

"On the way," Cox answered. "There's morphine in one of these other first-aid kits. The crew chief knows which one!"

"She's out cold," Murphy said, looking down at the tiny aviator, "besides, no morphine with a chest wound."

Cox only nodded and concentrated on his flying. If nothing else happened, he would get her to the evac hospital. She would be okay. She had to be okay. These fuckin' LRRPs, they attracted metal like a fuckin' magnet! Red lights winked at him all across the instrument panel.

★22★

The launcher loomed up like a prehistoric metal beast. Harlan thought for a second that it would run right over the BTRs, but at the last moment it halted. An officer of the RVSN, the Raketnye Voiska Strategicheskogo Naznacheniya, the Strategic Rocket Forces, jumped down from the left rear door and stomped up to Harlan. The long intercom cord from his black canvas tanker's helmet flailed around his black coveralls like a snake. Four stars on the olive-colored shoulder boards identified him as a captain. The young officer was clearly upset by this delay.

"What the hell are you doing?" he shouted at Harlan. "Are you insane? You have no authority to stop Rocket Troops!"

Harlan, in the uniform of a captain of Internal Troops, stood his ground placidly. "Perhaps not, comrade," he replied calmly, "But we are increasing our security in this area due to attacks by renegades. Your identification?"

"I do not need identification, you idiot. Move your vehicles, you are occupying my site, do you understand?"

"No, I do not understand, comrade, what site is that?"

"This site, this place, is a launching site for these weapons!" the young captain hissed, pointing to the open area behind Harlan. "Move your vehicles at once."

Harlan just stood there and looked at the red-faced Russian for a second. This was a stroke of luck, certainly. The trick now was how to exploit it best. Harlan wreathed his face in a smile.

"Of course, comrade, immediately." Harlan turned and motioned the BTRs back off the road.

"My men and I will be happy to provide security for your position, Captain. As I said, there are reports of renegades in the area."

"I do not need your protection, Captain," the RSVN officer answered haughtily, then paused and asked quietly, "What reports of renegades?"

Take the hook, sucker, Harlan thought.

"There are reports of attacks on supply convoys by a group of renegade soldiers. As yet, we do not know the location or strength of the gang, but we are searching for them."

When the BTRs were off the road, the lead launcher/transporter lurched forward. The two men stood aside as the enormous MAZ-543 eight-wheeled transporter rolled through the roadblock. The rocket captain seemed lost in thought.

Probably thinking how long he would have to rot in a Gulag if he lost these Scuds to a bunch of renegades, Harlan thought, maybe he'll get to find out.

"Perhaps you can be of assistance, Captain," the rocket captain said brightly, "my armored escorts were drawn off to reinforce the front. You can take their place."

"Exactly so, comrade," Harlan answered, saluting the captain, who halted the MT-LB and climbed aboard.

The second launcher brought up the rear. Harlan looked for the trucks bearing the reload missiles for the launchers, but there were no other vehicles. The reloads must be waiting at the next firing position. The launchers would "shoot and scoot," firing their missiles and immediately moving to the next launching site to avoid any counterfire from the enemy.

Fuck the reloads, Harlan thought as the second launcher rolled past, they're not worth much without the launcher.

As the two rocket vehicles passed the BTRs, Ikehara pulled one of the BTRs back across the road. The other BTR stopped as Harlan held his hand up and walked over to the machine.

"Teddy, take your BTR over the crest of the rise and turn it around so you're hull down on us. We're going to give these guys a surprise. Fire when I do, concentrate on the MT-LB."

"Exactly so, Comrade Captain." Tedder grinned, then slid down into the personnel carrier.

Harlan looked down at the two missile launchers as they turned off and backed across the road, parking near the tree line. The MT-LB command vehicle moved forward across the road from the launchers and parked near the trees on that side. As the vehicles stopped, crewmen leaped from the side doors of the launchers and began to set up. It would take only a few minutes to ready the missiles for launch.

Tedder gunned the BTR's engine and chugged over the slight rise. A minute later, the small turret of the BTR popped up over the rise for a moment, then slid back down out of sight. Tedder had picked a fairly level spot off to one side of the road. He had good protection and could easily cover the other BTR's withdrawal.

Harlan walked across the road to where Ikehara was standing next to his vehicle.

"Could you see it, Comrade Captain?" Ikehara asked as Harlan walked up.

"What?" Harlan asked, confused.

"I thought for sure you'd be able to see my hard-on from across the road." Ikehara was beaming.

"They are a prize, Ike," Harlan answered, an infectious grin breaking out on his face, too. "Let's let them get set up good then we'll jump 'em."

"Roger that."

Ikehara climbed back into the BTR and Harlan could see him inside checking the AT-7 launcher. There were eight more AT-7 rockets inside, more than enough to handle three nearly defenseless vehicles.

Harlan walked around to the far side of the BTR and entered through the side door. Once inside, he stepped up into the turret and unlocked the 14.5mm gun. There were one hundred rounds in the ammo tray, armor-piercing incendiary. Ikehara had moved over by the open side door. The AT-7 was resting across his legs. In the rear of the BTR, Nolan sat watching the rocket troops through the vision block.

"We'll give them ten minutes to get busy, Ike," Harlan said, dropping out of the turret to sit across from the grinning Hawaiian, "then we'll jump them. I sent Teddy and the rest over the rise to cover us. Trade places with Nolan so you can pop up out of the rear hatches. Use the AT-7 on the MT-LB. I don't want them calling for help. Walt, get up front and start 'er up when I yell."

Nolan slid quickly by and climbed into the driver's seat. Ikehara moved the AT-7 launcher to the rear of the troop compartment and slowly opened the two large roof hatches. This done, he casually stood up in one of the hatches and lit a cigarette.

Harlan dismounted and walked slowly up the rise. At the top of the rise, Anderson was lying in a clump of grass, watching. Tedder was standing in the open turret hatch of the BTR.

"Teddy, when you hear us shoot, move up and cover us."

"Got it," Tedder answered, the excitement clearly audible in his voice. Harlan never ceased to be amazed by how much his people enjoyed their work. Even here, behind enemy lines with no support, they were itching to get on with it. God bless SF, he thought as he walked nonchalantly back down to his own BTR.

The rocket crew had sited their machines by the time Harlan got back to the personnel carrier. The missile on the far launcher was starting its elevation sequence, rising slowly from the carrying position to the upright firing position. The rear doors of the MT-LB opened and two men came out carrying a small package. They moved away from the vehicle, then knelt down to work on the device. One of them set up a tripod-mounted instrument that looked like a surveyor's transit. In a few seconds, a large balloon swelled full and the two men released it. It drifted high up over the trees trailing a small box at the end of a tether. The officer began tracing it with the instrument.

"Weather balloon, Captain," Nolan called softly as Harlan walked up. "This looks like a fire mission to me!"

Harlan entered through the side door and immediately stood up in the turret.

"Fire this mother up, Walt, but wait for my order to move out."

"Roger that," Nolan answered as he started up the engine of the BTR. Harlan unlocked the turret and slowly swung it around toward the launchers, keeping the gun at maximum elevation. He hoped it would look as though he was scanning the sky for aircraft. Even if it didn't, it wouldn't matter in a few seconds. When the gun was in line with the launcher, Harlan stooped down and called to Ikehara.

"Ready, Ike?"

The Hawaiian was crouched in the center of the personnel carrier, the AT-7 cradled in his arms. He turned to Harlan and gave a thumbs-up.

Harlan stood up in the turret and grasped the trigger of the 14.5mm. He took a deep breath, let it out, then yelled, "Fire!"

* * *

One damn delay after another, Igor T'sinko thought as he sat in the open rear door of the MT-LB and watched the two launchers slowly back into position. First, it was an air raid on that railhead. Then a tank column that went on forever, and, finally, those moron Internal Troops parked on his launch site! If he got these missiles ready for firing by 16.00, it would be a miracle. With any luck, the firing order would be delayed as had everything else. T'sinko stood and walked slowly across the open space toward the lead launcher. Already, the launch crew was lowering the support jacks at the rear of the launcher. Leveling of the vehicle would take five or ten minutes, then they could initiate the launch sequence and wait for the firing order.

I suppose I should not complain, T'sinko thought as he watched his crews at work. It could be a lot worse, I could be with that bunch of Spetsnaz animals that my brother has to serve with.

T'sinko had wondered many times in the last few days where his brother might be. The family had not heard from him in weeks. Maybe he was still in Central America. That would be best, the war would be less likely to touch him there.

T'sinko walked over to the *yfreitor* (senior private), who was checking the launch controls.

"Is everything in readiness, *Yfreitor*?"

"Yes, Comrade Captain," the young technician answered, "I am calibrating now."

The corporal's voice was tight with nervousness. It was good to be in the rocket troops in peacetime. The pay was better and the privileges greater. In wartime, the danger was extreme, and the job repellent. T'sinko chose to ignore the moral implications of his weapons. His job was just to get them up, though where they came down, and what they destroyed, was the enemy's problem.

The sound of an engine caught T'sinko's attention. On the rise at the edge of the clearing, one of the Internal Troops's BTRs was leaving. The other was parked across the road. T'sinko hoped the one on the road would follow the other. Internal Troops always made him nervous. It was common knowledge that the worst Central Asians were regularly drafted into MVD units because they were known for their obedience, stupidity, and cruelty. They did everything they were told without thinking. They would kill the enemy, prisoners, or disobedient Soviet troops with the same great pleasure.

Let those two BTRs go and chase renegades, T'sinko thought, and get their noses out of my ass.

"Comrade Captain," the *yfreitor* called, "we are ready to initiate firing procedures."

T'sinko looked over at the second launcher. Its crew was still lowering the jacks, but it would be ready, too, within minutes.

"Begin elevation, but hold for firing orders, *Yfreitor*."

"It is done, Comrade Captain."

Perhaps they would be ready in time, after all.

A puff of smoke from the BTR on the road caught his eye.

"What the hell are those Mongol mongrels up to now?" T'sinko said aloud as he turned. He watched disbelieving as a missile streaked from the BTR and slammed into the MT-LB. The doomed vehicle jerked under the impact and disappeared in a large cloud of black smoke. It took T'sinko a second to realize he was under attack.

As he stood transfixed, the 14.5mm stuttered from the turret of the BTR. T'sinko turned as red fireballs raced past, ripping into the launcher. The slugs, each as large as a thumb, walked up in a jagged line toward the elevated missile. The *yfreitor* grabbed T'sinko, pushing on the stunned officer.

"Get down, Comrade Captain," the young corporal screamed, "get . . ."

The world suddenly went a bright orange and fire swept over the crew of the SS-1C and its amazed officer.

Harlan dropped the barrel of the 14.5mm and centered the sight on the base of the SCUD missile that was now nearly vertical. He fired, the blast from the 14.5mm ringing inside the BTR. Before the first red tracers even reached the launcher, Harlan heard the *whoomp* of the AT-7 and saw the missile slam into the MT-LB. He concentrated on the SCUD directing one short burst after another at the thin missile.

The MT-LB erupted into a cloud of black smoke as the Saxhorn missile went home. Ikehara had connected with the vehicle dead center on the side, just behind the engine. Smoke poured from every hatch. There would be no calls for help from it.

Harlan forced himself to ignore everything but the launcher. He was dimly aware of figures scurrying around the launcher, ignored the pinging of their rifle shots on the side of the BTR. Finally, a tracer round found what Harlan was looking for. The fuel tanks erupted in a ball of fire that consumed the missile, the launcher, and everyone within fifty meters of it. The ball of black-tinged flame rose over the launcher site, a boiling pillar of fire.

The crew of the second launcher was running now. They were trying to get the second launcher started and out of there, but they were wasting their time. The launcher, poised for firing, had its jacks down and the engine off. It was a sitting duck for the Kreuzadder's guns. In the back of the BTR, Ikehara had traded his AT-7 for a Dragunov SVD sniper rifle and was standing up in the open roof hatch, picking off crewmen from the launchers. Harlan was lining up the 14.5mm on the second SCUD when a stream of red tracers streaked by and slammed into the cab of the launcher. Tedder was firing, too. Harlan laid his sights on the control compartment in the center of the vehicle. He poured three long bursts into the missile control center, then pulled the gun up to hit the missile itself. Tedder had the same idea, and bursts from his gun were working their way back along the launcher and up onto the missile. The remaining rocket crewmen fought back in earnest now. Harlan heard a steady pinging of rifle slugs on the metal skin of the BTR. He suddenly felt very exposed and stuck his head down inside the BTR.

"Hit it, Nolan! Get us out of here!"

Nolan slammed the BTR into gear and whipped it around on the road. Harlan slewed the turret around and found himself aiming at the top of Ikehara's head. The Hawaiian was still firing at the remaining SCUD crewmen.

"Get down, Ike!" Harlan screamed from the turret. "Drop! Get down!"

Ikehara, intent on sniping Russians, seemed not to hear. Harlan, pumped up and as excited as Ikehara, fired a burst right over the sergeant's head. That got his attention. He fell into the BTR so fast Harlan wondered if he had been hit.

"God damn it, blow my head off, why don't you?" Ikehara screamed. He turned the handle on a rear side firing port and shoved the snout of the SVD out, firing as best he could from the narrow port.

Harlan went back to work on the missile. The launcher was smoking from both the cab and the control area, and Harlan couldn't understand why it had not blown up. As he fired another burst at the SCUD, his curiosity was satisfied. The launcher seemed to rear up like some reptilian bronco and disappeared in a ball of flame identical to the one that its companion had produced. It stood on its tail for a moment, then crashed down out of the depths of the fireball that leaped again into the sky. Most of the defenders disappeared in the wall of flame that raced along the ground on either side of the launcher. The ones not burned alive were easy prey for the 7.62mm machine guns of the BTRs. In less than two minutes, it was all over. Both SCUD launchers burned like bonfires and the MT-LB poured black smoke into the sky in a column that rose hundreds of feet.

Pain was T'sinko's whole world. He could not think about anything else. He could barely move. The blast from the first launcher had wreathed him in flame. The tank coveralls had been nearly burnt off him. His head, uncovered, was burned all over. He had inhaled some of the fire, now the pain was as fierce inside his throat as on his smoldering head.

Bastards, how could they? Renegades! They were the renegades!

T'sinko gasped for breath. The fire in his throat caused it to swell, to cut off his air. T'sinko tried to scream, but could not force the sound out. He lay writhing on the cold ground, slowly joining his crews in death.

As Harlan's BTR crested the rise, Tedder poured one last long burst from his 7.62mm into the dead launchers and backed down from the rise.

Opening the hatch above him, Harlan shouted across to Tedder.

"Teddy, get that thing turned around. Let's get out of here!"

Tedder, wild-eyed and feral-looking, only nodded and spoke down into his vehicle.

Harlan called down to Nolan in the driver's seat.

"Wait, let's put some distance between us and those crispy critters, head north up this road until we find one going west. I want to be far away from here by dark!"

Nolan gave a quick thumbs-up and gunned the BTR down the road with Tedder in hot pursuit. Ikehara's round face appeared in the turret, split by a smile that was scary to look at.

"Suck on that, Atomic Bitch!" he screamed. "AAAAOOOOOOWWWWW!!"

★ 23 ★

The sudden, staccato honking of the air-raid warning siren
scared Caporal-Chef Henri Bouchet half out of his skin. This
time, he did not hesitate. He dropped the hose and ran for the
makeshift air-raid shelter. The last raid on Liege-Bierset had made
a believer out of him. He had been outside when the MiG-27s
had come over, dropping gravity bombs that blew deep holes
in the runway and completely destroyed the remaining maintenance hangar. He had listened to shrapnel whining overhead as
he hugged the earth. Now, he ran with all his might toward one
of the covered trenches that served as a makeshift bomb shelter.
He would not be caught out again.

What is wrong with the antiaircraft gunners, Bouchet wondered as he ran. Why haven't they launched? Their launchers
were not even turning toward the raiders.

Missile attack! Bouchet realized as he dove through the door
of the shelter, another chemical attack! Inside the dark shelter,
Bouchet pulled open the mask case and quickly donned the
rubber mask. He had lived in the mask for the first three days
of the war, while his unit had decontaminated the base. Now it
looked like he would be stuck in it again. The others in the
shelter, seeing Bouchet's mask in the dim red glow of the emergency light, did the same. The airmen and mechanics had learned
the hard way to heed the warnings and advice of the decontamination troops.

"At least we won't have to wait long in here," Bouchet said

to the others slipping on their masks, "if it's missiles, they will be here . . ."

The opening slit of the shelter blossomed in a light so bright that it seemed to shine right through the twenty-four people in the shelter. Heads jerked convulsively, trying to keep their eyes from the searing white light. A scream was cut short by the fist of Shiva slamming through the top of the shelter.

In the space of a blink, the trench and its twenty-four occupants were ripped open and vaporized. A new sun burned 1500 meters above them, cremating the people, the buildings, and the dozens of vehicles and aircraft parked on the airfield. The fireball lasted only seconds, but that was much longer than the men and women of the Belgian Air Force at Liege-Bierset lasted. They died instantly when the fireball skimmed the earth over the main runway.

The force of the blast destroyed everything within the base perimeter except for the heavier concrete structures. Even these were seriously damaged, their occupants killed by the overpressure that burst heads and hearts.

The metal hangars and brick office buildings, already blasted by the fuel-air explosive attack on day one, blew away like card houses. Flaming debris, backed up by the awful heat of the explosion, set fire to the trees and brush that ringed the base. The fuel depot blazed brightly, sending a finger of flame up to light the tall, thin mushroom cloud forming over the base.

It could be worse, Sergeant Feliks Umrov thought as he turned his collar up against the cold wind caused by the forward motion of the car, it could be raining. The wind flapped the fur collars of his field coat against his face, stinging his face. The little battery-powered railcar hummed along the track silently. It would take another forty minutes to reach the next stop at Oebisfelde. They would take a rest there, get some hot tea, thaw their frozen backsides and faces. Another squad would take the car back to Gardelegen when the track was clear. At least the enemy's air attacks had stopped. The antiaircraft belts along the front had been very effective in keeping the bombers at bay. The few air attacks in this sector had been easily repaired with the prepositioned repair materials, the trains moving again in a few hours. The engineers . . .

Private Putalin grabbed Umrov's sleeve. "There, Comrade Sergeant, look!"

Twenty meters away, a man, barely visible in the dim moon-
light, was moving away from the tracks, into the brush. The
outline of a rifle showed on his left shoulder. Saboteur!

Umrov jerked the throttle control back, stopping the electric
car with a lurch.

Why were they so slow to acknowledge? Mitchell wondered
as he stowed the antenna in its carrying bag and hoisted the
heavy rucksack onto his back. I hate to wait around after I transmit. That's when you get caught, waiting around.

He had just started walking back to the team's OP when he
heard the shout. In Russian. Behind him. Mitchell ran or tried
to run with the pack pulling him down with each step. He
couldn't drop it, the DMDG was in it. Stay away from the team,
he thought as he fought his way through the brush.

The voice shouted again. The heavy pack seemed to push
him, then he fell. His mind was still alert, but his body was no
longer under his control. The ground came up. As he fell, he
could see his arms fly up over his head. Why were they doing
that? He tried to catch himself, but nothing would cooperate.
The ground hit him in the face and everything disappeared.

"Oh, shit," Paul Cohen hissed under his breath. Moving
down the rail was an open car of some sort. On it were maybe
half a dozen men. Cohen ducked slowly down behind the shrub
and reached out to touch Thompson, next to him.

"Thompson," Cohen hissed, "contact right!"

Thompson glanced at the car, then alerted the other three
Green Berets. They watched silently as the car passed, whispering down the rails. No one moved or spoke. In the car, the thin
whip of an antenna stuck up out of the crowd. The men had
rifles cradled in their laps or held upright between their knees.
Railway Troops, patrolling the line.

As the car passed, Ben McCullough wondered what was keeping Mitchell. The commo man had been gone too long already.
They needed to cross the rail line and start circling back to their
target. McCullough was lost in thought when the Russian
shouted.

"*Stoi strelyat budu!*—Halt or I will fire!" Umrov shouted at
the retreating figure. He jumped down to the ground and ran

after the saboteur. The squad was now clambering down off the car, running behind Umrov in a jagged line.

The figure darted to one side, running clumsily under the weight of a huge pack. Umrov brought his rifle up, looking over the sights in the darkness, centering them on the running figure. *"Stoi!"* He shouted again, then pulled the trigger. The four shots sounded like cannon fire in the dark. The orange flash from the muzzle left a blue circle in the center of his vision. He could no longer see the running man, but could not tell whether he had hit the man or just could not see him in the blue spot. The rest of the squad came up behind him.

"Putalin, take Lobanov and go around that way," Umrov ordered the private, pointing to the left. "The rest of you come with me."

As the two privates made their way off to the right, Umrov and the remaining squad members formed a short assault line and began walking through the brush where the saboteur had disappeared. On the right was open space, they would see him if he ran that way.

A saboteur, what a prize! Umrov thought, the major will be very pleased. Perhaps pleased enough to let someone else ride the security car and freeze to death.

Instinctively, the team moved on line facing the sound and began to move toward the commotion. The Railway Troops had spotted Mitchell.

McCullough could not see Mitchell running through the brush, his rucksack bouncing heavily on his back. Off to the right, a Soviet soldier broke through the brush and shouted for Mitchell to halt, then fired a burst at the fleeing figure. Mitchell went down like a tree. Malle had his rifle up, but McCullough put his hand out to stop the big weapons man from firing. They needed to get them all, not just one. In seconds that seemed like hours, the rest of the Soviet squad appeared. The shooter, apparently the leader, split the squad into two groups. As the split pair moved off, the others went on line and began to advance on Mitchell's body.

McCullough pulled Malle close to him and whispered, "Go around to the right and get behind them. Don't let any of them get back in that car."

* * *

Private Yukashev tripped over the body. The man had run only a few feet after Umrov fired. Now he lay facedown, his hands above his head, the rifle a few meters away.

"Yukashev, is he dead?" Umrov asked as the squad gathered around the still form.

Yukashev prodded the body with his rifle barrel. There was no movement, no sound. "Yes, Comrade Sergeant, I think so," Yukashev answered.

"Take off his equipment," Umrov ordered the squad, "make certain none of it 'disappears.' The major will want to see all of . . ."

Noise erupted from the left side. Putalin had found another saboteur! This would be a . . .

The storm of bullets ripped through the squad before they could even react. The grenade that followed the fusillade was unnecessary, it only added a final note to the lethal fanfare of revenge.

The Soviets were very near the spot Mitchell had gone down. One of them tripped and fell, crying out in surprise. The rest of the squad gathered around. They had found Mitchell. McCullough gave Malle another five-second count to get in position, then motioned the others to fire on his signal. He set the selector on his M16A2 to burst fire. Down the line, the other men waited.

McCullough nodded, then brought the rifle up to his shoulder and fired at the cluster of Russians still peering down at Mitchell's fallen form. He held the trigger down, then released it, pulled it again. The M16 roared and shimmied, a tongue of flame lighting up the brush in front of him. McCullough raked the muzzle back and forth across the small group of Soviets, pouring burst after burst into them.

The other Green Berets were firing now, too. Cohen shouted something at the dying Russians, but McCullough could not make out the words over the roar of his own weapon. The brush around the Russians jumped and danced, bits of leaves and branches snapping off from bullet strikes. The Russians writhed and fell, wracked by violent seizures brought on by the high-velocity metal. The ambush only took ten seconds, the time necessary to fire thirty rounds from an M16A2 rifle.

Putalin threw himself down on the cold ground as the torrent of firing broke out ahead. The squad had been ambushed! The saboteur had not been alone. Lobanov fell beside him, wide-eyed and terrified. Putalin had no desire to look for any more intruders. He pulled Lobanov by the shoulder and began to crawl back toward the car and the radio. If they could regain the safety of the car, they could perhaps get away and call for reinforcements. He prayed the terrorists had not captured the car.

He could see the outline of the car against the slightly lighter sky. No one moved around it. They were in luck. Perhaps the terrorists had run away after their cowardly attack. He and Lobanov had escaped, now they . . .

A few hundred bright flashes burst through Putalin's head, lighting the way for the pain that stabbed through his brain, seeking to burst out the front of his head. He heard Lobanov cry out, less from pain than fear. Then the bright flashes dimmed as Putalin blacked out.

He could hear them moving, scrabbling through the brush. They were crawling, scared and sloppy. Malle crouched on the cold ground . . . waiting. He drew his K-bar knife from its sheath, tied upside down to his combat vest. In a few seconds, the pair emerged from the brush, looking toward the car, seeking its relative safety.

Malle silently slid forward, tensing his muscles for the leap. The one Soviet looked up and began to rise. Malle sprung forward. In two fast steps, he was on the pair. He kicked the one rising in the back of the head with his boot, then fell on the other, twisting his head to one side and plunging the knife down into the hollow of the man's throat. The blade slid over the top of the Russian's sternum and sliced down toward his heart, cutting his aorta and piercing the windpipe. The Soviet began to thrash around, but Malle held him tight with one arm around his neck, choking the now mortally wounded soldier. Malle locked his legs around the man, trapping him. Flailing around on the ground, the two men looked like perverse lovers writhing in passion. Malle twisted the knife and jerked it free. The Russian grabbed at the blade, missed, and Malle plunged it down again at the Russian's chest. The heavy insulated field coat turned the blade. Malle stabbed again, harder. The knife bit into the coat, but did not penetrate more than an inch. The Russian finally began to fade both from the blood that filled up his chest and from the iron arm that choked off his air. Malle glanced over at the other Soviet. He was still out cold.

Lucky, Malle thought. If the other one had come around, this fight would have gone a lot different.

As he disengaged himself from the dying Russian, Malle used the unconscious soldier's scarf to tie his elbows behind him. As he cinched the scarf tight, the others came quietly up behind him.

"Jenkins!" Tucker's voice boomed through the white noise of several clattering computer printers working at once. "Jenkins! Call 'em off! The SACEUR's put out a FLASH message that, effective immediately, we are in a nuclear stand down. Send the recall to all ADM teams, immediately!"

"Jenna, honey, get on the horn to the base radio station and have them send code word REDLOSER followed by each team's specific recall code word to all the ADM teams!" Jinx said, flipping through the CEOI as he looked for the code words. "Have them broadcast the message at one-minute intervals. We want an acknowledgment from each team!"

Jenna reached for the secure telephone, then clutched at the edge of the table. Jinx heard her breath rasping again. She had recovered from the gassing, but she was still not right.

"Here, baby," Jinx said, taking the handset from her, "you take a break, I'll call the base station."

She looked up and smiled a wan little smile at him. "Thanks, Jinx. Sorry."

"No problem."

Jinx made the call.

Jenna worked her way through the CEOI book, finding each separate team's specific response code word and posting it on the status board beside each team's designation. If the teams were still alive, they would acknowledge as soon as they could after receiving the message. They were in luck, as most were in a time window where they would be monitoring their radios. Along with the acknowledgment would come a sitrep. The team would stay in place until further orders, monitoring the target and reporting any targets of opportunity. She would check off each team as the acknowledgment came in from the base station.

Jinx's fear was that a team had their device in place and would not be able to retrieve it.

An hour passed, then two. The fax, linked to the base station, suddenly peeped and began printing out the first acknowledgment from a team. In two more hours, all the teams had reported in, all but one—032A. Jinx called the base station and told them to transmit only with the code for 032A.

By 2030 that night, it was obvious that 032A was not in contact. The team had not indicated any trouble in its last transmission. Still, they could have been bagged before they could get off a message. Many teams simply disappeared after their insertion. Company G, the III Corps' LRRPs, had lost nearly a fourth of its teams. The 10th SF Group had lost several, as well. This ADM team might just be hiding or running. That was Jinx's hope, but not his fear. Regardless, the word had been sent up through the chain of command that only 032A had not responded.

"Sir, the CO wants to see you," said Jenna from the door.

Jinx walked into his commander's office and took the offered chair as Tucker hung up the phone.

"Needless to say, the folks at NORTHAG, and on up, are somewhat concerned about the nonreporting ADM team," Tucker began without preamble. "NORTHAG C2 has directed III Corps to release a Company G element OPCON (Operational Control) to us. They're to be prepared to go in and find 032A and stop them by any means necessary. The 504th MI Brigade has been notified and Company G has been alerted. You've talked to those guys, call them now and let's get the ball rolling. I want you to handle this, but report back to me at every stage, especially if there's any new developments."

Jinx picked up the secure mobile subscriber phone and was patched into Company G's headquarters. He asked to speak to the operations officer.

"Captain Ranwanz, sir."

"Captain, this is Major Jenkins. I spoke to you the other day."

"Yes, sir, how you doin!"

"Not so good, Captain," Jinx answered. "We've got trouble in River City. I guess you've been alerted to our situation here. I need your help. Could you and your CO come over here ASAP? This is big."

"Yes, sir, we have been notified. We've got things started on this end. There's a lot of coordination needed yet, but the teams will be ready as soon as they're briefed."

"That's what we need you here for, so we can expedite the coordination process," said Jinx.

"Your friend, BJ Kirkley, is going to be the ground element leader on this, he'll be coming with us. We're on our way now, sir!"

"Thanks much, out here."

If there was a God, the lost ADM team would make contact. Unfortunately, God had not shown any interest in the conflict so far. He was about to send his friend into a no-win situation.

They would be looking for men who didn't want to be found and were happy to kill pursuers. The Soviets would be looking for all of them with hundreds of rear-area security troops. A LRRP team could get to the target just in time to be blown up by an atomic bomb. Even if they found the ADM team, the whole crew had to get out alive.

Killing the enemy was no problem. Killing your friends was a bitch. This was the part where war became hell.

★24★

"You okay, Malle?"

The big German was wet with blood all across the front of his load-bearing vest and Gortex jacket. The big wet spot glistened in the dim light.

"What?" Malle answered. "Yeah, sure." He saw the others looking at his blood-covered chest, ran a finger across his ammo pouches, and looked at the wet stain on his fingers. He looked up at McCullough and then pointed at the dead Soviet.

"This is all his, sir."

"Oh," McCullough answered, "of course. What's the story on this one?"

"He's out for now, but he's not hurt bad, I think," Malle replied, kneeling down and shaking the trussed Russian. "I rung his bell pretty good, though."

"Sir, we can't keep this guy," Cohen burst in. "We have a mission, remember?"

"Do we?" Taggart asked. "The radio is fucked."

He held the AN/PSC-3 up. Even in the darkness, the hole punched through the aluminum radio case by the 5.54mm round was easy to see. Taggart turned the radio around, showing the larger jagged hole where the bullet had exited, taking bits of circuit board with it.

"We can try it out if you want, sir, but it looks fucked to me."

The team stood silent for a moment, waiting for McCullough

to make the call. In the time-honored tradition, the captain bought some time.

"Let's get these guys off the right of way, move out of here, then we'll decide. Let's not all stand here in a cluster. Get some security out!"

"Sir, what do you want done with Mitchell and the stiffs?"

"Take all of Mitchell's CEOI and crypto materials, commo gear, and whatever else we need. Wrap him up in his IMPS. We'll take him with us." McCullough took off his field cap and wiped his forehead with his arm. "I don't care what you do with the Reds. Use your best judgment."

"What about this POW, sir," Cohen asked again insistently, his voice filled with mixed anger and anxiety.

"We'll take him," McCullough answered as he walked away. "He can carry Mitchell."

The Russian moaned and stirred on the ground. Cohen shot the captive a look that his team mates had not seen before from the medic. Cohen was the guy that always had a joke or a wise-crack, the team's morale NCO. He was looking now at the help-less railway soldier with eyes that bore no compassion, no humor.

"Come on, Paul," Thompson said, taking Cohen by the arm, "let's get the other Reds over here. Come on."

Cohen looked back at Thompson. His expression was odd, a thin smile under sharklike eyes.

"Yeah, great," Cohen said slowly, "I've got an idea for those guys!"

Fifteen minutes later, all the dead Russians had been dragged back to the electric car. Cohen placed each dead body back in the car, tying them in place with their rifle slings and belts. He placed each dead man's weapon between the corpse's lifeless knees and wedged the weapon so it would not fall out. In min-utes, the car was once again filled with Railway Troops, just as it had been when it first appeared.

"Now for the cherry on this sundae," Cohen said. He dragged the dead Soviet that Malle had stabbed to death over to the car. With surprising strength, Cohen picked up the body and hung it over the front of the little car. The dead man's head dangled face up over the front of the car, the bloody gash in his throat mim-icking his open mouth.

Cohen wedged the man's feet between the other bodies in the front seat so it would not fall off its peculiar perch.

Across the tracks, the rest of the team stood watching. None of them had seen this side of the medic and they were unsure what to do. One thing they were sure of, it was time to move it. Cohen stood back from the car for a second, admiring his handiwork, then reached in and yanked the throttle back, wedging it full open with a Soviet Army cap. The little car started slowly, gradually picking up speed as it moved away down the rail line.

As Cohen joined the team, he was beaming, an impish grin spread across his face.

"That'll give 'em something to talk about," he said brightly. "The Flying Dutchman of the Russian railroad!"

"Come on," McCullough said quickly, "move out."

With Malle walking point, the team made its way south, putting as much distance as possible between themselves and the railroad. Several kilometers south, they would turn northeast and approach the target. For now, though, they just needed to get away.

Cohen followed the Soviet soldier struggling under the load of Mitchell's body. When the Russian slowed or seemed to falter under the burden of Mitchell's corpse, Cohen jammed the man's kidneys with his rifle.

Two hours later, the team was nearly three kilometers away. The pace had been hard, but much time was lost in the cautious crossing of danger areas. The team took up a hide position in a small copse of trees on the edge of a large open field. Everyone was breathing hard, their breath snorting out in clouds of steam.

The Soviet soldier was worse off than the Americans, his load had been carried over one shoulder the entire way. He was gasping and sweat glistened on his face. He had been careful to set down the body with great care so as not to offend his captors. Now he sat panting a few feet away from his grisly burden. Cohen was behind the captive, propped up on his rucksack, his rifle muzzle trained on the exhausted man's back.

"Malle," Cohen hissed at the weapons man a few feet away, "you still got that Hushpuppy?"

Malle looked around and nodded, pointing to the outside pocket of his rucksack that held the silenced 9mm pistol. Without taking his eyes from the prisoner, Cohen scooted over and fished around in Malle's pack. When he had the pistol, he moved back, slinging his rifle over his shoulder, the muzzle of the pistol always pointed at the Soviet.

"Hey, Cohen," Thompson said softly, "I would love to be there to see the face of the poor *bahnhofmeister* that first gets a load of that car!'' The engineer broke into the theme of a popular movie.

"Who you gonna' call? *Poltergeistbusten!*"

Taggart, on the other side of Thompson, laughed in spite of himself. He was worried about Cohen. The macabre display now rolling the rails had disturbed him. Cohen had wasted a lot of precious time on that weird business. Taggart wondered if the strain was getting to the medic or if he was just pissed off about Mitchell's death. No one had really mentioned Mitchell since the firefight, even though they had his lifeless body right in front of them.

Maybe Cohen is the only one who is really dealing with it, Taggart thought, at least he's acting out his anger.

Taggart's musing was interrupted by the captain, who squatted down and set the damaged radio in front of him.

"Okay, here's the deal," McCullough began. "The radio's out. It may transmit, but it doesn't receive anything. The SOP says that if you do not have radio contact, you abort. We are one and a half klicks from the bridge, it's just over that little hill." The tall team leader looked from face to face.

"Sir, what's your point?" Taggart asked.

"Whether to go on with this mission," McCullough answered.

"You're asking us?" Taggart said. "Captain, this is your team. We do what you say."

"I know that," McCullough said, a trace of exasperation in his voice. "This is a bit different, though. We're talking about violating SOP and using a nuclear weapon on our initiative. That's heavy stuff."

"Sir, you're not even thinking about aborting, are you?" Cohen blurted. "I mean, we got the go on this! We been lugging the damn thing around all over hell and gone and now Mitchell's dead! We got to set the thing off!"

Even in the darkness, McCullough could see the wild look on Cohen's face. Since the shootout and Mitchell's death, the medic had been different. The business with the car had marked the change in the man. He was far more interested in killing now than in healing.

"Malle? Thompson? What's your vote?"

The two sergeants looked at each other. They were used to operating with a lot of independence and manipulating officers to get their way, but voting on whether to follow orders was something new.

Malle took the easy way out. "Whatever you wish to do, Captain," the big weapons man said quietly, "I will do what you say."

Thompson, the engineer, stared off in the distance for a moment. He looked at the captain and said firmly, "We need to do what we came here to do. We haven't heard any different, so we need to continue the mission."

"That goes for me, too, sir," Taggart chimed in.

McCullough looked at the four men. They were professionals, every one. Their advice was always good. On the other hand, Standard Operating Procedures were invented for a reason. It was a tough decision. What finally made his mind up for McCullough was the mental picture of hundreds of T-80 tanks driving through NATO lines, blunting the big counterattack, killing thousands of Americans. Tanks that came down Autobahn 188 or crossed the railway bridge over the autobahn. Tanks that would have been slowed or stopped by his device. That thought, more than anything else, made the call.

'Okay, let's do it. We'll stay here tonight, recon the target tomorrow, and set it off tomorrow night."

There were nods all around.

Suddenly Cohen and the prisoner were on their feet. The prisoner was running and Cohen was bringing up the muzzle of the pistol.

I can't believe the captain is trying to wimp out on this, Cohen thought as the officer started blathering about SOPs and atomic attack shit . . .

The slight movement of the Russian's shoulders stopped his mental grousing. The Russian shifted his hands down by his butt and leaned slightly forward.

He's going to run, Cohen thought and started to reach out and grab the man. No, Cohen thought, go ahead, Ivan, make my night!

The captain was saying something about the attack when the Russian made his move. He pitched sideways and rolled to his feet, breaking into a fast sprint as soon as his feet hit the ground.

Cohen was on his feet, too, twisting sideways, bringing the 9mm up into a combat stance, right arm out stiff, left arm bent, the big circle of the silencer covering the fleeing soldiers's back.

Cohen pulled the trigger as fast as the gun would shoot. With the silencer in place, there was no recoil and only a soft popping sound. One subsonic slug after another hit the running Russian, toppling him. After he hit the ground, Cohen fired three more times into the man. The Soviet soldier lay in a heap, his legs askew, one arm up over his face as if to shield it from the fusillade.

Cohen lowered the pistol and looked at the dead man. He felt the others watching him and turned his head to look at the team.

"He tried to run," was all the medic said as he handed the pistol back to Malle.

"We saw," Taggart said, his voice empty of any emotion. Taggart turned to the others. "Okay, let's bury Mitchell and that guy," he said, jerking his thumb toward the dead prisoner, "then we need to set up shop here."

The others did not reply, but simply went about their tasks without comment. Malle and Thompson produced entrenching tools and began to dig a grave on the edge of the clearing. Cohen came over and took Thompson's shovel.

"Here, I'll do it. You can spell me."

The medic dug in the hard ground like a man possessed. Even Malle eventually stopped digging to get out of Cohen's way. Cohen dug for an hour before he had a hole big enough to accommodate the two dead men. The three of them placed the Russian in the hole first, then Mitchell's gear, then Mitchell. The captain took one of Mitchell's ID tags and then they covered the dead men with dirt and carefully camouflaged the filled hole. The captain made a sketch of the site noting the landmarks. After writing down the grid coordinates, he dropped the sketch and ID tag into a small plastic bag.

"You guys recover this if I buy it, okay?"

They all nodded.

"Anybody know anything to say?" Thompson asked.

"Nope."

"Huh-uh."

"Not really."

The four enlisted men looked at McCullough.

Looks like I'm on, McCullough thought as he stepped over to the new grave.

"Our Father, who art in heaven, hallowed be thy name . . ."

* * *

One thing for sure, Jinx thought, the LRRPs will need some serious firepower to take with them, or they won't have a prayer.

"Jenna!" Jinx shouted down the hall. "Get in here, I got a mission for you."

The blond Specialist 4 appeared in the doorway a moment later.

"What do you need?" she asked skeptically. She had been noticeably less perky after her experience with Soviet nerve gas.

"I need a handful of SAWs—squad automatic weapons—and some M203s," Jinx answered, sitting on the edge of the desk. "Got any idea where we can get some?"

"Yep, the 93d Evac Hospital just down the road," she answered immediately. "They'd be happy to get rid of 'em. The things pile up there from wounded brought in. The medics have had a couple of people shot by accident trying to clear the weapons."

"How do you know all this?" Jinx asked, surprised at her quick response.

"I like medics," she answered slyly. "They're young and they're usually clean. I'll need an officer to go with me though, they won't give a bunch of weapons to a Spec. 4."

"Take Captain Haskell with you."

"Roger that. Be right back."

With that she spun out the door and down the hall. Jinx heard her corral the hapless captain on her way.

The coordination visit with Company G's CO and ops officer had gone well. Jinx and BJ had greeted each other like long-lost brothers, but the rest of the meeting had been slightly awkward for them both. Jinx played the "echelons above God" staff officer as he outlined the mission and BJ forced himself into the position of "just another snake-eating grunt" reluctantly being briefed in matters far out of his depth.

As the visitors were leaving and BJ said with a laugh, "We'll kick some more Russian ass like we did at Hood," it dawned on the two Company G captains who Major Richard Jenkins was.

Jenna was back in two hours. Over each shoulder, she carried two M16s with M203 grenade launchers attached. Behind her, Haskell staggered under the weight of four M249 squad automatic weapons.

"Here you go, Jinx!" Jenna said breathlessly, dropping the weapons on the desk. "The ammo's outside in the jeep."

"I had to sign my life away for these things," Haskell moaned as he let the light machine guns slide to the floor.

Jenna promptly kicked him in the shin, eliciting a yelp. She glared at the young captain, then shot a glance at Jinx.

"He told me we could get 'em easy if I would give their S4 a blowjob!" she snarled.

"I didn't *order* you to!" the wounded captain whined. "It was just a suggestion." Jenna kicked his other shin, bringing forth another howl.

"That's enough, Jenna," Jinx said quickly, "don't hurt him. You guys did real good." Jinx picked up one of the 40mm grenade launchers. "These things may save a friend of mine's hide," Jinx said, his voice filled with things unsaid, "and mine, too."

The serious tone of Jinx's voice stopped the battling Bickersons in mid-wrangle. With a flurry of "sure thing"'s and "no problem"'s, they left Jinx to his dilemma.

★ 25 ★

"Ain't that some shit?" Nolan said as he and Ikehara watched the lopsided battle unfolding below them. Ikehara grinned in reply.

In the wide draw between the two low hills, the Soviet supply point was being pounded by a T-80 and a 2S6 approaching from the west. The attackers were supported by two small groups of infantry who were laying down very organized suppressive fire while their armored comrades closed with the beleaguered support troops.

"Wonder who these guys are," Nolan asked, "to be scabbing our jobs?"

"Recruits, my man, recruits," Ikehara answered, sliding backward down the rise. "Stay here and watch 'em, I'm going to move up the team."

Mamud winced as his tank's gun roared again. The BMP 200 meters away jumped up like a shot rabbit and a cloud of black smoke blossomed on the front slope of the personnel carrier. The BMP slumped back down and burst into flames.

"*Allahu akbar!*" came the cry from the troops riding on the T-80. Mamud wished they could have saved the BMP. It would have been useful, but at least they had captured another tank intact. The surprised T-72 crew lay dead where the guns of the riflemen had caught them running for their tank.

The fire from the infidel support troops was slackening, now, as the 2S6 pounded their positions, its four 30mm guns plowing the earth, digging the Soviet bastards out like rats from a sewer trench. Now they would have some supplies and fuel, and maybe a Russian or two for sport.

"What's up, Ike?" Harlan asked.

"Looks like a bunch of renegade Soviets jumping a supply point to me, Comrade Sir." Ikehara grinned.

"Hot damn!" Harlan laughed. "Let's give 'em a hand!"

On the horizon, the thick column of black smoke pointed like a finger to the burning track.

"Gorkiy Leader, there, on the right, smoke!"

"I see it, Three-Eight."

The pilots of the two Mi-27 "Super Hinds" banked right, opened their throttles, and aimed the noses of their helicopters on the column of black smoke. The big camouflaged gunships were responding to a plea for help from the material support battalion.

Even in the rear areas, this was not the first time they had been called to assist in repelling a ground attack, but this one was different. The attackers were in Soviet vehicles! The Mi-27s would close in less than a minute.

The firing from the defenders was slacking now. Mamud's riflemen were still raking the few remaining positions, keeping the infidels' heads down while they closed the remaining hundred meters. The 2S6 had stopped, its 30mm guns quiet. Ali was saving the big guns, using his RPK-74 machine gun to rake the remaining Russians.

How easy! Mamud thought. His cheer was doused by the sudden noise of rotors and the flash of two combat helicopters overhead. Damn!

As the big helicopters swept over, the remaining defenders now took heart and began firing with fresh enthusiasm, thinking the tables had suddenly turned.

"Gorkiy Leader," the headphones crackled, "I see only our troops, Comrade Captain, where are the attackers?"

"I do not know, but someone has attacked them," the pilot answered. "There are dead everywhere and a BMP on fire. Break left and make another pass."

"Just so."

* * *

Harlan's BTR was nearly at the crest of the rise when the Hind flashed overhead, turning.

"Holy shit!" he yelled. "Get on 'em! Shoot!" Harlan unlocked the 14.5mm turret and swung it around. The slope hid the Kreuzadders from the Hinds, but only for a second.

The Mi-27s had not fired on the first pass, too close to tell friend from foe. Now they both turned to the left for another pass. Their 57mm rockets and twin 23mm guns would rip Mamud's tiny force to shreds if they were not destroyed quickly.

Ali was already tracking the lead helicopter, seeking the Mi-27 visually. The gunship was nearly head-on when the 2S6 fired, its 30mm guns working like pistons on either side of the big boxy turret. Mamud focused his attention on the other gunship that was now coming around behind its mate.

"Gunner, engage helicopter left!" Mamud screamed down into the turret as he pulled his own 12.7mm gun around to engage the trailing Mi-27. He knew that the 12.7mm was useless against the heavy frontal armor of the Mi-27, but he would die trying, anyway.

In the turret, Talat punched the automatic loader and slammed one of the special high-explosive fragmentation antiaircraft rounds into the gun's breech. He attempted to track the helicopter, but it was too fast, too close. He fired anyway . . . and missed.

"Three-Eight, there is the enemy!" the pilot shouted. "The T-80 and the 2S6. Engage!"

"Engaging the 2S6," came the reply from the pilot of Gorkiy 38.

As his Mi-27 spun to the left, the gunner flipped the arming switches for the missiles and rocket pods on both wings. He would let the T-80 taste a dozen 57mm rockets while he locked an AT-6 missile onto it. The AT-6 would take the tank apart like a toy. Then he would deal with the 2S6, if it was still there after 38 got through with it.

In the 2S6, Ali clung to the hatch's rim, firing at the Mi-27 on the left with his RPK-74 as the turret slewed around, tracking the Hind on the right. A second later, the 30mm guns roared, their tracers arching out, each round coming closer to the turning

Mi-27. The big helicopter was almost head-on when the first tracer hit just above the cockpit. A missile exploded from the starboard rail, inbound at supersonic speed. Before he could react, the Mi-27 was hit by more of the 30mm shells. It jerked to the right, causing the AT-6 missile to streak overhead out of control, exploding behind the 2S6. The gunship continued unsteadily forward for a second, then plunged to the ground, slamming in on its right side.

"The other!" Mamud screamed as he fired again at the remaining gunship as it came back around. "The other!"

Harlan's BTR was at the crest of the small hill when the Hind loomed up and swept over in front of him. The angle hid him from the Hind's crew, but Harlan wasn't concerned about hiding. The Hinds were attacking his recruits!

"Stop, Nolan!" he screamed down at the driver. Harlan slewed the 14.5mm down and held the trigger back. The red fireballs arced out after the Hind, seeking the unarmored side doors. Like a gardener with a firehose, Harlan directed the stream of tracers at the Hind. In half a second, the stream swept across the back of the attacking helicopter. Harlan held the Hind in his sights, pouring the heavy machine-gun rounds into the machine.

The cursed machine was almost on them and Mamud's gun was out of ammunition. More was stored in boxes on the turret's side, at his fingertips, but he would not have time to reload before the helicopter destroyed them.

"Talat!" Mamud screamed into the intercom. "Shoot, shoot."

In the turret, Talat was struggling to feed another antiaircraft round into the loader. He might get a round off, but even then, it would be a snap shot. Allah would have to guide it for a hit.

Mamud saw the nose of the Mi-27 swing around and waited for the puffs of smoke from the rockets that would send him and Talat to the Kingdom of Martyrs. What he saw, instead, was a stream of red tracers streak up from the crest of the ridge. The tracers overtook the Mi-27 and clung to it like sparrows chasing a crow. The gunship twisted and swept up in a hard turn to return the deadly fire from their rear. So caught up in the duel was he that Mamud cried out in surprise when the tank's gun roared.

In the turret, Talat had succeeded in loading the antiaircraft round. He had tracked the twisting Hind, punched the laser rangefinder, and now had his shot. The 125mm proximity-fused round took less than a second to reach the Hind. Its warhead detonated twenty meters from the helicopter and caught it in a spray of tungsten steel flechettes each the length of a finger. The fingers of death ripped through the helicopter's crew, electrical, hydraulic, and fuel systems, killing them instantly. The flying tank fell like a dropped boxcar and burst into flames just below the slope of the ridge.

"Allahu akbar!" came the cry from the crew of the 2S6 and the riflemen. Allah had destroyed the helicopters and saved them from defeat. It was a sign from him to destroy the rest of the infidels. The infidels, in turn, realized they were doomed without further support and tried vainly to surrender. Mamud's Uzbeks did not offer them that alternative. They cut the Russians down like the dogs they were, saving not even one for interrogation or sport.

Harlan approached the supply point slowly, his gun pointed at the sky, not wanting to make any hostile moves or gestures to these people. He was after these guys' hearts and minds, after all.

One hundred meters from the supply point, Harlan stopped the BTR-80 and dismounted. He and Nolan walked slowly across the open ground toward the attacker's T-80. The commander of the T-80 slid over the reactive armor blocks, down the skirting plates on the tank's side, and stood waiting, his arms crossed over his chest. When Harlan was within ten meters, he stopped and gave the tank commander a badly deformed Soviet salute.

"Good day and congratulations on your victory over the Russian dogs," Harlan said in Russian heavily tinged with an Estonian accent, "I am Gregor Flack, formerly of the 488th Motorized Rifle Regiment, and now an enemy of the Soviet Oppressors!" He mentally crossed his fingers, this could be touchy.

Harlan waited for the man to react, sizing up the tank commander. The man was not tall, few Central Asian tankers were. He had a slight beard and mustache, but his main feature was a single eyebrow that covered both eyes, eyes that now measured Harlan with a cold questioning. His general appearance was that of a Central Asian, a Kazak or a Uzbek. That was good, Harlan's Estonian routine would be more likely to succeed with someone from so far away. Finally the man spoke, his voice harsh and flat.

"I am Mamud Tajidin, Commander, by the grace of Allah, of this band of Mujahiddin," the man said. "Thank you for helping destroy the helicopter."

"Your excellent gunner destroyed the *dristui*," Harlan said ingratiatingly, "we merely distracted him."

The two men regarded each other silently for what seemed like hours, but was only seconds. Mamud finally broke the silence.

"Please share in the supplies we have captured from these infidels. They will help you on the way to your destination."

Harlan took a few beats before answering.

"Thank you for your generous offer, but we are not bound for any destination. We merely seek to kill as many of the Russian bastards as possible for the enslavement they have forced on our homeland. We seek to join with others who bear the Russians some malice."

The Uzbek again regarded Harlan in silence, looking through him with a thousand-meter stare. Finally, the tank commander broke into a sly grin.

"Perhaps that would be possible," he said, his voice betraying no hint of emotion. "We will talk about that."

"Excellent," Harlan answered and stepped forward, his hand extended.

Mamud stepped up and shook the offered hand. As if the gesture had been a signal, the Moslem infantrymen all cried, *"Allahu akbar!"*

Harlan stepped back and smiled, then turned and gestured to the remaining two BTRs on the ridge.

So far, so good, Harlan thought to himself as the Mujahiddin crowded around him, so far so good.

Bodnya stood over his map. On it was a tracing paper overlay, and on the overlay, a series of small black triangles were drawn with a date and time.

The triangles represented attacks on Pact units that were not the result of enemy action, attacks that came from within. At least two of the attacks seemed to have been the work of the same bandit gang. The convoy driver who had survived the ambush and the security troops who had so unsuccessfully guarded the SS-1C launchers had described similar attackers. If both attacks were the work of one group, who were they? What was their motive for attacking? If they were just deserters, why did they not simply run? The overlay and a report on this new threat had been delivered in person by a colonel from the KGB Directorate in Potsdam. He had ordered Bodyna to redirect his pursuit efforts to terminate this totally unacceptable threat. Renegade Soviet soldiers could not be tolerated and must be stamped out immediately, by any means. Of course, word of the existence of renegades must not be allowed to spread and all rumors would be stamped out. The colonel had briefed Major Butakov, the *zampolit*, and Captain Yakushev, the Special Section officer, on exactly how to handle rumor mongers within the ranks.

Bodnya's musing was interrupted by Lieutenant Zimin, the communications officer.

"Comrade Commander, a report has come in from the 3rd Shock Army's chief of the rear. A supply point signaled that they were under attack," the young officer explained. He pointing to a spot on the map thirty kilometers to the northwest, "The supply point is here. A pair of Mi-27s responded to the call, but their report was confusing and they did not return to their base. There has been no contact with the supply point or the helicopters since 13.00."

"Who did the support troops say was attacking them?"

"Only that they were under attack by tanks and infantry. Then their radio went dead."

"What did the helicopters report?" Bodnya asked.

"They were talking nonsense, Comrade Commander."

"What did they say, exactly?" Bodnya said, trying to keep his exasperation from showing.

"They said they were attacking a T-80 and a 2S6."

"What else?"

"Nothing else, Comrade Commander. Security troops have been dispatched to the area. Their report will be relayed to us."

Bodnya stood silent for a moment, staring back at the map.

"Bring that to me immediately when it arrives. That will be all, Lieutenant."

"Yes, Comrade Commander."

As the young lieutenant left the room, Bodnya stood at the map, measuring distances with his commander's ruler. The spot where the supply point was attacked was in a line with the convoy attack and the missile site attack.

Three reports of Soviet units attacked by other Soviet troops, he thought, traitors, renegades in their own rear area. He now had authority to operate anywhere in the 3rd Shock Army's rear. The traitors would be brought to heel.

The ruse seemed to be working perfectly. After looting the supply point, the renegades had moved several kilometers away. Now, Harlan's men were partying with the Mujahaddin on some vodka found in one of the pillaged trucks. The Mujahaddin, all devout Moslems, were not drinking, but Nolan and Tedder were. All were regaling one another with the day's events. Mamud and Harlan were perched on the captured T-72, watching their troops in silence.

Nolan, trying to dance to a Uzbekian tune, had fallen down, and everyone was hooting at him.

"All soldiers are the same, eh, Mamud." Harlan laughed.

"I fear you are correct, Flack," Mamud answered, tripping over the guttural European name. "Even the soldiers of Allah are still flesh and blood."

"What happened to the rest of your unit, Mamud?" Harlan asked gingerly. He didn't want the Uzbek to feel like he was being interrogated.

Mamud turned his silent stare on Harlan. Finally, he turned his eyes back to the party and spoke.

"One of the atomic weapons of mass destruction of the Western forces hit our regiment in an assembly area last night. These few and I were stragglers," Mamud went on. He pointed at the 2S6, "The antiaircraft gun had engine trouble; we stayed back to work on it. That is why we are alive." He pointed to the riflemen who were still laughing and hooting at Nolan. "Some of the others were in their vehicles when the bomb went off. As they say in the Gulag, they are alive, but they do not feel much like fucking."

Harlan chuckled at the phrase from the labor camps.

"And you, Flack, what about you?"

"We grew tired of Russians pushing us on to die for them. The enemy's air attacks had destroyed a third of the battalion, and we were nowhere near the front. Our major was a real *pizda*. My comrades and I decided that he was the real enemy, he and all Russians. We killed him, so now we are renegades." Harlan paused a moment. "We cannot kill all of them, of course, but we can kill some. We had a good start with that little *pizda* major."

Mamud was still staring at him, but a thin smile had crept onto his face.

"Yes, we too did away with our *ferengi* officers. We seem to have that in common." Mamud was silent for a moment. His face took on the look of a rain cloud forming. "They are such liars! Russians cannot tell the truth! Do you remember, Flack, the days of *glasnost*, of *perestroika*?"

Harlan nodded.

"My uncle Bilal was in the 13th Guards Tank Division in 1989, stationed in Hungary. Much ado was made about the loading of tanks onto railcars for transport back to Russia. The Russians said, 'Look how we disarm! All we want is peace!' Do you know what my uncle Bilal said about that? The tanks they loaded onto trains were either defective, or going back for modifications to install the new armor that explodes." He was referring to the reactive armor. "They were going back to Russia anyway. It was all a lie for the journalists!"

Harlan said nothing but only nodded, not wanting to interrupt the sudden diatribe.

"In my country, in Uzbekistan," the young Moslem said for emphasis, "the Russians hide their cruelty from the world. They test their atomic weapons there and cause the babies to be born deformed. After they sprayed chemicals on the cotton plants, one child out of four died an infant. Many women could not contain their grief. In one year, over 200 women burned themselves to death. What kind of men make war on women and infants? Russian men!"

The young Uzbek suddenly looked sheepish, embarrassed at his emotional speech. Harlan quickly spoke to reassure him.

"In my country, Estonia, it was much the same. The Russians promised much, but gave nothing. Certainly, the old flags came back and some political parties were permitted to form, but in the end, when Gorbachev went, the tanks came. It was the same in Georgia, the Ukraine, too. Talk never gets rid of Russians, only guns."

Mamud did not answer, but sat watching the impromptu party. The two men sat silently for several moments before Mamud slid off the tank and faced Harlan.

"We seem to have much in common, Flack. We will talk again." Mamud grinned slightly, then turned and walked away.

The Mujahaddin leader was hard to read, but so were most people from the Soviet Central Asian republics. Living under the Soviet yoke for so many decades had taught them to keep their mouths shut. His outburst had been a good sign. The question of leadership of this ragtag band had not arisen, and for now, Harlan was willing to let it wait. A confrontation now would accomplish nothing. The primary goal, the establishment of a fifth column in the Soviet rear area, was actually in progress. For now, that was enough.

★26★

"Here's the deal, BJ. We've had contact, sort of, with our missing team, ADM-032A, who are going to set off an atomic demolition device here"—Jinx pointed to the blue sticker on the map near Oebisfelde—"there's a railroad bridge over a highway there. The team's job is to close both the highway and the track."

Jinx sat on the edge of the desk and rubbed his forehead. He had come down to Company G's forward operations base to make the final coordination for the mission and deliver the weapons. He had asked Captain Schultz, BJ's CO, to let him talk to BJ alone.

"As you know, we got the order to recall the ADM teams right after the moratorium, and only this one team has not acknowledged. I thought they had been bagged until they transmitted a routine message a hour ago. They can't receive, but they are going ahead with the mission anyway. If they set off that ADM, the Soviets will probably knock the shit out of us again. They've got the German government running scared. The nukes, or, actually, their radiation, are worse than anyone had expected. If we give them this excuse, they'll jam it down our throats."

BJ whistled through his teeth. "I only see two problems, Jinx. One, these guys don't want to be found. Two, this is a hell of a waste of recon teams, to have to go out and fix somebody else's fuckup!"

"Right." Jinx turned and leaned against the map. He could see about a dozen problems with running a mission behind Soviet lines, and inside East Germany at that, the least of which were the two BJ had named.

"I don't like this shit either, BJ, but if we can't stop that team, the Soviets will nuke a lot more of our people."

"Oh, thanks, Jinx!" BJ snapped. "Make it my fault if we get nuked again! Believe me, Bud, it wasn't my idea to use the fuckin' things in the first place. I got to see one up-close and personal. My whole team took enough rads, our kids'll probably look like toasters. Don't lay a trip on me, okay?"

"Sorry, BJ, we're up against the wall."

BJ leaned against the map himself, looking down at the floor. The awkward silence hung in the room.

"Shit, okay, we can do it," BJ said slowly, straightening up, "but I can't guarantee that we'll find them, or that they won't set the damn thing off anyway. When are they supposed to set it off?"

"Day after tomorrow, 0500. To coincide with the big counterattack."

"What?! You mean I have two days to put together this operation, get in there, find these guys, and stop them from setting off a nuke?"

"You got it."

"Fuck me!" BJ said, incredulous. "What big counterattack?"

"The one you don't know anything about."

"Of course," BJ replied. It was better for folks like BJ not to know too much. Their risk of capture was always great.

"BJ" Jinx stared at the dark wood ceiling "if you can't do it the easy way, you'll have to kill them."

BJ stared at Jinx. "Who?"

"The ADM team. If you locate them, but can't link up with them face-to-face, or if they refuse to call it off . . . you'll have to kill them."

"Fuck you, Jinx."

"I'm sorry, guy, but that bomb cannot go off. Even if it means that all of you have to get captured."

"Or killed. Fuck you very much!"

"No one here needs to know that," said Jinx. "Don't even tell your teams until you're on the ground, okay? We don't need any rumors about this getting out."

"Yeah," muttered BJ, looking back at the floor.

"I've got all the pertinent data on the mission for you," Jinx said quietly. He handed the dejected LRRP a folder. "It'll tell you what you need to know. If you need anything else, let me know. You guys have unlimited access to resources for this."

"Yeah, thanks," BJ said over his shoulders as he headed for the door. He stopped in the doorway and turned back to Jinx.

"There is something you can get me, a bullhorn."

"A what?" Jinx answered incredulously.

"A bullhorn. Can you find me out?"

"Yeah, sure."

"Fine, do it."

The young LRRP turned and disappeared out the door.

It was hard to believe that this was all of Company G that was available. Out of eighteen teams that had come to Germany just days before, only about two thirds of the teams were still alive. Not many of them were wounded; wounded men didn't usually get out. Teams that reported more than one man wounded never seemed to come back. The inability to leave a man behind was thought to have killed some complete teams.

These nine men were it for this mission. BJ's team was just back off a mission, and the other five men were the remnants of two teams that had been chewed up by Soviet or East German rear security troops. They were scheduled to be reinforced with graduates of the Selection and Training Section in a few days, but were on hold for now.

Despite the danger, the losses, the seeming lack of success, BJ was happy to see a perverse sense of humor still existed with the troops. Murphy was wearing a torn white T-shirt that bore the hand-lettered slogan: "It's always hairy in the rear!"

BJ hoped the nine men would be able to keep their sense of humor about this job. As they sat in the tiny school desks, BJ looked them over.

Norman Sterling was running the other team. He was as good a recon man as there was, in BJ's opinion. In three missions, he had brought back his team, or most of them, when no one else could have. Captain Schultz had put him in for the Distinguished Service Cross after that mission at Lüneburg. Sterling's team had found an East German tank battalion and laser-designated it for a company of Apaches. The team had been discovered, stayed put, and continued laser-designating tanks instead of running. Sterling had killed an entire East German squad by himself, been slightly wounded, then carried his radio man out on his shoulder. His team had lost two dead and two wounded, but the Soviets had lost an entire tank battalion.

Left from Norm's team was Alex Robinson, the senior scout, and Jesus Alvarez, the radio operator Sterling had carried out. Both Sterling and Alvarez were still recovering from their wounds.

The other two leftovers, Dale Purcell and Clarence Slade, were from a team that never got inserted. Their Blackhawk had been hit by antiaircraft fire on the way in. The copilot, gunner, team leader, senior scout, and radio operator had been killed. The chopper had barely limped back. It crash-landed in the middle of a Dutch armored unit that rescued the survivors. The pair were pretty shook up, but they were okay.

All in all, not the best crew to go looking for Green Berets in enemy territory.

"Well, I guess you're wondering why I have called you here today," BJ began, amid groans at the tired old joke. "We have been handed a hot potato that we can't put down. We, these two teams, are to find a Special Forces team operating behind enemy lines and bring them back out."

"They don't got radios?" Alvarez asked.

"Not working."

"What's the hurry? Those Green Beanies are supposed to work behind the lines, aren't they?" Slade wondered aloud.

"Okay, here's the deal," BJ began. "They are an ADM team, that's Atomic Demolition Munitions, working inside East Germany. They've got a man-carried atom bomb that they are supposed to set off on this bridge." BJ pointed on the map to the crossing that was ADM-032A's objective.

"We have to find them and call them off. We just declared a moratorium on all nukes and this team will violate it if we don't stop them. NATO is afraid that the Soviets would use their attack as an excuse to hit us with another round of nukes." BJ paused to let this news sink in. "Like I said, their radio's fucked, so we have to go in and get them. Charming, huh?" Judging from their expressions, the other LRRPs were not charmed.

"*Madre Dios,*" Alvarez whistled softly.

"Yo momma," from Slade.

The rest were silent, waiting for the details. The nine men were clearly not happy with the assignment. BJ looked over at Wally Kosinski. He had snapped out of his mental state once the team had been recovered. BJ was concerned about taking him along on this one, but they needed every man. A "shrink" had checked and okayed him; all the team members were going to keep an eye on him.

"We're jumping in," said BJ. "A Combat Talon from the 7th Special Operations Squadron will be the insertion aircraft. Each team will have a different drop zone." That perked them up. No one had expected to get a combat jump out of this.

"BJ, this sounds like *Mission: Impossible* to me," Sterling said quietly. "I don't see how we can do it without getting all of us waxed."

"BJ, you must be kidding," Hickey blurted, "this is a sucker play. There's no way this will work."

"I'm not crazy about it myself, Shannon," BJ shot back, "but there it is."

"Well really, what's the difference?" Norm Sterling injected. "Every time we go out, it's the same. We go looking for people who don't want to be found. This one is only different 'cause they're our people, not the bad guys. They may even be happy to see some friendly faces!"

"Maybe so, Norm," BJ went on, "here's the plan. I'll be happy to hear any suggestions." BJ spread the map over one of the small desks, folding it to show the area around Oebisfelde. The others crowded around.

"Norm, your team's drop zone is here, northwest of the objective." BJ outlined a clearing six kilometers from the bridge. "We'll go in here, south of it."

"Where the fuck is this place, man?" asked Hickey.

"It's in the British sector," said BJ.

"BJ, your DZ is right next to this road," Sterling interrupted. "You need to pick someplace a bit less visible."

"I'd like to, Norm, but there isn't one close to the objective. The Talon will only be in the area for seconds, and we'll hot foot it out of there *macht schnell*."

"You better move like greased lightning."

BJ didn't mention that if one team was observed, it would serve to draw away any rear-area security troops in the area, giving the other team a better shot at finding the Green Berets. He suspected that the other LRRPs were smart enough to figure that out themselves.

"The Combat Talon will drop us an hour before dawn tomorrow morning," BJ went on. "We have all day and most of the night to find them. If we can't locate the team, we will move to the objective and disarm the device ourselves. Keep in mind, if we have to do this, that the ADM team may have booby-trapped the area.''

"What if those snake-eaters think we're the bad guys and go after our ass?"

"They speak English, yell at them."

"Oh, yoo-hoo, Mr. Green Beret!" Murphy trilled in falsetto. "I'm here to save you, please don't shoot me!"

"That's good, Murphy," BJ cracked, "you do it just that way, those Green Beanies will know you're not a Russian. No self-respecting commie would talk like that. No way."

"Fuck it," Murphy snorted, "let's do it."

"Sure," Hickey drawled, "who wants to live forever?"

"Gentlemen, I'm Brian Hagerty, a weapons specialist from Livermore Labs. I was sent here after the war began to access the ADM teams' performance and the effectiveness of the ADM devices. I'll be briefing you on atomic demolition munitions."

Great, thought BJ, a nuclear weapons user's satisfaction survey.

The man's dress and manner said Ivy League, probably MIT or maybe Cal Tech. He was wearing a pair of khaki pants, a ski sweater, those weird rubber duck boots, and a dark green down parka. A cap with earflaps and fur-lined leather gloves completed the ensemble. With him, he carried a briefcase and a large round nylon bag.

His fresh-scrubbed face and immaculate clothing were in severe contrast to those of his audience. They wore dirty BDUs, had stubble on their faces and the faint aroma of slept-in sweat. The faint aroma was not lost on the visitor who wrinkled his nose for a moment, then decided to ignore the smell as he would not be there long.

Hagerty opened his briefcase and withdrew a series of folded paper posters, which he set on the small table.

"The device in question is a Special Atomic Demolition Munition or SADM. We usually call it a sad-em." Hagerty smiled patronizingly. "It is available in a range of yields from .01 kiloton to 5 kilotons. That means equivalent from 10 tons to 5000 tons of TNT."

"We know what a kiloton is," BJ spoke up. "Tell us about the thing."

"Of course." Hagerty unfolded one of the posters. On it was

a line drawing of the device. "As you can see, the device is cylindrical, with a spherical top. This drawing is actual size. The device is twenty-four inches long and about eighteen inches across. It weighs slightly less than one hundred pounds."

He passed around the poster. The device, as it was referred to, was a featureless metal cylinder. The only external feature was a combination lock dial recessed into the flat bottom plate.

"The device comes in a special pack for carrying, a rucksack, I believe you call it."

"That's what we call it," Slade drawled, grinning at the other LRRPs.

"Yes, well, at any rate, the device is packed in a Styrofoam layer to protect it from impact when parachuting. The device is removed from the packing for arming, then replaced in the pack."

Hagerty paused, waiting for questions or response from the small audience. The motley group just sat there, impassive.

"All right," Hagerty went on, reaching for the nylon bag, "the device is armed by setting two timers."

Unzipping the side of the bag, Hagerty removed a plastic mockup of the device. Hagerty turned the mockup over and pointed to the combination lock dial recessed into the flat bottom plate.

"When the correct combination is entered on this lock, the entire bottom plate may be removed." Hagerty turned the plate and pulled it off, setting it on the table next to his briefcase. "The plate has an O-ring seal to keep out moisture, dust, and debris."

Moisture, dust, and debris, thought BJ. You can always tell a lab man. In the field, that O-ring would have to keep out water, dirt, and shit.

Hagerty now moved in front of the table to give the soldiers a better look at the business end of the device. He fished a gold Cross pen from the breast pocket of his parka.

"As you can see," the young Ivy Leaguer went on, warming to his topic, "the arming panel consists of two timer windows, one for hours and one for minutes, two timer winding handles, a detonator retaining well, a detonator well, and a toggle switch."

As he spoke, Hagerty pointed out each feature with the tip of the gold pen.

"The timers are set by turning the winding handles clockwise. The timers are mechanical."

Hagerty looked up at his students. "Can any of you tell me why the timers are mechanical rather than digital?"

"We don't give a shit," Norm Sterling snapped at Hagerty, "just tell us what we need to know."

"Yes, well, they're mechanical because radiation from the device can make digital timers erratic," Hagerty recited, a bit shaken by the atypical response to his canned lecture. "At any rate, the times are set by turning the handles until the proper number of hours and minutes appear in these windows."

As the civilian droned on, Sterling leaned over to BJ and whispered, "Who is this guy, Mr. Rogers?"

BJ stifled a laugh and looked over at Sterling, his face a twisted parody of the children's show star.

"Can you say yuppie cocksucker?" BJ crooned. Sterling laughed out loud, causing the entire group to look around at him.

"Sorry," he said in mock contrition. BJ's face was a mask of innocence.

Hagerty looked at the impassive faces of his reluctant, no, his surly students. He had given this lecture dozens of times before to Atomic Demolition Teams, but they had all been rapt pupils. These raunchy little pricks were like a class of juvenile delinquents.

"When the delay times are set in the timer windows, the knobs are fixed in place by thin copper wires inserted through the holes in the ends of the handles and secured to tie-down points around the rim. Each wire is twisted its full length, with precisely three twists per quarter inch. These wires are secured to two points on the rim to prevent them from turning due to vibration or tampering."

"Mister, do these wires make the bomb go off if they're cut?" Alvarez asked.

"No, they only hold the timer handles. The reason that . . ."

"Then forget about them," BJ broke in. "We don't give a damn about the number of twists or what kind of timers it's got, just tell us how the bomb goes off. Our job is not to set the damn thing off, but to keep it from going off, so skip the fine print and tell us what we need to know about disarming the damn thing."

Hagerty stopped and straightened up. His face was coloring and his hand had formed a fist around the gold pen.

"What I'm trying to do here," he said through clenched teeth, "is to compress a seven-day school into one short briefing. If you will be so kind as to let me go on, I'll . . ."

"You'll waste a lot of time we don't have," BJ interrupted again. "We have to go out there and find people who don't want to be found and avoid a whole bunch more, then deactivate their bomb if they've already planted it and try to maybe come back alive. Just tell us what we need to know and skip the rest of the course. And remember this, we are the ones who are doing this little job, if something you tell us is wrong and that bomb goes off, it'll be your ass. Captain Schultz'll see to that."

Hagerty looked around at the LRRP captain. Schultz had been surprised by BJ's outburst, but instantly put on a look of casual cruelty. "That's right, these boys are like my own family," Schultz said solemnly, silently thanking heaven they actually weren't.

As Hagerty turned back to the LRRPs, Schultz mimed sticking his finger down his throat. Hagerty's face seemed to collapse a little. He took a deep breath and went on.

"Well, in that case, we'll start with how the bomb works." He drew out another drawing and passed it around. "The bomb is an implosion type, which means that it is in the form of a ball surrounded with explosives. When the explosives go off, it compresses the nuclear material to create an atomic explosion. The Nagasaki bomb was of this design."

At the mention of Nagasaki, the LRRPs exchanged glances. Now they had a reference and the information seemed much more relevant.

Now I've got ya', you little scumbags, Hagerty thought as the students suddenly perked up.

"In order for an atomic explosion to occur," Hagerty continued, "all the explosives must detonate at once. If the explosion is not simultaneous, the atomic reaction will not occur."

All the LRRPs were gathered around one desk now, looking at the drawing. Now that the lecture was over, the class could begin.

"Arming the device is simple," Hagerty explained. "You take the detonator from the detonator retaining well and place it in the arming well on the other side." Hagerty stepped into the circle of soldiers and pointed on the mockup to the various parts he was describing.

"Then you flip the toggle switch at the bottom to 'on.' That starts the timers. When they get to 'O,' *boom!*" Hagerty yelled. Nothing. Usually when he yelled *boom!* in class, they all jumped. These guys just looked at him like he was retarded.

Tough crowd, Hagerty thought, moving on, a real tough crowd.

"So how do we deactivate the thing if we have to?" Sterling asked.

"You don't," Hagerty answered. Every eye was on him now. "Once the timers are running, they cannot be stopped."

"Even if you turn off the switch?" Hickey said, a note of anxiety in his voice.

"No, the switch merely activates the system, it doesn't have to stay 'on.' "

"Then how do we turn the fuckin' thing off?" BJ asked incredulously.

Hagerty stood thinking for a second. "I guess the only way to turn it off is to interrupt the firing sequence somehow."

"That sounds tricky," Sterling said amid nods from the others.

"Well, not really," Hagerty said, trying to reassure the suddenly nervous LRRPs. "If you burn through the outer case with something, you could set off part of the explosives prematurely and prevent the atomic reaction from occurring."

"What's to keep the part you set off from setting off the rest of it?" Robinson asked, speaking for the first time.

"Nothing," answered Hagerty, "but the detonation would not be balanced, so it would not implode the device. D'ya see?"

"Not really," BJ replied, "but we'll take your word for it."

"So if we find the thing set to go, we can use thermite grenades to deactivate it?" King asked, trying to nail down the real information.

"That's right."

Finally, thought BJ, finally we get the straight poop we need for this gig.

"I want every man to carry a thermite," said BJ, "just in case."

"Anything else we need to know, Professor?" Sterling asked as the other LRRPs moved to their gear and started for the door.

"Only one thing," Hagerty answered. All the men stopped,

waiting for the kicker, the "other shoe" to drop. "If the device is not already running, you need to bring it back. We don't need for Ivan to get the device intact. If you thermite it, the blast should destroy most of what the thermite doesn't, but otherwise, we want it back."

"We'll do our best, Mr. Hagerty," Schultz quickly injected, pumping Hagerty's hand. Schultz looked at BJ and jerked his head toward the door.

"Okay, guys, let's do it," BJ said loudly, moving everyone out the door. "Get your shit and leave us go amongst them!"

"Beej, I'll carry it back it you want me to," offered King as he followed BJ out.

Hagerty was let standing by himself in the room. The only reminder of the LRRPs presence was the sour odor in the air.

Hagerty turned and collected his drawings and mockup.

What a bunch of weird assholes, he thought as he gathered up the props of his little act.

★27★

It had really been too easy, Harlan thought, laughably easy. The freezing rain had helped, of course. Bundled against the cold and hunkered down in their vehicles, the troops of the 334th Motorized Rifle Regiment hadn't noticed the two extra tanks and the BTR that fell in at the end of their column during some confusion at a river crossing. The rear security element was still some distance behind them. For three hours, Harlan and Ikehara had trailed the column in the darkness, waiting for a good spot to jump them. The rain had stopped and now a thin line of gray behind them announced the coming dawn.

The road here ran through a cut in the forest. On each side, the trees rose up like a wall. Ahead, one tank and personnel carrier after another were dropping over a slight rise. Harlan signalled to Ikehara to slow down. As his T-80 topped the rise, Harlan could see twenty tanks and APCs below him on the narrow road. A mile ahead, the road curved sharply to the left and the column rumbled around it. The column had slowed slightly in the muddy slew that covered the road. Harlan signalled the other tank to come alongside and backed slowly down the slope. When the hull of his tank was just below the slope, he stopped and called to Ikehara in the other tank.

"You take the back door, Ike, I'll take the front," he shouted over the engine noise. "Fire on my shot."

Ikehara nodded and slipped down in the turret. Both tanks were hull down now, twenty meters apart on the rise. The BTR had backed into the woods just off the road. Mamud's ten Kreuzadders now made their way through the trees to the crest of the rise. Three men had RPG-7s, the rest had RPG-22s. They would take on the APCs and leave the tanks free to kill the heavy armor. Walter Nolan, acting as the gunner, waited until the riflemen were in place, then swung the long tube of the 125mm gun toward the spot where the road curved into the trees.

Ten seconds later, a T-80 pulled into the reticle of his sight.

"Target!"

"Shoot"

"On the way!"

Nolan pulled the gun trigger. The tank rocked back with the recoil of the huge smoothbore gun. It took the penetrator less than a second to reach the doomed T-80.

Valery Koslov was tired. Forty-eight hours without sleep had drained him. Now he dozed in the tiny tank commander's seat, the drone of the turbine lulling him, inviting him to sleep. His head nodded forward, the motion waking him. Startled, he looked down to see the gunner, Tutsl, grinning up at him.

"Napping, Comrade Sergeant?" the gunner taunted him. Koslov disliked the gunner, but was powerless to get rid of him. The man's uncle was a *zampolit*. Koslov was stuck with the arrogant *churka*.

"In no way, Tutsl," Koslov replied, "just considering your chances for promotion."

Tutsl jerked his head backward to hit Koslov in the balls. The gunner was just in front of and below the commander's seat, rearranging the big shells in the carousel that fed them up to the automatic loader. Anticipating the move, Koslov shifted to the back of his seat. The back of Tutsl's head missed Koslov's crotch by millimeters.

"Ha!" Koslov shouted, slamming his knees together on Tutsl's head, pinning it between his thighs, grinding the earphones into Tutsl's ears. The gunner howled and reached up between Koslov's knees with both hands, trying to free his trapped head.

Koslov grabbed the gunner's helmet and began thrusting his hips, rubbing his groin against the back of Tutsl's head.

"Ahh, Tutsl, you are even better than your sister!"

At this exclamation, the driver, Simok, turned to see what was going on above him. His laugh boomed through the tank, making Tutsl fight even harder. Koslov continued to cry, "Oh, ahh, oh," humping Tutsl's head.

"I will get you, Koslov," Tutsl screamed, his voice muffled by Koslov's legs. "You are . . ."

The impact of the penetrator interrupted Tutsl's tirade. It struck just above the turret ring on the left rear side of the turret. There was no reactive armor cover there, only a few centimeters of steel. The hardened penetrator spiked through the turret and blasted the interior of the T-80 with fire and white-hot steel. Burning metal pierced through into the ammunition storage below the turret, igniting the stored rounds.

Inside the tank, Simok and Tutsl died within a second, ripped to bits by the blasts. Koslov was spared this fiery end. A piece of metal the size of his thumb had ricocheted off the gun and hit Koslov in the face. It ripped through his head, exiting through the top of his canvas tanker helmet. Koslov was already dead when the ammunition went up.

The blast from both tank guns had come so close together that they had sounded like one shot. The trailing tank in the column had gone up first, it was barely a hundred meters away. When the tanks fired, a flock of rockets had streaked out of the woods, seeking the troop-carrying BMPs. Half a dozen BMPs were now burning. The RPG gunners were quickly reloading while their comrades began to lay down AK-74 and RPK-74 fire on the remaining BMPs.

As the automatic loaders forced fresh rounds into the tank guns, Harlan and Ikehara sought new targets. They fired as soon as the breech closed and the gun was ready. The column was effectively trapped. The burning tanks at each end blocked the road and the thick forest kept the column from dispersing.

Fish in a barrel, Harlan thought.

One of the BMPs had sought cover by backing up in front of a burning tank. It was a risky move, the tank could go up in moments. Still, it was some protection. The riflemen piled out of it and sprinted for the woods. Hidden by the black smoke from the burning tank, they all made it to the safety of the trees.

"Faster, God damn it!" Harlan screamed at Nolan. "Come on!"

"Loading, sir!" came the reply.

It seemed that the interval between shots was getting longer. Harlan knew that the auto-loader was working properly, the distortion in time was only the effect of his own adrenaline. The two Kreuzadders were killing tanks as fast as they could shoot and reload. The Soviets were stuck, and knew it. One alert tanker had spun his turret around and fired at Harlan's tank. The shot had gouged the dirt ahead of the tank and glanced off the slope of the turret, tearing off reactive armor bricks. Harlan had barely registered the sound. He and Ikehara fired together at the T-80. Harlan's penetrator gouged the thermal sight off the T-80's turret, but failed to penetrate. Ikehara's HEAT round hit the rear deck and set fire to the fuel. The commander of the T-80 was not ready to quit. He fired another round, but again missed. Harlan fired again, putting a second HEAT round into the T-80 that stubbornly refused to die. The crew of the now-burning tank gave up the fight and threw open their hatches, slithering off the sides to escape. Several other crews had bailed out of their T-80s before they were even hit. Mamud's gunners had killed most of them. The RPGs were still hard at work on the BMPs. Only two appeared to be undamaged. Their rear doors were open, dead troops lying in heaps behind them. Mamud's machine gunners were raking the column now, looking for survivors.

Senior Private Simon Rossovich had just about pissed himself when the shooting started. He had been asleep, or nearly so, when the first explosion jerked him back to reality. He heard the tank behind them get hit. The BMP and platoon commander, Lieutenant Blionov, had yelled at the driver to back up off the road. The men of Rossovich's squad had been thrown around the interior of the BMP like rag dolls by the violent maneuvering, but they had the doors open and were spilling out the back before the BMP stopped. The flight for the trees had been wild. There was no cover and no support. They had run like rabbits. Now the lieutenant and their squad commander were missing. Rossovich was the ranking man.

Up the gentle slope, they could see, through the smoke and the trees, muzzle flashes from the two tanks that were chewing up their company. Across the narrow road, smaller flashes twinkled in the trees, the chattering of the machine guns drowned out by the deafening cracks from the tank guns. It was impossible! How could the enemy have penetrated so far? And only two tanks! Traitors! The rumors were right!

Rossovich gathered up the surviving squad and pushed them up the hill. If they could flank the attackers, perhaps they could kill the bastards.

* * *

Harlan flinched and yelled at the pain. His elbow had grazed the gun breech. The gun was so hot, it was smoking.

Another round or two, it will be hot enough to cook off the rounds, Harlan thought as he rubbed the scorched spot on his black coveralls and jammed his head against the gunsight. He squeezed the trigger, and another T-80 bought the collective farm.

"Teddy, get ready to haul outta here!" Harlan yelled. He could see tanks from the head of the column begin to emerge from the woods at the road's bend. The tank jumped slightly as Teddy dropped it into reverse.

"Ready!" the driver yelled back.

One more shot, then we're out of here, Harlan thought as the breech snapped shut.

Rossovich placed the RPK-74 machine gun next to a fallen log and spread four riflemen alongside it. He told the gunners to watch him for their signal to fire. Rossovich, with the RPG gunner in tow, continued up the slope toward the two tanks.

As they approached the crest of the hill, Rossovich signaled to the machine gunner. He opened up on the tree line across the road. Using its fire to distract the attackers, Rossovich and his rocket gunner ran for the crest of the hill.

The sudden fusillade from across the road surprised Mamud. He had not seen the infidels in the trees. Still, he had expected some to escape.

"Ali!" he yelled to the RPK gunner to his left. "There, across the road."

Ali shifted his fire from the long line of burning vehicles to the fallen log where the muzzle blast of a machine gun was clear. Ali fired half a burst at the smoke, then changed magazines and fired another full magazine. The RPK stopped firing. Mamud shifted three riflemen to fire across the road at their exposed flank and began pulling the others back through the trees to cover the BTR.

Through his gunsight, Nolan saw the tracers race back and forth across the road.

"Infantry, port side!"

While the reloader began its cycle, Harlan stood up in the hatch and swung the 12.7mm gun around. Movement beyond Ikehara's tank caught his eye. He fired right over Ike's tank, splanging a few slugs off the turret. Ike's voice crackled over the radio.

"What? What?"

"On your left, Ike!" Harlan screamed into the mike. "Pull back now!"

Ikehara's T-72 pitched backward down the slope. The turret spun to the left, its coaxial machine gun raking high through the trees.

Harlan caught a glimpse of movement and swung his gun to bear. He fired just as the RPG rocket exploded from the tube. The rocket hit Ikehara's left tread. The explosion sheared the track and the tank shed the tread as it rolled backward.

Frustrated and scared, Harlan dropped back into his hatch as rifle bullets pinged off the turret.

"Nolan, target left, RPG!"

Nolan spun the turret to the left and fired the main gun at the spot where the smoke from the rocket still lingered in the still air. The tank round was not the right load for engaging troops, but the blast would get their attention. At the same time, he held down the firing switch on the coaxial gun, raking the trees.

"Now, Teddy," Harlan screamed into the intercom, "kick it!"

Rossovich was elated. The RPG round had knocked a tread off one of the attackers, now they would finish it.

"Quickly," he hissed at the RPG gunner, "aim at the base of the turret."

The main gun on the second tank thundered again, the blast making the RPG crew flinch. Kostin, the RPG gunner, was cocking the launcher when he looked up. Rossovich was leaning against a tree, oddly still. Kostin stopped, looking at the senior private. Rossovich's feet were not on the ground. The senior private was not leaning against the tree, he was nailed to it. The long, finned spike from the tank gun had knifed through one tree trunk and nailed Rossovich's head to another. He hung there now, a puppet on a nail.

The whipping of 7.62mm rounds through the trees broke Kostin's reverie. He suddenly felt exposed and scared. Grabbing up his RPG, Kostin ran back through the trees.

There was no more fire from the woods. Harlan raked the trees again for good measure. The counterattack had spooked him and now his T-80 felt very vulnerable.

Ikehara's crew had piled out of the crippled tank and was sprinting for the BTR. A moment later, the little Hawaiian rolled out of the turret and climbed up to Harlan.

"You scared me for a second, Ike," Harlan shouted. "I thought you weren't coming."

"I left a present for the folks who recover that baby!" Ike smile. "My old friend Willy Pete behind the ammo door." Ike stepped around to the back of the turret, covering the road and using the 12.7mm for support.

"Let's go, Comrade Captain!"

"Okay, Teddy, let's see how fast this thing will go in reverse!"

The BTR had already started back down the road. Harlan's tank followed in reverse, keeping the thick armor toward the Soviets.

All in all, it had been a great ambush. The Soviets were cut to pieces, at least a dozen of their tanks and APCs destroyed against one tank lost and two Kreuzadders wounded. Enough of the Soviet crews had escaped to carry the tale of the traitor tanks that had struck from behind.

I love it when a plan comes together, Harlan thought. It was only then that he noticed how badly his hands were shaking.

★28★

They were still there, down the slope of the hill, cautiously working their way up. They were good, too. No talk, no thrashing around. Trackers. Thompson slithered back over the crest of the hill and quickly made his way down to the gully below.

"They're still on us, Cap," he whispered as he slid down beside McCullough. "Got a dog with 'em."

"How far, Bob?" McCullough hissed back, his eyes on the crest above them.

"Maybe thirty to forty-five minutes."

"Shit, these guys are tenacious."

They had been leading the German Battle Group troops north, away from the knoll where the device was cached, to shake them. So far, the East Germans had not been fooled. They were still there, getting closer. Luckily, they were not working with a helicopter, or the team would have been caught already. This game of cat and mouse was putting their timetable even further behind. They needed to recover the device, emplace it, and set it off before they lost any more of the team.

McCullough turned and looked at the other four remaining Green Berets. His gaze finally stopped on Malle.

"Gunter, stay here and give our friends a little surprise. We'll meet you at the cache."

Malle nodded and dropped the heavy pack off his back. He dug into the large central pocket as the other team members shouldered their rucks and started off toward the next ridge.

"Nothing fancy, Malle," McCullough said softly as the team melted into the trees, "just give them a reason to go home."

Malle said nothing but looked up and smiled. McCullough trotted along after the rapidly disappearing team.

Inside his pack were the surprises he wanted for the pursuit force. Malle took a white phosphorus grenade, a claymore mine, and one of the new pursuit deterrent mines. He stuffed the grenade and PDM into his jacket pockets and slid the claymore into a trousers cargo pocket. From a side pocket on the pack he took a Ziplock bag that held twenty feet of detonating cord. He crimped a blasting cap on each end. The last item he retrieved was a small glass vial.

Slinging his M16 over his shoulder, Malle made his way quickly up to the crest and cautiously peered over the edge. The pursuit team was halfway up the slope now, following the team's trail. A black German shepherd busily searched for the team's scent.

Slipping slowly over the crest of the hill, Malle slithered down the slope and found a footprint left by one of the team. He opened the vial of oil and poured the thick syrup into the print, covering the entire depression with a coating of the aromatic liquid. The briefing he had gotten on tracker dogs said that the oil of eucalyptus would deaden the dog's sense of smell, but not knock it out. The dog would go on seeking a scent normally, but would not be able to smell a thing. It was a better technique than the old way, putting cocaine in your footprint. That threw the dog off, too, but the handler could tell his dog was screwed up. The only other dog deterrent that seemed to work was tiger shit in your tracks. Even dogs who had never seen a tiger could tell by the smell of the big cat's shit that they did not want to meet one. The dog usually ran away, scared shitless, as it were.

Malle moved back up the trail, lacing another print with eucalyptus oil. When the two traces were well doctored, he fished the explosives out of his pockets.

Gunter set the claymore up just off the trail and used thick rubber bands around the phosphorus grenade to secure it to the front of the claymore. This done, he slipped one end of the detonating cord into the primer well of the mine and played out the remaining twenty feet up the slope of the hill to the PDM. If the PDM went off, it would set off the det cord and the claymore, too.

The PDM was an adaptation of an artillery cluster bomblet

round, called area-denial artillery munitions, and designed to be fired by 155mm howitzers. The ground version had a pin and lever like a grenade. When the safety level came off, the mine would wait sixty seconds, then self-deploy four nearly invisible trip wires. The slightest touch on one of the wires would set off the PDM. When detonated, a fragmentation grenade was propelled up out of the mine case and exploded two to eight feet in the air. If undisturbed, the mine would self-destruct after forty-eight hours. The mine was grenade size, so each team member could carry more than one. Gunter had four of the PDMs in his pack, as well as two claymores.

When he had the detonating cord securely taped to the PDM, Gunter pulled the pin, holding the safety lever down. He came up into a crouch, released the lever, and ducked back out of the wires' range. He had picked up his gear and was already moving out to join the others when he heard the faint pop that meant the PDM had armed itself.

Malle picked a sizable tree trunk to hide behind in a spot where he could see the crest of the hill. He reached around for his M16, then thought better of it and pulled the 9mm pistol from its holster. Malle's M9 pistol had threads on the front of the barrel to accommodate the Hushpuppy silencer that he usually carried in a pocket sewn to his holster. The stubby silencer was still screwed on the muzzle of the pistol. The Hushpuppy had been designed during Vietnam for just this situation—silencing guard dogs—Hush Puppy.

Malle checked the magazine, there were still seven rounds left after the eight that Cohen had pumped into the unfortunate POW. With the pistol at his side, Malle waited for the results of his handiwork.

Truppführer (Squad Leader) Ernst Grennau heard the pop as he was trying to gain a good foothold on the slope. He spun up against the tree next to him, waiting for an explosion. None came. The other squad members had not even heard the noise and were still moving slowly up the hill behind him. Obermann and his dog just topped the rise and disappeared over the other side.

He held up his hand to stop the squad, then tugged his ear to tell them he had heard something. They waited for his forward signal.

Grennau's ears strained for more sounds, trying to locate the source of the pop. Had he imagine it? It might have just been a branch falling, or even the dog. No, it was a pop, a man-made noise. Grennau could feel the adrenaline starting to course through him, an electrical feeling. The woods, so quiet a moment before, now seemed louder than his uncle Franz's machine shop. Grennau strained to hear each sound. He could hear the other combat men below him. Must they be so noisy! Their movements sounded like thunder to his adrenaline-pumped ears. His own breath roared in the frosty air, steaming like a locomotive. His eyes searched the crest of the hill for a movement, an outline, anything that would give away the source of the pop. Surely the enemy could hear them, see their breath.

Finally he signaled ''danger—front,'' and the *truppführer* ordered the squad to fan out on line on either side of him. The squad quickly moved into position. All were watching him, waiting for his signal. He motioned for them to move up to the hilltop. As one man, the line started up the slope.

The dog appeared first, bounding over the crest with the handler being pulled along in tow. The German shepherd was nosing frantically around the team's path. Maybe he had missed the eucalyptus altogether. Malle slipped farther behind the tree and waited.

It didn't take long for the dog and handler to reach Malle's position. The handler was watching the dog, not where he was going. A big mistake.

The dog was only ten feet from the tree when Malle stepped out. The eucalyptus must have worked or the dog would have been alerted long before. Malle brought the silenced pistol up and popped two rounds into the dog. The dog yelped and collapsed. Malle pulled the muzzle on up to the surprised handler, who now stood openmouthed, staring at the dog killer. Malle walked three rounds up the East German's torso. The handler jerked backward, stopped by the leash that anchored him to the hundred-pound canine corpse.

No one else had cleared the ridge. Malle turned and followed the path his team had taken.

The squad was nearly to the crest of the hill when the mines went off. There were two explosions, a smaller one in the air, the other, much louder, nearby on the ground. To Truppführer Grennau, the sounds were drawn out and dull, a sudden blow to the head more than a sound. His eyes jerked to the left, toward the noise. Kampfmann Hohlbeck was nearest the air burst. In slow motion, he flew backward down the hill until a tree stopped his flight. Senior Kampfmannen Mueller and Reinke were next in the skirmish line and both fell, screaming and writhing in a shower of metal and a huge white cloud that sent glowing tendrils cascading across the crest of the hill. Above Grennau's head there was the whine of flying metal. Bits of bark and clipped branches fell around him as he dived instinctively to the ground. Down the line, the other soldiers opened up on the crest of the hill, firing blindly at enemies who were far away.

One of the glowing white streaks fell across Grennau's left leg. The pain was immediate and awful. The white phosphorus burned deep into his leg, searing a jagged hole as it went. At first, Grennau stared at the burning wound as if it were some sort of morbid curiosity, then screamed and clutched at the leg. A mistake. A piece of the sticky phosphorus burned his palm. Grennau almost stuck the palm up to his lips, but caught himself in time. He thrust the hand down onto the cold ground, hoping to smother the fire. It did not work. The pain only increased. He tried to stand, fell on his side and slid a few meters down the hill. The pain was past enduring now. He screamed and rolled into a ball, sliding a little farther down the hill. He could feel hands on him, turning him over. A voice far away was calling to him, but Grennau could only hear the sound of screaming, his screaming.

Malle heard the explosions behind him. He looked back over his shoulder to see the wisp of white smoke at the crest of the hill. Shots popped farther down the ridge, AKMs by the sound of them, firing wild. There were screams, too, muffled by the trees and the distance, but loud enough to hear.

Malle stopped behind another tree, watching to see if any of the pursuers topped the ridge. The screaming continued, louder if anything. On the ridge crest, there was no movement.

Only one, maybe two wounded, not counting the dog team, Malle thought. Oh, well. At least it would slow them up. They would check every likely ambush spot now. Still, it was disappointing.

The screaming grew fainter, and the shooting stopped altogether. Malle waited another minute, watching. Nothing moved on the hilltop. Smiling, Gunter Malle went on down the ridge to rejoin his team. The Combat Group troops would be back, but by then, his team would be on the other side of the target.

Malle caught up with the team on the next ridge. McCullough was studying a small folded map square while the others formed a tight perimeter.

"So, Gunner, did you give our friends a present?"

"Yes. They were very surprised, but they did not want to party much."

"We need to pick it up a little," McCullough said, replacing the map into the flap pocket of his rucksack. "Those guys'll be back with their friends, this time to crash the party, and we need to be far away when they return."

It was dark when they finally reached the cache. McCullough had the team rest for an hour, then they moved out to a spot where they could recon the target the next day before emplacing the device.

★29★

The MC-130H Combat Talon II touched on the dark highway and stopped short, reversing its props to cut down the distance needed to stop. Its belly and sides were painted infrared-absorbing black. Only the upper surfaces bore the dark green and brown camouflage patter of other Air Force transports. As it slowed enough to turn, the teams moved as rapidly as their parachutes allowed them and stumbled up the lowered ramp for a hot on-load. Both teams were inside the plane in ten seconds. The half-dozen Headquarters Platoon members followed them in with their lightly loaded rucksacks, some men carrying two. As they darted back out the ramp was raised, and the big transport was airborne again in moments. On the ground, the plane was a sitting duck. In the air, it was nearly invisible.

Delk Weir, the 1st platoon sergeant, went down the seated line of jumpers checking their seat belts and aiding the burdened men when needed. Weir would be the jumpmaster.

BJ and Weir made their way forward to the flight deck through the mass of electronic equipment that made the Combat Talon such a formidable special operations ship. The plane could do everything in the way of special operations support, including airborne insertion, high-speed aerial delivery, refueling of special ops helicopters, and HAHO—high altitude high opening—drops. It was crammed with radar, electronic jammers, and navigation equipment of all sorts. The flight deck reminded BJ of a video arcade. There were eight separate multifunction displays, plus the panels for the jamming gear, the terrain avoidance radar, the infrared detection system, and a host of other gadgets that BJ didn't even want to know about. The plane could operate day or night, and in the worst weather.

On the flight deck, the navigator took the drop zone information and fed it into his computer. Once locked in, the computer could fly the plane to the release points and back without any help from the pilots. "No hands," the crew called it.

"This is interesting," the navigator said as he keyed in the data. "This is just about the same place we dropped a bunch of Green Beanie types a few days ago."

"Really," BJ answered.

The navigator did not pursue it. He knew better than to get too much information above what he needed to know.

How ironic, BJ thought as he walked back to his seat. This is the same plane that dropped them in. Small war.

The plane roared through the night, the small red lights in the cargo bay giving the interior an eerie, dreamlike quality.

In the cargo bay, the two teams were checking the rigging of the containers for their new weapons and talking excitedly. Jinx had provided the extra firepower. The new long-range surveillance unit TOE, in the Army's peacetime wisdom, had stripped the recon teams of their M203 grenade launchers, saying that since they were not supposed to make contact, they did not need so much firepower. But if a team was compromised and had to fight its way out, the 40mm grenade launcher was a big plus. To rear-area troops, unaccustomed to high-explosive detonations, the little 40mm rounds sounded like mortars. On this mission anyway, the conventional wisdom did not apply.

Jinx had delivered four M249E1 squad assault weapons and an equal number of M16s with M203 grenade launchers attached. The teams settled on two SAWs and two M203s per team. The radio operators would carry only an M16 since they carried the heavy radio. BJ had also broken out a case of PDM mines to discourage any nosy pursuers. Each man was traveling as light as possible with only a few days' rations, but extra grenades and ammo. They weren't burdened with all the surveillance and NBC-monitoring gear they normally carried. The extra firepower was comforting, even if it was just a drop in the bucket compared to the firepower that could be brought to bear against them if they were caught behind the enemy lines.

In his team, Hickey and King had the SAWs; he and Kosinski had the M203s. His assistant team leader and the big radio operator sat running through the care and feeding of the automatic weapons, trying to acquire in hours what they should have had in months of Stateside training. BJ thought about the endless battles Hagger had fought with the state headquarters over the lack of training support. Those old penny-pinchers would not shake loose a nickel, especially for airborne or combat training. All they wanted the Guard units to do was push their pencils, keep their paperwork up-to-date, and meet the recruiting goals. Whether the units knew a damn thing about their wartime missions was immaterial. They seemed to miss the simple premise that if a unit conducted meaningful training, its recruiting was all but done for them. Units that trained aggressively attracted recruits like magnets, and retained them.

Now those old men were safe in the States, while the teams were here in Germany, struggling to accomplish the mission with half-trained radio operators in the Communications Platoon and recon teams whose members had not been permitted to attend the many U.S. Army and NATO combat courses. Hagger's dire predictions had been correct, he just wanted to stay around long enough to rub their noses in it.

BJ tried not to think about the captain, either. Schultz had rolled over so many times, it was hard to respect the man. He was doing his job over here, but it was a bit late. He was a lot better than some of his recent predecessors, though.

BJ shook the poisoned thoughts from his mind. None of that stuff had anything to do with this mission. He walked to his seat on the red nylon bench and buckled in. Time now to focus on the job at hand.

The flight was a snap, really. Since the nuke strikes, commo and radar acquisition on both sides was a mess, every unit was scared of its own shadow, and the coordination and momentum on both sides had been lost. The Soviet air defense units were still sweeping, but their AWAC assets had pulled back farther east for protection and were less helpful in picking up intruders along the forward edge of the front. The Combat Talon threaded its way through the jumble of radar, hiding in the terrain where possible, jamming radar signals when necessary. They were certain to make the drop zones and equally certain to be where they were supposed to be. The big question was ADM-032A. If they had been captured or killed, this was a wild-goose chase. If they were still going ahead with their mission, they would fight like tigers if anyone approached them.

At the airbase, there had been rumors of a cease-fire. That didn't affect this mission, of course. If they failed and ADM-032A set off their bomb, the chances of a cease-fire were nil.

No, no pressure here, BJ thought holding on to the red nylon webbing as the big plane lurched down another hillside.

If we do okay, he mused, the war could be over. If we fuck up, our side gets nuked again. He looked at the others holding on for dear life. Their faces were blank. Were they thinking the same thing or just waiting to get out of the flying bucking bronco?

"Well, Scarlett," BJ said softly to himself, "if you think about this today, you'll go crazy. Think about it after the war."

Numb. His butt was completely numb now. Senior Lieutenant Kir Gurenko had been at his console in the An-72/74 airborne radar aircraft now for nearly twelve hours. His neck hurt, and his butt was out of radio contact with his body. The An-72/74 was a small plane, a variant of a twin-engine light transport. It did not have the room to move around that their comrades had on the big Il-28s or even the old Tu-26s. This plane was cramped, crammed with too much equipment and too many men.

When would this flight end? he asked himself. Better not to wish for an end, really. At least they were still alive. Most crews of airborne radar planes were dead. The enemy had excellent weapons for tracking radar and attacking it. He had heard two senior officers talking about an American missile called Harm. It homed in on Soviet radars from a distance of forty kilometers. They had said it had claimed most of the radar planes that had been lost. The others had been shot down by massed fighter groupings hunting the radar planes.

Since the NATO gangsters had attacked with weapons of mass destruction, the radar planes had been pulled back to protect them, which was fine with Gurenko. An extra belt of MiG-29s and Su-27s was comforting. Comfort, what was that? He could not remember. He could remember a small, warm unmarried officer's room in the dormitory outside Moscow, and an even warmer medical attendant, Riva. Where are you now, Riva? Somewhere safe, I hope. Perhaps when . . .

The flash at the nine o'clock position of his screen jolted him back to the war.

"Comrade Captain, I have a target bearing 268 degrees."

The blip was there on the next sweep, too. Captain Drachev was making his way back to Gurenko's console.

"Here, Comrade Captain," Gurenko pointed, "it is here."

The sweep came around again. This time the screen was clear.

"Where, Gurenko?" Drachev demanded. "I see nothing."

"It was here, Comrade Captain. I saw it for two sweeps."

The captain stood over Gurenko.

"Perhaps you are just tired, you imagined it," the captain said, stretching. It was obvious that the captain was tired, too. Standing bent over, watching the operators' consoles over their shoulders, was very tiring.

"No, Comrade Captain, I saw it."

"Altitude and direction?"

"Very low, headed southeast."

"Perhaps the enemy is masking himself in the ground clutter. Watch the screen and increase the gain in the ground clutter. It may be a cruise missile or a ground attack fighter."

"It is done, Comrade Captain."

As Drachev made his way forward, he stopped at the radio console. Above the console was a map of Germany. Their flight path was marked in red. Drachev noted their position and measured the distance to the phantom on Gurenko's screen.

"Izotov, contact the Air Defense Command. Tell them they may have a low-level intruder moving southeast near Gifhorn."

"Exactly so, Comrade Captain."

"Izotov," the weary captain added, "notify also the Rear-Area Command. They may want to look for paratroopers."

"Comrade Captain," another operator called, "I have a flight of high-speed aircraft, bearing 330 degrees."

Drachev took a deep breath, stretched again, and made his way back, bending over another operator to look at another scope.

"Stand in the door!" shouted Delk Weir, motioning to BJ.

The adrenaline had hit like a syringe full of amphetamine. You could feel the buzz coming from every man in the plane. BJ shuffled forward, gripping the cold outer skin of the plane with his fingers, crouching in the doorway.

The icy wind pulled at his face, stinging his eyes. BJ did not notice the wind or the darkness or the trees flying by so close underfoot. He was looking at a place so far away it could only be felt. He felt it now; felt it every time he jumped. He was out of the plane and twisting into the darkness before his mind even registered the shout and the slap on the leg.

Above him, the low-altitude chute sprang open, jerking BJ upright, his head coming back between the risers to check the canopy. This was purely a reflex. At 500 feet, if the main chute did not open, there was no time for a reserve chute. Seeing the perfect circle above him, BJ fumbled under his reserve for the quick release straps that held his rucksack. Finding them both, he pulled hard and felt the rucksack fall away, then stop with a jerk at the end of the lowering line.

BJ brought his feet together and looked down, trying to judge the wind direction. Before he could make out anything on the ground, the rucksack hit. BJ had just enough time to straighten up and bend his knees for his parachute landing fall. The ground was hard, very hard. The PLF spread the shock up the length of his leg and across his back, but BJ still felt like he had been hit with a bat. It was more like feet, butt, back. The chute collapsed almost on top of him. He could hear the others landing around him, hear grunts as they, too, slammed into the hard dirt of East Germany.

In five minutes, everyone was accounted for in the small clump of trees on the side of the DZ. With their parachutes and helmets stuffed in kit bags, the team moved off into the forest to hide the chutes in a brush pile. SOP called for them to bury their air items, but there was no time to waste scratching in the hard dirt just to hide the stuff.

King took the point, leading the team silently into the forest.

It's broken and I'm fucked, Slade thought as he sat up, the pain from his ankle shooting up his leg like a hot steel rod.

He had heard the ankle pop as it twisted off a rock when he landed. Slade ran his hands down the ankle and foot. It didn't seem to be bent off to one side, but it hurt like hell to touch it at all. Slade leaned back on one elbow and disconnected his equipment with one hand, wriggling out of the parachute harness and unlatching his weapons container on his left side. He sat listening for sounds of the other LRRPs.

This was the reason, among others, that parachute insertion was not the preferred method of entry. What do you do with a slightly injured man many, many klicks behind enemy lines?

Hearing nothing, he slowly sat up, then rolled over and got onto his knees. The movement hurt his ankle like hell, but Slade ignored it. In the blackness, he could see nothing. He nearly jumped out of his skin when Alvarez said, "Waiting for the bus, amigo?" right in his ear.

"Damn ya, Alvarez, you scared the shit out of me!" Slade almost shouted. "Where're the others?"

"Right over there, numb nuts, you want to join us?"

"Love to man, but I'm hurt. Broke an ankle on the jump."

"Oh, man!"

"Get Sterling over here, would ya?" Slade asked, easing himself down on the hard ground.

"Yeah, be right back."

I'm fucked, Slade thought again as he tried to find a position for the ankle that didn't hurt.

They bundled him up in his Gortex bivisack just inside the tree line and prepared a well-concealed hide in a small clump of brush. The senior radio operator switched his M16 for Slade's fitted with an M203. He would be okay there as long as there was no sweep by any rear-area folks. Sterling had offered him some morphine, but Slade told the team leader to keep it for someone who was really hurt.

Five minutes after the team moved off, the silence on the drop zone was the loudest thing Slade had ever heard.

★30★

"Uri, we are chasing shadows," Omar Silenko said quietly. "Even the most stupid raw recruit knows that our weapons of mass destruction have destroyed the Americans and that even now the British and Germans are struggling to save the pitiful remnants of their forces. We have won the war and yet here we are groping around in the darkness whacking pears with our pricks. Soon you and I will be back at our homes, plowing the furrows of young farm girls!"

Uri Berkutov snorted, then said softly, "Shut up, Omar, if Ensign Kovpak hears you talk like that, he will whack your prick with a rifle butt. If you really think the main enemy has been destroyed, you too are beginning to believe the *zampolit*!"

The other squad had come up and now the two squads formed a long line abreast and slowly moved off the road into the trees toward the open area that had been marked as a possible dropping zone.

They would find nothing again, Omar was certain, just as they had found nothing on a dozen previous sweeps. The enemy was routed, why must they muck around in the dark?

Slade thought for a second he had dreamed the sound. The cold, the pain, and the immobility had put him to sleep. Now he was wide awake, his pulse pounding in his ears. He scrunched down farther in the brush and rolled on his side, bringing the M16 over in front of him. He silently searched with his hand for the pouch that held two frag grenades and a white phosphorus.

236

Finding them, he straightened out the grenade pins so they would slide out easily, then laid the three grenades up by his head. If he was lucky, they would not find him. If they found him, they would be unlucky. He would see to that.

There was the tree line and beyond it the open fields. Almost finished. In an hour, they would be back in the trucks and on their way back to the farm where the 1st Company was bivouacked. The barn was not heated, but it was warmer than the woods. Beside him Uri was grumbling, shifting the heavy flamethrower around on his back. The shoulder straps on the rig were not comfortable for carrying a twenty-four-kilogram LPO-50 flamethrower. They dug into your shoulders and cut off the circulation to your arms. Uri shifted the whole thing upward to take the weight off his shoulders for a minute. He wanted to give it back to his new friend. Omar was a Kazak, a stranger to Uri, but the little man spoke good Russian and always had humorous stories to tell of his conquests of young farm girls. Uri doubted most of them, but it was fun listening to him and the misuse he made of some Russian words. Omar and another flamegunner were from the 3rd Company, but somehow Ensign Kovpak had obtained their loan along with their flamethrowers. Uri suspected it had something to do with the case of jam they had found in an abandoned house.

"You see, my friend," Omar whispered, "nothing. We are chasing shadows."

Uri seemed not to hear. When Omar looked over at his friend, Uri was staring back up into the brush behind them.

"Omar, one of those shadows just moved over there," the slight Georgian said. He hitched up his flamethrower and unhooked the riflelike projector from his harness. "Cover me, I am going to have a look."

"You will see only trees, my friend," Omar replied, unslinging his AKS-74, "but if one of them moves, I will surely shoot it!"

As he hefted the heavy rifle on his hip, Uri moved down the slope toward a dark clump of brush.

That's it, Slade thought as the Russian came toward his clump of brush, he's seen me.

Slade thumbed the selector on the M16 to burst fire and waited motionless. He would let the Russian make the first move.

* * *

The team flattened out when the sound of shots came drifting over. Every man looked back toward the trees where Slade was cached. A long tongue of fire shot up over the trees, followed by the sounds of more shooting and the muffled *crump* of grenades.

"Come on, move it!" Sterling hissed at the others. "Let's go!"

They were still out there; he could hear them moving around. He could see three of them dead. The flamethrower, his buddy, and the one that had come up on the right. They were dead for sure. He might have hit some others, he had heard screaming after the grenades had gone off. That flamethrower had scared the hell out of him. Thank God he had gotten the flamer first!

The others would take their time now, looking, circling, waiting. Slade knew the drill. He was dead. At least he had taken some of them with him. Now he would take a few more. He rolled up and slipped the white phosphorus grenade up under the frame of his rucksack. He pulled the pin. The weight of the gear and rations in the rucksack held down the safety lever. When they moved the pack to search it, they would get a surprise. That done, Slade pulled the magazine from his rifle and put in a new one. He would make the ten bursts count.

Alim Gondarch inched forward, the heavy flamethrower pressing him into the dirt. On either side, Alim could see the others in his squad moving forward, too. Two long minutes had passed since the shooting. No one had come out of the spot, so they were going in to get them. Alim pushed the projector ahead of him and slid forward, trying not to make a sound. His breathing sounded like the roar of the flamethrower. He thought that the enemy must hear it, too! His heartbeat sounded like hammer blows in his ears. How could his own body make so much noise? He hadn't heard these sounds when they had fought in the city! Of course, it had been so loud there, he was lucky to be able to hear at all now.

On the hillside, Alim could see a still figure. He could make out the slim outline of a flamethrower sticking up over the body. It had to be Omar. The enemy bastards had killed him. After what they had endured, it seemed stupid to die on a hillside in the middle of the night.

* * *

There, off to the right.

Slade could just see the movement beyond the trees. He swung the barrel of the M16 toward the dark shape and waited. No hurry now. It would all be over in a minute. He looked up through the thin branches at the sky. Only a couple of stars were visible. That was okay. He just wanted to see one. Slade took a deep breath. The pain was returning a little now. It didn't matter, either. The shadow moved again, another moved beyond it.

"Come on, fuckers," Slade said softly, "let's party."

Alim jumped when the rifle fired. To his right, a figure went down. Beyond the fallen one, another rifleman fired into the brush on full automatic, only to pitch backward as another burst hit him. Alim could see the brush shaking as the enemy weapon fired. The enemy was in that small pile of brush!

Alim switched on the projector and pointed the snout toward the brush pile. He pulled the trigger. The hose bucked as the thickened fuel streamed out of the nozzle, lighting up the night ahead of him. As the first blazing stream arced across to the brush pile, Alim pulled the trigger again, sending another 3.3 liters of burning fuel into the now-blazing brush pile. When the loud hissing of the flamethrower stopped, a scream came from the brush pile, followed by a choking sound, barely audible over the crackling of the burning brush. Alim hugged the ground and waited. No more firing came from the pile.

In a moment, Sergeant Nevsky came up, got Alim's report, and walked up to the now barely burning pile. He waved the others up. In the center of the brush pile was a dead man. His face and upper torso had been burned away, but the rest of him had been partly protected by some sort of shelter that now smoked and smelled of burning plastic. Next to the man was an American M16 rifle, its handguard melted by the heat.

"Well done, Alim. You have roasted an American spy!" Sergeant Nevsky called out.

"I serve the Soviet Union," Alim replied weakly. He could not take much pride in the incineration of the man, even if he was the enemy.

"Well, let us see what this American was doing so far behind out lines." Nevsky bent down and hooked his rifle sight through the frame of the enemy soldier's melted nylon pack, pulling it out of the burning brush.

The crackling of the fire masked the quiet "ping" of the phosphorus grenade's safety lever.

The team was moving when they heard more shots and screams echo in the distance. Whatever had happened, Slade had put up a good fight. The bad news was that now someone was out there looking for them. After the firefight, they would surely be back.

"Comrade Senior Ensign," the young senior private called softly, "we have received a report from the group searching the area south of Neuferchau. They have engaged an American force and sustained casualties."

"Are they still in contact?" Kovpak asked as he downed the last of the cold tea.

"No, Comrade Senior Ensign, the fighting is over. They are returning with their wounded and dead."

"How large an enemy force did they encounter?"

"At least a platoon," the radio operator replied. "The group suffered many dead and wounded during the engagement, including Sergeant Nevsky who was killed by a booby trap the American bastards left on one of their own wounded."

"Call battalion headquarters and report the engagement," Kovpak said, pulling at his ear. "Make sure that headquarters knows they were Americans, but never mind the casualties, say that you do not know about that."

"As you wish, Comrade Senior Ensign."

Neuferchau, Kovpak thought, where are these people going, and for what purpose? Perhaps it was time to mount a real hunt, to put the whole wolf pack on the prey.

"Comrade," Kovpak added as the radio operator began his transmission, "tell the battalion commander I am on my way to his headquarters."

"Just so."

I want to look at the map of the area around Neuferchau, Kovpak thought as he turned up his collar and walked out into the cold wind. What is there that these Yankees want?

★31★

"Comrade Senior Ensign, should we not have other platoons with us?"

The sergeant was clearly nervous. The rumors of rear-area attacks were spreading and enlarging. This morning, Kovpak had heard that an American Marine Division was raiding at will behind Soviet lines. It was amazing what stories were concocted by fearful minds. A skirmish became an offensive, a probe became a campaign.

"Sergeant, surely you do not wish to share the glory of our capture of the other American terrorists with the other platoons?"

The look on the sergeant's face indicated that he would be pleased to share the honors—and the dangers. Amid all the rumors, the fact that the ambush had been only a single enemy soldier had gotten lost. The real loss was that the enemy had been killed before he could be questioned. Something was going on in the 1st Company's sector, but what it was remained a mystery.

Kovpak had convinced Captain Yurasov to cast his net wide, then pull it tight when it caught something. The two men had poured over the map, looking for hide areas likely to provide refuge for the terrorists. Tonight, Kovpak's platoon was patrolling the wooded areas southeast of Oebisfelde. The area was at the extreme north end of their area of responsibility. Yurasov had assigned each platoon a sector. Kovpak, in command of 1st Platoon, had drawn the north sector, putting him the farthest from any reinforcement. Kovpak assumed that was because his troops were better soldiers, less likely to need any help.

They had dismounted their trucks on the road that ran from Kathendorf in the south to Meisterhorst in the north, moving into the wooded area to the west. Now they moved slowly in squad subunits, combing the dark woods for hidden infiltrators. They had been in the woods for only half an hour before one of the men in 2nd Squad found the abandoned campsite.

Campsite was too grand a word, actually. There were some broken branches, a patch or two of scuffed dirt, and a pair of corpses.

The dead men were buried on the edge of a tiny clearing. One had been shot repeatedly in the back. His uniform was that of the Railway Troops. He had no weapon, no combat gear at all. He had probably been a prisoner, although there were no signs of interrogation.

The other was an American. His uniform bore no insignia, indicating that he was probably one of their "green berets." He had been shot in the back, at the base of the spine. An empty pack and the dead man's combat equipment, except for his weapon, were buried with him. The American's body had been laid on top of the dead Russian in the shallow grave. The identity tag around his neck read "Mitchell, Sylvan NMI."

"Comrade Senior Ensign, shall I contact company headquarters and report this discovery?" the apprehensive sergeant asked.

"And report what?" Kovpak asked. "That we have captured two dead men?"

The dead American's pockets yielded no information, nor did the pack and equipment. The Soviet soldier was the puzzlement. How did a soldier of the Railway Troops come to be in this hole in the woods? Kovpak was no detective, but he had spent his life outwitting detectives. Perhaps he could puzzle this mystery out.

"Place the American's equipment and clothing in the pack and bring all of it along." Kovpak fixed the nervous sergeant with a cold stare. "Make sure that *all* the American's gear is accounted for."

"It is done, Comrade Senior Ensign!"

"And make certain everyone is alert! These men are only recently dead. I do not want any of 1st Platoon to join them!"

As his squads moved out to finish the sweep through the woods, Kovpak tried to fit this piece into the puzzle.

An hour later, the three squads reached the far edge of the wooded area. Kovpak called a halt and sat down on the cold ground to rest a minute and look over the ground beyond the woods.

"Sergeant, give me the night-vision device."

The sergeant unslung his AKS-74 with the night-vision scope mounted above the receiver.

Kovpak put the weapon to his shoulder, settled into a comfortable sitting position, and slowly scanned the flat fields to the west of the wooded area. The image in the tiny greenish screen was hazy around the edges, but the center of the image was clear enough to make out details. There was nothing to see, really, just the autobahn that ran east to west off to the north and the railroad that crossed over it in the distance. As Kovpak watched, a train appeared from the east and made its way west, laden with BMP-2s and air defense artillery vehicles. Kovpak followed the train with his scope until it crossed over the bridge and disappeared from sight. He was just about to turn the scope off when the movement under the rail bridge caught his eye.

The day had gone slowly. The team had rotated the watch on the bridge, two on, three off, with one of the pair of watchers changed every hour. There had been nothing to see except frequent convoys on the autobahn and trains carrying tanks, self-propelled artillery, and fighting vehicles. The tanks were mostly T-72s being shipped from the western military districts of the Soviet Union. The traffic on the autobahn consisted of long truck convoys and engineer units.

Taggart dutifully recorded each sighting. McCullough took the data and prepared an encrypted message. There was no way of knowing whether anyone would receive the data burst. All they knew for sure was that the radio would not receive. There was no way to test its transmitter. They would transmit just before they moved out for the bridge, in case some Soviet radio intercept outfit was listening.

They took the time to study the layout of the bridge. The right of way on either side of the track was cleared of all brush for ten meters. The track itself sat on a gravel bed that extended a meter on either side of the rails. It was standard gauge with steel cross-ties.

There was no on-site security, but motorized patrols of East Germans in gray uniforms checked it often and at irregular intervals. It would be impossible to follow the tracks to the bridge overpass unobserved. The approach would have to be made overland.

Sundown came early. The team waited until it was completely dark, then slowly made their way out of the hide. They moved silently, slowly, and with total security. Malle carried the device. The big man carried the hundred-pound device like a daypack.

A ditch that ran roughly parallel to the highway gave them cover to get close to the bridge. They waited until a security check was made. From the ditch, they moved one at a time, the other four covering the moving man from the ditch and then from the underside of the bridge. Just after midnight, the team was up under the western side of the bridge. There was a flat ledge under the bridge about eighteen inches wide. Malle gently placed the device on the ledge, then slid down to make room for the two diggers.

Malle and Thompson provided security on each side, while Cohen and Taggart dug the hole the bomb would rest in. The two men dug slowly, keeping the noise of the digging to a minimum. At night, sound could carry a long way. McCullough sat with the device, looking for all the world like a worried papa and his unholy child.

When they finally had the hole dug, Cohen and Taggart replaced Malle and Thompson on guard. The weapons man and the engineer would place and arm the device.

The two sergeants eased the device out of its rucksack and slid it, still in its Styrofoam packing material, into the hole, the rounded end of the cylinder first. As they did so, a sound reached them, a faint rumbling from the east.

The train swept over three minutes later, shaking the bridge. A cloud of dust filtered down under the bridge as the train sped over. The team pulled up under the span, hunkered down against the dust, their fingers in their ears to keep out the noise, waiting out the passage of the train. It took five minutes for the train to pass. When the noise stopped, the men shook the dirt from their clothes and equipment. Malle slipped off the poncho he had thrown over the device and went back to work.

He turned the combination lock and removed the flat base plate, exposing the arming panel. Malle turned the timer handle on the hour timer, setting it for four hours. He then turned the minute timer and set it for thirty minutes. Thompson had the timer wires ready to go. Malle slipped a thin copper wire through each end of the timer handles and wired each to tie-down points on the rim of the arming panel. The wires were to keep the timer handles from moving once they had been set. That way, vibration or accidental movement would not set the device off prematurely or allow the planned delay to be changed.

Once the wires were in place, Malle turned to McCullough.

"Ready to arm, Captain. You want to inspect?"

McCullough looked at the face of the device. The times were correct, the wires in place.

McCullough took a deep breath and let it all out. He looked at both NCOs. They seemed totally unconcerned that this was an atomic bomb that they had just rigged. A picture of the device going off flickered through McCullough's mind, followed by the picture of those tanks attacking.

"Prepare to arm device," McCullough said firmly.

Malle was reaching for the detonator when the shots rang out.

"They're close, Beej. I can feel 'em."

"Close don't count, Murph," BJ whispered back. "We got to get our hands on them."

"They're already come an' gone, man," King muttered. "We need to get that bomb out from under that bridge and burn it. Then we can go home."

"That's where we're headed, Ty," BJ whispered. The bridge was about two kilometers away, far enough under the best conditions. BJ's main fear was that they would run into the ADM team and end up in a firefight with them. It would be tough to explain the nuclear moratorium over rifle sights.

"Murph, take the point," BJ whispered in the man's ear, "let's take it slow and keep our eyes open."

Murphy nodded and switched rucksacks with King. The pointman did not carry the radio. BJ could tell that Kosinski was miffed by his use of King and Murphy to run point, usually his duty. BJ just could not bring himself to trust the man on point yet. He wanted to see how he handled himself. Murphy slipped out of the security position. One by one, the rest of the team followed, walking in the stooped, slow-motion combat style.

They stayed along the tree line, just inside, using the dark foliage of the evergreens for concealment. The last 200 meters to the bridge was flat and wide open. They would crawl that stretch.

After two long hours, they came to the last stand of trees before the bridge. The first four men dropped to their bellies and crawled to the edge of the tree line to eyeball the target. King remained back covering the rear with his SAW.

"There it is," Murphy hissed. Even in the darkness, the bridge and road were easily visible, shiny ribbons in the dark landscape. BJ put his rifle up to his eye and turned on the AN/PVS-4 night-vision sight. The bridge was not guarded. That struck BJ as odd, but the Soviets could not put guards on every bridge and road intersection. Even they did not have that many troops. He focused the scope on the underside of the bridge, watching. After a minute, a flicker of movement caught his eye. They were there!

"Got 'em!" BJ said softly. "They're under the bridge, just like they're supposed to be."

BJ switched off the night-vision scope and started to move forward. Hickey's hand stopped him and pulled him down slowly. Hickey was pointing off to the right. BJ strained his eyes to see, scanning the darkness. Nothing. He slowly brought up the night scope and switched it on. In the direction Hickey had pointed, a group of men was moving down the shallow ditch that ran end on to their position. Through the scope, it was easy to make out their AK rifles and RPG-16.

"Oh, shit!" BJ hissed.

"How many, BJ?" Hickey asked.

"Two squads," BJ answered. "How'd you see them, Hickey?"

"Caught some movement out of the corner of my eye."

"Lucky."

Through the scope, BJ could see the squads deploying along the ditch. Two men continued on down the ditch to a spot fifty meters away from the others. BJ could make out the RPG-16 that one of them carried. A fire support team.

"Come on," BJ whispered, "let's move. This party's going to start without us."

The team slid out of the tree line, making its way not toward the bridge, as they had planned, but toward the ditch. If they could surprise the Soviets, they might save the ADM team. Even if they didn't save the team, they still had to fight the Soviets. Either way, the deal sucked.

God bless you, Jinx, for our extra firepower, BJ thought as they slithered down the rise, God bless you.

"All squads are in position, Comrade Senior Ensign," his nervous sergeant whispered.

"Excellent. Tell them to wait for my command."

"Just so!"

"Send this message to the company commander," Kovpak instructed the radio operator, "tell him we have the enemy located and invite him to their capture."

"Exactly so, Comrade Senior Ensign," the radio operator answered, changing the frequencies. "We are going to take them alive?"

Kovpak looked down at the young Ukrainian's excited face. "There is always the possibility that we may do so."

The young soldier looked confused, but instantly put on a mask of professional indifference. It did not pay to even look like you disagreed with the plans of an officer. He transmitted the message just as Kovpak had instructed.

Soon, my little foxes, Kovpak thought, soon I will have you. How sad that you should raid the hen house, only to run into a pack of wolves!

The ditch that held his squads ran almost parallel to the autobahn. The fire support group at the far end was farthest from the bridge. When the blocking force was in place on the other side of the road, Kovpak would assault the bridge with the troops in the ditch. The Americans would be caught like rats, and the risk was small. If there were more Americans in the area, the battalion commander and the rest of the battalion would deal with them.

I wish I still had those firebugs with me, Kovpak smiled to himself. They would give these Americans a warm welcome to the German Democratic Republic. Kovpak was suddenly reminded of the smoldering, wild-eyed American who had led the Contra attack on the training base in Nicaragua. The man had burst through the burning wall of that building like some demon from hell. If the man's old machine gun had not been empty, Colonel Bodnya would be dead now. How odd that he should think of the man now.

The thought of Nicaragua brought back a quick flood of memories of the Fort Hood mission. Memories of Fort Hood brought back memories of the American woman he and the colonel had shared. Was it really only two, no, three weeks ago that we were in America? It seemed like a lifetime ago. Rather, it seemed like a film he had seen at the cinema.

The soldier at his radio looked up and started to speak. The faraway look on the face of the senior ensign made him stop. The ensign had an odd smile playing about his lips. He chuckled, then shrugged.

''Comrade Senior Ensign . . .''

''Yes, what is it?''

''The blocking force is in position.''

''Then let us take these gangsters!''

Murphy and Hickey were only twenty meters from the Soviet fire support team. Crawling on their bellies, they had slowly come up behind the two Russians, who seemed oblivious to their two stalkers. The rest of the LRRP team was strung out in a line perpendicular to the ditch. With luck, they could catch the Soviet squads in a deep kill zone while they were still far enough away from the bridge and the team of Green Berets working under it.

Hickey and Murphy were tensing for a rush on the Soviet fire team when the green flare arced up over the bridge. The RPG gunner raised his launcher to his shoulder and aimed it at the bridge. Murphy, directly behind the man, buried his face in the dirt, waiting for the backblast of the weapon. It never came. Hickey dropped the SAW, sprang forward with his Air Force survival knife, and drove the blade into the Russian's kidney. The man's scream was drowned out by the roar of the AKS-74s and RPKS-74s.

Hickey left the knife in the gunner and turned to jump the assistant. Grabbing the man's rifle with both hands, Hickey flung himself backward. The Soviet had a grip on his rifle. He came along after Hickey, who rolled down on his butt and back, put up a foot, and sent the astonished Russian flying over his head to land on his stabbed comrade. The two Soviets fell in a heap, the one with Hickey's knife in him howling in pain. Hickey rolled onto his feet now, wading into the pair on the ground with the AKM-74's rifle butt. The two Soviets were out cold in a second. Hickey jumped back out of the ditch and ran up to secure the SAW. Back in the ditch, he popped out the bipod and set the light machine gun up to cover the ditch.

Across the field, the two squads were assaulting on line. They moved quickly, firing short bursts from the hip. The recon team let them get twenty-five meters from the ditch, then opened up with the M203s and the SAWs.

Half a dozen Soviets bit the dirt in the first volley from the team. The others, confused, but disciplined, veered toward the ambushers.

Oh, shit, BJ thought as the green flame arced up over the ditch. Why couldn't they have waited two more minutes?

As the line of Soviet soldiers climbed up out of the ditch and started across the open area toward the bridge, BJ, King, and Kosinski scrabbled down the rise, spreading out and searching for anything that would give them some cover. King was the first one down behind a clump of brush. He brought the M249 up and extended the bipod, then stretched out behind the machine gun, waiting for BJ's signal.

BJ stepped in a hole and fell to his knees, catching himself with one hand. He had not seen the hole, but now slithered back to see if it was big enough to hold him. It wasn't, but it was better than nothing. Off to the right, Kosinski dropped to his knees and sighted around a small mound.

BJ could not see the ditch, but there had been no shooting and more important, no RPGs from it. Murphy and Hickey must have gotten the RPG team.

"Fire!" BJ screamed at the team. He pulled the trigger of the M16, firing off single shots as rapidly as he could pull the trigger. It was easier to aim single shots at this range than wasting bullets on full-auto. The LRRPs opened up on the Soviet assault line, now caught out in the open by the team's hasty ambush.

King put a steady stream of tracers up and down the ragged line of Soviets. Two grenades from the M203s thumped out, their small charges detonating behind the Soviet line. Soviet soldiers were falling now, but the others turned, attacking the attackers, even though they had a broad open space to cross to get at the ambushers.

A few of those farthest away continued to assault the bridge, their original target. King and Kosinski hammered at them from the knoll. With the night-vision sight, BJ picked off a rifleman who had just fired his BG-15 grenade launcher at Murphy and Hickey. The Soviet twitched backward, them stumbled and fell forward. BJ put two more rounds into the still figure, then looked for another target.

Hickey and Murphy were working on the rest of the Soviets that had turned to assault the ambush. Hickey's SAW stitched back and forth across the running figures. Murphy's grenades were not having much effect, so after firing three, he concentrated on his M16, firing three-round bursts at each running figure.

BJ scanned the assault line through the AN/PVS-4 sight. One figure was waving the others on, shouting.

The leader, thought BJ as he laid the shaking crosshairs on the figure one hundred meters away. God, I wish I was a trained sniper, even at this short range. The figure paused. BJ blew out half a breath and squeezed the trigger. The figure spun and fell. BJ searched for the fallen leader. He could not see the man on the ground.

"Damn it," BJ said to himself, "where is he?" At least he had hit the sucker.

One by one, the Soviet line was falling. King was still firing his SAW, putting short bursts into individual targets. Kosinski was doing the same with his M16, saving his 40mm grenades. Two Soviets had set up an RPKS-74 machine gun and opened up on the slope, trying to give support to the ambush breakers. Murphy silenced the gun with a round from the captured RPG.

There had been no fire from under the bridge. The ADM team was still hiding up under the span.

As the team mopped up the few Soviets still alive and firing, BJ dug into his ruck and pulled out the bullhorn. Its bell was smashed into an oval, probably from the landing, and the microphone on the back end was loose. BJ pulled the trigger and blew into the mike, hearing the rasp from the front end. At least it still worked.

BJ pointed the bullhorn at the bridge and yelled into it, calling the ADM team.

"God damn, sir," Thompson nearly yelled, "there's a firefight goin' on out there!"

"Thanks for the bulletin!" McCullough answered. He had nearly pissed on himself when the first burst had shattered the silence. Across the open field, red tracers streaked from right to left. The sharp bangs of exploding 40mm grenades punctuated the rattling of machine guns.

Every mouth dropped open when the voice on the bullhorn called, "ADM Zero Three Two Alfa, Abort! I say again, Abort!"

★32★

"ADM-032A, this is Sergeant BJ Kirkley of Company G, 143d Infantry," the voice said over the bullhorn, "we are here to tell you to abort your mission! Do you acknowledge?"

"What do you think, sir," Thompson asked, "do we acknowledge?"

McCullough did not answer. He was still stunned by the sudden developments that had just taken place in front of them.

After a pause, the voice came up again. "Captain Ben McCullough, 10th SF Group, you are ordered by Special Operations Command, Europe, to abort the detonation of your zero point one kiloton Special Atomic Demolition Munition. Do you acknowledge? If so, use your flashlight to signal 'yes.'"

"Holy shit, sir, he knows your name," Cohen said, stating the obvious.

"He knows a lot more than that," McCullough snapped.

Ten minutes later, the man with the bullhorn slipped under the bridge accompanied by one of the largest black men McCullough had ever seen.

"Captain McCullough? I'm Sergeant Kirkley, this is PFC King." BJ extended his hand to the captain, who shook it gingerly.

"You're with who, again?"

"Company G, 143d," BJ answered, "we're III Corps LRRPs. We were sent by SOCEUR to bring you back. NATO and the

Soviets have declared a nuclear moratorium. If you set off your device, it could cause another nuclear exchange.''

''And we're just supposed to believe you?''

''No, sir, we have the recall code for your team. If your radio had been operational, you would have received this message.'' BJ handed the captain a sheet of paper with three lines of code groups.

McCullough handed the message to Thompson, who began flipping through the CEOI book.

''Who's Mickey Mouse's wife?'' Cohen blurted.

BJ looked at the tense little medic. ''Minnie, and she's fuckin' Goofy,'' he replied, giving the punchline of a popular old joke.

Cohen's eyes darted over to King. ''Sir, this one could be an Angolan!''

King shoved the barrel of his SAW between the medic's glasses' lens and his left eye.

''I could be yo' mama!''

''Gentlemen!'' McCullough said, getting the medic by the sleeve and pulling him off King's muzzle.

''Sir, this message is the abort code,'' Thompson said, carefully putting the CEOI book back in its waterproof bag. Cohen stiffened, still clutching his weapon.

''Is this guy okay?'' BJ asked, jerking his thumb at Cohen.

''Sometimes,'' McCullough answered, smiling at Cohen. ''Medics, you know.'' He could feel the tension in Cohen. The man fairly vibrated with distrust and hatred.

''I guess my old A-team sergeant was right,'' BJ said warmly, ''there's two kinds of folks in SF, medics and the rest of us.''

Thompson laughed at the old saying. It was truer now than ever before. The joke seemed to break the tension for everyone except Cohen.

''Sir, we need to get the fuck out of here,'' said BJ, ''and take that thing with us.''

''You're right,'' said McCullough. ''Half the Soviet Army's going to be on us now if we hang around here.''

Cohen slipped behind McCullough and Thompson. The CO and Thompson might be fooled, but he wasn't. These bastards were good, but he could spot a ringer a mile away. These guys were GRU for sure, even the black guy. He was a nice touch, though.

It won't work, though, Cohen thought, we didn't come this

far for nothing! You didn't kill Mitchell for nothing. These guys may be fooled, but not me.

Cohen sat with his knees pulled up in front of him, his back to the device. Thompson glanced over at him. Cohen smiled and made a show of removing his cap and wiping his face with it.

"Come on, let's bag this baby and get out of here," McCullough said to Malle.

"Here, Gunner," Cohen injected, "I'll give you a hand."

These gullible bastards may believe this crock, but they don't fool me, Cohen thought as he helped Malle pull the device up out of its hole. As they were getting the rucksack in position, Cohen let the device slip. It rolled down the embankment as Cohen yelled, "Damn it!" and jumped down after it. The medic caught the device by the hour timer handle as it slid down the slope, turning the handle, adding a few hours to the time set. He turned his back to the others, slipped the detonator into its arming well, and threw the toggle switch.

"Got it," he called back up to the startled team. "Thompson, bring down that end plate. Let's seal this thing back up."

In a second, Thompson slid down to him. Cohen took the end plate and quickly dropped it in place, spinning the knob to lock it. It was too dark to see the timer dials. It really didn't matter.

"There," he said, beaming, "now this mother's secure."

The two men pulled the device back up to its perch.

"Is it ready to travel?" BJ asked as the two men rejoined the group.

"Yes," McCullough said, embarrassment in his voice after the clumsy handling of the device.

"We'll meet you across the road, then," BJ said as he and King started down the slope.

The big captain nodded. "Be right there."

When they had their gear on, McCullough sent the team on across the road. Malle was carrying the bomb. McCullough waited for a couple of minutes to watch the back side of the road as the team left their perch under the overpass. Seeing nothing, he then jogged across the road where BJ waited for him.

"I sent the others on."

McCullough nodded and the two men jogged slowly up the rise.

"Comrade Sergeant, should we move up?"

"No," Sergeant Somolov answered firmly.

''But we have not heard from the senior ensign.''

''And we will maintain our position until we do.''

Somolov looked at the anxious private.

''Comrade, no one ever went to the guardhouse for following orders.''

★33★

What a place to be wounded! The abuse would be intolerable. Even the colonel would not be able to resist the temptation. He would not report it to the *feldsher*. Perhaps no one would notice the stain on his camouflage uniform trousers.

Kovpak gingerly slid the second field dressing over his right buttock. It hurt—badly. The thumb did not hurt at all. The pain from it would come later. At least the lower half of his left thumb remained. Loss of the whole thumb would make him a cripple. Still, it could be worse. A few centimeters either way and the slugs would have ripped his chest, or his groin. It was embarrassing to be shot in the ass, but a disaster to be gelded.

Where had the other enemies come from? He had seen no movement from the rise, only under the bridge. It was obvious that the Americans had been more than just a small team of terrorists. American Rangers had repeatedly attacked in strength behind the Soviet lines, assaulting a division headquarters a few days ago. His ambushers must have been part of some similar unit.

Now, if he could locate the radio, he must warn the battalion and send for the response force. The Americans were still in the area, he had seen them come out from under the bridge and slip off over the rise from which his platoon had been slaughtered.

If the Scout-Diversionary Platoon could reach him quickly, they could track the Yankees. Where the hell was his 3rd Squad?

It took Kovpak almost ten minutes to find the dead radio operator and raise the battalion headquarters on the radio.

256

* * *

"Comrade Commander, Senior Ensign Kovpak is on the radio," the breathless operator gasped, "he says his platoon has been ambushed by a large American force. He has taken many casualties and has been wounded himself."

Bodnya was on his feet before he even realized it.

"Where is Ensign Kovpak?"

"Near Bergfriede, Comrade Commander."

"Contact the other companies. Have them converge on the area. Alert the response force and tell them to assemble immediately, then alert our German friends in the Frontier Troops. I want their two standby Mi-8s here immediately. I will accompany the response force to assist Ensign Kovpak. Tell the Frontier Troops control post that there is a large American divisionary force on the ground and that they may attempt to retreat through the border defenses."

Wounded, how seriously? Bodnya wondered as he pulled on his combat equipment. By the time he emerged from his room, the Scout-Diversionary Platoon was already falling into four ranks in front of the headquarters. Their trucks were warming up next to the barn, the exhausts blowing steam in the cold air.

"Comrade Senior Lieutenant, you may turn off those trucks. We will fly to support our comrades tonight." Bubovik's face split into a wide grin. A heliborne assault!

"Exactly so, Comrade Commander!" the lieutenant exclaimed brightly.

He could feel the blood running slowly down the backs of his thighs, warm at first, then cold as it slowed and soaked into his insulated trousers. The cold was beginning to really hit him now that the flush of battle had faded. Was he losing much blood? It was hard to tell, since he could not see the wound. The wounds hurt now, the pain dull and throbbing. He could keep the hand up to stop the throbbing, but it was hard to keep your butt up in the air. Except maybe if you were a staff officer!

That thought cheered him enough to look for his errant squad. Perhaps the Americans had killed them, too. Kovpak shouldered the radio and began to walk toward the highway, using an RPKS-74 for a crutch. The weapon's gunner, who lay spread-eagled on his back, had no further need of it.

As he neared the highway, he could hear the sound of trucks approaching.

* * *

"Comrade Captain, I need your opinion on something."

The look on Nolan's face told Harlan that something was up. He climbed into the BTR through the side hatch that Tedder held open for him. Tedder stayed outside, casually standing guard.

"What is it, Walt?" Harlan asked, settling onto a bench.

"I just picked up a message on their rear security net, in the clear. I think it's a pursuit outfit."

"After us?"

"No, sir, after some folks about here."

Nolan pointed to a spot on the map. The spot was about twenty kilometers from their position.

"What are they saying?"

"They think they have these guys bagged, they want support units on call."

Harlan sat for a minute. "Who are the guys they're after?"

"Sounds like a LRRP team or maybe SF."

That pretty well made the decision. If the Soviets had an SF team cornered, Harlan would go to their aid. The mission cover was one thing, but SF blood was another matter.

"Well, let's saddle up then." Harlan rose and started out of the BTR. He turned in the door. "I don't know if I can sell this to the Muj. If I can't, we'll do it ourselves."

Mamud was waiting for him beside the 2S6.

"What is happening, my friend?" the little Mujahaddin asked.

"The VV are hunting someone nearby. I will take my men and join them. Perhaps we can help the prey get away."

Harlan saw the Uzbeks bristle at the mention of Internal Troops. The VV had made a name for themselves in every Soviet Socialist Republic. They were under the control of the Ministry of Internal Affairs, but nonetheless were soldiers. It was the Internal Troops who put down riots and quashed dissent. The Russians purposely stationed Internal Troops of specific ethnic origins in areas where the population was of a different ethnic group, antagonistic to them. The theory was that it was easier to shoot a stranger than a neighbor. There was little love lost between the local population and the Internal Troops.

"Inshallah, we will return. If not, Allah be with you, my friend."

Harlan turned and started back to the personnel carrier. He had not taken half a dozen steps when Mamud called to him.

"Do not think that we will let you have these dogs to yourselves, my friend," Mamud said, "we will have our share, too!"

Indeed you will, my friend, Harlan thought as he turned and waved at the Uzbek.

He had not thought the Muj would sit there while Flack's people took on the Internal Troops. Their pride, plus a hatred for the Russian bastards, would not let them sit out this fight. The Internal Troops had killed hundreds of Uzbeks in 1989 during the ethnic rioting. Aside from the killings, the Internal Troops had prevented the Uzbeks from ridding the Fergana Valley of the despised Turk-Meskhetis.

Harlan would have gone on anyway if the Muj had decided to sit this one out, but he was glad that he didn't have to.

★34★

"I hate this," CWO3 Howard "Hellhound" Harris said as he watched the readout dials come up. "First they want you to do one thing, then they want you to do another. I wish they'd make up their fuckin' minds."

Harris was increasingly annoyed with every order, every mission. He and his pilot, Captain Alan "Bat" Masterson, had flown far too many hours every day of the war. Their nerves were on edge and their reaction times were dropping. Harris thought that they would run out of Hellfire missiles days ago, but the little tank killers were a priority item for overseas shipment. As fast as they could be palletized and loaded, they had been flown from depots in the U.S. to Germany.

They had a full load of eight on board today, but Harris wondered how long the supply would last. At least they had a seemingly endless supply of 70mm rockets.

The techs were unwrapping a batch of the new 70mm flechette rockets now. Harris had fired one in a training course a year before, but the flechette rounds were just coming into the inventory as the war broke out. A much smaller version had been used in Vietnam and then shelved. The new flechette warhead acted like a flying shotgun. Fused for proximity burst, the rocket fired hundred of small steel spikes ahead of it in a cone-shaped pattern when it detonated. It could be used against lightly armored vehicles, troops in the open, and, most importantly, against other helicopters.

The Soviets had been hunting NATO attack helicopters with

a vengeance. Both the new Mi-28 Havoc and Ka-34 Hokum attack helicopters had radar for targeting other helicopters. The Ka-34, called the "Hokum" by NATO, was a dedicated helicopter hunter. Lacking a specific helicopter to meet this threat, NATO had fitted Air-To-Air Stinger missiles to many of the unarmed scout and transport helicopters. AH1S Cobras were also ATAS-equipped, and functioned as aircap for some flights of Apaches and other NATO attack helicopters, freeing them up for tank killing. The flechette rocket would give the Apaches more air-to-air capability of their own.

"Lighten up, Harris," the pilot answered, "you're just tired, like all of us. Look at the bright side, the nukes have quit falling."

Harris snorted. Yeah, the nukes had quit falling. So what? The ones that fell ruined both sides. He didn't know what the Soviets had taken, but he had flown over that airbase in Belgium. Liege something . . . That place has been flattened. The base had disappeared. The little town five kilometers away had been blown away, too. They had flown by upwind to keep any fallout away from their ship. God knew how many people, civilians and soldiers alike, had been burned by that radiation. Seeing that destruction, Harris had felt for the first time the sickening feeling that they were not going to win this war.

The Soviets had thousands of miles of depth behind them, room to retreat, to regroup, to form new armies. NATO had its back to the Atlantic from the beginning. Compared to the Soviet Union, Europe was tiny. Without nukes, they would not be able to hold the Soviets, and even if NATO used more nukes, it would be the Soviet's allies in the Warsaw Pact that felt the fire, not Mother Russia. Either way, the Soviets won.

"Ready when you are, C.B.," came Masterson's voice over the intercom.

Harris banished the gloomy thoughts from his mind. That kind of thinking belonged to someone else. His job was to kill Russian tanks and, tonight, to shoot up an entry corridor for some sort of deep penetration mission.

That's what I need, Harris thought to himself, a little deep penetration would fix me up fine right now.

He flipped down the night-vision goggles and waited a second for his eyes to adjust to the blue-green glow of the tiny TV screens. The dark green attack ship lifted into the darkness and skimmed the trees to the east. He would be back in an hour, hopefully for a meal and a long sleep. Hopefully.

The pain began right behind his eyes. Masterson knew it was from the night-vision goggles. Straining his eyes to see more through the twin scopes, he brought on the pain himself. It was impossible not to. The night vision showed you the shapes of things outside, but your brain had to interpret the shapes. There was also the persistent threat of telephone wires and power lines. It was almost impossible to see the wires themselves . . . in time; it was the poles and steel towers you looked for. To hit a wire was to die, so you strained as hard as you could to pick them up far away. The harder you looked, the more it hurt.

Masterson switched on the intercom.

"How we doin', Hellhound?"

"Running hot, straight, and normal," the gunner replied. Harris was using the Apache's TADS night vision, a much larger version of the personal NVG worn by the pilot. With it, he could make out terrain features by both visual and thermal images.

"See that gap, Bat?" Harris asked. "That's the strike point for the launch."

Their mission tonight was to fire a pattern of rockets at an area where Soviet air defenses covered a specific sector of the front. Each 70mm Hydra rocket had a multiple munition warhead that carried nine small antiarmor bomblets. The rocket would scatter them over the area where the Soviet air defense unit was parked. The effect was an instant mortar barrage on the vehicles, which would destroy some of the antiaircraft battery and keep the survivors' heads down while the deep penetration mission went through.

Masterson's flight of four Apaches did not need to see the targets. The on-board computer would launch the rockets at the correct angle for a hit. His Apaches would be gone before the rockets detonated, spewing their bomblets onto the target area.

After the suppression mission, they would fly fifteen kilometers north and attack a Soviet tank regiment with their Hellfire missiles. Again, the Apaches would never even see their targets.

They would launch the missiles from behind cover, then run for home. The missiles would be guided by laser beams aimed at the tanks by Army scouts hiding in the woods. The Hellfires would home in on the reflected laser light and destroy whatever the laser fingered. The Apaches could designate their own targets, but they had to be in sight of the target to do so. Masterson knew that Harris didn't care if he ever saw a Soviet soldier or vehicle. If he could go on killing them without ever seeing them, that would be just fine with him.

As they came up to the strike point, the on-board computers took over, pitching the noses of the ungainly helicopters upward and to the right. Each Apache carried thirty-eight rockets for a total of 1368 submunitions. The flight fired together, the rockets rippling out of their tubes and arcing across the night sky like a swarm of hellish fireflies.

When the last rocket cleared its tube, each Apache wheeled and headed for the next target, bobbing and weaving over the dark deadly terrain. The entire mission would take only forty-five minutes, but Masterson was already soaked in sweat and exhausted. Maybe after this one they could get a little sleep and some hot chow. Doubtful, but maybe.

"Radar's flashlighting!" Throckmorton's voice broke with the sudden anxiety.

"What kind, Paul?" Lew McFarlane replied. The co-pilot's voice was calm and reassuring, the type of voice that airline pilots liked to cultivate.

"A 2S6, maybe two," Throckmorton replied. "Hard to tell, but they're flashlighting like crazy."

"Where's our suppressive fire?" Al Dunwoody, the pilot, broke in.

"Should have been there by now," Throckmorton said, glancing at the bright glowing dial of his Rolex. "I hope that those Army pukes don't screw up, we need . . ."

On the horizon off to the left, a cluster of tiny cloudlets appeared in the air, dark against the sky made bright by the night-vision scopes. The little clouds were smoke from the rocket warheads bursting, sowing the ground below with their deadly seeds.

"Look at that! I'm sorry we can't see what it looks like on the ground!"

"Fuck that. If you can see them, they can see you!"

"I know, I know," McFarlane answered, reciting the litany, "if they can see you, they can hit you; if they can hit you, they can kill you."

Captain Dunwoody did not reply, but pointed the nose of the Boeing V-22 Osprey toward the notch in the wood line where they would penetrate the Soviet air defense net. The tilt-rotor V-22, designed specifically for special ops insertion and extraction, was manned by the Air Force's 16th Special Operations Squadron. Dunwoody hoped there would be no wait time. Waiting got you killed as surely as being seen. He hoped these LRRPs would be waiting for them at the pickup zone. He should have been more careful what he wished for.

"Target!"

Aleksandr Aleksandrovich P'talkin had just about nodded off when the voice on his headphone screamed, scaring Aleksandr so badly that he jumped, striking his shoulder on the right feed chute.

"Target," the voice shouted again, "200 degrees magnetic, single aircraft!"

Aleksandr flipped the arming switch on the four 30mm guns, slaving them to the radar. The turret automatically swung to the left, the guns pivoting up on either side of the big turret of the 2S6.

Single target, he thought, at least it's not a flight of fighters.

The turret stopped and began oscillating back and forth, the radar searching for the contact. The guns were set to fire as soon as the radar locked on a target. Aleksandr was now an observer, not a gunner. He sat waiting for the loud roaring of the 30mms.

Instead of a roar, Aleksandr heard a ripping sound overhead. He tripped the latch on the small hatch and stood up in the opening, searching the dark sky. Overhead, a cluster of small smoke puffs had appeared, like flak bursts.

What idiots, Aleksandr thought, if they were right over our heads, we would be firing . . .

The first explosion was such a surprise that Aleksandr thought it was his own guns going off. He realized it wasn't when two of the small submunitions went off on the turret top of the 2S6. One of the small bombs detonated over the ammunition feed chute on the right side, the same chute on which Aleksandr had banged his shoulder. His chest was struck by side spray fragments from the bomblets. Inside the turret, the 30mm shells in the path of the fiery jet exploded, turning the turret into a crucible of fire and flying steel. Aleksandr's legs were ripped by hundreds of bits of metal, burned by the fire of dozens of exploding 30mm shells. He hardly had time to scream before the force of the explosions popped him out of the turret like a cork out of a bottle. Aleksandr hit hard on the cold ground. Pain shot through his shoulder now, matching the burning that rushed up from his legs. As he lay on his side trying to catch the breath that had been knocked from him, he watched the other vehicles in the battery explode, riddled by an unseen force.

Who? he wondered as the pain became the focus of his thoughts, who could do this to us unseen?

The 2S6, burning full length, erupted in a ball of fire that put an end to Aleksandr's blurred speculation, as well as his life.

"Sir, we got company," Thompson said as the blacked-out truck lights crested the rise.

"Where?"

"Movin' up the highway, sir, trucks, no armor." The engineer disappeared, rejoining King in the observation post.

"Shit."

"Got any suggestions?" BJ asked McCullough, deferring to the man's rank.

"Maybe one."

McCullough dug in his pack and came out with two of the PDMs.

"I remember an old trick from Ranger School where I served on the Opposing Forces Detachment for a while," he explained. "We set up a fake camp, put a man under the fire in a spider hole, and let the students sweep through the camp. We used to 'kill' a bunch of 'em when they stood warming their hands over the fire. Then, we'd ambush them when they came back out the way they went in. It always worked."

"Too bad these aren't Ranger students," Murphy grumbled. He was obviously not impressed with the idea.

"No, this might work," BJ countered. "We don't have to kill 'em all, just keep 'em off us for a while till the pickup."

"If we set up a fake camp with our gear, and then scatter these babies around," McCullough said, holding up one of the PDMs, "we can slow them up at least and maybe kill a bunch of them in the bargain."

"Sounds kinda lame to me," Murphy muttered.

"Got a better plan?" BJ snapped at the corporal.

"Nope."

BJ looked at the others. All were nodding their agreement. He looked back at McCullough. "Then let's do it."

Both teams shed their packs and the SF troopers pulled out

their individual shelters and the LRRPs their bivisacks. They quickly set the little shelters up in the trees and camouflaged them just the way they always did on a mission.

McCullough dug a small hole a foot deep in the center of the ring of shelters and placed three heat tabs at the bottom. He covered the heat tabs with a few small branches, lit the tabs, and threw on a big handful of pine needles. By the time the others had finished the perimeter, a small bed of coals burned dimly in the hole. The fire was invisible outside the perimeter, but it would provide the smoke that would hopefully lead the Soviets into the trap.

Murphy and Malle were putting the PDMs out as Thompson and King burst back into the clearing.

"The trucks stopped just down the road!" Thompson said breathlessly. "Looks like about a company." Behind him, King turned and continued to watch the enemy's direction.

"Let's move it then!" BJ snapped.

The two teams quickly slipped out of the clearing in team order, the SF team leading, BJ's team following. McCullough and BJ remained behind until everyone else was out of the clearing.

"Ready?" McCullough asked as he dropped two pine cones onto the tiny fire.

BJ nodded, then the two of them went around the clearing, pulling the pins on the PDMs, working their way around to the spot where the teams had exited. The two men quickly followed, stopping only to arm the booby-trapped claymore mine Hickey had rigged in his shelter.

Twenty-five meters from the clearing, they passed Malle, who had stayed behind to cover them. The three then jogged off after the rest. Behind them, soft pops signaled the arming of the PDMs.

"Off the trucks, quickly," Senior Lieutenant Kashevarov barked as the trucks slowed.

As the two platoons piled off their trucks, Kashevarov spread them out in platoon order. He gave the two platoon leaders their final instructions and the 3rd Company began its sweep through the woods.

"Comrade Senior Ensign, would you be so kind as to lead your squad? They will be the fire support group."

A slighted look crossed Kovpak's face. Kashevarov smiled

and quickly added, "I need an experienced combat veteran to supervise the supporting elements. The Americans are unpredictable, they may counterattack from any direction." Kashevarov's expression was sincere, no trace of condescension.

"My squad and I will be happy to support your assault."

That young officer will go far, Kovpak thought as the lieutenant walked away. Instead of "you are too wounded to fight," he says, "I need your experience." The man knows how to save face and how to curry favor.

Kovpak turned to his dejected squad. They stood like whipped dogs next to the truck. Kovpak had reamed them when they had walked up to see who the trucks were stopping for. He had been furious that they had not fired a shot when their comrades were butchered. Their whining claim that they had only followed his express orders had not blunted his wrath. Now they looked like officer cadets caught with a smuggled copy of *Playboy*.

"Here is an opportunity to redeem yourselves. Make certain you take advantage of it. None of you performed this way in Texas!"

As the understrength company began its sweep of the forest, Kovpak limped along behind, each step literally a pain in the butt.

They were a half a kilometer into the woods when 1st Platoon reported that they smelled smoke from their left flank.

Kashevarov turned the company and moved 2nd Platoon up alongside 1st Platoon, keeping Kovpak's squad back. This done, the company moved quietly toward the smell of burning pine.

The camp was almost invisible. Kashevarov had built camps like this himself, blending into the earth. The campfire was stupid. Spets would never build a fire so far behind enemy lines. These Americans were so spoiled!

Kashevarov silently spread the first two platoons out on line and moved into the center. He studied the camp through his night-vision scope, looking for the sentries. They were good, he could see no movement, no telltale silhouettes. It did not matter. They would be on the camp before the sentries could alert the others. On his signal, all the BG-15 grenadiers would fire and the platoons would assault. Kashevarov slipped the PG-431 illuminating rocket out of his jacket pocket and looked quickly up and down the line. He raised the projector and fired it up through the thin pines.

The popping of the flare was answered by the dull thuds of

the grenade launchers. Immediately, fifty AK-74s and RPKS-74s opened up as the troops began to assault the little camp.

"Sounds like they took the bait."

"I hope it keeps 'em busy long enough."

The pickup zone would be the clearing on top of the small rise. McCullough sent Hickey and Cohen ahead to recon the site and report back. The fifteen minutes the men were gone seemed like an eternity. Hickey returned, reported the PZ was clear and that Cohen was there watching it.

The two teams moved up, settling in the trees just down the crest on the far side of the slope. Malle, King, and Hickey stayed on the front slope as a security outpost.

"What a great ruse," Cohen muttered under his breath as he lay beside a pine tree, watching the pickup zone. "The fuckers are really putting on a show." The G-2 people from SACEUR had put on enough dog-and-pony shows about disinformation and masking. How the others could be taken in was beyond him. It didn't matter, now.

"You'll get our show when little SADM goes off in your fuckin' headquarters," he chuckled to himself.

The assault had been wild. The cornered Americans were not completely surprised. As his men entered the camp, grenades went off all over. An American claymore mine fired, raking the area with screaming steel. Kashevarov's men fell, even as they shredded the Americans in their shelters.

The fight was over as suddenly as it had begun. After the first flurry of grenades and the mine, the enemy evaporated. Kashevarov counted ten casualties, mostly wounded by fragments. Two men were dead, caught by the claymore mine. Kashevarov had the remaining troops of the 1st Platoon secure the perimeter, then had the survivors of the 2nd Platoon search the camp.

A few minutes later, the platoon leader came over to Kashevarov, a look of confusion on his face.

"Comrade Commander, there is no one in the camp!"

"What? No one?"

"Not even any bloody trails," the junior lieutenant answered. "The terrorists left their equipment, but they are not here."

A trick, thought Kashevarov, an excellent trick. He turned back to the sergeant.

"Have the equipment collected, we will take it back to the battalion headquarters."

Kashevarov knelt down next to the tiny fire. Dirt had been kicked in it during the assault. It was out now, but still hot to the touch. The fire could not have been very old. The Americans had moved out just in front of his Spets. Where were they now? Surely not far!

"Senior Sergeant, assemble the remaining members of 1st and 2nd Platoons," Kashevarov called to the sergeant. "Leave a squad here to protect the wounded. We are going after these gangsters!"

It took several minutes to assemble the men and resupply them with ammunition from their wounded and fallen comrades. By the time this had been accomplished, the trail of the Americans had been discovered, heading west.

Kashevarov and his cobbled-together platoon set off after them. He would use caution, this time. The Americans were wily and unpredictable. It did not matter, he would find them.

"Got 'em!" Murphy exclaimed, looking up from the decryption one-time pad. "The bird's on its way!"

"Let's hope it doesn't take all night getting here," Kosinski butted in.

"What's the matter, you don't like it here in the German Democratic Republic?" Cohen piped up.

"Not much, Bud," Kosinski shot back, "especially when I have to risk my ass looking for little lost atomic boys."

The Green Beret bristled at the remark, but BJ stepped in before things could get ugly.

"Kosinski has been on the receiving end of a nuke, Sergeant," BJ told the medic. "He's a little gun-shy, now. Anyway, he don't need to hear about it from you."

The little medic shut up.

This guy's wrapped too tight, BJ thought as he looked at Cohen, who had developed a real interest in his M16. The medic sat field-stripping the weapon, wiping it with a tiny rag stored in the buttstock.

BJ looked toward the eastern sky. There was no telling how long it would take to get the extraction ship in. At least the V-22 would be here quicker than a chopper.

"Sergeant Kirkley, I think we may be in trouble," the SF

captain said as he scuttled into the clearing and dropped onto one knee.

"What?"

"There're three squads moving across the open area," McCullough said quickly, "with a fourth behind."

"Whatcha think?" BJ asked.

"Looks like we didn't get as many as we had hoped," McCullough answered. "This bunch looks like a recon platoon fishing for targets, to me. When we open up, they'll fix us with suppressive fire while another element maneuvers in on our ass, probably from the flank or rear."

"Sounds like we're fucked!"

"My thought, too, unless the cavalry gets here . . . fast!"

Sergeant Taggart joined the two men.

"Sir, we need to put together a reception for these fuckers."

"What have we got?"

"My team has two SAWs and two 203s"—BJ ticked off the arsenal on his fingers—"we got two more claymores, too, and some Willy Pete."

"We got one claymore and our 16s," Taggart added.

BJ smiled at the Green Beret sergeant. "Too bad we can't use that nuke of yours!"

"We tried to use it, but *noooooo.*" Taggart chuckled. All three of them looked at Cohen, who sat looking out over the PZ.

"Uh, yeah." McCullough chuckled nervously, then got immediately back to business. "Sergeant Kirkley, we'll set up a hasty ambush with the claymores inside the tree line and put the troops farther back behind them."

"Roger, sir."

"If we put the SAWs on the flanks, they can hit the entire kill zone, then cover the flanks," Taggart added. "The 203s can support them when they pull back."

"We'll fire the claymores first," BJ jumped in, "then hit 'em with the SAWs and 203s. The 16s can take anyone who gets into the trees. We withdraw on the green flare."

"What green flare, Sergeant?" McCullough asked. "We don't have one."

BJ dug into the leg pocket of his BDUs. He pulled out a nylon bag containing the team's air/ground marker kit. Inside were a pen-flare launcher, six tiny screw-in flares, a small signal mirror, a strobe light with filters, and a folded piece of marker panel. He pulled out the pen-flare and held it up. "It's not much, but it'll have to do."

"Sounds good," Taggart answered, "let's do it."

The three men returned to their teams and ran down the plan. BJ looked up as the captain trotted over.

"Sergeant, why don't you leave one of your team here at the PZ with the radio," McCullough suggested. "I'll leave Sergeant Cohen, we'll have a PZ party here if our bird shows up."

"Yes, sir."

"Wally," BJ hissed at Kosinski, "you stay here with laughing boy and watch the PZ, okay? Murph, give him the 'romeo.' "

Kosinski nodded and took the radio from Murphy after he had switched it to FM voice mode so he could talk to the V-22.

The sound of Cohen's voice grabbed everyone's attention.

"No way, sir, pick someone else," the medic said, his voice plainly audible, far too loud for their current situation.

McCullough was whispering urgently at the little medic who only shook his head, picked up his rifle, and started to walk off. McCullough jerked the medic around and spoke sharply to him, jabbing his finger into Cohen's chest for emphasis. Between them, the rucksack carrying the device sat upright. For a moment the two men just stared at each other, then Cohen nodded and McCullough walked off. Cohen shouldered the device rucksack and walked dispiritedly over to BJ.

"PZ party?" the little medic grumbled.

BJ pointed to the clump of grass where Kosinski was setting up the radio. The Green Beret nodded and walked away.

★35★

Kashevarov had halted the squads one hundred meters from the tree line. They had been following the trail of the fleeing Americans. It was an easy trail, the Americans were making no effort to hide their tracks. Crushed grass, scuff marks, boot prints in the patches of snow, they all pointed to the small tree-covered rise ahead.

Kovpak made his way to the front of the column, where Kashevarov was searching the tree line with the night-vision scope.

"Can you see anything?" Kovpak whispered as he dropped down on one knee by the senior lieutenant.

"Nothing," Kashevarov replied, not taking his eyes from the scope. "That does not mean they are not there."

"Indeed," Kovpak replied, thinking to himself. No one knows that better than me!

A full minute passed before Kashevarov put down the weapon with the scope and looked at Kovpak.

"I believe that they are running," Kashevarov said quietly. "They are running like rabbits!"

"Perhaps that is what they wish you to think."

"Perhaps, but I believe not," the young officer said firmly. "We surprised them in the woods back there and now they seek to place distance between us and them."

"May I suggest, Comrade Commander, that we enter the woods in assault formation, just in case the rabbits have set a snare of their own?"

The lieutenant looked at Kovpak, thinking, weighing the time they would lose against the security they would pick up. He also considered the little ensign's experience, he had heard the stories being circulated by the soldiers. He decided for the security and experience.

"Very well, Comrade Senior Ensign, we will take your suggestion. Remain with . . ."

The lieutenant leaned over and looked at Kovpak.

"Comrade Senior Ensign, are you all right?"

"Yes, of course."

"You do not look good,"Kashevarov said. "Remain with your squad in the rear as a fire support group, should the need arise."

"Exactly so, Comrade Senior Lieutenant," Kovpak said, then turned and made his way back to his 3rd Squad, who knelt on the cold ground, waiting for orders.

"We are to remain back and provide supporting fire for the platoon, if they need it. I think they will," he said to no one in particular.

The nine men nodded and spread out on line readying their weapons.

For his part, Kovpak was happy for the short rest. His thumb was throbbing badly now and with each step, his buttocks felt like an electric wire was being lashed across them. The field dressings had slipped from the walking. Twice, Kovpak had to stop to adjust them. They were soaked with blood.

"Lieutenant Kashevarov does not expect any contact, he believes the Yankees are running," Kovpak explained to the squad. "I hope he is correct. If he is not, we will provide covering fire for his platoon and sweep around the enemy's flank. If the platoon is surprised, we will surprise the attackers." The squad nodded its silent acknowledgment.

Ahead, Kashevarov's squads rose and deployed on line in squad order. The men began a slow advance to the tree line.

"Come, my reluctant warriors," Kovpak said to his squad. "We will move to a position from which we can better support the platoon."

Kovpak led his squad off to the right, angling toward the side of the rise. He pushed his squad, seeking to clear the open area, in case the Americans had another surprise planned. The damned Americans were so unpredictable! They fought when they should run and ran when they could easily vanquish! Tactical norms were useless when fighting Americans, there was nothing normal about them.

* * *

"Here they come!" Hickey hissed as he slid into the shallow ditch. "They're about twenty meters from the tree line!"

Hickey's OP had been at the end of a small ditch that ran toward the tree line. At the end of the ditch, it was possible to see beyond the trees into the open area. Gunter Malle flipped down the safety bails on the three claymore firing devices. Malle would fire two of the claymores, McCullough would fire the third. The claymores would be the signal for the ambush. BJ, sighting through his night-vision scope, would give the order to fire the claymores. The eight men were spread over a forty-meter line. On each end, a team made up of a SAW and an M203 grenadier would provide the heavy firepower, while the riflemen in between would pick off individuals. They had placed their three claymore mines just inside the tree line, aimed at the gaps in the trees where the Soviets would enter the woods.

The ambush would withdraw when they saw the green pen-flare. King and Malle would throw white phosphorus and frags to cover their withdrawal.

"I hope this works, Sergeant," McCullough whispered to BJ. "If it doesn't, we won't have anything left to throw at 'em."

BJ nodded. At least we won't have the weight to carry when we run like striped apes, he thought as he put the M16 up to his shoulder and waited for the first Russian to appear in the shimmering green screen of the scope.

They appeared all at once, on line, looking good. At least half of the platoon was in the kill zone. BJ waited another few seconds for even more of them to enter the area where the claymores' fans of steel overlapped. Time began to stretch out as adrenaline began to take hold of his senses. Struggling to control his now-rapid breath, he laid the crosshairs of the sight on a soldier carrying a BG-15 grenade launcher.

"*Fire!*" BJ screamed as he fired at the grenadier. The three-round burst stitched the Soviet from navel to sternum.

Next to BJ, Malle and McCullough squeezed the claymore "clackers," pumping the detonators in their fists. The mines roared, ripping through the ranks of the Soviet platoon. Russians began flopping, some flopping backward, dead or wounded. Others flopped forward onto the ground, returning the fire of the ambushers. The Soviets recovered quickly, leaping to their feet and rushing forward to break the ambush.

The squad automatic weapons on both ends of the ambush

raked the Soviets, their tracers crisscrossing the area inside the tree line. Short bursts from the riflemen felled one Soviet after another. Tracers ricocheted off of trees. BJ used the night-vision scope to snipe at individuals. He easily killed the two men who tried to set up their RPKS-74 behind a log. The machine gun was pointed directly at BJ who sighted down the long barrel of the RPKS-74, shooting both men in the head as they attempted to fire at the Americans. The second man got off a burst just as BJ's round hit him above the right eye. He twisted, firing the RPKS-74 in an arc that crossed McCullough and Malle. Malle never even looked up, intent on killing the other Soviets that still rushed through the trees, but McCullough jerked to the right and clutched at his side high up near his armpit. The captain gasped, then went back to fighting, moving much slower than before. A handful of Soviets had gotten through the narrow center of the kill zone and were rushing the American positions, screaming and firing long bursts from their AKS-74s. McCullough killed one man point-blank with the last two rounds from his magazine, then dug at his combat harness for the single fragmentation grenade he carried. Another Soviet suddenly appeared and was almost on top of McCullough when Malle skewered the Russian with his bayonet, tossing him over to one side like a hay bale.

We are wasting more time, Kashevarov thought impatiently, the Americans are putting more and more distance between us. He had agreed to this on-line movement only because the senior ensign was in such bad shape. The man had the ear of the battalion commander, and it would be better to lose the Americans than to run the commander's friend to death. But still, his experience . . .

The line was moving well as they entered the trees, each squad on line and in good order. The squads were not widely spaced, Kashevarov did not want to lose anyone in the dark woods and waste more time looking for them.

It was darker in the woods, but only a bit. They would sweep to the crest, then return to a column formation and start off again in earnest after the Americans.

Poor Kovpak . . .

The blasts shook the ground. Kashevarov cringed reflexively. Around him, the trees were shedding bark and his 2nd Squad was falling, their bodies twisting in slow-motion, ripped by invisible steel.

Someone was screaming ambush and Kashevarov realized it was him. He shoved his rifle out in front of him and fired, raking the trees in front of him with automatic fire. The magazine was empty before Kashevarov could take more then two steps. He released the empty plastic magazine and was latching in a full one, running forward, Private Spednev by his side. They ran, screaming and firing at the flashes that lit the darkness in front of them.

Spednev stumbled, then twisted and fell, landing on his back. The wind whooshed out of the man. Kashevarov suddenly saw the American who had killed Spednev. The American was on his knees, firing right in front of him. Kashevarov pulled the trigger. Nothing, the magazine was empty. He rushed the American with his empty rifle. He would bash his head in.

From the right, a figure moved. Kashevarov never saw the M16 until it suddenly sprouted out of his belly. Then he was flying, the dark ground tilting wildly beneath him. He hit the ground hard.

Inside, something was wrong. There was a hot pain in his chest, burning deep all the way to his back. It would not let him catch his breath. Kashevarov rolled over onto his knees and tried to rise, tried to raise his rifle. Where was his rifle? There, on the ground. He reached for it. Blackness fell on him.

Suddenly there were no more targets to shoot. BJ quickly scanned the kill zone, looking for live Russians. There were a few wounded still moving around, but none firing.

"Save the WP!" BJ shouted. There was no need to waste it on the dead and wounded. BJ fished the pen-flare out of his pocket and thumbed the plunger off. The tiny green spark flew out over the trees. Before it landed in the open area, the eight American soldiers were pulling back through the trees to the clearing on the far side of the ridge.

"Move!" Kovpak snapped. "Move! There!"

They were running now, sprinting for the tree line on the right side of the rise. Off to the left, Kashevarov's platoon was catching hell from someone and giving it back, too. They would flank the ambushers and roll up their ambush line.

They ran through the tree line, expecting to be fired on. All the firing was off to the left. The Americans did not have enough men to cover the entire tree line.

"Straight on!" Kovpak bulled the squad on when they tried to turn toward the firing. "Get behind them!"

The 3rd Squad was eager to get into the fight. Since the embarrassment at the bridge, they were looking for a way to atone for their poor performance. They plunged through the trees, up the slope. The firing had stopped now. A few single shots rang out, American rifles, not AKs. Kovpak turned the squad to the left.

"Up there, on the crest," he panted. "We will catch them . . ."

Kovpak stopped. His legs suddenly felt very heavy, his head light. Around the edge of his vision, tiny lights twinkled, then turned into black lace curtains. The curtains closed. Kovpak felt himself fall, but could not move to stop it.

"What shall we do, comrades?" Somolov asked as they knelt by Kovpak's still body.

"We will continue the attack!"

"But the others."

"Forget the others! We are here, the enemy does not expect us, we will surprise and kill them!"

The squad moved forward, watching to the left for the ambushers and to the right for other Americans. It was unlikely that there were two ambushes set up, but one never knew about Americans.

On the right, a clearing opened up. The slope was clear there.

"There, we will catch them when they cross the open area."

The squad spread themselves among the trees that bordered the open slope. They would not have long to wait.

"Lemon," Kosinski said, his voice loud in the sudden stillness that followed the roar of the firefight.

"Meadowlark," came the countersign.

"The bird's inbound, BJ," Kosinski reported as the ambush party filed in, BJ on the point. Behind BJ was King with his machine gun, then Malle, assisting the wounded officer.

"How long?"

"Moments away!"

"You called 'em in while we were down there?" BJ asked, hooking his thumb back the way they had come.

Kosinski nodded. "Uh-huh."

"Optimist," BJ said, looking around for the Green Beret medic.

"Cohen," BJ called to the medic, "your CO's hit. Take care of him!"

The medic spun up from his watch position, grabbed the aid bag out of his rucksack, and trotted over to where McCullough was easing himself down against a tree.

"Where're you hit, sir?" Cohen asked calmly. This he knew about.

"Up here, Paul." McCullough coughed. The captain's breathing was ragged. Cohen pulled off McCullough's combat vest and shucked his Gortex and BDU jackets off, wrapping the latter around the captain's shoulders. The wound on McCullough's chest was the size of a nickel. A pink froth ringed the hole, a classic sucking chest wound. The froth was air blown out through the blood. As air entered the chest cavity, it pushed the lungs over, compressing them. Blood from the wound collected at the bottom of the chest cavity, farther compressing the lungs. Chest wounds were progressive. Air pressure outside the lungs would finally collapse the lungs, suffocating the patient.

Turning McCullough, Cohen found the exit wound on his back. The exit wound was larger, the size of a half dollar.

"No sweat, sir," the medic lied, "just a flesh wound."

Cohen pulled two field dressings from his bag and handed one to Malle.

"Pull off the plastic wrapper and hold it up against the back wound," he instructed Malle.

The weapons man was already doing it, ripping out the side and end seams, making the dressing into a flat square of plastic, relatively sterile on the inside. Cross-trained like all Green Berets, Malle knew quite a bit about combat first aid, too. When both dressings were unwrapped and ready, Cohen placed his plastic square against the chest wound. Malle did the same with the one in back.

"Hold 'em both," Cohen said, "gently."

As Malle pressed the plastic square against the wound, Cohen reached around the wounded captain with both arms.

"This may hurt, sir," Cohen said soothingly.

McCullough just nodded. Cohen squeezed the man in a bear hug, forcing out the unwanted air from McCullough's chest, the air bubbling out under the plastic dressings. McCullough groaned loudly, the hug hurt. When no more air came out, Malle pressed both palms against the plastic so that no more air could get in. As he held the airtight seal on the wounds, Cohen taped each square in place, then tied the field dressing over them.

"How you doin', Captain?" Cohen asked as he tied the dressings in place. McCullough nodded, his face screwed up with the pain.

"Hang on, sir," Malle encouraged, "help is on the way!"

McCullough nodded again, then coughed, a small spray of blood splattering on Cohen.

The aircraft was on them almost before they heard it.

"There," Somolov pointed left to the origin of the sound.

The groan was loud. At least one of the Americans was wounded badly. They could hear the voices, faint, but very close.

The sound of an aircraft rose from the treeless slope. Somolov immediately pointed toward the rising aircraft sound. The squad hastily deployed along the tree line, facing the grassy slope. They could easily see the rest of the tree line. The rise appeared to be kidney-shaped, with the cleared side curved inward.

"Excellent, comrades, we will catch them and their aircraft," Somolov whispered as the Soviets took up their positions.

"Sweet Mother of Jesus!" Kosinski said as the V-22 loomed up the rise. The tilt-rotor plane was much larger than it had seemed in photos. The huge upturned props pounded the air. The big camouflaged plane hovered right above them, turning around, dropping down in front of them. As it turned, BJ moved everyone out into the clearing. Malle carried the device. Cohen helped the wounded captain, staying close to his patient.

They were running for the open mouth of the troop bay when automatic weapons began to rattle on their right flank.

"Now!"

At Somolov's shout, the squad opened fire on the strange aircraft and the running figures. One of the men on the ground turned and fired his rifle at them. Another turned his machine gun and fired continuously as he ran for the hovering aircraft. The man with the rifle fell, rolled, and continued to fire from the ground. The machine gunner made the rear of the aircraft and knelt down, raking the tree line with his gun. Another

American joined him, firing. Somolov heard the slugs ripping into the ground and trees. He buried his face in the dirt as the burst walked over his position. Next to him, the *yfreitor* screamed.

Somolov looked back up and raised his rifle to fire at the machine gunner. A column of flame jumped from the front of the strange aircraft. Red tracers in a continuous line streaked into the tree line. The ground roiled like it was being plowed by an invisible harrow. Small trees splintered and fell, cut off at the base. As the glowing stream of steel swept over each position, the Soviet soldier there died, torn to shreds. Somolov pressed himself to the earth. The ripping sound of the bullets tore over him. His leg caught fire, the pain rushing up his left side. Somolov screamed as the red ripsaw moved past.

"Move!" BJ screamed at the two teams. "Move!"

They were all running now, seeking the relative safety of the V-22. Kosinski was firing his M16 from the hip, raking the trees. Beyond him, King had his SAW in action, firing a continuous stream of 5.56mm at the attackers.

Malle swept McCullough up over his shoulder and ran for the V-22, the others right behind him.

Kosinski suddenly fell, rolled over, and kept firing, laying down cover for the teams. As Hickey reached the open troop bay of the V-22, he joined King, the two SAWs stitching the tree line.

The rattle of the two machine guns was suddenly overshadowed by a loud rasping sound from the front of the Boeing Osprey. The noise was like a loud continuous foghorn, the effect of 7.62mm rounds firing at 4000 rounds per minute. There was no distinct sound from each shot, only one continuous roar. A solid stream of tracers flashed to the edge of the trees and walked rapidly down the tree line, ripping and digging up the ground.

"Let's go!" BJ yelled at the two machine gunners as he ran up to the aircraft. The others were inside, all except Kosinski.

"Wally!" BJ screamed over the roar of the engines and the blasts from the minigun. "Come on!"

Kosinski was lying facedown, not moving. His hands were on his rifle.

"Jesus!" BJ yelled as he turned to run to his fallen friend. A pair of huge hands grabbed BJ's web gear from behind and jerked him back, pulling him into the moving bay of the aircraft. BJ twisted, trying to break loose. The floor tilted forward sharply and the big plane surged up into the sky. BJ lost his balance and fell to one knee.

"Wally!" BJ screamed as he fought to get to his feet. The ramp swung up and shut out the dark howling void.

"He was dead, BJ," King said, putting his arm around BJ's shoulders. The big black man took the M16 out of BJ's hands and thumbed it onto safe. "I'm sorry, man."

BJ slumped to the floor and just sat there. They were out, or at least out of there, but Wally was dead. The whole deal sucked real bad.

"Norm, look!" Alvarez hissed as the T-80 and 2S6 clanked down the road. The team had heard the two vehicles before they could see them and were worried that another rear-area security patrol was looking for them, this time armed with real firepower. After Slade had been found and killed, the team had headed away from the bridge. If they were being tracked, there was no reason to take the trackers right to the ADM team. They had evaded, staying away from the roads, hiding during the day and moving at night. They had made one radio transmission, just to let the FOB know they were still alive.

When the two armored vehicles clanked into sight, it was obvious they were not part of some ground-pounding security force or, worse, Internal Troops. They were probably just stragglers, trying to catch up to their parent unit.

Everyone was so busy watching the tank, they almost missed the trucks. The nine trucks were led by a command car. When it was obvious that the tank was not going to pull off for the column, the trucks halted. An officer leaped from the command car and ran up to the tank, where the tank commander waited, standing in his hatch.

They were too far away to hear the conversation, but the officer on the ground was reading the tank commander the riot act, yelling and pointing back down the road the way the tank had come. Finally the tank commander nodded and spoke into his intercom. He then turned and motioned to the commander of the 2S6, pointing to the left side of the road. The 2S6 commander nodded, and the quad 30mm tracked gun lurched off the road to the left. The tank churned off to the right, clearing the road for the trucks.

As soon as the road was clear the command car sped off, with the trucks lumbering along behind. As the column passed, both the tank and the antiaircraft gun pivoted, churning the hard ground with their treads, facing back the way they had come. They were joining the column.

Captain Shepelev's 2nd Company had almost run headlong into the T-80 as the column rounded the bend. His first thought was to clear the road. He ran up to the battered tank, it looked like it had seen a lot of action, and glared up at its commander.

"Get this tank off the road, that gun, too!" he screamed over the noise of the tank and the column of trucks. "We must pass quickly."

"Of course, Comrade Captain," Harlan answered. "What is your hurry?"

"That is no concern of yours!" the officer shouted. "Just move your vehicles!"

It was not possible to tell just what this captain was, but it was a sure bet that he was one of the folks whose radio traffic Nolan had intercepted. The soldiers in the back of the trucks were all wearing camouflage uniforms and looked like a tough bunch.

"What?" Harlan yelled down, holding his ear.

"That is of no concern of . . ." The captain stopped and looked at the tank for a minute as though he had never seen one, then walked to the side of the road and peered at Mamud's 2S6. He promptly climbed up on Harlan's tank and perched right in front of him on the turret slope.

"I hereby order your tank and the 2S6 accompanying you to join this column and provide supporting fire for our attack on a gang of terrorists who have already ambushed two Soviet units and killed many servicemen," the captain proclaimed. "You will fall in at the rear of this column and take your orders from me."

"Just so, Comrade Captain," Harlan answered, "we will gladly help you fight these gangsters."

Harlan thumbed the intercom mike. "Off the road to the right, Teddy, then spin it 180 degrees when the trucks pass."

Harlan spun the commander's cupola and motioned Mamud off the road to the left. Mamud nodded and dropped back inside his gun turret. It only took a minute to get the two tracked vehicles off the road. By that time, the little captain was back in his command car and gunning it down the road.

Inside the tank, Tedder threw the right tread into forward, the left tread into reverse. Harlan gripped the sides of the cupola as the tank shuddered through the turn around. When the gun was pointed at the rear of the column, Harlan thumbed the intercom again.

"Nolan, can you see the command car?"

"Roger!" came the reply.

"Shoot it, then the trailing truck. What have we got loaded?"

"HE frag!"

"Shoot!"

Nolan laid the thermal sight on the small command car, centering the car's nose in the crosshairs. It was so close, there was no need for fancy fire control. Nolan pressed the trigger. The tank rocked back. Before it came to a halt, Nolan had the next HE-fragmentation round loading. The blackout taillights of the trailing truck glowed bright in the thermal sight as the driver slammed on the brakes. Nolan swung the gun to the right and fired at the left taillight. The truck was so close that the noise of the gun firing and the noise of the round hitting were part of the same sound.

Across the road, Mamud's gunner worked the 30mms from the front of the column to the rear, ripping the GAZ-66 trucks like paper toys. One after another, the trucks were torn to shreds or exploded in bellowing fireballs.

Harlan swung the 12.7mm around and raked the column from back to front as the troops spilled out of the vehicles and sprinted for safety. Mamud was standing in his hatch, firing an RPK-74 machine gun at them as they spilled out of their doomed trucks.

"*Madre*, look at that," Alvarez whispered, "those tankers are kicking ass on their own dudes, man!"

"What the fuck is going on?" Sterling asked.

"Looks like a discipline problem!" Robinson chuckled. "I hope those are the assholes that got Slade!"

"Talk about your interservice rivalry!"

On the road, the troops in the trucks were getting slaughtered. Caught flat-footed by the attack and thrown around in the back of the trucks by the sudden stop, they were a bit slow in dismounting. The tank and the AA gun chopped them to bits. The 30mm guns ripped through the line of trucks like a big paper shredder, the tank gun disappearing one truck after another. The few troops who got out of the trucks had to run through a curtain of machine-gun tracers.

Sterling slithered back from the crest pulling the others with him.

"Gentlemen, I think this is an excellent time to get the fuck out of Dodge!"

The four LRRPs shouldered their packs and trotted off through the darkness.

★36★

The landing area was dark, as usual. Masterson eased the Apache onto the hard surface, cut the power, and slumped back against the seat. The second half of the mission had gone well enough. They had found the tank regiment, fired all their missiles, and turned for home listening to the scouts' reports of destroyed tanks. Then, just over the FLOT, one of the Apaches just blew up. No warning, no signs of ground fire, nothing. It just blew up and cost him two friends and an irreplaceable helicopter.

Well, I'm still alive, he thought as he pulled the releases on his safety harness, I've walked away from another one. Outside, the round face and perpetual grin of his crew chief, Sergeant Tod Johnson, appeared. Johnson popped open the hatch, letting the cold night air into the stuffy cockpit.

"Welcome back, sir," the young sergeant said brightly, as he always did when Masterson came back from a mission. It was a habit that was increasingly annoying. He thought Johnson sounded surprised every time he and Harris came back alive. Masterson began to push himself up out of the cramped cockpit.

"Might as well stretch for a minute, sir," Johnson said as he filled the Apache's tanks, "I think you're going right back out again."

"Mind if I pee first?" Masterson snapped back at the perpetually perky buck sergeant.

"Oh, no, sir," the kid shot back, "help yourself!"

"I'm going to the latrine," Masterson said as he walked away, "can I bring you anything?"

"Oh, no, sir, thanks," Johnson replied.

"Yeah, hotshot, you can bring me a discharge," the crew chief muttered under his breath, "I heard you had a bad one last month." Pilots, he thought, what a bunch of prima donnas! The only difference between an Apache and a Hoover vacuum cleaner was that a Hoover only had one dirt bag in it.

Under the Apache's stubby wings, armorers were already removing the empty rocket pods and Hellfire tubes and replacing them with loaded 70mm pods. Rearming would take only a few minutes, since the 30mm gun had not been fired. Loading the big belted shells was a time-consuming task.

"Grab a quick bite, Bat, you're going back up. That special ops outfit needs help getting out. More of the same interdiction fire."

"Why do we get to do it?" Masterson asked angrily. "Isn't there another outfit that can give us a hand with this? Anyway, when did we get into the special ops business? I thought we were tank hunters."

The Battalion S3 stood and looked at the pilot. The man had circles under his bloodshot eyes, his flight suit smelled like an old jockstrap, and he was surly almost to insubordination. Stateside, he would have jerked a knot in this pilot's tail.

"You're doing it because it needs doing," he replied, his voice cold and detached. "As for working with special ops, we are in whatever business the Army tells us we're in. I know that you haven't got much sleep and you've seen a lot of action, but tough shit, welcome to the war. That's why it's called Hell. Those LRRPs or spooks or whatever they are have been behind enemy lines, living on the cold ground, surrounded by the bad guys. They don't often get to come back, from what I hear. If we can help 'em, we sure as hell will. Sometime we might need help ourselves. Now, get some chow and take it to the briefing room with you. You take off in fifteen minutes."

Masterson stood looking at the "Three" for what seemed like a long time. He had never heard the man snap at anyone before, much less him.

"Did you hear me, Captain," the S3 repeated, "get some chow and report to the briefing room!"

Masterson snapped up straight. "Yes, sir." He watched as

the major stomped off down the hall, slapping a bunch of papers against his leg.

Shit, Masterson thought, some guys just can't handle the pressure! He turned the other way down the corridor, making for the mess hall on his way to the briefing room.

The briefing was short and sweet. Masterson's flight would again hammer a sector of the Soviet air defense zone to open a hole for the V-22 Osprey carrying the special ops folks out of Soviet airspace. Some nights it seemed like it was all Soviet airspace and NATO was just borrowing part of it.

Six of the new flechette rockets had been loaded in the Apaches' outboard pods. If the Apaches intercepted any pursuing helicopters, they were free to engage them with the new rockets or with the Stingers on their stubby wingtips.

Outside, Johnson was still standing there smiling. Even in the dark, Masterson could see the bright, even teeth. He was starting to despise the man. Harris was already in his seat up front.

"Ready to go?"

"I guess so," Harris replied.

Masterson peered through the darkness at the other Apache in his flight. The crews were climbing into their cramped seats, tired and, he suspected, suddenly afraid after the loss of the other ship.

I should be afraid, too, Masterson thought. Maybe I would be if I weren't so damn tired. He turned and climbed into the pilot's seat. Johnson buckled him in, then leaned back and smiled.

"Have a good flight, sir."

What an asshole, thought Masterson as he flipped the switches that brought the big killing machine to life and opened his preflight checklist book on his knee.

"Harris," Masterson asked, keying the intercom, "why did we have to get a crew chief who's an asshole?"

"Aren't they all?" Harris laughed as Masterson lifted the chopper's tail and skimmed over the trees.

"Strike point coming up, Bat," Harris said quietly over the intercom.

It had taken less than thirty minutes to reach the firing strike point ten kilometers behind the enemy lines. Harris already had the figures laid into his firing computer and now, as they reached the firing point, the chopper slowed, pitched nose up for the proper elevation and fired automatically. The Hydra rockets rippled out of the tubes, the fire from their motors lighting the Apaches with a flickering yellow glow. The 142 rockets fired by the two Apaches streaked off toward their targets seven kilometers away. Over the target, each rocket would spread its submunitions over a square 500 meters wide. Each submunition could knock out a vehicle. The air defense unit on the receiving end would be out of commission more than long enough for the special ops bird to get through.

"Rockets away, Skipper," Harris reported over the intercom. His voice fairly sang. Harris loved pulling the trigger and watching the weapons fire. The pleasure would be short-lived. Masterson would have them on the way home before the first rocket hit.

"Odessa One Seven," the voice of the Ground Control Intercept controller jabbed in his ear, startling the pilot, "come to course one-nine-five. Target is single aircraft flying two-six-five magnetic, seventy kilometers. Acknowledge."

"Control, Odessa One Seven acknowledges," Viktor Tovin answered automatically, "coming to one-nine-five." He flipped the radio to intercom. "Elimov, arm weapons for air combat."

"Arming," answered the gunner, Pauli Elimov.

To the right, Max Kron, Tovin's wingman, turned, following Tovin's Hokum in the darkness. Fifteen kilometers behind the two Hokums, the controller in the Mi-27Z command-and-control helicopter, downlinked to an AN-74 "Coaler" aerial command aircraft, watched as the two air-attack helicopters turned toward the last-known track of the American aircraft that had picked up the enemy force at Kathendorf. The course was more a guess than anything. The American would surely take the fastest path back to NATO lines, following the cover of the hilly terrain. The vector would cause the two Hokums to intercept the intruder in the vicinity of Hameln. There the helicopter's MMR (millimeter wave radar) would be able to detect the target. The Hokums would engage it with their air-to-air missiles and 30mm guns.

Tovin, the pilot of the Odessa 17, was very good. He was rated a sniper, the highest rating for a Soviet pilot. His Hokum section had accounted for dozens of NATO helicopters, and even two ground attack jets. He would easily catch and kill this intruder.

In the front seat of the Hokum, Elimov switched on the radar and watched it make two sweeps. Then he quickly switched it off. The enemy had too many weapons that tracked radar emissions, especially airborne radar. Elimov only ran it every thirty seconds or so for two quick sweeps to see if any targets appeared. If they did, he would switch from scan mode to attack, narrowing the beam to a thin corridor directly ahead of the sleek helicopter. Once in range, the infrared seeker of the SA-14 or the larger AA-8 missile would take over to guide the missile into the target aircraft.

For now, the airborne controller was their eyes. They would follow his directions until they were nearly upon the target. The controller was a mixed blessing. He could order pilots into combat with impunity, sitting safely behind his console kilometers away from any danger, and had no "feel" for what was actually happening to the men he directed by radar as they fought for their lives. On the other hand, he could also muster reinforcements and other support for a flight that was in trouble. Most importantly, he was a convenient scapegoat for any botched intercepts.

Their intercept should occur in the next few minutes. Elimov could see the thin ribbon of the Weser River gleaming in the distance. Hameln would come up soon. He smiled as he remembered the childhood story of the Pied Piper of Hameln, who cured the town of rats. His Estonian grandmother had thrilled and terrified him with the tale on many a cold winter evening. It had been one of his favorites, next to Peter and the Wolf.

Tonight, he and Tovin would be the pipers, cleaning the sky over Hameln of a flying rat. The Yankees would pay the piper with blood!

He suddenly realized that he had not recently conducted a radar sweep, lost in childhood thoughts. Elimov flipped the switch on the millimeter wave radar. The sweep instantly lit up with two blips! The aircraft were less than a kilometer away, below them!

"Targets!" Elimov shouted. "Ten o'clock low!"

"Skipper, we've got a radar at two o'clock!" McFarlane said as the warning tone on the AN/APR-39 radar-warning receiver warbled in his headphones. The white line pointer on the receiver's face pointed to the right, slowly moving counterclockwise. "Looks like airborne radar," McFarlane added, "not real fast, probably helicopters."

"Hunter/killers," Dunwoody said quietly. "Here's where it gets interesting." The pilot switched the terrain-following radar to its search mode. Immediately, two blips appeared on the screen. Dunwoody switched the radar back to terrain-following. "Watch 'em on the threat receiver, Lew. If they switch their radar off, we'll watch 'em on ours."

"Wright, you and Throck get back there on the guns," McFarlane said to the loadmaster sitting at the back of the cargo bay. "We may get to use those babies."

"Roger," Wright answered. He stepped aft to the 7.62mm minigun, locked in its storage position forward of the V-22's portside door. The minigun was the same weapon used as door guns on the Nighthawk helicopters. Its six barrels could fire from 1500 to 4000 rounds a minute. A metal container held 1750 rounds of 7.62mm armor-piercing and tracer ammunition. He had used most of it on the extraction, covering the teams.

He checked the counter on the ammo storage. The indicator pointed just above 200 rounds. "Gun ready, Skipper. We're really low on ammo port side."

"Throck, how're you doin' for ammo?" the copilot asked.

"Seventeen hundred rounds," came the engineer's report from the starboard gun.

"Stay on 'em, guys," the pilot replied. "We'll let you know if you have company. If you can, transfer some ammo to port."

Thank God the weapons were already armed, Elimov thought as he thrust his head forward onto the night-vision scope. Tovin was already nosing the Ka-34 over, pivoting toward the intruders as he warned the other ship.

The two intruders were too close to shoot with the AA-8s. It would be guns or perhaps an SA-14 if they had time to get a lock. Elimov gripped the gun trigger and searched his scope for the targets. There they were, two Apaches! The enemy ships were banking to the right, crossing in front of the Ka-34s. The range had closed to 500 meters.

Tovin's voice rang over the intercom. "I have gun control."

Elimov shifted his grip on his control stick, flipping the switch from gun to missile, the trigger now firing the eight SA-14s. As the American helicopters moved into the center of his scope, the pilot opened fire with the Ka-34's NR-30 cannon. The flash from the muzzle would have blinded Elimov if he had not had his face down in the night-vision eyepiece. The Ka-34 trembled as the gun poured fire at the Americans. The tracers showed as bright streaks across the screen. Both Ka-34s were firing at the nearest Apache. The fiery tracers filled the sky around the squat, ugly American gunship. Flashes twinkled on the side of the ship, the 30mm shells ripping through the armor.

The burst caught the Americans by surprise. As the two Hokums raced past the Americans, the stricken Apache was nose down, mortally wounded. The other Apache had been turning right, looking for the attackers. They would pivot and come up behind the American for a missile shot. Even if the American ran, their radar would find him.

Elimov heard Tovin on the radio again.

"Controller, this is Odessa One Seven, we are engaging Apaches northwest of Hameln. Repeat, engaging two AH-64s northwest of Hameln."

The voice of the controller in the Mi-27Z broke in over Tovin. "Odessa One Seven, disengage! Repeat, disengage. Primary target is approaching from the west, distance twenty kilometers. Engage primary target!" Tovin said nothing in reply, but spun the Ka-34 back toward the remaining Apache. Elimov was thrown against his restraining harness by the centrifugal forces, but still kept his eyes on the radar, searching for the American. A huge white blossom filled the right half of the screen, chaff fired by the fleeing Apache.

Returning to the forward-looking infrared, Elimov found the Apache, a warm blur on the screen. He pulled the missile trigger to its first position, uncaging the infrared seeker in the nose of the first SA-14 missile. A second later, the target-lock tone warbled in his ear. Elimov pulled the trigger all the way back, firing the missile from the starboard outboard pod.

"Missile fired!" Elimov called out.

"Control, Odessa One Seven engaging primary target," Tovin acknowledged the distant controller's command.

When the engineer and loadmaster began checking their guns, the pucker factor in the troop compartment began to rise.

"Oh, shit!" Murphy moaned as he realized what the loadmaster was up to.

"Looks like visitors," BJ answered.

"I hate this!" Murphy hissed. "You can't shoot back, you can't even see the fuckers! You just have to sit here and get your ass shot off!"

"At least this thing has guns to fight back with," Ben Mc-Cullough injected.

"Yeah, if the gunners can shoot around a corner to hit a missile boring up our ass!"

In his seat near the forward bulkhead, Cohen sat confused. The firefights were part of the plan, he was sure of that. This plane was the ringer. It didn't seem possible that the Russians could have picked one up intact. Spetsnaz! That was the answer. One of their teams had gone in and snagged this bird from a NATO airfield! Of course! But who's flying it? The Russians would kiss off a few grunts to snag a nuke, but where did they get the pilot for this thing? Maybe they kidnapped him in the bargain. It didn't matter. When the Russians revealed themselves, the others would see how wrong they had been. That didn't matter either, since they would all go up when the device went off. Cohen smiled and stretched out, putting his head on the seatback. Nothing to do but relax now.

When the two gunners suddenly jumped to their guns, the tension in the V-22 peaked. BJ could smell the fear coming from both the LRRPs and the Green Berets. On the ground, they were the best, but up here, they were just meat along for the ride. A couple of men crossed themselves. BJ wondered if they were Catholic or just hedging their bets. The V-22 jerked violently to one side.

Here it comes, BJ thought, it'll all be over in a minute. He noticed the medic stretched out in his seat. Cohen's hands were clasped behind his head, his eyes closed.

Either this is the coolest bastard in the world, BJ thought to himself, or he's nutty as a fruitcake.

On the radar screen, a large blip appeared, approaching rapidly. They would get this one! The target was crossing to their left. Elimov brought the night vision to bear on the enemy plane.

At first he thought he was seeing things. The enemy plane had two engines mounted on the ends of short flat wings. The engines sported the largest propellors Elimov had ever seen. The props were as long as the wing!

"Target in sight," Elimov called out. "Engaging."

The AA-8's missile seeker was already warbling. It had acquired the intruder very quickly.

"Firing!" Elimov called as the long white missile ripped off its launch rail in a ball of flame that engulfed the entire wingtip. The missile streaked away at twice the speed of sound toward its fleeing target.

Behind the strange intruder a cloud of chaff blossomed, followed by a pair of flares that arced away from both sides of the plane. A steady stream of chaff and flares were ejected from the dispenser on the plane's whalelike tail. The AA-8 continued to track steadily for a few seconds, then, fooled by the chaff and flares, went wide of the target, exploding harmlessly behind it.

"Harris, this is an attack helicopter, that's what the 'A' stands for. Now find me those fuckers!"

Harris was still shaking. The Hokums had come out of nowhere. The other Apache had been hit before he could even react. Their own ship had barely missed a missile hit. The heat seeker had been fooled by a flare, passing just under the ship and exploding with a muffled thump ahead of them.

Masterson had redlined the Apache, dashing out of the area, trying to shake the Hokums. It was quickly apparent that the Soviets were not following. They were after the V-22!

Masterson had put the Apache through a high-speed turn that wrenched Harris' stomach the way the aerial duel had wrenched his nerves. Now Masterson was rushing back to join the fray. It wasn't as if they were unarmed. They had four Air-To-Air Stingers, six flechette rockets, and their 30mm chaingun.

"Find 'em, Harris!" Masterson yelled. He slipped the big attack chopper between trees, clipping the tops with the wheels, and then skimming the fields. Harris ignored the ground rushing by just under his seat and scanned the sky with his FLIR—forward-looking infrared scope. Using the White Hot setting, which made hotter objects, like helicopters, appear white against a black background, Harris scanned back and forth in front of them searching for the Osprey and its pursuers.

"Got 'em!" Harris shouted as three white dots, one large and two small, appeared at the top of his screen. "Bandits, eleven o'clock high!"

The targets were closing at 200 mph. Masterson pulled up on his stick.

"I'll try to get between 'em!" he shouted. "Shoot as soon as the Osprey is past. If you can't get tone, use the flechettes!"

"Got it!"

The V-22 had quit firing chaff and flares. Probably out, Harris thought.

The Hokums were closing now, maneuvering for the kill. If they got there in time, it would be close.

"Permission for a gun pass," Kron asked Tovin.

Tovin almost said "Denied" but changed his mind. Drachev was a good flyer. He had the killer instinct. Why not let him hone that instinct on this fat intruder?

"Granted," Tovin replied, "kill him, Odessa One Eight."

The V-22 was at the limit of gun range. Kron gave his Ka-34 everything it had, closing the gap to the intruder.

Now, Tovin thought, shoot!

The V-22 flashed overhead. The lead Hokum was coming up fast now, trying to get a shot at the fleeing Osprey. If they could get a little closer before he launched . . .

Masterson jerked up the nose and thumbed the weapons action switch to Stinger.

"Harris, give me a lock ASAP!" Masterson said. "That Osprey's gonna get it!"

"Tone!" Harris called as the Hokum bore down on them. "Firing."

The thin missile sprang from its launch tube and streaked off after the Hokum trailing a stream of white smoke. Harris selected the next missile for firing as the first one closed with the lead Hokum. The first missile was nearly on the first target when the second one locked on the trailing Hokum.

The five-foot missile slammed into the lead Hokum like an arrow. It hit the Russian just under the port engine. The Russian blew up in a huge orange fireball.

"*Awwright!*" Masterson yelled. "Now for number two."

A bright streak appeared below Kron's ship, slamming into the Ka-34's left side. The white blast lit the entire side of the craft.

Odessa One Eight vanished in a ball of fire. Elimov yelled, the bright light hurting his eyes as he watched the attack through the night-vision scope.

The V-22 still raced on, undamaged. Where had the missile come from? Tovin wondered. Some ground launcher, left far behind? Hopefully.

"Gunner, ready for missile attack!"

"Ready, Comrade Senior Lieutenant!"

Tovin threw the throttles forward. This American would pay for Kron's death. As soon as the AA-8 missile had lock, the American would die.

The second Hokum was passing overhead now, closing the gap to the V-22. It didn't matter, they were coming up behind him.

Masterson spun the Apache and pulled over. The helicopter responded, pinning both men in their seats.

"I got lock," Harris groaned as gravity ground him into his armored seat. "Tone."

"Take him, babe!" Masterson shouted.

Harris forced his head forward. The second Hokum was plainly visible in his heads-up display. The target shimmered near the center of the screen where the Stinger-targeting indicator shone. Harris pressed the trigger. The second Stinger flashed off into the darkness. The missile selector automatically keyed up the next Stinger in line. The second missile was half-way to the target when the missile-lock tone sounded again and the indicator reappeared.

Harris fired again. The missile raced to join the one bearing down on the Russian. As it turned out, it was a wasted Stinger.

The Soviet fired flares, seeking to distract the Stinger the way the V-22 had fooled the Russian AA-8. The Stinger was not fooled. Its seeker head was programmed for the temperature of an Isotov turbine engine exhaust. It ignored anything hotter or cooler. The thin missile hit and detonated behind and below the Hokum's left engine, sending fragments into both the engine and transmission. The Hokum slowed shuddering, fighting for power. When the second Stinger slammed into the fuselage, it merely killed a bird that was already dying.

Tovin pressed the missile trigger to its first stop, waiting for the missile to lock on the target. On the starboard wing, the infrared seeker in the nose of the AA-8 sprang to life, liquid argon cooling its surface so that any warm object in front of it would register. Tovin waited for the tone that would tell him the missile was ready to streak past his window and blow the intruder out of the sky.

"*Target!*" Elimov screamed. "*Nine o'clock low!*"

"Flares!" Tovin called back.

The night sky suddenly exploded. A blow hit the left side of the Ka-34. The windscreen suddenly cracked into a dozen spiderwebs on its left side. Bits of something whipped over Tovin's head. His instruments showed what he already knew. The port engine was out. The transmission was making noises. The stick felt odd in his hand. Tovin gave the starboard engine full power. The noise from the transmission grew louder. The Ka-34 lurched again. Tovin's voice rang over the intercom.

"What is to the left?" the pilot screamed. "What?"

Elimov did not know what. The radar had been hit. The night vision was dark, too. The pilot had cut hard to the right, now jerked the Ka-34 back to the left. The craft was vibrating badly.

"Radar out," Elimov shouted. "Night vision as well! Only the infrared!"

"Hold on, Pauli!" Tovin said, his voice unnaturally calm. "Hold on."

Elimov was amazed to hear the pilot use his first name. Tovin never did that . . . A sledgehammer hit the stricken Ka-34. The nose tipped over and the dark ground below filled the windscreen. In the intercom, Tovin was screaming something. Elimov was not listening. He could not take his eyes off the sight of Germany rushing up at him. He was staring at it when the Ka-34 dug a long shallow grave for both him and Tovin.

"Out-fuckin'-standing!" Masterson hooted. "Let's go home, babe, it's Miller time."

"I'm ready," Harris replied. When those Stingers had hit, he had felt a thrill like nothing he'd felt before. It was more than just we-got-them-first, it was more sexual than that.

The word "Ace" popped into his thoughts. As Masterson turned the Apache back east, Harris was already deep into a fantasy. On the horizon, a thin pink line heralded the approaching dawn. Dawn was always the best time for valiant dreaming.

"God!" Harris said over the intercom. "A cigarette would taste great right now!"

★37★

"There!" Bodnya pointed to the spray of red tracer that shot up into the sky. "There they are!"

"Comrade Colonel," the pilot said into the intercom, "there is hostile fire there."

"Comrade Pilot," Bodnya shot back, "if you do not land there, there will be hostile fire in here. Do you understand?"

Never have I seen such cowardly pilots, Bodnya fumed. First the German bastards would not come, then they did not want to fly where there was fighting. The frustration was maddening. Kovpak could die of old age before these bastards got to him! Could he really expect more? These were not Afghan veteran pilots, just a bunch of Germans used to chasing after their own citizens!

The pilot of the Mi-8 nodded and pointed the nose of the big transport helicopter where the sparks had risen from the woods.

By the time the helicopters swooped in over the crest of the rise, there was no more firing. The wheels had not touched the ground before the Scout-Diversionary Platoon was out of the two helicopters and running for the trees. Bodnya and his radio operator followed partway across the clearing and stopped behind a bush.

Shortly, one of the Scout-Diversionists returned to the wood line and waved at Bodnya.

By the time Bodnya reached the tree line, the Scouts had located Kovpak's 3rd Squad. Four of them were dead, their bodies riddled with wounds. Three others were wounded. The other two were tying field dressings on the wounded.

"Where is Ensign Kovpak?" Bodnya demanded of the survivors.

"Over there, Comrade Colonel," Somolev, the sergeant, answered. The sergeant was wounded in the head, his face half hidden by a poorly secured dressing. "He passed out during the attack."

"And the Americans?"

"Gone," the sergeant answered, "in an airplane that hovers."

Bodnya ran through the trees, searching for his friend. It was not possible that Kovpak was dead. He had been through so much, he could not be dead.

Bodnya almost missed the wounded Ukrainian.

"Pavel!"

Dropping to his knees, Bodnya thrust two fingers against Kovpak's throat. The pulse was still there, weak, perhaps, but there.

"Feldsher! Over here!"

The medical orderly came running at the colonel's shout.

"See to Ensign Kovpak!"

"Comrade Colonel, there are many wounded," the medic replied, looking back to the crest, "I am told that there are more in the woods to the east."

"Treat the senior ensign first, do you understand?" Bodnya hissed into the medic's face. "If he dies, you will answer to me."

"Exactly so, Comrade Colonel!" the medic blurted. He would ignore the others if necessary to treat this ensign.

Bodnya walked back to the wounded sergeant and took his report, then walked down to the cleared spot where the helicopters sat with their rotors still turning. Bodnya climbed up on the nearest one and spoke through the pilot's window.

"There are more wounded on the next rise to the east," he shouted over the noise of the engines. "Take your helicopter and pick up everyone there. Bring them back here. We will return to the battalion headquarters from here."

The pilot nodded and twisted the throttle, bringing the engine up to speed. Bodnya jumped down and walked out of the rotor area, not looking back to watch the helicopter take off.

The *feldsher* had Kovpak on a litter and was carrying him

toward the other helicopter with the aid of one of the Scouts. The wounded members of Kovpak's 3rd Squad either walked or were carried by other Scouts. A squad of the Scouts had gone in search of the remainder of Kashevarov's 2nd Platoon. They were back in minutes, calling for the *feldsher*. There were more wounded along the tree line on the far side of the ridge. An ambush, the wounded men had said.

Who were these tigers? Bodnya asked himself. Were they really so good, or had his men blundered so much? Kashevarov's company were not the best troops in the world, but they were not virgins, either.

None of that matters right now, he reminded himself, Pavel needs to be taken to a hospital. He walked over to the helicopter and stuck his head into the troop compartment.

"Who is missing?"

"No one, Comrade Colonel," came the reply, "even the dead are loaded on board."

Bodnya climbed in and instructed the pilot to fly to the other side of the knoll to pick up the wounded and dead there.

Amazing, he thought as the helicopter lifted off, so many dead. Where was the 2nd Company? They should have been here in time to support these poor bastards. He would have the company commander's head for his failure.

And you, Comrade Battalion Commander, he asked himself, who will have yours?

"Crossing the FLOT," the loadmaster said calmly, "be home in thirty minutes."

The man was so cool, you'd think it was a tour bus, BJ thought to himself as he watched the aircrewman stow his gun and prepare the V-22 for its landing. There was nothing to prepare, really. Mostly he just wanted the gear secured and all the weight near the center of gravity. The machine landed easier if it was balanced, the loadmaster, Sergeant Wright according to his flight suit, had explained.

The LRRPs and SF were hardly as cool. Both teams were exhausted mentally as well as physically. Some, including Malle and Taggart, sat with their eyes closed, miming sleep. Murphy, Hickey, and Thompson were wired, chattering like bluejays. Cohen looked like—what? The man looked as if he were having an out-of-body experience. Cohen needed psych work. Too bad he couldn't have died for Kosinski. McCullough was propped up on the nylon seat, awake, but out of it. The little medic had done all right by the wounded man, he would give him that. Cohen suddenly looked over at BJ and gave him a smile and a thumbs-up. Something about the man's smile made BJ's skin crawl.

King looked over at BJ and saw the odd look on his face.

"What it is, Beej?" King said, holding a fist in front of him.

"What it was, Ty," BJ answered, rapping his knuckles on King's and trying to put on a happier face.

"What it will be, bro."

King held his palm out. BJ gave him a slow "high five" and grinned. The huge black man launched into a poem.

"Yea, though I walk through the vale of shadowy death, I fear the evil. I pack a rod and protect my staff. I shall not commit."

BJ laughed at the butchered psalm.

"Where'd you get that?" BJ asked.

"Buddy of mine made it up," King answered. "He was talking about women, though."

Both men laughed.

Laugh, you commie bastards, Cohen thought to himself as he watched the two GRU men doing their little act, you'll be laughing in hell soon.

The landing was conventional. Through the Osprey's tiny window, BJ could see Jinx waiting on the tarmac with an ambulance for McCullough. A Humm-V sat next to the ambulance. As they taxied up, three men got out of the Humm-V and walked quickly toward the V-22. The big tilt-rotor had barely stopped before the three men were pounding on the door. The loadmaster opened it and the three climbed in. The first face BJ recognized was Brian Hagerty. BJ looked over at King who was noisily miming fellatio with an imaginary organ.

Hagerty seemed not to notice. "You got it?" he asked BJ eagerly.

BJ hooked his thumb back over his shoulder at Malle. The two NCOs with Hagerty walked over to the big German, flipped their EOD credentials, and gathered up the rucksack with the device in it.

While the EOD men were talking to Malle, the rest of the two teams were slowly stumbling out the back of the V-22. Now that the immediate danger was over, they were exhausted, almost too tired to function. The medics were hustling in to fetch the wounded.

"Casualties?" Jinx asked as he shouldered BJ's weapon and walked away from the Osprey.

"One LRRP killed, one Green Beenie killed, one wounded." The words were so simple, but what they meant was so complex. The two dead were just two more out of thousands, the wounded man one of thousands more. They were just mere numbers to the war, but they were friends, team mates, close friends that would be missed.

"We're not goin' out again without a little rest," BJ said, suddenly turning and jabbing a finger into Jinx's chest. "We have had it!"

"You're not going out at all," Jinx quickly replied to defuse the tirade that was obviously coming. "We're in stand down—a cease-fire."

BJ stood openmouthed. "You mean it's over?"

"For now."

"*Ha!*" the laugh exploded from BJ's face. "We stopped 'em!"

"Well, guy, not really," Jinx said quietly.

"Whatdya mean?" BJ asked, uncomprehending. "They gave up, didn't they?"

"No," Jinx answered, his voice almost a whisper, "I mean we're in a cease-fire, no one knows any more than that. Neither side has withdrawn, we've just stopped shooting."

"*What?*"

A chorus of "oh, man!"'s, "fuck me"'s, and "shit"'s! issued from the troops as they heard about the cease-fire. The five men were already dirty and exhausted. They had been alternately terrified and exhilarated for days now. Their nervous systems had been pushed to the limit. Now they seemed to shrink, to sink in upon themselves. They had worked so hard for . . . nothing.

"So what's the deal now?" Hickey asked. His eyes had already taken on the thousand-foot stare, the pulled-back-from-reality look so common to combat veterans.

"We wait and see." Jinx shrugged.

The ambulance roared past them, headed for a four-lane highway that ran along the edge of the large concrete parking lot. For the first time, BJ realized he did not know where they were.

"Jinx," he said, stopping to gaze around, "where the hell are we?"

"Ibbenburen," Jinx answered, "it's just east of Osnabrück,

about fifty klicks from the Netherlands border. That road is Autobahn 65.''

''Where's Company G?'' several voices asked at once.

''On the way here now,'' Jinx reassured the team. ''They're rounding up civilian buses and trucks now to bring the folks left at the forward operations base.''

''How many teams are still inside?'' BJ asked. The weight of the world suddenly seemed upon the exhausted platoon sergeant.

''Nine, not counting yours.''

''What happened to Sterling's people?''

''Last contact. Just said, 'Evading, one KIA.' ''

''Shit.'' The word was filled with doom and despair.

''We'll get 'em out, BJ,'' Jinx said reassuringly. ''We're working on an agreement allowing both sides to go in and recover special ops teams. We'll have to take Soviet observers along, but we can go in and get them.''

''Then why did we just get our ass shot off bringing those guys out?'' BJ spat angrily. ''Why is one of my men dead if we can just waltz in and pick them up at the bus stop?''

''The cease-fire goes into effect at 1000 tomorrow, I mean today,'' Jinx corrected himself. ''Until then, it's still a shooting war.''

''Fuck me!'' BJ moaned. ''Fuck all of us!''

''Here,'' Jinx said as he slipped a pint bottle of peppermint schnapps out of his coat pocket, ''a little antifreeze might be in order.''

BJ took the thin bottle, unscrewed the cap, and tossed it over his shoulder. He took a long swig, then stood with his eyes closed, feeling the warmth of the liquor flow down the length of his body. He handed the bottle to Murphy, who took a swig and passed it on.

Behind them, the pilot and engineer of the V-22 were walking around the tilt-rotor, surveying the damage. Throckmorton ran his hand down the side of the Osprey, feeling the holes gouged by the 5.45mm rounds from the AKS-74s. Dunwoody was studying the pocked engine nacelle on the wingtip. Throckmorton turned to the pilot and loudly exclaimed, ''God bless DuPont, the makers of Kevlar!''

The LRRPs all turned and looked at the two flyers. Hickey, holding the bottle, raised it in a toast.

''God bless No-Name Industries, the makers of BDU shirts.''

Hickey took a healthy swig of the schnapps.

"Kill it, there's more."

As the LRRPs went through the schnapps, Jinx jogged over to the four Green Berets who stood looking around for some sort of reception party. Jinx spoke to Taggart, who nodded. The two men shook hands and talked a moment, then Jinx trotted back.

Jinx put an arm around his dejected friend. "Come on," he said, guiding BJ toward a Humm-V parked against the side of the factory whose parking lot was being used as a dispersed airfield. "If we hurry, we can catch a friend of yours before she gets evac'd."

Something was wrong, really wrong. No one could fake all this. Cohen's thoughts rolled and fought like two kids at a picnic. This can't be real. It can't. I armed the bomb. They have to be Russians so the bomb can kill them. They can't be Americans. First do no harm.

"Cohen!" Thompson yelled. "Didya hear that? We're in a cease-fire!"

Cohen looked at the others. Malle, Taggart, and Thompson were slapping one another on the back, shaking hands, generally congratulating one another for surviving. Cohen felt his insides go cold. A metallic taste came up in his mouth, the taste of fear. The bomb. Where was the bomb?

"Hey, Bud," Thompson was saying as he and Malle walked over, arm in arm, "whatsamatta you? You don't look good."

"Cheer up!" Malle boomed, "The cap'n's going to be okay, and it's over!" The two threw back their heads and whooped.

"It's not over!" Cohen blurted. "It's not over!"

"Sure it is," Thompson said gleefully, "cease-fire."

"The bomb," Cohen said, the pitch and volume of his voice rising. He grabbed Malle's combat harness, pulling him down to eye level. "The bomb!" Cohen stammered.

"The bomb is on its way back to the States," Malle answered, giving the agitated medic a confused look as he broke the frantic little man's grasp. "It's not our problem anymore."

"It's armed!" Cohen screamed. "It's running! I, I . . ." Cohen's eyes rolled up in his head and he crumpled to the cold asphalt. Malle and Thompson dropped to their knees to help their friend. Seeing the medic fall, Taggart came running over.

"What is it, babe?" Taggart asked.

"The bomb," Cohen answered weakly, "the bomb is armed. I armed it under the bridge. GRUs, those GRUs . . ."

The three Green Berets looked up at one another.

"Jesus Christ!" Taggart shouted. He jumped to his feet and ran toward the communications van set up on the edge of the field.

Fatigue, fear, and madness finally overwhelmed the little medic and he passed out. Malle sat own and cradled his friend's head in his lap. Thompson sat down and the two men just sat looking at each other. There was nothing to say. They were up the creek with no canoe.

The ride was very short. Fifteen kilometers west, the NATO forces had transformed a section of autobahn into an international airfield. The road was straight for 5000 feet, a rarity in Germany. It existed because it had been planned as an emergency airfield when the autobahn was constructed. The two westbound lanes were the runway, the eastbound lanes the taxiway. On a feeder road, a cluster of trailerlike buildings had been set up, with another cluster of tents next door.

"325th Evac," Jinx said as they turned off the autobahn. They had left the teams back at the parking lot landing zone, promising to be back in an hour.

The tent compound was the holding area for medical evacuations out of the European theater. A steady stream of ambulances ran between the tents and the taxiway. Air Force C-130s, empty after bringing in combat supplies, would fill up with wounded before returning to England, rerigging their cargo bays to handle litters.

The inflatable superheated tent was filled with dozens of metal racks that held one folding litter apiece. It took BJ several minutes to even find her. For a second, he wondered if she was alive. She looked so small, so hurt, lying there, wrapped in blankets on the green canvas stretcher. When he reached down to touch her face, her eyes opened and a smile spread across her tiny pale face.

"Hi, BJ," she said brightly, "where'd you come from?"

"Texas, ma'am."

She laughed, then coughed, clutching her left side with her arms.

"Don't make me laugh, sweetie," she moaned, "it hurts too bad."

"Donna, you gonna be okay?"

"Oh, yeah, I'm all right," she said reassuringly, "I got lucky."

"Yeah, how?"

"Well, between the windshield, my flight vest, and my bodacious ta-tas, the fragments didn't have enough steam to get into my heart."

She smiled at the pained look on BJ's dirty face. "Little did those commie creeps realize that my heart is my least vulnerable organ!" She laughed again, clutching her side.

"Bullshit." The look on BJ's face said that he thought otherwise.

She reached out from under the blankets to take his hand in hers. When she reached out, BJ could see the bandages that covered her entire left side, wrapping up over her shoulder. Even with the bulky bandages, the left side of her chest was much smaller now than the right. BJ fought to keep his face calm, to keep the pain of that sight from her. The sight of those beautiful breasts wrecked by jagged bits of hot steel shot by some Russian bastard brought tears to his eyes. Hell, she was taking this better than he was.

She saw his sad expression and sought to cheer herself up by cheering him up.

"Anyway, the docs say I can get a replacement for this poor boob. I told 'em I wanted the giant economy size!"

BJ smiled. "You already had the giant economy size."

"I know, but I want this sucker to be bulletproof the next time," she quipped. "Anyway, I'm writing a story about all this for the *National Enquirer*."

Confusion rippled across BJ's face.

"I'm gonna' call it, 'Big Tits Saved My Life.' "

BJ shook his head and laughed. What an incredible woman, he thought, she's the one with her knockers shot off, and she's trying to make me feel better.

"So when are they evac'ing you?"

"ASAP, I guess. Usually the folks who are shot up bad go first. I'm practically walking wounded."

"Don't try it."

She smiled up and squeezed his hand. "Don't worry, I won't!" Her eyes searched his. "Don't worry, period. I'll be okay!"

A medic shouldered his way into the tent and read from a clipboard.

"Burton, Clyde; Maxwell, RT; Vasquez, Donna; Nicklas, Billy; you're next. Leave the protective mask here on the litter stand, you won't need it."

"That's what they all say," Donna said, shaking her head, her voice dropping into a macho impression. "Don't worry, honey, you won't need any protection."

"Jesus," BJ said, shaking his head, "are you sure you didn't stop some frags with your head?"

Donna smiled up at him and pulled him down for a kiss. A long kiss.

"I'll see you soon," she said as two orderlies in BDUs picked up her litter and started for the door. Outside, an ambulance was backed up to the tent door.

"How?" BJ called after her. "How will I find you?"

"You'll think of something, that's your job, remember?" she called back as she and the two medics disappeared into the ambulance. BJ walked to the door and watched as the ambulance drove the short distance to the waiting C-130, whose props turned slowly as it sat on the highway. As the men unloaded the litters and carried them up into the plane, BJ saw a tiny hand waving from one of them. He waved back, not knowing whether she could even see him.

"I'll think of something," he said softly as her stretcher disappeared up the ramp. "You bet I will, babe."

"BJ!" Jinx suddenly screamed at him from the Humm-V. "Come on, we got a major problem!"

BJ trotted back to the Humm-V. Jinx was already in it, with the vehicle in gear.

"Come on, we gotta get back," Jinx shouted as BJ clambered in. "That bomb you brought back is hot! One of the Berets just happened to mention that he armed the damn thing before you extracted them."

"Mother pus bucket!" was all BJ could say. Jinx kicked the Humm-V into motion.

★38★

Let's see, Brian Hagerty mused as they roared down the E3 Autobahn, we'll be an hour on the ground at Twenthe, then eight hours on the flight to Dover. Ten more hours, and I'm home free. The Humm-V was sailing down the right side of the road, which had been cleared for military traffic. Across the median, thousands of German civilians sat in their cars, mired in the huge traffic jam. All civilian traffic had been shunted to the left side of the road to keep it out of the way of the military traffic. The left side of the autobahn looked like a long parking lot stretching toward Belgium. It would take an hour or so to reach the Belgian border, then just a few minutes to reach Twenthe Airport. There was a knot in Hagerty's stomach that had come up when he had landed in Europe. He knew that it would not go away until he left. Wrecked tanks and personnel carriers littered the roadside, grim remains from Soviet air attacks. Here and there, Hagerty could see the burnt remains of dead helicopters and planes where they had gouged into the picturesque scenery.

Sergeant Kilmer, the driver, signaled for a turn. As the Humm-V turned right onto the two-lane road, Hagerty shielded his eyes, searching for a road sign. There it was, Highway 54. It ran all the way to Enschede, west of the airport. He glanced into the back of the Humm-V. Sgt. Franks was holding on to the ruck-sack that held the device, cradling it in his arms as they turned the corner. Hagerty had worked with EOD men before, teaching them about atomic munitions the way he taught those LRRP animals. EODs were always low-key, but this pair was unusually

laid back. They looked like Mutt and Jeff. Kilmer was tall and
lanky, a hint of Tennessee mountains in his accent. Franks was
stocky and obtuse. He talked like an aging hippie; Hagerty had
not heard the word "groovy" in years. For all of that, they were
the perfect pair for this job. They did just what he told them.
Hagerty leaned back in his seat and shaded his eyes with his
cap. Soon, very soon, he thought, I'll be out of here and
safe.

"Jesus, Jinx, they could be anywhere!" BJ whined. "Hell,
we could be anywhere!"

"We're in the right place," Jinx answered, trying to sound
more confident than he really was, "I just hope they're not already past us." The Humm-V was parked across Highway 54.
The EOD team would pass this way, if they had not taken another road, gotten lost, or already gone by. The large number of
ifs made Jinx queasy.

"What are we going to tell these guys?" BJ asked. BJ was
nervously tapping his foot on the Humm-V's door sill while fin-
gering one of the thermite grenades.

Jinx propped his foot up on the center console. "We might
start with the truth," he answered. "I know that's risky, but it
might work this time."

BJ shot him a look. "Well, okay, but I better do it. You may
not remember how."

Jinx just grinned in reply. BJ's running on empty, Jinx thought,
watching his young friend fidget. Stress and fatigue were starting
to get the best of fear and exhilaration. Jinx had that hollow
feeling, too. The longer they sat here, the heavier his limbs and
eyelids felt. After they took care of this bomb business, they'd
both get some sleep.

Of course, if they messed it up, he chuckled to himself, they
would get a very long sleep. That's it, he thought as his eyes
slowly shut, think positive. His eyelids felt like lead.

The sound of a Humm-V woke him. BJ was already out of
their vehicle, walking down the asphalt with his M16 unslung
from his shoulder, ready to fire. Jinx took out his Beretta, jerked
the slide back to chamber a round, and slipped it back in the
holster.

"Please don't let me need this," he prayed under his breath.

* * *

Brian Hagerty was absently studying the scenery when Kilmer slowed. The delay getting around the civilian traffic jams had slowed them up. Now they were making good time.

"Checkpoint, sir," he drawled as they neared the man walking down the center of the road. Hagerty looked up and started. The dirty apparition walking down the road was the same surly bastard who'd brought back the SADM.

"Oh, no," he groaned as Kilmer brought the Humm-V to a stop. "What now?" Hagerty climbed out of the Humm-V to confront the armed specter. This bozo was not going to delay his leaving this charnel house. No way.

"What's going on here, Sergeant?" Hagerty demanded.

"Kirkley, BJ Kirkley," BJ answered, "I'm afraid we have a problem with that device of yours."

"That device is none of your business, Sergeant," Hagerty snapped back. "Your job was just to bring it back."

"That's more than I wanted to do, mister," BJ answered, fighting down the anger that suddenly flashed up. "I'm just here to tell you your bomb is armed and ready to go. Do you understand? It's hot, it's live, and the timer is running. I have grenades with me to disarm it. Shall we get on with it?"

Hagerty studied the man. He was wild-looking, dirty, exhausted. If his story was true, why would the Army send this man to find the bomb instead of MPs or EOD people like Wilmer and Franks. Something was fishy here.

"Do you have any authorization to destroy the device, Sergeant Kirkley," Hagerty asked quickly, "any orders?"

BJ started to speak, then glanced off to the side as Jinx walked up and interrupted.

"Major Jenkins, Mr. Hagerty," Jinx answered, his Texas twang cloying with courtesy, "I got a radio message that your little A-bomb is all set and ready to blow. Apparently, one of the ADM team armed the little thing and forgot to mention it to anybody. My instructions are to intercept you and destroy the device."

Jinx put his hand on BJ's shoulder. "Sgt. Kirkley here was with me and volunteered to come along." Jinx glanced over to see BJ staring at the two EOD men who had climbed out of their Humm-V.

"Gentlemen, I'm sorry," Hagerty said firmly, "but I am not authorized to turn over this device to anyone. I am required to deliver it to the special ammunition section at . . ." Hagerty caught himself, then went on, "At a base in the United States. I am afraid I can't let you touch it at all."

BJ stared at the civilian. The man was the pure distilled essence of every bureaucratic asshole in the world. The fucking bomb was ticking and this dork wanted to argue paperwork. BJ felt the heat rising in him, felt his control slipping as a flood of adrenaline surged into him. BJ felt his vision constricting. Jinx was saying something to the Ivy League bastard, but BJ didn't really care.

"Didn't you hear what I said, you silly cocksucker?" BJ shouted at the startled civilian. "You're riding around with a ticking A-bomb! Give it here!"

Hagerty stepped back, surprised. He turned and called to the two EOD men. "Stop them!" he shouted to the two technicians. "They want the device!"

The two EODs reached for their weapons. The driver had a pistol and the other reached into the Humm-V for a 16. BJ had the drop on them before they even got to their weapons.

"*FREEZE!*" he shouted. "*HANDS ON YOUR HEADS!*"

The EOD men quickly complied.

"Driver, toss that pistol away," BJ called to the taller of the two EODs. The driver reached down with his right hand to unsnap the holster. "Left hand!" BJ shouted. The man slowly reached across with his left hand, never taking his eyes off BJ, and pulled out the pistol with two fingers. He tossed it gingerly into the dirt along the road.

BJ gestured with his rifle barrel. "Move away from the vehicle!" The two EODs were quick to comply. BJ turned to the civilian. "You get back there with them, yuppie fucker!" Hagerty walked slowly backward, his eyes wide with fear.

Oh, fuck, Jinx thought as BJ walked the civilian back to the vehicle, this is turning to *caca mundo*.

"Sgt. Kilmer, Sgt. Franks, you're both witnesses!" Hagerty was shouting. "These two terrorists are stealing the device from me!"

"Shut up, Mr. Hagerty," the driver cautioned.

"That's right, Mr. Smartass Yankee Bigmouth," BJ barked, "shut up and get back there." The three men moved slowly away from the Humm-V as BJ advanced, his weapon trained on them. Behind BJ, Jinx was grappling with the heavy rucksack that held the hundred-pound atom bomb. Over his shoulder, BJ heard a loud clunk and a muffled "Jesus."

At the sound, BJ looked back. Hagerty dug in his pocket, came up with a little pistol, and fired. The M16 leaped from BJ's hands and, tethered to his shoulder by the snap link, swung around behind him. A second later, Hagerty's hand snapped to the right, his pistol cartwheeling out of his grip and clattering across the asphalt. Hagerty screamed and grabbed his forearm with his left hand. Both BJ and Hagerty were screaming from pain and surprise. BJ reached behind him and pulled the M16 back around. The front handguard was split near the front sight.

"You little bastard!" BJ screamed. "You broke my rifle!" Hagerty looked up, his face screwed up with pain. His mouth was open and noises were getting out, pained noises. "I'm shot," he observed. There was surprise in his voice. From the right sleeve of his parka, bright red blood began to drip onto the pavement. The two sergeants with Hagerty wisely stayed put.

BJ looked over his shoulder at Jinx, who was still leaning over the seat of the Humm-V, his pistol trained on the trio across the road.

"Nice shooting, Tex." BJ laughed. "Shot that six-gun right out of his hand just like the Lone Ranger!"

"Not very good shooting," Jinx replied sheepishly, "I was trying to kill him." Hearing that, Hagerty's head snapped around to Jinx.

"Tried to kill me!" he shouted. "You'll hang for this, both of you! I'll see you hang!"

"Shut up, Mr. Hagerty," Kilmer said quietly. "Please shut up."

Hagerty looked back at the EOD sergeant, then back at BJ, who raised his eyebrows and nodded. The civilian reluctantly shut up and sat down on the pavement in defeat. BJ held the rifle with one hand and reached down to the first-aid pouch on his belt. He popped it open and tossed the plastic-wrapped bandage to Hagerty.

"Here, put this on your arm," BJ said. "If you don't know how, read the directions on the wrapper."

Hagerty glared at BJ, then picked up the bandage and began reading the directions. Franks, the other EOD man, began talking him through it.

Behind BJ, Jinx wrestled the heavy rucksack out in front of the Humm-V, pulling it with his left hand, the pistol still clutched in his right.

"Okay, BJ, now what?" Jinx asked as he stood, wiping the cold sweat off his face.

"Cover 'em," BJ answered as he backed toward the bomb.

"None of the three look too dangerous, now," Jinx observed as BJ slung his rifle and knelt down, tugging the device from its padded cradle.

BJ tipped the device up onto the flat end plate and pulled the rucksack off of it. For the first time, Jinx got a look at the item that was causing all the trouble. It was amazingly nondescript. The device looked like a big, black .45 bullet.

With the device out of the bag, BJ ran back to their Humm-V to fetch the thermite grenades. He ran back with a grenade in each hand and another tucked under his arm, then stood panting as he looked at the bomb.

"How'm I gonna tie these things on?" BJ moaned. "The fuckin' thing's gonna go off before I get my shit together!"

"There's tape in the Humm-V," the taller EOD man said, "in the tool box."

BJ looked up at the man. The man still stood with both hands on his head, near the side of the road. "Why are you bein' so helpful?" BJ asked suspiciously.

" 'Cause if you're gonna blow that thing," the driver answered calmly, "I want you to do it right."

"Kilmer, I forbid you to help these terrorists!" Hagerty shouted from where he sat tying the tails of the field dressing around his arm. "You work for me, do you understand?"

"Shut the fuck up, you little weasel!" BJ shouted. He walked over to the Humm-V and pulled out the hard plastic tool kit from the back. Inside was a roll of green "hundred mile an hour" tape. As he walked back to the device, BJ looked over at the fuming civilian.

"Did your mother have any children that lived?" BJ asked, laughing. The two EOD sergeants laughed with him. Hagerty dropped into a deep sulk.

Kneeling next to the squat little bomb, BJ ran his hand around it. There were no external features at all, no clue as to its inner construction. BJ looked up at Kilmer.

"Any suggestions?" BJ asked.

Kilmer dropped his hands.

"Actually, yes," he replied, "I'll help, if you want me to."

Hagerty shot Kilmer a look, but Kilmer didn't even see it. He appeared to have dropped the civilian from the discussion.

"Come on," BJ said, gesturing with one of the thermites, "we need to get on with this."

Kilmer walked over and knelt by the bomb. Behind the Humm-V, Jinx moved around so he could cover Kilmer as well as Hagerty and Franks.

"Okay," Kilmer began, "let's tape one thermite here just above the base. How many of them you got?"

"Three."

"Okay, one near the base," Kilmer went on, "and two on the other side about two thirds of the way up." He pointed at spots on the bomb's case. "Call the bottom one twelve o'clock, put the others at four o'clock and eight o'clock," Kilmer instructed, looking up to see if BJ was following him. "Pull the pins one after another, not all at once. That'll make sure that the reaction can't occur." BJ handed the man the thermite grenade and the tape.

"Here, you do the diaper," BJ said, "I'll hold the baby."

Kilmer took the grenade and strapped it to the bomb with the thick tape. It took him only a few minutes to strap the grenades in place. When the last one was taped on, Kilmer stood and put the tape roll in his pocket.

"That's it," he said, turning his palms up.

"Okay, Hagerty and Franks, into that Humm-V," Jinks shouted, pointing with his pistol at the vehicle parked in the crossroad, "BJ, you and Kilmer take that Humm-V and get down the road. I'll do the honors here and bring this one down."

BJ stood and stared quizzically at his friend. Jinx glanced over and saw BJ's look. "You brought the damn thing back," Jinx explained, "I'll do this."

BJ just smiled, picked up his broken rifle and waved the two men on the roadside toward their Humm-V. Kilmer walked along with BJ, ignoring the scowl from Hagerty. Jinx stood by the device as the group reached the vehicle. Kilmer got behind the wheel and the Humm-V sped off down the road.

Jinx holstered his pistol and reached down. For a second, he had a vision of the bomb going off just as he reached for it. He ignored the vision, reached around the device, and pulled the pin from the bottom grenade. He waited until he heard the hiss of the burning thermite, then pulled the pin on one of the grenades on the near side. When it began to shoot sparks, Jinx pulled the pin on the third grenade, turned, and ran to the Humm-V.

He jumped in, turned the starter switch, and heard—nothing. Jinx looked up at the device. Sparks and flame from all three thermites danced around the black case. Jinx turned the switch off and thought for a second about jumping out and running. He gave the switch one more hard turn and the motor roared to life. Jinx slammed the machine into gear and gunned it past the device, which was now completely obscured by smoke and sparks.

Jinx was almost to the intersection when the device exploded. Jinx looked in the mirror and saw the squat black slug bouncing across the pavement, trailing smoke. He gunned the Humm-V around the corner. BJ and the others were parked a hundred feet away.

As he pulled up, BJ walked over with Hagerty. The civilian had calmed down quite a bit, since there was nothing he could do now anyway, and he had a scapegoat, Kilmer, if he needed one to cover his own ass.

"L. L. Bean here says he needs to look at the bomb to measure the radiation," BJ said, hooking a thumb at Hagerty.

"Climb in," Jinx said, patting the passenger seat.

Hagerty got in and the two men drove back down to the intersection.

"Stop here," Hagerty said as they turned the corner, "I want to get a reading here." He reached into his jacket and took out a radiac meter. Hagerty held down the switch and swept the small Geiger counter back and forth. The digital counter ran numbers up and down, but Hagerty did not seem concerned.

"Drive down to the device," he ordered, seemingly in command. "Where did it end up?"

"Right over there," Jinx replied, pointing to the shallow ditch that ran along the road, "where that smoke is."

Jinx stopped the vehicle. "Why don't you go on from here?" he said to Hagerty. "I'll wait."

Hagerty, his face a mask of annoyance, got out and walked down to the smoking device, scanning back and forth with his meter. He walked up to the case, touched it gingerly to see if it was still hot, then turned it so the flat end plate faced him. Hagerty took a small notebook from his pocket and knelt by the device. He looked at the end plate, then at his notebook, then took out a pencil and wrote on the baseplate above the combination lock. This done, he put away the notebook, bent down, and turned the combination lock. The baseplate fell away. Hagerty peered at the face of the bomb, then stood, scanned it once more with the radiac meter, and walked back to the Humm-V. When he got in, Jinx could see the man's face was the color of chalk. His hands were trembling. Hagerty suddenly turned and faced Jinx.

"Thanks!" he said, extending his hand.

Jinx shook it and asked, "For what?"

"The device had less than a minute left on the timer," Hagerty said, his voice cracking. "It would have taken us and half this country with it."

All the cockiness was gone from the man, now. Hagerty realized that, had he gotten his own way, he would now be explaining all this to Saint Peter while the hot dust that had been his body settled slowly on eastern Belgium.

Jinx snorted and punched the man on the shoulder. "Welcome to the war, Ace," he said quietly. "What do we do with that thing?"

"Leave it," Hagerty said, looking over at the device, "I'll get a team out here to recover it."

"No problem," Jinx replied as he kicked the Humm-V into reverse and turned it around. He hoped that Hagerty was too freaked out to see how bad Jinx's hands were shaking.

★39★

Jinx and BJ spent the next two days rounding up their far-flung teams. The Soviets agreed that both sides would pull out their special ops people, accompanied by observers from the other side.

So far, very few Soviet teams had been extracted. All the NATO teams had responded to the cease-fire order and were hiding, awaiting extraction. The Soviets wanted the NATO teams to turn themselves in to the nearest Soviet unit for repatriation. SOCEUR nixed that idea. Jinx, flying in a Blackhawk marked with United Nations colors and insignia, had been picking up Special Forces and LRRP teams, accompanied by a succession of Soviet KGB and GRU officers. The Soviets had been smug, but not unpleasant. They could afford to be cordial, they had won.

Today, they would pick up Norm Sterling's team of LRRPs, the second team sent in to find McCullough's ADM team. BJ was going along to assure that the team they picked up was the real McCoy, not a group of ringers. The Soviets had already tried that trick once.

As they stood waiting for the extraction chopper, BJ was clearly in a mood.

"What's up, guy?" Jinx asked casually.

"Everything, Jinx," BJ answered, "the whole thing sucks. We did so much, lost so many people. For what? For nothing. We didn't win, we didn't lose, we just did it for nothing."

"Yeah, guy," Jinx answered, "I know. I been there before."

BJ looked over at Jinx and laughed. "Yeah, I guess you have."

Jinx turned, his palms up and outspread. "Hey, I'm two for two! But I suspect this is just the first round of this fight!"

BJ just shook his head.

Over the trees, they could see the helicopter with its U.N. globe on the side.

"Fuckin' U.N. pukes," BJ spat. "They give me a pain. Most of 'em act like they're glad the Reds won."

"They can hardly act any other way, can they?"

"I guess not," BJ replied, "but it chaps my ass to have to listen to a bunch of crap from some jerk from Sad Sackistan."

The Blackhawk touched down in front of them. Behind it, two AH-1S Cobras landed. The Allies were playing by the Russians' rules, but they were not whining around like whipped dogs. The Cobras went along on every extraction flight, and they were armed to the eyeballs.

The door of the Blackhawk slid open and Jinx reached up to get a grip, pulling himself and then BJ into the chopper. The crew chief shut the door as Jinx handed the pilot his list of pickup coordinates.

That done, Jinx settled onto the bench seat and strapped himself in. BJ was chatting with the crew chief. As the chopper lifted off, Jinx took a moment to check the U.N. observer, a captain from the Indonesian Army. He sat impassively next to the side window, not speaking to either group of soldiers. BJ ignored the Indonesian, examining instead their Soviet counterparts of the day. It took a second, then recognition dawned.

BJ felt the blood pound in his ears, the adrenaline suddenly surging through him. The face in his bad dream was suddenly right there in front of him.

"YAAAAAA, Jesus Christ," BJ screamed through the intercom. *"You!"*

Kovpak had not even noticed the Americans. He was trying to find some position on the bench seat that did not hurt his butt. There was no such position. The doctor had wanted to put him in the hospital, but Kovpak would have none of it. This cease-fire was a time of great opportunity, and he had no intention of wasting it in a hospital bed, being ridiculed for getting shot in the ass.

When the young American sergeant had screamed in his face, Kovpak stopped thinking about his butt and looked up, staring at this wild man.

BJ jumped forward, reaching for Kovpak's throat, but his seat harness held him on the bench. His hands flew to the release. In his excitement, he was having trouble getting the simple quick release undone.

"Hey, hey, hey, what's the problem, BJ?" Jinx asked as he put a restraining hand on his friend. The Russians across from him were suddenly nervous at BJ's outburst. The smaller one, an ensign with a bandage on his left hand, looked at BJ warily. It was then that Jinx looked closely at his Soviet counterpart and saw the man from Nicaragua.

"Jesus H. Christ!" was all Jinx could say.

"So, my friend, we meet again," Bodnya said quietly as he recognized the American he had last seen in a gymnasium in Texas, "it seems we cannot escape each other."

Jinx just looked at the man for a moment. The Russian wore the uniform of a Soviet lieutenant colonel. The striped undershirt and the badge on his tunic said Guards Airborne. The little weasel next to him had on senior ensign boards and was clearly in pain.

"On the contrary, we always seem to escape each other," Jinx answered.

The Russian laughed. "Indeed."

"You little fucker!" BJ shouted at the Soviet ensign. "You almost blew my head off!"

"Yes, I apologize," the uncomfortable little man replied. "It was dark, and I could not aim very well . . ."

Jinx could feel BJ tensing. He put a hand on BJ's chest to calm him.

The four men just sat for a few minutes looking at one another. They were all in the same business, more or less. They were all good at their jobs. They were on opposite sides. Jinx thought of all the Second World War reunions where American veterans had gotten together with German veterans on the battlefields they had shared in Europe. He wondered if he would be able to put this fight behind him enough to do that in a couple of decades. He hoped not.

The Russian colonel broke the silence.

"This area where we are going to pick up your team was my battalion's area of responsibility."

This revelation perked up BJ's interest.

"Is that right?" the LRRP exclaimed. "Well, that's real . . ."

"We have the pickup signal," the pilot of the Blackhawk interrupted, "they're just across the highway."

The chopper cleared the trees and settled onto the concrete roadway. It was barely on the ground before four figures darted from the trees and ran for the helicopter. Jinx slid open the door and stepped out onto the road, waiting for the team. BJ joined him, never taking his eyes from the little Russian ensign.

Norm Sterling was the first to reach the chopper.

"God damn, I'm glad to see you, BJ!" Sterling exclaimed as he shouldered his pack into the chopper and turned to help Alvarez out of his gear. "We thought we were gonna have to walk out!"

"No way, Norm," BJ answered, "who's not here?"

Sterling turned and looked at BJ. "Slade bought the farm. He broke a leg on the jump. The Reds found him cached off the DZ."

BJ stood looking at Sterling. "Yeah, Kosinski got it on my team."

"Wally?" Sterling asked. "Aw, man."

"Yeah."

The two sergeants went back to loading the team's gear into the chopper. Jinx stopped Alvarez as he tried to climb into the Blackhawk.

"Unload your weapons out here," he said to the LRRP team, "no live ammo in the chopper."

"Fuck that!" Purcell snapped.

"That's the rule," BJ answered his men. "The Russians've got a pair of observers on each extradition chopper, so no ammo on board."

"BJ, I don't trust these Red bastards," Sterling said, his voice rising above the engine noise.

"It doesn't matter, Norm," BJ replied, "it's pretty much their party, now. We dance to their tunes."

The LRRPs moved off a few meters from the chopper and began to dump their ammunition.

"Grenades, too?" Sterling asked dejectedly.

BJ nodded. A look of supreme humiliation and despair flashed across Sterling's face.

Shorn of their firepower, the team crawled into the chopper. The look on their faces stuck into Jinx like a knife. It was the same look he had seen on the faces of Hmong tribesmen in Laos, on the faces of Montagnards in Vietnam, on the faces of Contras in Nicaragua, on the faces of everybody the U.S. had used and abandoned in one little war after another. The Russian's voice broke into his musing.

"These men are all of this team?"

Jinx turned and climbed aboard, giving the pilot a thumbs-up signal.

"Yes, this is all of them."

Jinx slid the door shut as the Blackhawk lifted off and turned for its base in the west. No one spoke on the trip home.

When he saw the T-80 and the 2S6 roll up, Corporal Salvador (Sally) Carsten spit off to one side of his fighting vehicle. What do the Red arseholes want this time? he wondered. Every five minutes, another bunch came along to meddle in his business.

The two vehicles were a hundred meters away when they ran up a white flag on each antenna and clanked to a halt. Their gun barrels were at maximum elevation.

"Sally, do they want to surrender to us?" Patrick Abner, the driver, asked.

"I dunno, Pat," Sally answered, "I'll ask 'em." He slid off the side of the track and waited for the Soviet officer who was walking up to him, a big smile smeared across his face.

The big Russian stopped a few feet away and saluted. Carsten was about to speak when the Russian said in perfect American English, "Good morning, Corporal. I am Captain Harlan of the 10th U.S. Special Forces Group. My team wishes to 'surrender' and to rejoin our unit."

Carsten stood openmouthed at this amazing declaration.

"If you would call up the 588th Military Intelligence Detachment," the "Russian" went on, "wherever they are, they can vouch for us. As you might suspect, we are not carrying our ID cards."

It took over two hours, but the American officer who finally came on the line identified the Russian and his friends perfectly. The short, dark troops that accompanied the Americans formally asked for asylum, which was immediately granted.

As the Americans clanked away in their Soviet vehicles, Carsten turned to Abner.

"Pat, this wasn't the worse morning of this stupid war, but it was the most peculiar."

Abner just nodded.

* * *

A command car was waiting for the helicopter at the base. As the Blackhawk touched down, the car drove up. The two Russians stepped out, followed by Jinx and BJ. The LRRP team exited the other side of the chopper.

The Russian colonel turned and faced Jinx.

"I see that your name is Jenkins," the Russian said over the whine of the Blackhawk's slowly turning rotors, "my name is Guards Lieutenant Colonel Akexsei Michailovich Bodnya." The colonel gestured toward the ensign, who still seemed to be in pain from some unseen injury. "This is Senior Ensign Pavel Kovpak."

"Richard," Jinx replied, "Major Richard Jenkins. This is Sergeant BJ Kirkley."

The four men stood looking at one another for a minute. They would never have another opportunity to size one another up so casually. The weasely ensign reached into his tunic pocket and pulled out a Sony Walkman, adjusting the headphones and smiling benignly at the two Americans.

The Russian officer finally spoke. "We may well meet again, Comrade Major," he said in a tone that held anticipation, "I doubt very much that this is all over."

"I know it's not," Jinx replied emphatically.

"So, until then." The Russian nodded, then turned and climbed into the command car, followed by the ensign. As the car pulled away, the ensign's face appeared in the window. He gave the two Americans the finger as he drove away.

★Glossary of Military Terms★

ADA—Air Defense Artillery.

ADM—Atomic Demolition Munitions.

APC—Armored Personnel Carrier.

Army—Soviet operational formation composed of three to five motorized rifle and tank divisions plus support units. May be termed a combined arms army (more motorized rifle than tank divisions), tank army (more tank divisions), or shock army (same as a tank army).

BDU—Battle Dress Uniform.

BMP—Soviet full-tracked infantry combat vehicle.

BTR—Soviet eight-wheeled armored personnel carrier.

C^3I—Command, Control, Communications (cubed), and Intelligence.

CCP—Communication Checkpoint.

CEOI—Communications-Electronics Operating Instructions.

CO—Commanding Officer.

Corps—A NATO formation composed of two to four divisions plus support units.

Division (NATO)—Tactical formation composed of (usually) three brigades, artillery command, and support units. Organization, strength, and equipment vary greatly between the NATO countries.

Division (Soviet)—Tactical formation composed of three regiments, artillery regiment, and support units. Non-Soviet Warsaw Pact divisions are similar.

DMDG—Digital Message Device Group.

DZ—Drop Zone.

FLOT—Front Line of Own Troops.

Front—Soviet strategic formation composed of three or four combined arms and tank armies plus an air army and support units.

GRU—*Glavnoye Razvedyvatelnoye Upravlenie*—Chief Directorate of Intelligence of the General Staff.

KG—*Kampfgruppen*—Battle Groups of the Working Class or ''Workers' Militia''—East German.

KGB—*Komitet Gosudatstvwnnoy Bezopasnosti*—Committee for State Security.

LRRP—Long Range Reconnaissance Patrol.

LRS—Long Range Surveillance.

LZ—Landing Zone.

MI—Military Intelligence.

MOPP—Mission Oriented Protective Posture.

MRE—Meal, Ready-to-Eat. Freeze dried replacement for C-rations.

NATO—North Atlantic Treaty Organization.

NCO—Noncommissioned Officer—sergeants.

NORTHAG—Northern Army Group—NATO command controlling the five national corps in northern West Germany.

NVG—Night Vision Goggles.

O&I—Operations and Intelligence.

OP—Observation Post.

ORP—Objective Rally Point.

POMCUS—Pre-positioned Material Configured to Unit Sets.

PZ—Pick-up Zone.

SAS—Special Air Service—British.

SAW—Squad Automatic Weapon.

SF—Special Forces.

SOCEUR—Special Operations Command, Europe.

SOP—Standard Operating Procedures.

Spetsnaz—*Spezialnoye Naznachenia*—Special Purpose.

S&T—Selection and Training.

TL—Team Leader.

TOC—Tactical Operations Center.

USAREUR—U.S. Army, Europe.

VOPO—*Volkspolize*—Peoples' Police—East German.

XO—Executive Officer.

Zampolit—Deputy Commander for Political Affairs.